Praise For

After Happily Ever

"Safrey's fantasy novel explores the lives of three fairy-tale icons long after their happily-ever-afters...In centering older women as powerful, multifaceted protagonists, the story is both feminist and empowering, demonstrating that value and agency do not diminish with age. A refreshing reimagining of fairy-tale figures that redefines what it means to claim your happy ending."

—*Kirkus Reviews*, **starred review**

* * *

"Safrey rightly places her fairy tale princesses in the center of their own stories as they each do the work to build their own happily ever after in this hopeful novel of quiet but powerful rebellion that is perfect for our times."

—A.C. Wise, award-winning author of *Wendy, Darling* **and** *Hooked*

* * *

"Fairy-tale aficionados will eagerly devour this reinterpretation that explores how the past shapes the present."

—*Booklist*, **starred review**

* * *

"Safrey offers a delightful feminist take on the continuing lives of protagonists after the traditional fairy tale has ended. Sharp characters and a twisting plot create an empowering and enchanting tale inspired by iconic princesses."

—*Library Journal*

"Jennifer Safrey gives new meaning to the word 'fairest' in this once-upon-a-time tale that shows us what lies beyond 'happily ever after.' She masterfully weaves together themes of female friendship, aging, magic, and power into a novel that kept me in thrall to the end. What a great read!"

—Kerri Maher, USA Today bestselling author of *The Paris Bookseller* and *All You Have To Do Is Call*

* * *

"*After Happily Ever* is an exquisitely clever take on middle-aged princesses inspired by three iconic fairytales. Sprinkled with wit and humor, this tale sends each princess down a path of profound personal growth. Well-paced, with plenty of fun twists and turns, this book reveals the daily lives of reliant princesses and pushes each one toward her true power. An enchanting read and an inspiration for women of all ages."

—Christina Mercer, award-winning author of *Arrow of the Mist*

* * *

"A captivating magical adventure, a clever fairytale upending, and a rousing feminist anthem, Jennifer Safrey's *After Happily Ever* offers us a poignant reminder that life's middle stories can be its most stirring."

Katie Williams, *Kirkus Reviews* Prize finalist and author of *My Murder*

* * *

After Happily Ever

An EPIC NOVEL *of* MIDLIFE REBELLION

JENNIFER SAFREY

Sibylline Press

Copyright @ 2025 by Jennifer Safrey
All Rights Reserved.

Published in the United States by Sibylline Press,
an imprint of All Things Book LLC, California.

Sibylline Press is dedicated to publishing the brilliant work of
women authors ages 50 and older.
www.sibyllinepress.com

Distributed to the trade by Publishers Group West.

Sibylline Press
Paperback ISBN: 9781960573179
eBook ISBN: 9781960573186
Library of Congress Control Number: 2024941274

Book and Cover Design: Alicia Feltman

**Sibylline
Press**

For the women of Generation X.
Because we deserve to believe in fairy tales.

NEVE

Neve rode alone to the castle, accompanied by her determined—and adorable—woodland guard. Two fluffy rabbits sprinted alongside Biscuit's hooves, along with a pair of young deer with barely sprouted nubs of antlers, a fluttering mix of sparrows and bluebirds, and one small but confident lumbering bear.

Neve had once lain under glass in the woods for a year, under the watchful eyes of all the creatures of the forest. Now, the great-great-great-grandchildren of those animals had inherited the instinct to protect their princess. They peered into her bedchamber every morning with wide, innocent eyes through the glass of her double doors, waiting for her to open her eyes and rise.

It wasn't that Neve was ungrateful or unmoved by their attention, but she had sometimes wondered what it would be like to experience a day or two that didn't dawn with the reminder of her death.

Neve didn't travel long distances without a soldier or two, or her husband if he was free of duty. She preferred to have someone reliable at her back. But the distance from her castle to that of her sister-in-law Bry was quite short, and she trusted her forest friends to alert her of danger, even if most of them were simply too small to fight for her.

She wouldn't ask them to. She could fight.

She hadn't had to—yet. But she could.

Upon arrival, she handed over her horse to one of Bry's waiting servants, who edged away from the bear carefully. Neve took a moment to nuzzle and pet all her furry friends before sending them on their way.

* * *

Bry welcomed Neve into the lush sitting room, rather than having servants escort her in.

"You look lovely," Bry said, her hands on Neve's shoulders. Neve, who didn't usually allow anyone other than Brockton to touch her, compelled herself not to flinch.

"Come," Bry said, as she took her hand and led her into the room. "There will be tea when Della gets here. In the meantime, what can I offer you?"

"I'm fine, honestly," Neve assured her.

"I suppose you haven't had a very long journey here, have you?" Bry smiled.

"Not quite, but I appreciate your efforts." She did. But Bry's attention to everyone's needs was disconcerting. Then again, her dinners, balls, masquerades, and parties were legendary in the kingdom. It was her personal, unique touch that the guests talked about for weeks afterward.

"I have a gift for you," Bry said. "Wait here a moment, and I'll be back."

"Bry, your company is gift enough."

Bry shook her head and laughed as if Neve had said something that made no sense, and dashed from the room.

Three dessert place settings of etched glass lay on a tablecloth on a small wooden table, and heaps of strawberries and gingerbreads and iced currant cookies filled serving dishes. Once upon a time, Neve would have been conservative about choosing which she would eat so she could fit easily into her gowns, but lately, she ploughed through dessert tables without a care, sampling everything.

Bry blew back into the room, carrying a large pie with a mountainous golden crust. Steam rose from the hole on top, and so did the aroma of cherries.

"I had my cook make you her best pie," Bry said, holding out the dish. She seemed to struggle a bit under the weight and placed it on a side table. She then dragged the table a few inches forward for Neve to better admire it. "I thought perhaps you could bring it to Brockton to share?"

Years ago, one of Neve's seven uncles had made her a cherry pie, and though he'd been so proud to present her with it, and he was an excellent cook, she'd found it wasn't her favorite. But her sister-in-law's face was now so eager that Neve didn't have the will to let her down. "You are so generous and sweet," Neve said. "Sweeter than any of the desserts in this room. Brockton will love the pie. Thank you so much."

"Oh, I'm so glad it made you happy!"

"Yes," Neve said, accustomed to assuring her sister-in-law that everything she gave, prepared, gifted, was perfect.

Bry squeezed Neve's hand and sat beside her on a richly upholstered chair. Unlike Neve, who sank her hips and shoulders into the chair, Bry perched on the edge of her seat, ever ready to spring up and bring someone whatever they needed. Or what she thought they needed.

Neve smiled at her. Bry folded her hands in her lap and leaned forward. "Are you having a good day so far, my sister?"

"It's not bad," Neve said. "But it's unremarkable in its sameness. You know."

Bry rolled her eyes. "I do know." She patted her hair. It was pulled back, always with the same tortoiseshell comb.

Neve first met Bry when they were both young brides and new to Foreverness. Back then, Bry's hair had been a cascade of startling and brilliant red. Neve couldn't recall the last time she'd seen Bry's hair down, and she wondered if the color remained as vibrant. Bry's face was exquisite, a field of small, delicate freckles, her eyes bright, big bluebells. Tiny smile lines creased the outer corners of her eyes, but otherwise, her face was unmarred by her forty-nine years.

Er, her one hundred and forty-nine years.

Perhaps because Princess Briar Rose Charming had slumbered for most of those years, time had forgotten to touch her face.

"Would you mind if we opened a window?" Neve asked. "I'm feeling a bit … warm."

Bry leaped up, unlatched the ornate double windows, and pushed them wide open. "Is that better? Shall I fetch you a fan?"

"No, no," Neve assured her. "It's perfect. How is Lucan? And Dawn and Thea? Are they well?"

Bry took her seat again. "Lucan is training his men," she said of her husband, the youngest Charming brother and commander of the King's Protection. "Dawn and her husband are well, and her talent—she spins magic, I tell you. Every garment is more beautiful than the last. Most seamstresses work because we need clothing in polite company." She laughed. "But Dawn's work isn't necessity, of course. Rather, it's … art. I'm her mother, so of course I'm biased, but it astounds me. She creates all day long."

"It must be joyful to be able to do something no one else can do as well, and have the freedom to spend your time perfecting it."

They were both silent a moment before Bry added, "She certainly keeps her little sister in style. Thea can't get enough of astonishing everyone around her."

Neve grinned. "I love that. She's as creative and unique as Dawn."

"She is."

"Any love to soon announce?"

"No, she hasn't found a prospect yet, despite the fact that noblemen line up outside our castle walls to lose at chess to her." Bry chuckled at her daughter, genius at both the game of skill and the game of flirtation. "She wants a love match, and I promised her I wouldn't arrange it. Between us, I would be sad for her to leave our home, so though she is well past coming of age, I secretly hope it's not soon. Is that selfish?"

"It is not. Thea is the brightest candle in every room she's in. If she were my child, I would hold on tightly as well."

A clatter on the cobblestone and shouts outside startled Neve, and Bry went to the open window and peered down. "Ah, here's Della. With her entourage."

Della never went anywhere—even a simple tea with her sisters-in-law—without fanfare and opulence.

"They're rolling a carpet to my door for her," Bry reported, still looking out the window.

"She's ridiculous," Neve muttered.

"She's a sight to see, but she's loved."

Neve shouldn't fault Della for being the best at what they all were. Della Charming was a princess for all the people—an ideal slice of perfection. She allowed everyone in the kingdom many opportunities to see her, touch her hair, and talk to her.

"I'm only surprised she isn't walking on flower petals," Bry said, her hand on the white linen curtain. "Oh ... my mistake. She is. They're tossing them down now."

"How many horses for her coach?" Neve asked, closing her eyes for a moment. "That can't be only two I hear."

"Six. And a dozen footmen in livery behind her. She's being helped from the coach now. Her shoes! Gleaming rose gold. You should see them."

"I will," Neve said. The parlor was about to get very full of Della's presence.

There was a commotion downstairs and a swishing of skirts and footsteps on Bry's circular staircase. The sitting room door opened and a man in sharp uniform stepped in. "Her Royal Highness Della Charming!" he called in a volume more fit for a crowded town square than two women in an intimate setting.

Della swanned into the room and dropped her arms to her side, allowing two of Bry's servants to slip off her rich wool cape. She thanked them and put a hand on each of their shoulders like a friend before they hurried out, closing the door behind them. Della smiled warmly. Her bright yellow dress flattered her flushed skin, and a rose gold tiara winked at them from atop her upswept blond hair. There was some aging in her hair now—as in Neve's own dark hair—but the gray strands only lent a subtle silver shimmer in Della's case.

"My sisters," she said. "I am so happy to see you. Forgive my tardiness." She kissed Bry on both cheeks.

"You aren't late," Bry said. "Neve only just arrived. Your shoes, Della! I could see their beauty from the window."

Della pointed a delicate foot and turned it this way and that. "I suppose I *am* known for my shoes."

"Oh, that sparkle! That reminds me," Bry said. "I have a gift for you, Della. I'll go get it." She was already out of the room before finishing her sentence.

"That woman can't sit still for more than a moment," Della said, dropping into the chair Bry had vacated. She began to peel off a long white glove. "Neve. Tell me how you've been."

Neve was never sure whether Della wisely perceived Neve's aversion to physical affection, or if Della had her own issue with her. Neve suspected it might be the former because Della was ever gracious, but she would not have been surprised to find out it was the latter. Everyone would agree, particularly Della herself, that Della would be a legendary asset to the throne as the queen of Foreverness. But she'd married the second-born Charming. Brockton had confided to Neve that his brother Colby harbored lifelong resentment at being second, and Neve had wondered more than once if that resentment had been passed on to Della.

If so, Neve wished Della would be crass enough to voice her jealousy, because Neve would have eagerly told her she also wished the responsibility would fall on Della—or on anyone but Neve. Della was far worthier and less fearful. But without a confrontation, Neve had no reason to say it, and so kept it to herself.

"I'm well, Della. You know, I sometimes leave my home believing I look presentable, and then you show up. It's hardly fair."

Della laughed gently.

Bry returned and presented Della with an exquisite shawl. Della wrapped it around herself, looked down at it, and back up at Bry. "Tell Dawn it's beautiful," she said. "I shall wear it until it's nothing but little spindly threads. She is an artist."

"Indeed," Bry said. Her face was full of sunbeams as she spoke about her daughter. Della, also a mother, smiled with the experience that Neve didn't have.

She and Brockton had assumed it would happen. They waited for it to happen. When it didn't after a few years of marriage, they tried a little harder to make it happen. When it still didn't, they decided to not let the circumstances affect them. Neve was grateful that Brockton, the heir to the throne, wasn't too concerned about his ego or his legacy—after all, with two royal brothers, two royal nephews, and no perceivable political threats to Foreverness, the Charming succession was assured. Brockton was disappointed, but he was ever pragmatic.

Neve had feigned disappointment when it became apparent no children would be born to them. But she really wasn't. She hadn't had much to model motherly behavior after, and though she was sure she wouldn't have been a terrible mother, she was also sure she wouldn't know how to be a good one. It was hard enough to worry every day of her life that she might meet her end. If she'd had to worry about the safety of a defenseless baby as well, she would have been driven into madness.

And she hadn't told one soul this, but she'd never really wanted children. She wasn't a child given to playing with dolls or thinking of names for her inevitable babies. She just didn't want any of it, and nature somehow understood. Luckily no one asked her about it, because no one would dare be that impolite to the future queen.

"Your sons, Della?" Neve asked. "Are they well?"

"Oh," Della said. "Those two are far, far too busy to write to their poor mother."

Neve snorted at the word "poor," and Della also smiled belatedly at her word choice. "Oh, you know what I mean," Della said. "They are useless. But their wives are angels, and they write often from their kingdoms."

Neve didn't ask how Colby was and was certain Bry didn't plan to, either. They couldn't presume to know what was happening in the privacy of Della's castle, but the shadow that passed over Della's fine features at any mention of her husband's name had stopped her sisters-in-law from asking for him long ago, even out of mere politeness.

Bry poured each of them a cup of fragrant tea. "The king's birthday is upon us in a fortnight."

"I assume you have the party planned already, full menu, theme, and all?" Della asked.

"I do," Bry said. "The theme is ... Dreams Come True."

Neve raised a brow very slightly over her teacup as she sipped, but Bry caught it. "You don't like it?"

"It's a perfect theme," Della said, rescuing Neve. "That's what King Hopkin is most proud of, after all."

Bry sat back, mollified. "All right. If you're certain."

"Foreverness gets its very name from the happy endings it's renowned for," Della said.

"Neve?" Bry prompted. "I'd love for us to all agree."

Neve didn't want to distress Bry, who put every drop of her energy into making others happy. And it wasn't as if the theme itself was a problem. Dreams did come true in Foreverness, and the princesses' only daily task was to be the living embodiment of the dreams of every woman who lived in the kingdom. Della was effortlessly the best at it, and Bry tried the hardest, but Neve, the future queen, rarely made public appearances.

It wasn't safe.

Bry waited for Neve's response, and Neve tried to understand her own annoyance. Perhaps it was just the similarity to the king's last birthday theme, The Happiest Land, and the birthday before that, Wish On a Star.

"It's wonderful, truly," Neve assured Bry, patting her hand. "You are a brilliant hostess."

"Of course she's brilliant," Della said. "Dreams do come true. For example, what would have happened if Lucan hadn't kissed Bry? She'd still be snoring."

"I don't snore." Bry looked horrified.

"How do you know?" Della asked.

"Lucan has never said I snore."

"Would he, though, if you did?"

Bry sank back in her seat, wide-eyed and open-mouthed. "What if I do?" she whispered. "What if I do … and Lucan can't sleep? He has been looking tired lately …"

"Then he can very well sleep with a pillow over his head. You can't help what you do in your sleep. You're missing my point." Della looked at Neve again. "What would have happened if Brockton hadn't wandered through the woods and decided to kiss a girl lying there dead?"

Neve's lips twitched. That celebrated kiss had been a fiction. While helping to carry the coffin containing Neve's corpse, heir Prince Brockton had tripped on a rock, the bit of poisoned apple flew out of her mouth, and she awoke, banging on the lid and sending his spooked men fleeing into the forest. She'd agreed to tell the story that Brockton had kissed her awake—like his younger brother Lucan recently had at Sylvan Castle—because as the heir to the throne, Brockton said, tripping over his feet was "not a good look." They'd kept that secret safe in their marriage for more than thirty years.

But Della was correct that Neve would still be dead if Brockton hadn't found her. Neve opened her mouth to say so, when the door to the sitting room slammed open and a half-dozen large men in armor clattered into the room.

All three women pushed their chairs from the table and leaped to their feet. Bry turned her face into her shoulder and held up her arm as a weak shield. Della stepped forward, likely to demand explanation, but Neve pushed in front of her, pulled the dagger from her sleeve, and extended the weapon, with her other arm reaching back protectively at her two sisters-in-law.

No one breathed for a half-minute, in which time Neve realized these men were King's Protection soldiers, but she didn't stand down. The intrusion was a surprise, and trust turned a princess into a court fool.

"Your Highnesses," one man said, "forgive us."

"Of course," Bry said, briskly brushing off her fear in favor of etiquette. "Er, tea?"

"Tea?" Della repeated. "You men crash into this small room of gentlewomen as if it's a rowdy tavern at dusk, and then you stand around like mute simpletons? We await your explanation. *And* your proper acknowledgments."

The men all bowed quickly, then eyed Neve and shuffled uncomfortably, clearly unwilling to speak while they were held at bay by her meager little weapon. Neve knew three women and a small blade were nothing against six armored men, but perhaps Della could summon her godmother while Neve distracted them, and then—

Bry laid a warm hand on Neve's shoulder. "It's all right," she murmured into her ear. "We're safe."

Neve breathed hard. These men easily could carry out death sentences right now, if they'd been ordered, and a princess was often the last to know ...

"They're uncouth and inappropriate," Bry kept whispering. "That's the way of men. But they're the king's men. They take orders from Lucan. They're not here to harm us." She slid her hand to Neve's upper arm, which was still steadily holding her weapon aloft. She rubbed Neve's sleeve, softening the muscles and applying just enough pressure to encourage Neve to slowly lower the dagger to her side. "We're safe," Bry said again.

Neve took in and released a long, loud breath. She needed something bigger than this lame little dagger from now on. But how to carry it concealed ...?

"Your Highnesses," the man repeated. "King Hopkin has taken ill."

Neve blinked.

"You needed six armed men to tell us this?" Della asked.

"Hush," Bry said to Della, and then to the soldier, asked, "How ill?"

"The situation is grave," the soldier said.

"I don't understand what you say," Bry said. "He was fine this morning. My husband took breakfast with him. The sovereign is hale and hearty, and in good spirits."

Several soldiers winced. The one who'd been speaking for them clarified. "He did have a good breakfast and was looking forward to the day. He dressed, met with his advisors, and then he left for the stables. Halfway there, he was stricken and fell facedown into the dirt."

Neve took a step back and nearly fell into Bry, who covered her own mouth with her hand in horror.

"Have our husbands been summoned?" Della asked.

"Prince Brockton was informed immediately, and he has sent for his brothers and for the three of you. He said to make haste, but to tell no one of the situation. Not even your children. The prince said it is not for Foreverness to know." He paused before adding, in a tone of respect and regret, "Yet."

It was a criminal offense to talk of a king's death, but it was near impossible not to when it was imminent.

And if it was imminent …

Panic gripped Neve's heart. If it was imminent, she would shortly be …

No.

They would go to the king's side, and he would improve. Sometimes, older people fell. Their bones were weaker. It didn't mean they would—

"All will be well," Neve heard herself say. "We are on our way to Eterne Castle. All will be well, I'm sure of it. Let's go."

"We will take my coach," Della said, wrapping the shawl from Bry tighter around herself and putting on her gloves. "You will accompany behind us," Della told the soldiers, and they acquiesced, because it never occurred to anyone to contradict Della, or to volunteer a better idea.

Della turned to Neve and looked her in the eye. Then her

gaze traveled down to the dagger in Neve's hand and back up to Neve's face. "We won't speak of this again," Della said. "Unless you care to."

"Not particularly," Neve said.

Della nodded, and when she turned away, Neve hurriedly slid the dagger into her sleeve, the cold metal reassuring and familiar against the thin skin of her forearm.

Bry shuffled them into the hall and led them outside, where they crowded their full skirts and heavy hearts into Della's coach.

* * *

Neve knew every line of her husband's face, and though Brockton's expression was controlled and authoritative, she detected the current of sadness that moved underneath it.

When the princesses entered King Hopkin's bedchamber, Brockton stood at his father's bedside. "My wife. My sisters. The king wishes to speak with each of you. I'm going to see if Lucan and Colby are on their way."

He moved to Neve and kissed her cheek, lingering a second—just long enough to take comfort before leaving the room. Neve's compassion for her husband's grief was second only to her fear of her own future, and she felt deeply guilty for that.

The king coughed, and Neve saw Bry flinch ever so slightly.

King Hopkin was small in the bed, smaller than she'd ever seen him. He was pale, his eyes sunken into the dark hollows of their sockets. His lips were as dry and crackling as parchment, and even from across the room, Neve could hear him dragging in each breath.

"My daughters," the king said. "Daughters by ... marriage, of course ... but daughters who nonetheless epitom—epitomize and model perfection for all of Foreverness's women."

His speech was labored, but the long-serving Charming

king would no doubt push against the end as long as he could.

"Come here, Briar Rose," he said.

Bry knelt at his bedside and took his hand, covered in gold rings with jewels so bright, a bat could see them.

"Briar Rose, Foreverness's hostess," he said. "I task you to go on as you have, to continue bringing happiness and ... satisfaction to all in your always selfless way, with nary a controversial or con—confrontational word to anyone. I can leave this kingdom content if you can promise this."

"It is my honor, Your Majesty," Bry said. "Always."

She kissed his cheek and smoothed his white hair back as he said, "Della."

Bry moved away, and Della went to his side and leaned over his pillow. King Hopkin reached up with effort and took gentle hold of her forearm. "Della," he said. "Colby is ... not easy. I don't like to say it. But I know."

Della winced, so slightly that the king in his infirm state probably didn't see it.

"But the people love ... you," he said. "You are their most valuable princess, for you were once one of them. Your ... beauty and graciousness are legend. I ask that you con—continue to set an example for Colby, who will surely come around. I would rest easy knowing ... you are keeping him on the path."

"Colby is ..." Della started.

Bry cleared her throat nervously.

"... my beloved husband," Della said. "And a prince of this kingdom, without whom I'd have nothing. I promise you, Your Majesty, I will guide and help him to righteousness."

"Good girl," the king said, despite that it had been long years since any of the princesses had been girls. Della's chest rose and fell with a breath that seemed resigned. She patted the king's hand twice and walked back to the other women.

"Neve," the king said, but Neve was already on her way to his bed.

"Come closer, my daughter."

She sat beside him on the woolen blankets—far too warm and too many for this mild late-autumn day—and leaned in, angling her ear close to his lips.

"My death will mean your coro—coronation," he said quietly.

"Nonsense, Your Majesty," Neve said. "No one here is dying."

"Neve," he said, his voice a little stronger, "you don't fool me, and you don't fool yourself. You are about to become queen. You have always been a good … wife to Brockton. Smart. Clever. Strong. But … we both know what queens are capable of, so … continue to know your place. This is not Goldenstone."

"Thank the Lord," Neve muttered, and despite what must have been excruciating pain, the king chuckled.

"Thank the Lord," he repeated, "this is not Goldenstone. This is Foreverness, and we have a standard here for people—for women. Be a good queen and a good partner. Be the … happily ever they—we—all believe in. I need to know you are ready."

I'm not ready. I'm not ready. I'll never be ready.

"I'm ready," Neve said, so when his time came, the king could pass into the next glorious world unburdened.

That time came quickly—just a few minutes to midnight.

As Brockton and Lucan embraced, sorrow shaking their shoulders, and as Della and Bry clutched hands, sharing an expression of grief, every beat of Neve's fearful heart thumped, *I'm not ready.*

I'm not ready.

DELLA

The morning sun had barely cracked the sky's dark shell, but Della was already in her garderobe, peeling up the corners of gowns that hung on pegs in search of the one or two somber gowns she must certainly have.

Somewhere.

Her fingers lifted and moved through the mauve gown with drapey sleeves; the seafoam gown, square neckline, drop-pearl trim; the violet—

Ugh. Did she have *nothing* appropriate? Having nothing to wear was not a problem Della was accustomed to.

Her annoyance was interrupted by a soft knock on the door to her bedchamber. "Your Highness?"

"Yes, come in!" Della bit her bottom lip and flipped through her colorful options a little more harshly than a moment ago.

She heard the slight rattling of the shiny silver tray that was carried in every morning and set upon the small table by the tallest window.

"Good morning, Catelina!" Della called. She released the gowns with a huff and poked her head out. Catelina was setting out dishes and small platters. "Don't you look lovely today?" Della said, and the young maid, new this week to Della's household, blushed. "Would you mind fetching Eda for me? I—"

Eda rushed into the room and appeared momentarily startled to not find the princess sitting in bed, waiting to be helped into her soft dressing gown.

"Eda," Della said from the garderobe. "Thank goodness you're here. I need—"

She cut herself off. Brockton had made very clear that they were to keep the king's death in confidence until the entire family could gather this morning to briefly mourn in private and to make arrangements. His father, he said, had not wanted Foreverness to grieve long.

Eda, Della's efficient, longtime servant, moved to the garderobe and said very quietly, "I've already taken one black and one deep-blue gown to be flat-ironed, and you can choose which you prefer."

Della raised her brows. No need to question how Eda had anticipated her unusual needs this morning. The royal servants were discreetly aware of everything, even when they weren't meant to be. Eda left the garderobe and began to make up the bed.

Della yawned loudly and stretched her arms overhead, then circled slowly inside the carpeted room. It was a sad morning, but being in here—it was her joy and her comfort. She moved to the far end and opened the drapes to let the light fall over her collection. Her clothing, her jewels, her adornments—they all deserved to be in the light of day, where she could see and touch everything. She sighed with satisfaction at the rows upon rows of colorful gowns and cloaks on pegs, and the shelves upon shelves of headpieces and wraps and capes.

And shoes.

The shoes took up one entire side of the cavernous space, obedient footmen lined up and ready to serve their mistress.

Elaborate shoes with appliqués and encrusted jewels. Simple shoes in luxe fabrics. She brushed her fingertips over a few pairs. Dozens and dozens to choose from, more than she could wear in a lifetime—if she didn't change her outfit several times a day, which she, of course, did. The people—the women—of Foreverness wanted to see her in finery. They wanted to see her embodiment of their dream. It wouldn't do to disappoint.

A pair of dark silver shoes caught Della's eye. She picked one up and studied it, judging it the choice for today. She used her little stepstool to reach to the highest shelf and pull down a silver tiara, which was small but with a subtle sparkle. Understated.

Her sisters-in-law all had the same right to wear a crown any time they wished, though they usually didn't, outside of formal occasions.

To Della, every day was a formal occasion, and every day she wore a crown.

She'd earned it.

She emerged from the wardrobe and saw that Eda had placed a few peonies in a cup beside her bed, and on her blue velvet pillows were some nicely wrapped tarts for Della to enjoy tonight before bed.

Catelina stepped from the table and tied back the heavy drapes of the window beside it. The morning sun beamed across a table filled with mangoes, oranges, grapes, biscuits, and a selection of cheeses and jams. Catelina poured Della a cup of rose tea. She picked up the other cup and paused. "Will His Highness be joining you, or—"

Della looked up in time to see Eda, who'd come back into the room to open the rest of the drapes, quiet Catelina with dagger eyes. Catelina's face went red.

"Prince Colby has already left for the day," Della assured

her worried young maid. "He awoke very early." So early, in fact, that he never actually came to bed. But it was not something for Della to dwell upon.

After all, it had happened many mornings, after many nights, over many years.

"More importantly, Catelina," Della said, unfolding her napkin, "this is the most beautiful meal I have ever seen in my life."

Catelina giggled, and Della said, "What?"

"You said that yesterday morning, Your Highness."

"It was true yesterday morning. Just as it is true this morning. You do such wonderful work."

Eda finished securing all the drapes of the other windows and the bedchamber was filled with light, but Della didn't look outside. Instead, she examined the perfect room around her. Not a spot of dust anywhere, not a wrinkle in the bedcovers, not a smudge on the window, not a stray cinder in the fireplace. She pushed Colby from her mind.

"I will be in to do your hair when you are finished," Eda said.

Eda and Della customarily chatted together for longer each morning, but Della noticed she was all calm business, in deference to the tragic day.

Della hadn't been close with the king; Colby's contempt for him was open and didn't leave much room for Della to cultivate her own close relationship with his father. She felt sad for the loss of the sovereign and for the kingdom's imminent shock and mourning.

Catelina and Eda both curtsied and turned to leave.

"Wait," Della said, and handed them each an orange. They thanked her and left her alone.

Della popped a grape into her mouth and frowned at the empty teacup. What a fool Colby was.

And he was the first heir now, so he ought to recognize it

would do him well to try to at least appear worthy. Though, if the throne became his, it would be many years from now, and it would likely be a brief time before he succumbed to old age.

What a stupid, stupid fool. As if Colby could find better than this meal, this bedchamber, this life.

This wife.

BRY

ry awoke without opening her eyes. The consciousness slid in softly, her mind forming thoughts again after hours of silence, and Bry had that moment of disappointment she always had upon waking. Sleep was kind. It asked nothing of her. It wrapped her in soft comfort and protected her.

She never dreamed. She'd heard others talk of dreams, and she had no understanding how it even worked. Pictures and feelings and situations that weren't real? Feeling awake when you weren't? How was sleep not the warm escape for everyone that it was for her?

Once, she had invited a wise woman to come to one of her dinner parties, to entertain the noblewomen with fortune-telling. The wise woman proclaimed herself an interpreter of dreams, and all in attendance had clapped in delight and clamored to contribute their dream for discussion. The wise woman had moved down the table, weaving meaning into fanciful dreams of princes trapped in frog bodies, geese that lay golden eggs, witches' houses made of spun sugar. When she reached the end of the table, she looked at Bry, and all the guests held a single breath. Bry had given the smallest shake of her head, for she had no dream to offer. The wise woman had cocked her head in curiosity. Finally, the woman leaned in and spoke softly in Bry's ear, so no one could hear.

"Princess, you *are* the dream, come to life." Bry had blinked, and the woman moved away.

Eyes still closed now, Bry gradually gained awareness of her surroundings. She shifted her legs to feel the silk of her nightgown slide across her shins. She turned her head to feel the satin of her pillow under her cheek. Repose, her loyal cat, was curled up on her belly, and she reached down to pet his long tail. The scent of lavender filled the room, from the candles that burned down earlier in the night, and from the muslin sachet of dried lavender leaves under her pillow.

No light filtered in through her eyelashes; her specially made heavy window drapes covered every crack and kept her bedchamber as dark as a crow at midnight, no matter how bright the morning.

She tried to recall if there were some obligation she needed to rise for, but per usual, she didn't have any morning appointments. She often didn't emerge into the bustling castle until nearly midday. But today—oh.

The king.

Lucan's dear father.

Bry squeezed her eyes shut again, tempted to succumb to the peace of slumber, but she needed to rise, to dress, to meet her grieving family at Eterne Castle.

The door opened, and Bry gave a little sad smile. She heard Lucan walk to the window and open the drapes. Her eyelids brightened inside but remained shut as he walked to the bed and sat down. He always did that for about a silent count of five.

Then he touched his lips to hers, lingering for just a few seconds, and Bry let her eyelids flutter open.

Lucan's eyes widened convincingly, though neither of them was surprised.

"I'm awake," she whispered.

"You're awake," he repeated. "How did you sleep?"

"So well. What … what year is it?"

He laughed softly. She liked that her joke never got old for him.

And what she'd allowed him to believe all these years never got old for her, either. The satisfaction and the happiness on his face every morning were worth it.

"I didn't think you'd come in this morning," Bry said.

Lucan pressed his lips together, but Bry saw the bottom one tremble. "He wants—wanted—Foreverness to go on as it always has," he said. He cleared his throat. "For us to do what we've always done, to allow the perfection of this land to continue. And every morning, I wake you this way."

"Yes," Bry said gently. "You do."

Every morning since her sixteenth birthday—her hundredth birthday as a sixteen-year-old princess. Lucan remembered that day as the day he fought through the fatal bramble around Sylvan Castle, kissed the love of his life awake, and wrote his chapter in Foreverness legend.

Bry remembered that day as the day everyone in her castle in Eventide woke from their century of deep sleep to find their families and friends long dead, their lives gone, and blamed her. Her mother and father practically threw her at Lucan and told him he could have her, and she left her home kingdom with only Repose and her tears.

Young Lucan had been baffled that Eventide didn't celebrate him as a hero, but Foreverness did, and they welcomed her as a daughter. And Lucan loved her as fiercely today as he ever had.

Not telling him the truth of that day was such a small favor when he'd given her so much.

She'd made it her job to give Foreverness all she could, parties and galas and memories. She wanted—needed—this kingdom to love her. But she knew that love could so easily be taken away.

Repose circled around the bed, then sat in front of Lucan. The patterns on his fur began to shift, and colors swirled blue and violet under his skin. His purring grew louder.

"No," Lucan said, looking away. "Not today, Repose. No hypnotizing me to fall into bed. Besides, your mistress could do that to me any time she wants to." He kissed Bry once more and stood. "I'll see you at Eterne Castle, my love. I'm leaving now."

"I'll be there as soon as I can."

He left the room, and Bry watched Repose's colors for a moment, but looked away before he could lull her into drowsiness again. There would be so much heartache today, and she would do everything she could to ease it.

But she'd be back tonight, exhausted as always from doing so much for so many. Then she could sleep.

Sleep was where she felt free, with no obligations. Sleep asked nothing of her.

NEVE

Neve wanted to look away, but she knew she couldn't without guilt. Large brown eyes, filled with wisdom and innocence and concern, gazed into hers.

The fawn finally blinked. Slowly.

Two bluebirds perched on the sill. Singing. For at least a half hour now.

Once, some years ago, she'd asked her staff to hang drapes across the doors and windows at night, and she'd been awakened even earlier than usual by a cacophony of scratching and tapping by her agitated protectors. The window covers were removed the following day.

She got out of bed, pushed open the window, and knelt, allowing the birds to hop onto each of her shoulders. Their loud songs quieted into happy, humming trills. She opened the door and the rabbits hopped around her bare feet, their puffy tails tickling her toes. The fawn nuzzled its trusting head into her open palm.

"What will I do with all of you?" she murmured, and she smiled for the barest second until she remembered what happened last night.

Remembered what she now was.

She gave the fawn a last distracted pat and leaned to the window so the bluebirds could fly out. "See you tomorrow, friends." She ushered out the rabbits and closed the door.

She spread her toes in the thick rug before walking across the room. She was still a little unsteady from sleep, so as she passed the large tapestry on the wall, it caught on her hand and fell to the floor. The huge oval mirror underneath filled with smoke and light.

Neve rolled her eyes.

"Your Majesty," the mirror boomed in a deep, dramatic baritone.

"Honestly," Neve said. "Can you try for a volume more suitable for indoors? It's early. And regardless, it's a bit ... much."

"Your Majesty," the mirror repeated in a more casual, friendly tone. "From this day forth, you are Your Majesty and not Your Highness."

"Could you please not?" Neve hissed. "The king's—it is not public knowledge yet. I don't even know how it is your knowledge."

"It is my one job to see all, and to tell you what you desire most to know. May I tell you who is the fairest of them all?"

"No, thank you. I'm not interested." Neve gathered up the tapestry and tried to toss it over the top of the mirror, but it slipped off again.

"We have not talked for some time," the mirror said.

"We have nothing to say to one another," Neve countered, tossing and missing again.

"I cannot tell you who is the fairest of them all unless you formally ask," the frustrated mirror said.

"Why do you think I keep you covered? I don't want to ask. I don't want to know."

"Why not? All women want to know this."

"I don't." She looked around for the little upholstered stepstool.

"It is difficult to serve you, Your Majesty, if you don't ask me. Would you like to repeat after me? Mirror, mirror on the—"

Neve gave the mirror a stern look, and her stern look reflected back. "Let me explain something to you, piece of décor that has no business addressing me. I'm a few weeks away from being half a century old. If I let you name all the women in Foreverness fairer than me, I wouldn't get out the door before midday."

She dropped to her knees and saw the stepstool under the bed. She dragged it out and over to the mirror. As she stepped up with the tapestry, she could feel the heat of the mirror's enchantment through her thin nightgown.

"Your Majesty, I can—"

"It's not personal." She tossed the material over the top of the frame, relieved when it finally draped over the glass. "I just don't need the information you have to offer."

Because it was information that corrupted. Because the obsession with beauty turned a soul vain, jealous, bitter, angry, destructive. Murderous.

Whatever the mirror said next was muffled, and the magic cooled.

The fawn had come back to the door and was staring at the covered mirror, puzzled.

Neve shook her head. Normal for her was just not ... normal.

She sat on the edge of the bed and put a hand on her chest. *I'm not ready.*

When she stood again, she noticed that when she'd slid the stepstool out from under the bed, a sharp dagger had slid out partially with it. She bent, turned the point away from her, and pushed it back under, then shoved the stool in after it. She didn't need the servants to see the dagger, or to see any of the other weapons their new queen had hidden all around the castle, and the stables, and her coach, and in the garter around her thigh—even now, under her nightclothes.

DELLA

ella alighted quietly from her coach and waved off the footmen ready with her customary arrival pomp. The bells hadn't tolled yet to proclaim the death of their king and the ascension of his son, but there were always people milling around Eterne Castle, the center of this perfect land. King Hopkin had customarily allowed the good citizens to enjoy the grounds.

One young woman cried out, "Princess Della!" and many calls for her attention followed suit, the people moving closer to her.

Della was ever delighted to chat, to hug, to allow her dress and hair to be touched. She stayed for a moment or two longer than she should. Brockton had mandated silence, but the truth of it was that the affection softened the sadness of the morning for her. She worried for a moment that her dark dress would give something away, but one woman who fingered the sleeve marveled at the material, and it seemed they were not alerted by the color. After a few moments, Della excused herself with grace.

They waved at her as she walked across the drawbridge, over the deep moat around the castle. She watched her feet in their lovely shoes so that she wouldn't stick a heel between the boards and leave a shoe behind.

She'd done it before.

The door was open, and two soldiers in full armor gestured her into the Great Hall. A dozen trumpeters, six on each side, raised their horns to their lips and prepared to blow tribute, but upon seeing it was Princess Della, they lowered the horns and bowed their heads instead. She was embarrassed for being disappointed at the muted response.

"My family?" she asked a trumpeter. The king's death couldn't have been hidden from the Eterne Castle staff, and certainly if they were preparing to trumpet in the new king and queen, these men were included.

"In the purple room, Your Highness."

The purple room was somehow as grand as every other room in this castle, even though the focal point was merely a large table. It was where decisions were made, decisions that affected everyone in the kingdom and everyone in the Charming family. The people in the room were not at the table, however; they clustered in a far corner, arms around one another.

Della dashed to Bry, who was rubbing her tearful husband's shoulders. "Oh, Lucan," Della said, embracing him. "I'm so very sorry."

Lucan tried to respond but his throat restricted his voice, and when he stepped back from her, he covered his mouth with his hand, shaking his head.

Della hugged Bry, then Bry's eldest daughter, Dawn. When she stood back, Della swiped away a tear on her niece's face. Dawn offered a watery smile.

"Aunt Della," Thea said, stepping out from behind her parents.

"Oh, Thea." Della took both of Thea's hands in hers.

"Grandfather was so ... alive when I saw him last week," Thea said. "I just don't understand."

"Neither do I," she said.

"Do you need anything?" Bry asked Della. "Is there anything I can get for you? I'm sorry, I should have—"

"You're soothing your grieving husband," Della said with a sad smile. "It's all right, Bry. You can't do it all."

"But—" Bry began, and was interrupted by the trumpeters' loud, harmonious herald.

"Is such a cacophony appropriate?" Della muttered to no one in particular. "A funeral is imminent."

"So is a coronation." Thea took hold of her elbow and whispered to her. "That's the irony of a king's death, isn't it? No one knows whether to mourn the departed or celebrate the incoming. So they do both."

"Idiots," Della said through her teeth, and despite the somber room, Thea giggled softly.

Speaking of idiots, where was Colby?

The door opened, and Prince Brockton entered.

King Brockton.

With Queen Neve at his side.

Everyone in the room fell immediately into a curtsy or bow. Della didn't mean to hesitate; she really didn't. But Neve appeared truly despondent, her alabaster skin even paler, her rosy lips drained of color. Their father-in-law had just died, but though King Hopkin was ever kind to Neve, Della, and Bry, he hadn't had much room in his heart for anyone other than his sons and hadn't had room for anything in his agenda other than upholding the traditions of Foreverness, so Della didn't believe Neve's face was miserable with grief.

It must be something else. Confusion, perhaps? But she'd known this day was coming, if not exactly when.

If it had been Della, Della would have been fully prepared. She would have known what to say, what to do.

What to wear.

She would have been an instantly beloved queen.

As Neve would be. So why did she look as though someone had offered her an apple glistening with heart-stopping poison?

Neve looked right at Della. Della hurried to dip into her lowest, most reverent curtsy, eyes downcast. *Rats.* She hadn't intended to be insolent.

When she glanced up again, Neve was looking at Brockton.

"Please rise," he said, and gestured to the table. "Sit."

They each took a seat in a high-backed, purple velvet-cushioned chair. Brockton sat at the head of the table, Neve at his right.

He said nothing for a few long moments.

Then the bells began to toll, deep and heavy and final.

The shrieks of shock began with the people outside on the castle grounds. They would quickly reverberate throughout the land.

A few people in the room sniffled.

"It grieves me to have to get down to business on this cursed, dark day," Brockton said, and cleared his thick throat. "But I have no choice. Our father insisted that our ever-joyful kingdom not formally mourn, and I will honor that, despite our deep sadness. I will, however, delay the traditional coronation ceremony and celebration for two weeks. Out of respect."

The door slammed open, and Colby swaggered in.

Maybe "stumbled" was a more accurate word. There was no way to know if his drinking had started before or after the news of his father's death, but either was staggeringly inappropriate.

"Your Majesty," he slurred and collapsed into an exaggerated mockery of a bow, with one knee on the floor and one arm sweeping his hat grandly off his head. "My dear brother. Brother dear."

Della's mouth fell open. Were those leaves in his hair? What was wrong with him?

He stayed in the deep bow long enough for someone at the table to cough nervously, and then he jumped up, snapping his heels together. Then he clapped his hands once. "What have I missed, *King* Brockton?" he asked with a grin.

"Colby, sit down," Della hissed, but he didn't hear her, or pretended not to. She slid out the empty chair beside her, and he glanced at it before electing to stand in the corner, arms crossed, the grin never leaving his face.

She couldn't believe she'd ever found that fool face worth a night of fragile spells and elaborate masquerade.

Neve appeared even more pained. Brockton arched an admirably tolerant brow at Colby and carried on.

* * *

After Brockton adjourned, Bry left her children sitting with Lucan as she went about arranging refreshments to be brought to the common folk who were now pouring onto the grounds and surrounding the castle. Lucan's chin drooped to his chest, and Dawn and Thea flanked him, murmuring and drawing him close.

Della pushed away from the table. Colby was standing in the corner, gazing into space with a twisted smile. He'd been thankfully silent after his memorable entrance.

He'd lost his father, too. And though she knew full well this outburst wasn't just his way of mourning, she went over to him.

"Do you need anything?" she asked, keeping a kind face. "Some water?"

"There is nothing you can do," he said, "that will make any of this all right."

She winced a bit at his emphasis on the word "you," but she loathed a scene, and he'd made enough of one.

The door to the purple room creaked as Lord Everard, King Hopkin's head councilor, stepped into the room. He approached the new king and queen with deference, bowing and speaking low to them for a moment before moving toward Colby and Della.

Though she knew the names and faces of everyone in court, Della had never had compelling reason to speak directly with the lord for any reason other than polite greetings. And it was unkind, but she couldn't help wondering if his voice was as sharp as his countenance. When he walked, he sliced a path through the air with his pointed chin and nose. His lips were always pushed into a firm line, his eyes always squinting in discontent.

Lord Everard bowed to her cordially, then bent his head to Colby to speak quietly. Della backed away a few steps. When she saw a thin smile ghost across her husband's face, she wondered if she should judge the lord so harshly.

Colby's eyes met hers and hardened again.

She left the room, needing a moment to herself.

She circled away from the Great Hall and its infernal trumpeters and moved down the corridor toward the tall window at the end.

You're not going to be king. Della would never say it to Colby's face, but she said it in her head. *It's just as well for all of us. You have no diplomacy and no passion. But it's a pity I won't be queen. And I would have been a legendary one. Yet you don't see me making a scene, crying, drinking, pouting like a toddler. It's unbecoming of those of our position, which is still the second highest in the land.*

As she was scolding her husband in her head, it took her a moment to hear the real scolding. She followed the angry sound into the kitchens. Servants dropped their spoons and knives to the floor and hurried to curtsy. "Your Highness," they said, but she did not stop as she ordinarily would have. She picked up her pace and the voice got louder.

"Do you think that is sweeping the floor? Do you see those crumbs in the corner? Are you blind?"

You missed a spot, Cinder-slut! You're the stupidest child ever born!

Della rounded a last corner just in time to hear the servant woman say, "Well, lest you forget the corners in the future, perhaps you should eat the crumbs yourself, like a mouse."

The girl, no older than thirteen, shook her head. "No, please—"

The woman kicked the girl's knee hard, sending her with a gasp to the brick floor. "Eat them!"

The king's death. Colby's embarrassing display. The silvering hair she'd had to carefully arrange her tiara over. Neve's issues about whatever the hell she was having issues about. All the feelings that had been simmering under Della's calm countenance bubbled, boiled, and spilled out.

"*What* am I witnessing?" Della roared.

The woman turned, ready to argue, but when she saw the princess before her, she dropped low. "Your Highness."

Della knelt and put her arm around the frightened girl. "Are you all right, sweetheart? Are you hurt?"

"N-no," the girl said, standing with Della's help.

"Your Highness," the older woman began in a far more reasonable volume, "we hold the highest standards in the royal kitchen, and I needed to make sure she—"

"I don't need your explanation," Della interrupted, "for you can have no good one. She is but a child."

"She is willful and stubborn and—"

"The only willful and stubborn person I see here is you, who is still speaking when I told you not to." She looked around and saw the offending breadcrumbs in the corner. "Have you ever shown this child exactly how you want the sweeping done? Have you ever gently corrected her with patience until she swept a floor to your liking?"

The woman stayed silent.

"That was a question," Della said. "You may speak to answer a direct question."

"Who doesn't know how to use a broom?" the woman burst out.

"Someone who hasn't been shown proper technique. Someone who hasn't been taught what the standards are and how to meet them. Someone who hasn't been praised, and has only been abused, and as a result, sees herself as invaluable and incapable of good work."

Della turned to the girl. "Is this the first time she has laid a hand on you?"

The girl's eyes widened in fear, and Della had her answer.

She turned back to the older woman, whose shoulders had hunched into her dress as if she were expecting her own blow.

"There are two reasons I'm not sending you to your room to pack," Della told her. "The first is that I presume you haven't been taught properly either, and you emulate only what you've seen and experienced yourself. Second, you are not my staff."

If she *were* Della's staff, this wouldn't have happened at all.

"The new queen will hear about this," Della promised, and the woman flinched. "And I will recommend you undergo the training you should have had years ago so that you learn how to treat new servants. And you *will* learn."

What training? From whom? Della didn't know. The only person she knew who had properly and respectfully trained staff was herself.

"Yes, Your Highness," the woman stammered.

Della wrapped her arm around the young girl. "Come. I will have you reassigned elsewhere, and I will make sure you understand your duties so that when you are senior staff, you will repay the favor to new girls."

The girl leaned into Della's shoulder, and Della rubbed her upper arm. Most middle- and lowborn children did not have a fairy godmother to grant their wishes to escape torment and enjoy life.

As they walked, the girl's body lost its tension, softening to trust. So did Della's.

Everyone remembered Della as a lowly cleaning woman. That part of Della's legend was unforgettable.

From the moment the first delicate crown was placed on her head, Della had known her legend wouldn't end with a queendom. Destiny didn't have that in mind.

Tightening her protective arm around the girl, Della considered what that destiny might instead be.

BRY

The next morning, Bry wrapped her arms around her younger daughter and held her close. "Thea! What a joy to see you."

She felt Thea's body shake a little with laughter. "Mother, you speak as though I rode in from the top of a deserted mountain, rather than strolled from the other end of this very castle."

Bry stood back from her, hands on her shoulders. "This castle is unreasonably large. I'd live in a two-room cottage happily if it was with you, your sister, and your father."

"That just wouldn't work. After I put my clothes in the cottage, where would all of you sleep?"

"You get your clothing obsession from your Aunt Della," Bry said.

"Because she is *marvelous*," Thea said. "Speaking of marvelous, what do you think?"

She twirled in a circle, the skirts swirling around her feet. The violet satin brocade gown had a tight bodice and a square neckline that flattered Thea's slight shoulders, and it flared out at the waist into a full skirt covered with tiny white embroidered blossoms. She'd added a large amethyst pendant on a substantial gold chain, and long white gloves that clung to her upper arms.

Thea was never without a stunning outfit, thanks to Dawn. Neither was Della, for that matter, who often requested original gowns from her niece.

"You look like the most enchanting flower in the garden," Bry said.

"Hello!" Dawn cried, walking into the foyer.

Thea ran to the door to hug her sister, and their strawberry-blond heads touched. Thea was a year younger than Dawn, but they could have been twins, with their red-gold hair and their freckles and their wide, bright blue eyes. Dawn's eyes held the sparkling promise of a new morning. Thea's held the joy of the best day in one's life.

Dawn stepped back and took in the violet gown as Thea twirled again. "Gorgeous. I don't mind saying, I'm really good at this."

As a teenager, Dawn had discovered her talent in secret with a royal seamstress who'd taught her the basics. When Bry found out her daughter was using spindles, needles, pins on a regular basis, she was irate—and terrified—but when Dawn brought her first dresses out for her mother to admire, and Bry saw all the little bandages on her fingers, she realized her fear was unfounded. If her daughter had inherited her curse, she'd have succumbed to it already, judging by the number of times the spindle had jabbed her.

Even those first dresses she'd made had been so unique, with unusual color pairings and creative use of different patterns and fabrics, and Bry couldn't dream of suppressing her daughter's talent. Now Dawn made dresses for herself, for her mother, for many nobles—and mostly for Thea.

Dawn was headed to market this morning to find some fabrics and lace trim for some recently requested gowns. Thea was joining her because she loved going to the market for any reason. Bry had invited herself along because if her two daughters were having fun together, she refused to be left behind.

"You are beyond good at this," Thea affirmed now. "Luckily for you, you're a wealthy woman of leisure with hours upon hours of time to make dresses for your sister. Oh, I suppose I mean, luckily for me."

Dawn grinned. "Hello, Mother."

"Let's go, my daughters," Bry said. She covered her hair with her hat and held out each arm. Her daughters each took one, and they walked toward the center of town.

"It's a beautiful day," Thea said, "and I'm so happy to shop, but I feel like I shouldn't be. Grandfather—"

"Grandfather wanted Foreverness to go on as usual," Bry reminded her. "He would want to see you smile."

"In that case," Thea said, "when we get back, how about a game of chess?"

Dawn groaned. "Theaaaa. You know I play chess about as well as I can fly, and Mother is even worse. No offense, Mother."

"None taken. I'm quite hopeless at the game. But don't you get enough play time, Thea? Your skill is renowned. Scholars travel from beyond our borders to play with you. Not to mention military and clergy."

"All men," Thea said, " men who would have expected to lose, and did, to the prince once upon a time. But you should see their faces when they lose to Princess Thea. At least when you two lose to me, you don't feel the need to convince me how much luck plays a part or make the excuse that you happen to not feel your best today."

"You changed genders," Dawn said, "not brains. These stupid men are not as wise as they think themselves to be."

When Thea had told Bry and Lucan two years ago that she was a woman, Bry had not been the least surprised. She'd known Thea's entire life that her mind and spirit and character were feminine, delicate, sensitive, far more like her own than like Lucan's. Lucan had known it too, and Dawn, and they'd embraced their younger child's soul as original and beautiful. They would love her any way she felt true.

A sorceress of good was able to manifest the permanent transformation, and Prince Day at last became Princess Thea.

Though Bry tried her best, she'd been frustrated over the months to make mistakes that hurt Thea. She called her Day a few times, and each time Thea fled the room, sometimes angry, sometimes frustrated, sometimes holding back tears. Bry had finally trained her treacherous mind and mouth by staring at a portrait of Thea and saying her name over and over so she wouldn't make the mistake again, and she hadn't since, but she'd made others. She'd told her sisters-in-law about Thea's decision rather than letting Thea do it—she'd thought it would make it easier on Thea, but she realized too late it hadn't been her news to share. She'd also fussed over Thea so much before her first public appearance that Thea snapped at her that she was an adult and didn't need her mother hovering like a vulture.

Every time Bry blundered, Thea and Dawn both let her know—Dawn with a little more impatience than her younger sister. Bry insisted each time that she was trying so hard, that she wouldn't hurt her deliberately. She didn't want Thea to feel a mere shred of the rejection Bry had felt when she'd left Eventide.

What kind of mother would she be if she let that happen?

The kingdom had accepted Thea's change; after all, Foreverness was no stranger to human transformation. Spells and potions and curses made humans stronger, weaker, more beautiful, and more unfortunate-looking, as well as turned humans into frogs, crows, trees, and bears. A human changing from man to woman was something to barely blink at.

"It is their privilege to be in your brilliant presence," Bry said.

"Tell me about it," Thea agreed.

"Maybe ... maybe in time, it will change."

"Yes, just wait for men to figure out women are as smart as they are," Dawn said to Thea. "You'll wait so long, they'll find your dried-out skeleton sitting in front of the chess board."

Thea snorted.

"But—" Bry started.

"It's all right, Mother," Thea said. "I know you prefer to look the other way, and to not make a fuss, lest people decide they don't like you."

Bry opened her mouth to protest, but Thea held up a hand. "I said, it's all right. Men don't think highly of women. But at least I'm a high-ranking woman. Maybe not as high-ranking as I was before ... but still, I suspect I have it easier than most."

The trio arrived at the market, and Bry's daughters released her arms.

"I'm going to see Peat first," Bry said. "You two wander about. I'll catch up."

Dawn and Thea linked arms and disappeared into the crowd.

Moss Apothecary was just outside the entrance to the market, a small cottage with a thatched roof. Peat didn't keep particular hours; he was there any time one came. He always knew who was coming and when.

Bry pushed the door open, and an unfamiliar fruity scent wrapped around her. There didn't seem to be anyone around, but she often had to look down or up or into corners to find Peat Moss.

Not seeing him right away, she called, "Peat?"

"Princess Bry!" he called back. "I'll be out in a moment."

Bry began looking at bottles of oils on shelves, and in less than a minute she already carried two she intended to buy. "What is that scent? It's tantalizing."

"It's pineapple sage, Your Highness," he said from the back room.

"It smells nothing like clary sage."

"It doesn't," he agreed.

"Where did it come from?"

"That, I can't tell you," he said, his voice in the same room now, and she turned to see him hop onto the table in the middle of the room. He placed a little paw on his chest, and his bushy gray tail rose behind him as he bowed. "It is wonderful to see you."

She bowed her head back to him, returning his humble acknowledgment. "And you, Peat. You look well."

"Would you know for sure if a squirrel didn't look well?"

Bry stammered, and Peat dipped his head. "A joke, Your Highness. You are a kind soul who would find a compliment for someone no matter how they looked."

"Peat, for goodness's sake, will you please just call me Bry?"

"I will not," Peat said. "I am honored by the presence of royalty here, and I will enjoy every moment. What can I do for you?"

"Do you have anything for snoring?"

"Thyme," Peat said. "I will make you a potion if you wait a few moments."

"A small one. I am not even certain that I do snore, but ..."

Peat studied her with his small dark eyes. When she didn't finish her sentence, Peat said, "Perhaps you would like some lemon balm as well. It ... soothes worries."

Bry relaxed her shoulders. "That sounds perfect."

Peat leaped off the table and bounced from a chair to

another chair to a smaller worktable. He rummaged through jars and bottles. After finding what he sought, he began to crush leaves into a tiny bowl. "I am sorry for the loss of King Hopkin," he said. "He will be remembered by all."

There were other alchemists and healers in Foreverness, including some who used sub-par ingredients and charged much less for teas and potions. But everyone knew if you had a cough, a sore back, a heartache, anything that one good night of sleep couldn't resolve, Moss Apothecary was where one found proper relief. Peat had come to see the king in the hours before His Majesty passed, but he was past the point of healing. Peat could only offer herbs of comfort and drowsiness before he left.

"How is King Brockton faring?" Peat asked. "And Queen Neve?"

"They are sad," Bry said, "but they inherit a strong kingdom with no problems or strife. Things can go on as they always have."

Peat bent his head lower over his work. "All new rulers have changes they want to put in place, no?"

"Perhaps in other lands. But here, there is no need for change."

"Change is the order of the universe," Peat said. "Winter changes to spring. Caterpillars change to butterflies. Children grow into adults. Clouds give way to sun. Winters and caterpillars and children and clouds all have their time, but they must change eventually."

Bry fidgeted her hands together. "I agree with your logic," she said carefully. "I just—it's not my place to—I shouldn't—"

"Forgive me." Peat scurried to her and placed his little sharp-clawed paw on her hand for a moment. "I don't mean to distress you."

"You didn't. But it's not for me to have an opinion about

how Foreverness should be governed. Brockton and his councilmen are wise."

"Indeed, they are. I'm just a squirrel given to musing out loud."

"I appreciate your opinion," Bry assured him.

"And if you offered yours, I promise you I would appreciate it in return."

Bry smiled as Peat wrapped her purchases in parchment and secured them with twine. "As always, I'll put it on the Crown's account," he said.

"Thank you."

"Please remind your family that I am at their service. If they need anything."

"I will, but I'm sure I don't need to," Bry said. "You are a gift to this kingdom."

Bry left the cottage and walked into the bustling market. She moved from booth to booth—admiring, touching, inquiring—while one of Lucan's most-trusted King's Protection men followed her at a respectful distance, keeping watch. Two other guards had followed her daughters. The booths the princesses perused were on the perimeter of the main part of the market—the merchants who catered to buyers noble and royal. The rest of the market was for commoners, and Bry had never ventured there.

Bry saw Thea examining necklaces as Dawn flipped through fabrics and chatted to the shopkeeper. They didn't appear ready to leave yet, so Bry moved restlessly toward the center of the square. As she stepped onto the unruly, overgrown grass of the square, a chilling wind blew the forest-green hat from her head. The hat was a gift from Dawn, and Bry couldn't bear to be without it in the coming winter, so she chased it as it tumbled along the grass, carried quickly along by the determined gust.

When she was finally able to snatch it off the grass and

deposit it back on her head, she straightened and looked around, breathless. The crowd was larger here, and merchants were shouting competing prices and enticing potential customers to look at their wares.

Bry's dark cloak covered her rich gown, and though her identity went unnoticed by the commoners moving around the market and filling their baskets, the merchants had a discerning eye for the quality of the wool of her cloak. "My lady! My lady!" they began to call, trying to get the attention of a woman who might have a bit more to spend than most of the others in this part of the market.

The strong scent of wood and cinnamon stopped her, and she closed her eyes a moment, breathing it into her nostrils. She blinked her eyes open and moved toward a table with spices in jars. The jars were created with love, with raffia tied around their lids and little sprigs of flowers or herbs tucked into them. Each jar looked like a little work of art.

"These are beautiful," Bry said, brushing a respectful finger along the jars.

The shopkeeper was bent at the waist—her rump to Bry—as she rummaged through some supplies. "There are some small open jars on the right, there," she said, "if you'd like to smell any samples. I'll be with you in a moment."

Bry moved to the samples and picked up a small jar containing a crooked and clawed light-brown root. One part of the root had been sliced off and the smell from the jar was a strong pine. Galangal. She picked up another with bright reddish-orange shavings and the leathery, earthy scent of saffron wafted out. Bry brought it to her nose, and nearly dropped it when the shopkeeper stood, saw Bry, and shrieked.

"Your Highness," she breathed, curtsying low. "H—h— how may I serve you?"

"Your jars are lovely. They smell wonderful—high-quality

spices. But it's the way you wrapped them with love that makes me want to take them all home."

"Please," the woman said, sweeping her arm over her table. "Take anything you like."

"I will not," Bry said. "I will, however, purchase several for my kitchens. I'd like the galangal, the saffron, and I did smell some cinnamon—"

The woman produced a little jar with cinnamon sticks, and when she handed it to Bry, her trembling fingers brushed the princess's. She looked to be about forty and was wearing a simple dark-brown gown with a colorfully stained apron over it. Her fingers had the same stains, brown and red and bright yellow.

"Do you have anything else you'd particularly recommend?" Bry asked, trying to put the woman at ease.

"Well, I do have some black pepper. Many here sell black pepper, but mine is—"

"The best?"

"I wouldn't want to say that."

"You should want to, if it's true. If you were a man, you'd say it even if it weren't true."

The woman paused, taking that in, then burst into laughter. "Your Highness, that is a fact."

"I'll take some of the best black pepper in the market then, please."

"You are very kind," the woman said, and put all Bry's jars into a basket. She named a price that sounded far too low. Bry plucked two gold coins out of the little purse dangling from her wrist and handed them over.

"Oh, Your Highness, they say you are the most generous princess who ever lived. I appreciate it."

"I appreciate it more," Bry said, "and I will instruct my staff to cook a meal tonight featuring these wonderful spices.

What is your name?"

"Giselle, Your Highness."

"How long have you had this shop, Giselle?"

Giselle told Bry about her spice business—begun by her parents, and when her parents died, Giselle's husband, a farmer, allowed her to take over the business. Giselle had helped her parents for many years. Now her children were nearly grown, so he'd seen no harm in her taking over to provide them with extra money. As Bry asked more questions, and as Giselle told her more, it began to feel like two women having a warm chat, and not a commoner speaking to a princess.

"I'd love for you to visit for tea if you'd like—" Giselle said and stopped abruptly. Her face flushed bright red. "Oh ... oh, I'm so sorry, Your Highness, I forgot myself. I—"

"I would love to visit you for tea," Bry said. "The market is closed tomorrow. How about tomorrow?"

Giselle blinked. "I—I suppose I could make the place ready."

"Don't go to any trouble. I'll bring cakes. If you have tea, that will be perfect."

"I do," Giselle said. "I—I would love that."

"Do you have any friends or neighbors who'd like to join us for a ladies' tea? That would be lovely. I'll bring plenty for all."

"You want to come to my farm?" Giselle clarified. "And meet my friends?"

"Yes. Unless you prefer to come to the castle."

"No! Er, no," Giselle said, laughing. "I don't have a gown suitable for a visit to a princess. And I invited you, so ... please come ... to my home. Yes. Your daughters are also welcome, of course."

"Wonderful. It's gotten quite mild today, hasn't it? Unseasonable." Bry pulled off her hat. Her hair was pinned up like always, but the sun must have lit the red ember of it, because several people gasped.

"The princess," she heard in hushed tones from every side of her. "The princess!"

NEVE

Neve's hands were soft on the reins, not interfering as her horse picked her careful way over rocks and roots. Turning from the smooth dirt road in town to this transition path was bumpy, but Neve had done it hundreds of times, and she knew the path would smooth out as they moved into the woods.

The path was too narrow to ride side by side here, so Brockton waved her ahead. She heard his stallion snort behind her, and she smirked. Brockton loved that intimidating, muscular, ebony horse from the moment he'd laid eyes on it. But the horse—named Monarch—had proved a sensitive, mewling baby about everything in the forest: running streams, a robin's sudden chirp, a chipmunk skittering from here to there. Any time Monarch caught a pebble in his shoe, he moaned and limped dramatically. Brockton had to travel with a pick so when necessary, he could slide off Monarch's back and remove an offending pebble from his hoof. Monarch would gratefully snuffle until faced with the next peril: a swaying low-hung branch, or a particularly sinister baby rabbit.

Brockton didn't sell the horse or give it to one of the men who worked in the stable. He insisted that Monarch behaved like a professional in an open field and on a dusty road; he was just distracted when in the forest. He rolled his eyes and shook his head every time Monarch acted up, but he always soothed the spooked beast until the horse could move forward.

Neve loved her own mare, Biscuit, but she had more kinship with Monarch and his state of constant anxiety. There was no assurance of safety anywhere, really. You could live with someone who protected you in a secure kingdom, you could train with weaponry and arm yourself, but if someone set out to hurt you, they'd get to you sooner or later.

The bumpy path smoothed out into cushiony grass, and Biscuit plodded happily along. The woods were friendly here on the edges of town. Traveling farther and deeper brought one to the dark forest of The Unfathomed. And no one with any sense went there.

Not unless it was against their free will.

The path widened, and Brockton urged Monarch into a trot to catch up with Neve and Biscuit, then slowed to a walk beside them. Six members of the King's Protection kept a respectful distance behind them. As the future king, Brockton hadn't been permitted to travel anywhere without an escort, and as the new king, his guard had multiplied.

Neve pressed her hand flat to her right thigh—subtly, for Brockton was riding on her right—and felt the cool comfort of the dagger on her skin, secured under a garter.

"Did you sleep well?" Brockton asked.

Neve had awakened covered in sweat, but the night sweats were nothing new these days, dreams or not. Even during the day, doing nothing in particular, a heat would come over Neve so suddenly, burning her from the inside out, intense but brief. She'd mentioned it to Peat Moss a couple of weeks ago, and he'd given her some licorice tea and told her it was normal for a woman her age to experience these hot spells during the change.

She didn't even like the word "change." In fact, the thing she'd liked most about Foreverness was that it didn't change. It was the ever after, and ever after was secure and safe. It had kept Neve secure and safe.

"I slept as well as I am able," she told Brockton truthfully.

She was certain he had slept worse. She wanted to ask him which weighed heavier on him, the loss of his father or the inheritance of a kingdom, but she didn't.

She supported him always. He was destined to be a king of legend.

Brockton glanced at her. Everything about him was regal, from his tall seat on Monarch to his perfect nose to his gleaming hair to the important lift of his chin. The only time he wasn't regally composed was when he visited her bed and she—

Brockton interrupted her thoughts. "My Neve, perhaps after your visit today, you could study your books, refresh your knowledge of the laws and—because ..." His words trailed off.

After they had married, Brockton and his father had encouraged her to acquire the kind of education a royal boy would have. Well, they hadn't really encouraged her—they'd insisted. Brockton had told her that although he was a traditionalist and intended to rule Foreverness the way it always had been, he could see nothing but benefit in having a wife who was educated and from whom he could seek counsel. And he did often ask for and value her opinion on political and social matters, and when he did, she gave him careful, learned answers. More often than not, he took her advice.

"Oh, Brockton," she said now. "You didn't need to escort me today with all that's happened."

"No, I didn't. But I craved one peaceful ride with my wife before I begin a lifetime of rule."

"I understand. And yes, of course, I'll catch up on my

reading and current events. But there is not much to catch up on, is there? King Hopkin never tired of reminding us that the social and political waters of Foreverness are still and clear."

"I know," Brockton said. "And I'm grateful for my father leaving me a peaceful land to rule. But it would ease my mind if you do it anyway."

"I understand."

Neve appreciated the opportunity to do as Brockton asked and use her mind. What she was known for—what she'd died for—was her beauty. A princess had lots of dull social obligations, and she fulfilled them all, but they were not intellectually stimulating. She rarely used her mind for anything important or creative. What she did seem to use it for most frequently was to dream up scenarios she had to prepare for, scenarios that involved her assault, her kidnapping, her poisoning, her—

A butterfly skipped along the top of the grass, and Monarch danced in place, lifting his head, showing the whites of his eyes.

"Shh, boy," she said, as Brockton rubbed the steed's big neck.

Biscuit kept walking, unaffected by the butterfly or her equine companion. She just enjoyed the walk. Monarch could do the same, if only he let go of his unfounded fears.

The cottage came into sight, surrounded with swaying colorful wildflowers. The wooden windchimes above the front door clanked a tuneless, continuous song as the breeze moved through the air. Several miniature horses roamed through the grass, swishing their tails and chewing.

"I'll never understand," Brockton said, "why your uncles didn't want us to build them a grander, larger home. I told them I'd be happy to. After so many years of working in the mines, and caring for you, they deserve it."

"That's not what they want," Neve said. "They know we'd give them anything, but they want to live as they always have."

Shortly after her royal marriage, Neve had insisted on moving her uncles out of The Unfathomed, for she would never again set a foot in those woods, but she wanted to keep her close relationship with the men who'd raised her. They had agreed, but only if their home was re-created, brick by brick, so the relocation, the change, would feel less abrupt. This, Neve understood, and granted their wish.

Though he'd seen the small horses many times before, Monarch began to shuffle uneasily, so Brockton slid off his back and took hold of his bridle to walk him to the door. Neve did the same with Biscuit. But before they got to the door, it swung open. Uncle Bart stepped out and fell into a deep bow.

"There's no need to—" Neve began, but Brockton dipped his chin in acknowledgment, so she did the same.

"Is she here?" Uncle Forwin yelled from inside the house.

"No," Uncle Bart called back, staying low. "It's just my favorite chicken wandering by and I decided to bow to her egg-laying prowess."

"Witty." Uncle Forwin stepped outside and bowed as well, and they both rose.

"Perhaps the handsome King Brockton will appoint you jester, and you can take your wearisome jokes to court. I would regard it as a personal favor to me if you did, Your Majesty," he said directly to Brockton.

Brockton chuckled.

"We are deeply sorry for your sudden loss, Your Majesty," Uncle Forwin added.

"There will be songs sung about your father for generations," Uncle Bart added. "Truly."

"Thank you both," Brockton said.

Neve dropped Biscuit's reins to run over to them. She knelt to embrace each of them in turn.

They were her home.

"Where are the others?" she asked.

"Anselm and Terric are out back," Uncle Forwin said. "Gerard's in the kitchen."

"Ah, I'm jealous. Had I the time to stay and indulge in Gerard's fine cooking, I would," Brockton said. "I will send men back for you in a few hours," he said to his wife, kissing her on the cheek.

"We'll take good care of her," Uncle Forwin said. "It's nearly time for tea."

"Tea?" Brockton said, swinging himself up into the saddle. "Don't even try to fool me. The minute Monarch's rump is turned and we're heading out, you'll pull out the ale and play cards all afternoon. My wife can't sit still through tea with noble ladies, and it's mainly because she prefers old-man pastimes: cards, dice, backgammon, and ale."

"I'm sure I have no idea what you're going on about," Neve said.

"Like every visit, we'll first have tea," Uncle Bart said, "then Neve will needlepoint as we read aloud from the Bible."

"That's three bold lies in one sentence," Brockton said. "Luckily for you, I don't care what she does."

"I'd say it's lucky for you," Uncle Forwin said, "for even if you did care, Neve would do as she pleases."

"He's not wrong," Neve said to her husband. They looked into each other's eyes for a lingering moment. She trotted over, reached up, and took his hand, pressing it comfortingly between hers. "You are certain you don't mind if I stay here a while?"

"Of course not. They're family. I'll see you soon," Brockton said fondly. "Have fun, sirs. Don't let her take your gold this time."

"Eh, not worth getting cross about it when she wins. Our gold is your gold, after all. It's more a transfer than a loss," Uncle Bart said.

It was Neve's privilege to be able to support her uncles with the Crown's money—these men who opened their home and their hearts to Neve when she'd stumbled into their cottage as a traumatized twelve-year-old. They'd shared everything they had, even for not having much. She'd needed a home, and they'd quickly realized they wanted a child.

"Let's get on with it," Uncle Forwin said. "No use standing around chattering like magpies when I have ale to drink and coin to transfer."

Brockton left with the escort, and the three of them watched until he was out of sight. Then they walked to the back of the house.

"He has you somewhat figured out," Uncle Bart said, "but not completely."

Uncle Anselm and Uncle Terric were already back there as Uncle Forwin had said, but what he'd left out was that they were taking turns throwing axes into a badly constructed wooden wall twelve feet from the cottage. Most of their axes stuck with a chunk. Some of the axes simply thunked against the wall and thudded to the ground.

"Little love!" Uncle Anselm called as he and Uncle Terric rushed to her, a small carving knife and piece of wood falling from Terric's lap to the ground. She hugged them each in turn, grinning as she always did to hear the "little love" nickname from one of her short-statured uncles.

"Bow to your queen, you fools," Uncle Forwin said, and they rushed to do so.

"Brockton's not here," Neve said. "You can skip the formalities."

"Good. You're up," Uncle Anselm said to her. "I'll have you

know that my throwing has improved four-point-eight percent after putting into practice some calculations I've been working on. Foot position and the rotation of my shoulder. So—"

"Button up, Anselm," Uncle Forwin said. "At least three of the four axes on the grass belong to you."

"You didn't see it."

"Am I mistaken?"

Uncle Anselm twisted his mouth under his thick gray beard. Neve patted his arm. "I've no doubt you've improved."

Uncle Terric laughed. "It's so good to have you here indulging us," he said, then knelt to pick up his knife and small piece of cherrywood from the ground. She held out her palm, and he handed her his latest creation: a dove. Though it was only whittled to half-finished, the feather lines were intricate, and the eyes already held the wisdom that an inanimate object shouldn't. But she did notice the eyes were uneven, an unusual imperfection for Terric's precise artistry.

"Beautiful as always," she said, and when she gave it back, she noticed a small tremor in Uncle Terric's fingers.

Her uncles were getting older, after all. They'd each seen seven decades, and Uncle Forwin had recently seen the turn of an eighth. But one wouldn't know it by the way he now said, "Terric, quit your showing off. Let's throw axes."

Uncle Terric stretched his arms overhead. "I was only giving you all a little extra time to gird yourselves against my ax onslaught."

"It's little Neve's turn," Uncle Bart said. "Stack 'em up and step aside."

Neve shed her woolen wrap and dropped it on a cut tree trunk. The cool wind cut through her gown's light sleeves, but she didn't mind. She gathered her skirts in both hands and took her place beside the axes.

"Nice and steady," Uncle Anselm counseled.

Neve took an ax in her hand and rubbed her thumb along the rough wood. She focused on the crudely painted bull's-eye in front of her, and it morphed into Fina's exquisite, perfect, evil face. No matter what target Neve had in front of her—for axes, for knives, for archery—it was always Fina's face.

Her stepmother, Queen Fina, was long gone, but the threat to Neve never faded. Fina's council was still alive, and they knew full well Neve was alive. As long as she was, she could conceivably return to Goldenstone, though Neve had made it clearly known she'd never again set foot into her home kingdom—the kingdom whose now-deceased king had allowed their queen to murder her stepdaughter with impunity.

Her uncles had protected Neve with love and safety for five years, and just when Neve had allowed her happy life to ease her constant anxiety and vigilance, Queen Fina had returned to deliver death.

Neve hadn't let the anger cool, ever. The anger fueled her training and sharpened her skills. And she never again abandoned her cautiousness.

Her uncles stood by quietly, waiting for her to throw. She let the ax fly. It rotated once before sticking, hard, on the inside white circle. She picked up another and threw it, and it landed wide, sticking on the outside red circle. She threw all ten this way, some going wide, one dropping, and the last throw sliced through and stuck in the center of the bull's-eye.

"Men," Uncle Bart said, "why do we even bother?"

"We all play for second place," Uncle Anselm agreed, winking at Neve as he went to collect the axes.

"The difference is," Uncle Terric said, and cleared his throat, "that little Neve is never playing."

Neve swallowed, her own throat dry. It was one thing for her to dwell daily on her past and worry about her well-being every moment. It was another thing for her uncles to have to worry for her now. They'd earned their present life of leisure and ease.

"How are you?" Uncle Forwin asked, far too casually to suggest anything other than he knew full well how she was.

"Why would you ask me that?" Neve said.

He shrugged. "When we'd heard the other day that the king had fallen ill—"

"How did you know that?"

"Everyone knew," Uncle Forwin said, "that Hopkin was not long for this realm."

"You weren't supposed to know that."

Uncle Terric raised his brows. "Right, right, no one was *supposed* to know. But everyone did."

"The more people involved in keeping a secret," Uncle Anselm said, "the more likely it is the truth comes out. With three sons, three daughters-in-law, and an entire castle of staff taken into confidence, you thought it was going to stay quiet?"

"It's happening," Uncle Bart said. "Our little love, the best queen Foreverness will be lucky enough to have."

Neve began to shake her head, but Uncle Anselm nodded. "You are a smart girl. You always have been. And Brockton did well to hire the best tutors for you, though I did try my hardest to teach you."

"The royal tutors were very surprised at my proficiency in Latin, and reading, and arithmetic," Neve said, smiling at the memory despite herself. "And they were quite horrified at my knowledge of military tactics, rudimentary though it was. They had no intention of furthering my military education until the king eventually commanded it. He thought I would be a help to his son behind the scenes. It took a while before the tutors were comfortable discussing scenarios with me."

"Not only do you have brains, but you are the most beautiful child in half a dozen kingdoms," Uncle Terric insisted, squinting at his little wooden dove as he worked. "The mirror decreed it."

"The mirror decreed it when I was twelve," Neve said. "I am to be fifty not long from now."

"Are you saying some women have become fairer than you?" Uncle Bart asked.

"Some? I'd say very many," Neve retorted. "And that's for the best. Foreverness doesn't need a jealous and powerful queen obsessed with any woman who stands between her and perfection. It didn't do Goldenstone—or me—any good. At any rate, the people of this kingdom haven't had a queen since Brockton's mother died eighteen years ago. They want a queen like she was—temperate, agreeable, and steady. And yes, pretty enough. That will be my public job. I will counsel Brockton as he requires."

Uncle Forwin took an ax and threw it expertly into the center of the bull's-eye. His next throw was also close to the center, but lacked the force of the first, so it just clanked the target on the ideal spot before falling to the grass. "Sounds to me like a waste of everything you are."

"Forwin!" Uncle Bart admonished. "Don't be so ornery."

"I'm not ornery," Uncle Forwin said. His next shot stuck well, and he turned and lifted his chin to look Neve in the eye. "I'm honest. And honesty holds that a future queen who is smart, tough, resilient, and capable should be using all those traits to rule a kingdom. To solve problems."

Neve hesitated at the sudden fire in his eyes, then she looked away. She lifted an empty cup, filled it with ale, took a hearty sip, and wiped her mouth on her lacy sleeve. "Let me remind you, as queen I won't be ruling anything. I'll be little more than a head under a crown, and a warm rear end on an elaborate velvet chair."

"In Goldenstone, you wouldn't be a consort," Uncle

Forwin said, as if she didn't know. "You would be a queen regnant."

"You are the true heir to that throne," Uncle Anselm added, "and in Goldenstone, women can fully inherit the throne and rule."

"Yes, well, it's too bad then, isn't it, that I'm never returning to Goldenstone? They have a strange way of showing allegiance. For example, by shrugging off the assassination of a child princess. My guess is they'd shoot me through the heart with an arrow the moment I stepped through the gates and put me in the ground this time so I'd stay dead."

Neve realized her back teeth were pressed tightly together, and when she released them, the tension in her jawline eased. Uncle Forwin continued working through the pile of axes. Uncle Bart poured Uncle Terric another ale. Uncle Anselm watched Neve, his eyes warm.

She didn't often discuss her death with her uncles, both because it wasn't her favorite topic of conversation and because of the deep grief they had fallen into upon finding her body on their floor, half a golden apple beside her lifeless hand.

Uncle Walter had succumbed to his heartache two months later, as Fina's collateral victim. When breath had returned to Neve after a lifeless year under glass, she had rushed back to the cottage to find her beloved family had lost him as well, and the broken spell could not return him the way it had her.

"Goldenstone is behind me," Neve said, knowing the words were useless. "And as it happens, I have no interest in ruling. I just want to continue to enjoy the security I'm fortunate enough to have in Foreverness."

But even as the sensible words fell from her lips, her mind was screaming. As queen, she was an even larger target than she was as a child princess. Who knew who wanted her dead?

Fina had been survived by ambitious advisors who wouldn't want to see Neve return, and once they heard she was queen, they might fear a desire in her to return to Goldenstone and claim her right to that throne as well. She never would, but as long as she was alive, she was sure they'd consider her a threat.

"Anyway," Neve said, "it's your turn at the axes, Uncle Bart. Let's see how you've improved since our last game. Maybe you can stick one out of ten this time."

Uncle Bart guffawed and stood for his turn. It took a few minutes, but the mood lightened, and Neve laughed and drank as she always did with them. When they tired of throwing axes, they circled around the large, low wooden table and played cards with most unsportsmanlike conduct, taunting one another. Uncle Anselm tried to lecture them on probability and strategy, which they all ignored. Uncle Forwin slapped his cards down in anger every round and growled in frustration when they all found it hilarious. Uncle Bart's attempts at bluffing failed every time, and Uncle Terric's attention constantly shifted between his wood art and his cards. Uncle Gerard stepped out of the cottage to bring plates of fruit cobblers, juicy slices of ham, and gold-roasted cabbage and turnips. He sat for an occasional card round, chewing while he studied his cards, then returned to the kitchen for more.

During one loud but amicable argument, Neve slipped from the table and went inside. The simple window covers were drawn so the interior wouldn't get too warm, but in the light filtering around her, Neve could see the main room—an exact replica of the main room in the cottage where they'd once lived happily together. Though Uncle Walter had been gone already, her uncles had insisted on bringing all seven beds to this new home, so that his spirit always had an earthly and familiar place to rest.

Neve wandered into the small kitchen and watched Uncle

Gerard fuss over a rhubarb pie. "I eat better here than I do at the castle," she remarked.

"Good," he said, bending over to breathe in the pie, then patting her forearm with floury fingers. "Then I know I can always lure you back here by your stomach, Your Majesty Little Love."

"You speak as though I would ever need incentive to come."

"Well, I have a feeling your daily schedule is about to get quite busy."

Neve frowned.

Uncle Gerard waved a tea towel over the pie to cool it. "Almost ready."

"I can't wait."

Neve moved back into the main room and walked to the bed designated for Uncle Walter. She sat, then reached over to the next bed and took Uncle Layne's pillow into her arms. They'd lost him, too, four years ago.

She'd been lucky to have the love and care of seven generous men, who'd protected her from royal wrath as long as they could. Who'd seen to it that she grew up smart and capable and cautious.

But a large family meant her losses and heartaches would be many. She hugged the pillow to her chest. Uncle Walter had been empathetic and wise. She wouldn't have had to tell him about her royal trepidation—he'd have understood without a word and hugged her as long as she'd needed him to. Uncle Layne would have understood also, and he would have tried to fix it for her, the way he'd fixed broken pottery and fences and had sewed all her loose buttons. His amicable advice would have been a salve.

She asked silently for their presence, asked them to surround her with love, asked them to send her something, someone, to help her.

DELLA

ella took her usual seat in her cavernous dining room for supper. Catelina had helped her change into a satiny orange gown and twisted her hair into braids. Della had added sparkly heeled slides and a tiny tiara to make her grand entrance down her center staircase— to no one.

The table was covered with enough platters of food to satisfy six of her: fruits, breads, meats. A vase at the center of the table exploded with pink, red, and orange lilies.

She sat at one end of the table and was halfway through a little pile of grapes and cheese when Colby breezed in. He went straight to the table, plucked a strawberry from a plate, and popped it into his mouth. "Good evening, my only love," he said with a smile.

He moved to her end of the table and kissed her on the cheek. "You smell like a spring bud," he said, close to her ear.

"I know." *You smell like rancid rose oil and sour mead.*

The least he could have done, for the sake of politeness and decorum, was bathe before showing his duplicitous face to her. The cloying rose scent stayed in her nostrils as he took his seat at the other end of the table. The burst of lilies hid him from view, and that was fine with Della. "You are well?" she asked, pretending she was truly as ignorant as he believed. She almost wished she could blame unspeakable grief for his absence since the new king had called them all together, but it was just more of the same from the middle Charming.

"Pardon?" he called from his end.

"Never mind," she answered, louder, and filled her wine goblet. At least her husband remained discreet about his dalliances. The only ones who knew for sure were their staff, who loved Della and so remained quiet and kind. And of course, Della's godmother, Rhyannon, knew, but only because Della had told her.

Colby's behavior was obvious to Della, but not to anyone outside their castle; she'd never heard idle talk, nor could she identify any of his paramours. In public, he maintained his royal appearance. And as Foreverness's tax collector, he was in and among the public often. It was an unusual post for a prince, but Colby liked money, and he liked traveling and meeting lots of people.

Particularly female people.

It disturbed her that his contempt for his deceased father and for his brother had been on such open, foul display at Eterne Castle. Della hoped whatever Colby had gotten up to afterward had cleansed his soul somewhat, so he could continue to keep himself in check.

Colby said something, and Della called, "Pardon?"

"I have a gift for you, my love."

Della raised her eyebrows.

Colby rang the little bell beside his plate, and a maid rushed in. He gave her a small velvet box and she walked the length of the table to give it to Della. "Thank you, Saphira," Della said. "I must say your hair looks beautiful. So shiny."

Saphira blushed, curtsied, and left.

Della opened the velvet box and her eyes widened at the size of the ruby, nestled at the center of the gold filigreed locket. She slid her fingers under it to feel its weight. She used her thumbnail to pry the locket open, but—not unexpectedly—Colby hadn't placed a love token or note inside.

It was a beautiful piece, and Della enjoyed the rush of excitement that always flowed through her when she acquired something exquisite. The satisfaction of knowing she deserved it, that she was in a position to wear and possess anything she wanted her entire life.

She pushed her chair back and traveled the length of the table to Colby's seat. "Will you help me put it on?"

He stood as she pulled the chain from the box. She handed him both ends of the chain and turned her back to him. As he placed it around her neck and worked the clasp at her nape, his fingers lingered on her skin. She remembered when they first married—that rush of happiness came not only from his gifts but from his touch, his breath on her body, his sleeping beside her.

It was a distant and hazy memory. She'd since redirected her desire to her clothes, her jewels, her shoes, her carriage, her magnificent horses. Everything except her prince, because she'd learned he wasn't the prize. He provided her the prizes, perhaps even more often now than ever.

"Turn," the prince said, and she did. He stepped back and looked at the locket, not at her face.

"How does it look?" Della finally asked, though the weight of the gold below her throat was sufficient to remind her of her worthiness. She didn't need his hollow words as well.

But she played her part.

He did look at her face then, and her hair, and her décolletage. He said nothing at first. Then: "Exactly the way it's supposed to look. As always, you look the way you're supposed to."

"Thank you," she said. "How has work been?"

He patted her cheek as he sat again. "That's not for you to think about. Just be pretty."

Della had had to fiddle with her tiara several times this morning to make sure it hid the small little patch to the left of her hair part, where the strands had gone nearly white and where her maids painstakingly applied dandelion paste daily to try to mask it. She twisted her lips. The phrase "just be pretty" didn't take into consideration how much work and time "just" being pretty was. More and more every day. Every year.

Colby reached for a glass of water.

Despite her husband telling her not to think about it, Della added, "Perhaps you should take a little time off, and—"

"Duty calls," he said. "As the tax collector, I don't have the luxury of not working during crises. I daresay my father would have been more pleased to know I was ensuring business as usual."

As callous as it sounded, Della suspected Colby was right. King Hopkin had only ever received barely disguised disrespect from his second son and wouldn't have expected his deep mourning. And the king made clear to his daughters-in-law at his deathbed that what he wanted afterward was status quo. Foreverness frozen in its perfection, and for them to all continue playing their perfect parts in that.

Colby took up a small plate, heaped meats and bread on it, and stood. "I'll take this with me. Enjoy your supper."

"Surely duty doesn't call at this late hour," Della was unable to resist saying.

"It's less of a call," Colby said, "and more like a scream." He took a bite of bread and winked at her.

She picked up another small loaf and hurled it hard at his smug face, shattering the bones of his flawless royal nose.

No, she didn't.

Colby left the dining room without incident, and Della returned to her seat. She sipped her wine, but it had lost its appeal.

She'd only asked after his business because it was expected of a wife. She'd learned not to care what he did all night, but she'd never actually cared a fig about what he did all day.

His condescending response never changed, but today it aggravated her to no end.

Just be pretty.

She laid her hand on her chest and pressed the locket against her skin.

Lines around her eyes and mouth, grays in her hair, thicker flesh around her waistline and her thighs. She was loved by the people nonetheless, but how many years until her youthful beauty was a memory? Neve would be queen, and she'd have the throne and the respect of the kingdom upon which to rest her aging bones. Della would just be an old princess, no longer relevant.

She couldn't turn back the pages of time, but at least her looks were only one part of the image she and Colby maintained as a royal couple, and the rest of it was something Della had full control over. Their castle grounds had to be not just neat and orderly, but noteworthy—full of flowers not grown anywhere else in the kingdom. Della had designated several acres for the public to walk in, and even on rainy days, she could see people from her window, alone and in groups, walking along the paths and admiring the unusual flora.

The grand foyer was private, but a year after their marriage, she'd commissioned a foyer nearly as grand to be built just off the public gardens. The foyer had high gilded ceilings in pale blue, and lush blue carpeting that she replaced yearly. There were some paintings and sculptures there, but visitors mostly ignored the impressive art in favor of viewing the showpiece of the room.

The glass slippers.

The shoes were nestled on purple satin cushions in an enchanted box. Only Della herself could open the box, but she hadn't, not since the day the shoes went on display. She had no more use for them, but they were the stuff of dreams for the women and girls in the kingdom. Mothers brought their tiny toddling daughters and lifted them to see. Teenage girls ceased their giggling for a moment as they gazed on their own ambition.

Every woman, every girl, wanted to be a princess. Della had been born into nobility, but was nowhere near royalty, and had been forced into degrading servitude by her own family. But she had become a princess. The shoes were a reminder to all that the dream of elevating one's status—though rare—was possible. Boys were expected to go out and make their fortune. Girls merely hoped and wished a fortune could somehow make its magical way to them.

The foyer would open early tomorrow, with probably two dozen people waiting at the door to come in and visit her shoes. Visit her past.

Along with maintaining the castle grounds to the highest standards, Della saw to it that her household was immaculate and pleasant. Upon her arrival to Foreverness as princess-to-be, she had trained her new staff to attend to the smallest of details, and year after year, her veteran staff continued to train incoming staff the same way—ever improving in small ways. Everyone who worked in this castle—from the cooks to the laundresses to the chambermaids—understood that Della's household set the standards for the households of other nobility, and they worked knowing their littlest tasks were meaningful.

Della wasn't a fierce taskmistress, quite the opposite. These immaculate flowers, the flawless spread—perfection was achieved because Della genuinely respected the people doing the work. She addressed them each by name, she complimented them, she tried to make each of them feel seen and valued, not just for their contribution, but as a person.

Here are my dirty underthings, Cinder-slut. Launder them and be quick about it.

Oh, did I spill the sugar bowl? How careless of me. Make sure you get every speck of it off the floor. Looks like it will take a while.

I found some stray cinders in the fireplace, Cinderella. Did you think I wouldn't notice? You will pay for this in lashes. Remove your shift ...

There were echoes of her mistreatment in the way so many noblewomen talked about their staff. Della hosted occasional ladies' afternoon teas and dessert parties, and upon taking in Della's warmly decorated and spotlessly maintained household, the invited guests would immediately begin complaining to one another about their own lazy, incompetent, useless staff. Della listened with discomfort. If they used those degrading words in polite, etiquette-minded company, they were certainly meaner and more ruthless to the servants themselves.

Della slid off her chair and to her knees. She squinted at the wood floor, and swiped her finger across it, picking up nothing. She stood and walked to a side table, brushing her hand on its surface. Dust collected quickly and daily, but there was none here. To avoid beatings and berating at the hands of her stepfamily, Della the teenager had gotten quite good at cleaning floors—and windows and furniture and fireplaces. She would have done it all happily if she'd known she'd be a princess and teaching a staff to keep her castle. If she'd known she'd capture a prince's fickle and changeable heart long enough to secure her future.

She bowed her head and put her fingers on her temples. "Rhyannon," she whispered. "Rhyannon."

When Rhyannon appeared, it was without noise but with plenty of light and shimmer. Her expression was amused, but it always was. Her pink hair was plaited, held together with live butterflies, their wings fluttering. Her summery gown was woven with fresh, fragrant flower petals and her cape was a patchwork of every leaf that grew on Foreverness's trees. She defied age, or at least an estimation of age. Sunlight glowed off her dark-brown skin, and moonlight reflected in her eyes, even though they were indoors. She *was* nature, ever changing.

"Della, child," Rhyannon said.

"Rhyannon," Della said, "I need you to turn Colby into a decent human being."

"That's not a skill I have," Rhyannon said. "You know this, my lovely goddaughter. I can only transform outward appearances."

"Surely you can change mine, then. To my seventeen-year-old self, please."

"We've talked about this, Della. Come on." She took Della by the shoulders and steered her to the table. Della collapsed into her chair.

"Rhyannon, Colby had supper with me and—"

"That's unusual."

Della glared at her godmother, who blinked, causing glitter to fall from her lashes onto her cheeks. "What?" Rhyannon asked. She sat and poured water into a goblet.

"He looked at me like he wasn't completely happy with what he saw."

"Is that what he said?"

"No, he said the same all-purpose, flattering nonsense he always says. But ... he paused a bit too long in his assessment of me before he said it. It's only a matter of time, Rhyannon."

"Until what?"

"Until everyone feels as he does. Until Foreverness no longer regards me as a standard of beauty." It was bearing down on Della. "It might already be happening. I only need to look younger. I don't ask you for much."

"That's true," Rhyannon said. "Since your wedding, in fact, you've asked me for very little. Being a princess seems to take care of all one's basic needs and then some."

"That's right. So, just this. Yes?"

"Why can't I say yes? You tell me."

"Because you're a horrible, uncaring godmother."

"Perhaps if you keep acting like a child," Rhyannon said, "you will physically regress into one. Now, why can't I say yes?"

Della sighed. "Because your stupid spells are temporary."

"That's right. And it takes a lot of work to hold them in place. A spell as elaborate as making you look like a teenager—"

"Thank you *so* much."

"—would take constant physical effort on my part to keep it up and even then, it would expire in just a few hours. I couldn't do it daily. You'd need a sorceress for a long-lasting or permanent transformation, and even so, you're not guaranteed to look like Della Charming when she's done. You might look younger, but like a completely different person, and what if you look younger but you're not as beautiful?"

Della touched her face instinctively.

"It just wouldn't work," Rhyannon said. "You've been gradually aging for years. You haven't gone to pot overnight. Why is it important to you today? Because Colby looked at you for a half-second too long? He's probably still drink-addled from last night."

It was true that for some years now, Della was preoccupied with gazing at herself in the mirror, pushing the skin on her face up with her fingers and letting it drop with dismay. She'd continue to maximize what she had as long as she had it—in no earthly realm would Della Charming put herself out to pasture—but this was all she had.

Neve would be a good queen, brilliant counsel to Brockton, a boon to the kingdom. Della didn't want to be petty and jealous. And she certainly didn't want to think about her father-in-law's demise in terms of what it bestowed on someone else. Those were the thoughts of a bad, shallow person.

"Right." Della stood and smoothed down her skirts. "I need to undress."

"What are your plans tomorrow?"

"A ladies' tea."

"Sounds lovely."

"It's just another day."

"Is it?"

Della straightened and looked at her godmother. "What do you mean by that?"

"The kingdom is very different today."

"How?" Della asked, puzzled. "It is Foreverness. With a new king and queen, yes, but that is all."

"Is that all?"

Della waited, but Rhyannon didn't elaborate.

"I've never been fond of this," Della said.

"Of what?"

"Your infuriating little tendency to entice me to figure things out for myself instead of just telling me what you mean. I don't have the patience for this."

"That's a good start," Rhyannon said, and before Della could stomp her foot in frustration, Rhyannon added,

"Farewell, my goddaughter," and shimmered out of sight. Della walked out of the dining room and toward the grand staircase, mentally shuffling through her gowns to select one for tomorrow.

Just be pretty.

BRY

Bry relaxed on her coach's velvety cushions as it turned off the Foreverness town road and bumped onto a country path. Several plates of her kitchen's most wonderful pies and cakes sat beside her, and she put her hand on the furthest one to keep them all from sliding to the floor as the coach bounced side to side. On the seat opposite her, Dawn touched Thea's shoulder to steady herself.

"Thank you for inviting us along, Mother," Thea said.

"I didn't invite you," Bry clarified. "Giselle did. She's the owner of the most delectable spice booth in the market."

"So you've said." Dawn smiled. "I'm happy to see you're making friends."

"What do you mean by that?" Bry asked, looking down at herself, then back at her daughter. She always tried to be kind to everyone, but Dawn's statement sounded patronizing. Had Bry fallen short lately? Had people been talking? Had—

"There just isn't much opportunity for you—us—to widen our perspective, is there?" Dawn asked.

"What my sister means," Thea said, "is that we're subjected to the same faces of the same noblewomen at every party, every ball, every feast day, every tea, every—"

"Don't be rude," Bry admonished her younger daughter.

"Am I wrong?" Thea insisted.

"Whether you're right or wrong is not the arbiter of rudeness," Bry said. "And no, you're not wrong. But some of the noblewomen are ... lovely."

Dawn laughed. "Diplomatic as ever, Mother. Of course, you want to be above reproach. But between you, me, my sister, and a bunch of sweets, I'm sure we can agree we don't get to meet many new people with different interests and ideas."

"Mm-hmm," Thea said, looking out the window.

The coach hit a bump hard enough for Bry's teeth to slam together, and she winced. She didn't want to encourage her daughters in gentle mockery of the ladies at court, however private the coach was, so she merely said, "I am sure this afternoon will be an enjoyable and memorable one."

Dawn and Thea exchanged satisfied smiles. Bry was happy to see the gowns they had chosen were flattering and pretty—Thea in a blush pink, Dawn in a leafy green—but simple, without rich adornment and with minimal jewelry. Bry herself had done the same, in cobalt blue. It would be unseemly to arrive at a modest home in ostentatious dress.

"Your Highnesses!" the driver called. "If your directions were accurate, the farm is just up ahead."

"Thank you," Bry called back. Before Bry had departed the market yesterday, Giselle had drawn a painstaking little map for Bry, who'd passed it to her driver. She leaned away from the sweets and peered out the window.

The small home was just as Giselle had described it: a single-story structure made of earth, sticks, and mud. The grass was lush around the home, and several goats casually wandered, yanking up mouthfuls of it every few steps. There were no other houses in immediate sight, so all this farmland must belong to Giselle and her husband.

The driver pulled the coach to a stop, and jumped down to help the three princesses out, but they were out before he could get to the door, dividing the cakes and pies among themselves to carry to the house. "I am happy to help, Your Highnesses."

Bry had chosen to come along with her daughters without the assistance of a maid, and she refused the driver's help now as well. "Please return in an hour and a half," she said.

He bowed and hopped back into his seat as the three princesses walked to the door. With their arms full of sweets, they couldn't gather their skirts in their hands, but Bry was pleased to see her daughters were as unconcerned about it as she was. Despite their status, she'd vowed when they were babes that she would not spoil them, and there was no deeper satisfaction for a mother than witnessing her own job well done.

Giselle threw open the door when Bry arrived. "Your Highnesses!" she cried and dipped into a low curtsy.

"Ah," Bry said, "let's dispense with formalities. I find them tedious and time-consuming."

Giselle guffawed and rose. Her nearly black hair was pulled into an elegant bun. The streaks of gray reminded Bry of shooting stars in a midnight sky. "These are my daughters, Prin—ah, Dawn and Thea."

They exchanged pleased-to-meet-yous as Giselle took the sweets Bry was holding. "My goodness!" she exclaimed. "Such decadence my stomach has never known! Though you wouldn't know it to look at me." Her comment was accompanied by an affectionate pat of her own belly and such a joyous laugh that Bry had to join in. "I'll bring these to the kitchen."

"We'll help," Thea said, and she and Dawn followed Giselle to the far corner of the home. Bry needed a moment to adjust her eyes to the dim lighting—the trees around the home scratched out most of the bright afternoon sun, and candles lit the room. She realized there were four other women seated in small chairs in front of the fireplace, with the largest three chairs waiting, she assumed, for her and her daughters. A few young girls sat together on the floor, playing with dolls and paying no mind to the new women who'd walked in.

Dawn and Thea's comments about the noblewomen blew back into Bry's brain as she looked at the group. Any time Bry hosted a tea, the guests' dresses and jewels were chosen for distinction, each woman wanting to look the prettiest, the wealthiest, the most tasteful. In this room, however, the dresses were neutral, unadorned, while the women themselves held Bry's interest: They were a range of ages—and expressions, from nervous to wary to suspicious.

"Good day to you all!" Bry said, coming into the room. "I apologize if we are tardy."

No one said anything for a moment, and Bry remembered the way Giselle had stammered when she'd first met a princess.

"You're not at all tardy," Giselle said, bustling back into the room. "My guests were all quite early. Hoping, no doubt, to catch me in either a fib or the throes of madness when I'd told them three princesses were coming for tea."

Bry felt a tug on her hand, and she looked down to find a girl of about four, brown eyes wide in her brown face. "Well, hello, my darling," Bry said softly.

"Adelaide," a woman said, standing abruptly and nearly sending her seat tumbling to the wood floor. "I'm sor—sorry, Your Highness."

"Call me Bry. And there's nothing to be sorry for." Bry crouched until she was eye level with the child. "Hello, Adelaide. Do your friends call you Addie?"

The little girl was too shy to say anything more, and just looked at her own tiny bare feet, but she clutched Bry's hand tighter. Bry smoothed her other hand over the dark hair and turned to her embarrassed mother. "She is just like my Dawn was."

Dawn smiled and took a seat, and Thea sat beside her. Bry introduced them and continued to speak.

"As a child, Dawn would merely look at me with her big eyes—just like Adelaide—every time I spoke to her," Bry remembered. "If I hadn't clearly recalled her crying in the cradle, I'd have sworn she was born with no voice. Her hearing was fine, because when anyone called her name, she'd cock her head toward the sound. I did worry some that she'd been enchanted, perhaps." Bry laughed. "Then one day, she opened her mouth, and she never closed it again."

"Mother," Dawn said in reproach, but it was with a twinkle in her eye.

"It's true. You chattered about your day and about the birds outside and about something your father might have said that morning. And when there was no one around to talk to, you just sang to yourself while you played." Bry grinned at the women. "It turned out she had plenty to say. She just chose her moment to start saying it."

Adelaide's mother's face relaxed into a smile. "I am—I am glad to hear you say that. Addie is the same, so I have worried some. I'll look forward to that day she chooses to speak."

"Look forward to it?" another woman exclaimed. "Please. My boy never gives me a moment's peace with his constant nattering. I'd give anything to have him spend just two consecutive moments with his lips together."

All the women laughed, and the awkwardness thawed. Bry sat and pulled Addie onto her lap, and the little girl leaned her head back contentedly on Bry's chest while fingering the subtle lace on the cuff of Bry's sleeve.

"I'm afraid that was more my personality," Thea said. "Incessant talking from my first day."

"It still is," Bry quipped.

Thea gasped and placed a dramatic hand on her chest. "You wound me."

"Oh, she does not," Dawn said.

"You're right, she doesn't," Thea agreed, dropping her hand and shrugging. "It's all true."

The women laughed again. Bry was happy to see several of them slide their chairs closer to her and the rest of the group and lean in to introduce themselves.

By the time Giselle began to pour the tea, the smiles were warm, the conversation was noisy and spirited, and the room had brightened despite the sun dipping lower and lower behind the obtrusive trees.

* * *

"This is the most pleasant afternoon I've had in ... well, forever," Mirabel—Addie's mother—said, popping the last bite of cake in her mouth and licking apple icing off her fingertips.

Giselle grinned. "Oh, yes. I've happily neglected everything today, and it was well worth it."

The other women nodded in agreement. Bry's inner hostess was pleased to see they had enjoyed the sweets and chat. Dawn was leaning close to Kathryn, and they were whispering with foreheads close in that way that fast female friends did. Thea had moved to a corner table, where she was playing chess with Kathryn's teenage daughter, and Bry could tell by Thea's expression and gestures that she was impressed with the girl's mental acuity.

"I'm delighted that you invited us today," Bry said to Giselle. "This has been wonderful."

Indeed, it had. Bry had discovered these women's interests and talents were unique. Kathryn was an artist, and

Giselle had several of her charcoal sketches of owls and birch trees and fawns to show Bry. Mirabel was a singer, and with the women's enthusiastic prompting, she sang one of Bry's favorite hymns so elegantly and profoundly, it moved Bry to tears. Anne read more books in a month than Bry read in a year and had an astonishing knowledge of history and herbalism. Bry wondered if she could introduce her to Peat, but of course, Anne and Peat were already friends. And Thomasina told stories so hilariously that the bawdiest young men at court would be impressed.

But now, Bry noticed that beside her, Thomasina had gone suddenly somber, staring into the teacup on her lap. Bry waited until Giselle began speaking to another woman, then she leaned toward Thomasina and touched her hand. "Are you troubled, friend?"

Thomasina hesitated, then looked up at the princess, her eyes shimmering. "I—it just seems as though this tea is coming to an end."

"Soon," Bry said. "But we must do this again. Your story about your neighbor's dog made me laugh so, and I will insist upon hearing more of his exploits next time."

Thomasina quirked her lips into a smile that disappeared as quickly as it had come. "I just—I don't want to go home."

"Whyever not?" Bry asked. "Surely you will want supper."

"Your Highness—" she began.

"There's no need for titles, my—"

"Please tell me," Thomasina whispered, "for they say you slept for a century. How can I do that? How can I—because I want to sleep."

"What—"

"I want to sleep until he is dead and gone."

Bry noticed that the room had fallen silent, except for the sounds of the oblivious Addie and other children now frolicking outside. Even Thea and her chess student had stopped and were looking on.

Thomasina gripped Bry's hand so tightly, her fingers were turning white. "Please," she said again, her voice thick with tears. "Please tell me. I'll do anything."

No one asked Bry about that, ever. It was decades ago, but the ladies at court were far more likely to whisper about a scandalous past than to outright ask someone about it, especially when it concerned a royal family member. Even Neve and Della had never asked for specifics, though Bry had mentioned a few small details over the years.

"Thomasina," Giselle said in quiet warning.

"It's all right," Bry said, though she wasn't sure it was. To the crying woman, she said, "I am sorry to say that it was an enchantment cast when I was a babe. I ... I didn't even know about it until after I woke up."

A couple of women gasped and murmured.

Thomasina sniffled. "I am sorry, Princess. I shouldn't have asked."

"Don't be sorry. You are desperate; it is clear," Bry said. "Please tell us what is wrong. Who is it you fear?"

Bry glanced up at the other women, and she realized immediately that though their faces were full of sympathy, they were absent of surprise. They knew what pained Thomasina.

"My—my husband died," Thomasina said. "A few weeks back. It was an illness. Mercifully short, but sudden."

"Oh, my sweet," Bry said. "I am sorry."

"That's not—of course, I mourn him. But—"

She stopped, then sat up straight, still clutching Bry's hand.

"When he died, I prepared to take over the farm. I am a farmer's daughter. I've worked the land my whole life. I know what to do. But last week, my husband's brother rode to Foreverness, to my home. He said our farm—my farm—belongs to him now."

"What nonsense," Bry said. "I hope you told him to turn around and ride back home."

Thomasina smiled faintly again. "I did. But he told me that not only does his elder brother's land belong to him now, but—but everything belongs to him now."

"What ... what do you say?" Bry asked, horrified at where her mind went. It couldn't be.

Not in Foreverness.

"He said that I belong to him now. That we will be wed. He won't leave the house. He lives there. I am forced to make his meals, and I—"

"Please tell me that you are not forced to do more," Bry whispered.

"No," Thomasina said, "not yet. But we are to be wed in a few weeks' time, and then I ..." She took a deep breath and held Bry's gaze again. "He is destroying the land. He knows nothing about farming and refuses to listen to my counsel. He will ruin everything my husband and I created. He will ruin ... me."

A red, hazy veil fell in front of Bry's vision. "What right does he have—"

Giselle touched Bry's arm. "He has every right," she said. "Before arriving at Thomasina's, he saw King Hopkin, and the council confirmed his right to inherit his brother's land."

"He can't inherit his brother's *wife*!" Bry nearly shouted, then covered her lips with her hand and glanced out the window at the blissfully unaware little girls chasing each other in the grass. "She is not an *heirloom* to be passed down," she hissed.

"According to the king," Anne said, "there is no offense to God in marrying his brother's widow."

"Certainly not if she wants it," Bry said. "But—"

Thomasina tilted her head. "Your Highness, it is done. It is law. I have no escape. This tea with you all ... this is an unexpected respite. Perhaps we could do it again soon, and I would have it to look forward to, at least." She sighed. "I have a teenage son and daughter. I can't flee, and even if I did, to where would I flee?"

No one said anything for a moment. Bry caught Thea's eye and held it as she said flatly, "Well, King Hopkin is dead."

There were more gasps then, louder. But Thea didn't gasp, she merely raised an interested eyebrow.

"You can't say that!" Kathryn said. "I mean, Your Highness, you ... you can't say that. Can you?"

"Why not?" Bry said. "It is not traitorous. It is a fact. King Brockton rules now and—"

And Foreverness wasn't known for this sort of abomination.

"I am married to the king's brother. I will speak to Lucan," Bry said, but her voice wasn't as confident as she'd meant it to be.

And Thomasina heard it. "I thank you, Princess Bry. I truly do. You are as good and generous as everyone has said. But ..."

Her voice trailed off.

"But?" Bry prompted.

"But, princess or not, you are a woman," Thomasina finished slowly. "Though I will never see the inside of a castle, I can guess that your voice does not carry through those grand halls the way your husband's does. Or the new king's."

Frustration filled Bry until it seemed her heart and lungs would burst from compression. "This can't happen to you. This can't happen here."

"It happens," Giselle said wearily, "and it happens often. We don't blame you for your unawareness. You live among those who thrive here. I consider myself lucky—my husband allowed me to keep my family's spice business. But do you hear me? He *allowed* me. Had he not allowed me, that's all it would have taken to shut it down."

Bry imagined that beautiful market stall with the lovingly prepared spice bottles shuttering permanently, all on the whim of a man who had nothing to do with it. She winced.

"We all have stories," Kathryn said.

"Yes," Mirabel agreed. "Our own and others'. Though we love Thomasina and want to see her freed from this obligation, she is not an exception."

Bry said nothing for a few moments. Then she turned to Dawn. "Go out and inform our driver he will need to wait."

Dawn rushed out.

Bry sat back in her seat and looked each woman in the eyes, one by one.

She said, "Tell me."

* * *

That night, for the first time in her life plus a century, Bry couldn't sleep.

NEVE

Neve wrapped the cloak around herself tightly, pulled the hood low over her forehead, and dashed out the door.

The crowd that had been gathered at Eterne Castle since the king's passing, determined to publicly mourn him despite the decree to go on as usual, had dissipated when night had fallen, with only the deceased king's fiercest loyalists keeping vigil now. They huddled against one another for warmth and sang songs of dragons slain and fortune found, and love lost.

In their hour of mourning, they didn't notice their new queen slipping out of the castle and sidestepping in the darkest shadows, away from them all.

When she reached the brush at the beginning of the garden, she broke into a run.

The area was familiar—she'd walked it hundreds of times in leisure. But now she ran as if she were being chased by a demon. She was frightened, having rarely gone anywhere without a guard, especially at night.

The Aura Tree stretched its limbs over half the royal garden, protecting and embracing it. The tree was alive and lit from within, so it stood rooted in eternal daylight. Neve didn't stop running until she reached its white tree trunk, as wide as the wall of her bedchamber. She pushed back her hood and laid both hands and her forehead on the bark.

The tree bent its nearest branch to touch leaves to Neve's face. She felt the tree tremble a bit. Black veins crawled through the bark, widening until the entire trunk and all its branches were black. The leaves crinkled as they shrank back, trying to pull back into the branches they'd grown from.

Neve took a step back, dropping her arms at her sides and looking up at the tree that had transformed into Neve's black fear.

The tree didn't relieve emotions. The Aura Tree simply saw an emotion, felt it, and manifested it. Women who wanted to know how their suitors felt could walk them by to see if the tree manifested fluffy pink love or merely deep red lust.

Neve wasn't at all uncertain of her fear. She'd lived with it daily, but it was now too much for her body to handle.

She leaned her back against the tree and slid to the earth. Crickets chirped and stars twinkled, and the stiff leaves now sounded crispy in the evening breeze.

She'd seen Della summon Rhyannon a few times. She didn't know if Rhyannon would come for anyone else, or if she could help anyone other than her goddaughter. But Neve was queen now, so maybe Rhyannon would be obligated to hear her.

Neve closed her eyes and interlaced her fingers. "Rhyannon," she whispered. "Rhyannon."

The leaves were her only response. She put her hands over her heart and filled her mind with the vision of the fairy. "Rhyannon, I need you. Please help me."

She listened to the silence. This had been a foolish idea. She opened her eyes.

And Rhyannon was there.

"Your Majesty," she said in her tone of perpetual amusement. "Can I serve you?"

Neve blinked. "Oh."

"You're surprised? You summoned me."

"I didn't think it would work."

"Up until very recently, it wouldn't have. Della is my god-child, and she was the only one who could summon me. But now that you are queen, I'm beholden to you as well."

"I'd hoped so."

"And anyway," Rhyannon added, "I just happened to be here tonight. I come to the Aura Tree on occasion to charge crystals and ... do some other magical things that you need not worry about. And I saw you. I retreated to give Your Majesty privacy, but I heard your summoning."

"I'm the queen."

"So you are."

"I'm the queen, but I don't want to be."

"You did marry the heir to the throne. Barring a tragedy to you or him, this was inevitable."

"Yes, but I ... wasn't ready. It always seemed far off, like it would happen only when I was ready to accept it."

"Sometimes a thing needs to happen for you to accept it," Rhyannon said. She took in the Aura Tree. "Fear. What is it you fear?"

"I fear death. I fear assassination. My life was once taken from me. It was only foolish luck that broke the spell."

"It was a fated kiss that broke the spell."

Neve sighed. Her lower back still hurt occasionally from Brockton and his men jostling her when he'd tripped.

"Nevertheless," Neve said. "My assassins bided their time between attempts on my life. The second attempt was years after the first and after I'd found my uncles. I don't know if they're biding their time still."

"Even now?"

"Even more now."

"Is that why you carry a dagger?"

Neve's hand went to her thigh, but the strap holding the weapon in place was hidden under layers of gown and cloak. "How—"

"I can see things," Rhyannon said. "Is that your only fear? Assassination?"

"*Only*? Only that perhaps enemies have been waiting until I sat on the throne to target me again?"

"Who are the enemies? Fina is dead. You saw it with your own eyes."

Neve had seen it, the madness that had overtaken her stepmother, an evil that had consumed her after Neve's wedding. She'd delivered the mirror as a wedding gift and was promptly arrested by King Hopkin. Before he could send word to Neve's father, King Eustace of Goldenstone, Queen Fina had gone mad in her prison, and danced herself into flame and ash before Neve's eyes. Neve wondered if madness and evil were dormant in everyone, ready to be drawn out at any time by title, status, beauty.

Neve had all that, and now the throne.

"Fina had a loyal council of advisors who had no qualms about vengeance and violence. My enemies could be anywhere," she said. "I wear the crown now."

"The crown is different in Foreverness," Rhyannon pointed out. "You don't have power to rule like you would have in Goldenstone. Here, only men rule."

"That's a thing to be thankful for," Neve said. "For if I don't make decisions, I won't cause unrest."

"You won't have the opportunity to bring about good, either."

Neve shook her head. "That's not my issue at the moment. Brockton could easily make enemies who'd kill me to get back at him. I'm not any safer."

"No, you're not any safer," Rhyannon conceded. "But in that case, I would think you'd want to rule. If just sitting on a big chair looking beautiful is a dangerous post, then why not try to make a difference? Why not do more?"

"This kingdom doesn't need my activism. There is peace and prosperity here. Brockton inherits a strong land with strong people."

"As far as you know. In my vast experience, those under crowns and on councils know very little of the everyday workings and worries of their own lands."

Neve paused. Rhyannon's expression was still easy and amused.

"I believe what I'm trying to ask you is for help finding peace and strength in my heart so I can sit beside His Majesty each day in that peace and strength," Neve said. "Or perhaps there's a protection spell you can offer. But advice on how to shake the kingdom like a whimsical snow globe is not going to help me."

"Are you sure you want my help?" Rhyannon blinked, and the smallest bit of glitter fell from her lashes. "Because it seems you already speak with authority."

"I'm sorry."

"No," Rhyannon said, and her face went stern. "Don't be sorry. There are enough sorry people—sorry women—out there wringing their hands. You were born to be queen, and when someone tried to take that from you, you took it back by winning a battle with death and marrying into your royal destiny. Do not be sorry for anything."

"You are right," Neve said. "I am to be a model of virtue and goodness. But ..."

Rhyannon waited a moment, then, her face softening again, prompted, "But what?"

"But who is mine? I didn't have my mother. My stepmother was evil. And my father was a shameful coward."

The fairy godmother templed her fingers. "Very well,

Your Majesty. It was never my intention to deny you. I just needed to understand you a bit better to see what my limited charms can offer. I don't think I can protect you. I can create a spell, but I can't hold it for more than a few hours. That made Della's fortuitous formal evening somewhat ... deadline oriented. You're better off taking whatever your husband has to offer you as far as guards. He has the best, so be assured. And keep up your weaponry skills."

"How did you—ah. You see things."

"I didn't know for sure, but only an unwise woman would carry a weapon around without knowing how to wield it. And you are not unwise." Rhyannon nodded. "Now. If it's guidance you need, I can provide that. I can bring you into a dream state and show you the person who can help you with the advice you need going forward."

"Who is it?"

"I have no idea," Rhyannon said. "I don't even know if such a person exists. But if they do, they will appear to you. Then, when you come out of the dream state, you can decide to seek the person out."

"Very well. Let's get on with it."

"Just like that?"

"It's midnight at the Aura Tree, and I'm standing here with a fairy," Neve said. "I'm confident I am in the right place at the right time."

"Please sit." Rhyannon gestured to the grass.

Neve sat and scooted until her back was against the tree. Rhyannon put her own hands on the tree and whispered a few words, then went silent.

"What are you doing?" Neve asked.

Rhyannon said nothing for another long moment. Then she smiled up at the leaves. "I'm asking the tree's permission to do magic here."

"But you say you come here often."

"I do. But I wouldn't thoughtlessly walk into a dear friend's home without knocking, no matter how many times I'd been there."

Neve pulled her cloak more securely around her shoulders and chest.

"Close your eyes, and try to hear me without listening," Rhyannon said quietly. "Listen as if I'm singing you a lullaby. You don't need to follow my words. Just float on the river of your unconscious."

The fairy godmother began to chant in a foreign tongue that was impossible to understand but somehow familiar. The syllables wound into Neve's ears and through her mind in swirls until she felt herself falling, falling …

… landing hard on the earth, face down. She pressed her hands into the dirt and grass to lift her face. The Aura Tree was gone, and she was surrounded by dark trees with gnarled branches. Long roots moved under the ground toward her to pull her closer, pull her in, pull her into The Unfathomed.

"No," Neve said, and her voice came out a mouse's squeak. "No!"

The roots pushed up through the ground with earthy, hard tentacles that grabbed Neve by the thighs and elbows, wended around her chest, and branched across her throat.

Neve lowered her chin and tried to look at the roots that held her fast. Her dress was different; it was the dress that she'd gotten from her father on her twelfth birthday. It was declared a feast day in Goldenstone, and she'd loved her gown so much that she'd worn it many times in the weeks after, including the day the huntsman had taken her into The Unfathomed.

Her curveless girl's chest heaved in fear, and her girl's arms were weak, and now that Neve knew she was back in her childhood body, she no longer felt her dagger.

She was back where she'd been that day she'd had to run. Defenseless.

"No!" she screamed and struggled against the roots, but she heard Rhyannon's voice. It was ahead of her, and she moved toward it, afraid the roots would pull her back. But they moved with her, encouraging her.

She was escorted deeper into the woods. She didn't know if it was day or night because the dark leaves formed a ceiling that blocked the sky. The birds didn't sing; they mourned and moaned. The few flowers dotting the ground were black, with red blood dripping from petals. Growls and whispers from invisible animals filled the air.

Rhyannon's chant was loud now, and Neve stopped in front of a tree in her path. In front of the tree was a basket with a bottle of wine, a cake, and a bunch of pink and yellow flowers.

The roots holding her captive dissolved. Neve bent down to pick up the basket, but a wet snarl stopped her, and teeth snapped out at her from above the basket.

A wolf.

Neve fell onto the ground in her haste to back away, but now, there was no wolf. Where had it gone?

In its place, there was a young girl of perhaps ten with shiny black hair and innocent blue eyes. Her dress was drab, and her boots were ordinary, but her thick velvet hooded cape was the red of a carved heart.

The two girls stared at one another, eyes wide in shared terror of The Unfathomed.

A burst of sunlight filled Neve's chest and she gasped as her birthday gown was replaced by a royal purple brocade. Her fingers were covered in rings. She felt the weight of a crown on her head and the assuring coolness of the dagger on her leg.

The girl before her was no longer a girl—she had become a woman with long, wild black hair and sharp blue eyes.

Her trousers were well worn. Her shirt was sleeveless, and her muscles were defined like a young man's. Her face was streaked with dirt. The full red cape was gone, with only a muddy scrap of it wrapped several times around her left wrist.

Behind the woman, there was movement. The wolf slowly crept up—a wolf large enough to loom over her shoulder.

"No!" Neve cried again, but this time, not for herself.

The wolf drew back its lips into a menacing, hungry grimace, then relaxed its jaw and laid its head against the side of the woman's neck. She reached up and circled the wolf's neck with her arm, her fingers stroking its fur with love, her eyes never leaving Neve's.

"Are you the one I'm looking for?" Neve asked in a disbelieving whisper.

The wolf whined to its mistress like a helpless puppy. The woman gave no indication that she heard Neve's question and showed no inclination to verbally respond. She bent down and pulled the small cake out of the basket. She held it out to Neve. Crumbs fell out of her cupped hand.

Rhyannon's voice echoed through the breeze. Neve reached for the cake.

The invisible growling animals, the unharmonious birds, the dead black flowers, the twisted trees said into Neve's mind: *Rowan.*

Rowan.

Neve closed her hand and the cake smushed through her fingers.

Rowan.

Rowan the Wolf.

Rowan the Wolf.

Neve lifted her chin.

The woman was gone. The wolf grinned at her with knife teeth. Neve watched a long stream of drool slide out of its mouth slowly, slowly ...

It splatted on the ground as Rhyannon said, *come back.*
Come back.

Neve opened her eyes, shook her head, rubbed her face
with her open palms.

Rhyannon's eyelashes shed a little more glitter. "Did you
find the one?" she asked.

"I don't think so."

"You saw no one?"

"Not anyone real."

"That can't be," Rhyannon said. "That spell conjures real
places, real people, with your own perception, of course, so things
look the way you see them. If you saw someone, they exist."

"I was in The Unfathomed. I saw someone, but not someone who can help me. She isn't real. She's just a story that
adults tell children to scare them."

Rhyannon raised her brows.

Neve answered her silent question. "Rowan the Wolf."

The fairy nodded slowly. "I see. Now that you've been given
your guide, it's up to you whether you seek that person out."

Rhyannon turned to leave. Neve scrambled up from
where she'd been sprawled on the ground and, finding one
of her feet numb, hopped to the fairy and caught her arm.
"Wait. Rowan is just a story."

"The spell told you Rowan the Wolf is real, and she is in The
Unfathomed. It means whatever it is you need to hear, whatever
it is you seek to move forward in your new role, she has it."

"Maybe it was wrong—"

Rhyannon laughed, a tinkling and infuriatingly confident
laugh. "That spell is never wrong. But you don't have to find
her. Only if you want to."

Neve had expected to come out from under the spell reassured and calm, but her heart was pounding so hard it almost

hurt. She put a useless hand on her chest to try to still it, but the panic magnified with her memory of the dream. She'd once known The Unfathomed—the flowers weren't black, the birds sang sweetly—but the deception of the woods was worse than any dream. "People disappear into The Unfathomed, never to return. People *die* there."

"The king died in his familiar, safe castle."

Neve released her hold on Rhyannon's arm, and Rhyannon grasped Neve's hand in both of hers. "You are prepared and ready for any external attack at any time. But you have an enemy inside you, and that's your fear. Fear attacks you every day, and you surrender to it. Do you know the best weapon against fear? Knowledge."

Neve's brows drew together slightly.

"I would not counsel you to wander into the woods alone," Rhyannon went on. "That would be folly. Perhaps you could send some of the King's Protection into The Unfathomed to summon Rowan to you."

But even as the fairy offered this alternative, Neve knew it wouldn't do. The wild wolf woman she'd seen wouldn't be summoned by men.

Neve could ignore this dream—or vision, or whatever it had been—because how could a wild resident of The Unfathomed have anything Neve needed? But even as Neve thought this, she knew it was wrong. She'd felt a strong connection to the girl in the hooded cape, and to the woman she became. If Rowan existed, she had something Neve needed; Neve was certain of it.

And if she were to talk to Rowan, Neve would have to go back to the dark place in which she'd run for her life. It had taken her life. And it had seen the life return to her.

No Foreverness resident of sound mind ventured into The Unfathomed. Once a flourishing forest of joy that was known as the Emerald beside the Silvering Sea, it had darkened over decades into a prison that swallowed innocence. It cut open strong, young hearts and left them to bleed into the hard dirt.

Rowan the Wolf was there, and Neve had to find a way to lure her out. For there was no way in hell she'd take one step into that death trap.

DELLA

"My maid actually came into my parlor yesterday wearing a pink apron. Pink!" Gervaise said, and all the women gasped.

Teas with noblewomen were mostly a tolerable obligation because Della did enjoy being fawned over. But today, sitting with seven of Foreverness's most ambitious social climbers was a bit of a chore.

Especially since their conversation about members of their "terrible household staff" was more tedious than usual. Idalia's maid didn't fluff her pillows to maximum fluff. Gervaise's cook always served a dry pheasant. Petra's coachman cleared his throat far too often.

Della said quietly, "I don't understand what was wrong with the apron. I rather love pink."

Gervaise angled her head to Della in deference. "It is a beautiful color, to be sure. But my parlor is decorated in rich scarlet."

All the women nodded except Della, who raised her brows in question.

"A pink apron in a red room!" Gervaise said. "My goodness, it hurt my eyes. Couldn't she see she clashed terribly? I told her to remove her apron at once. But it was too late. I developed a severe headache and had to lie down for the rest of the day."

Della herself daily demonstrated the value of wearing flattering colors and looking one's best. But to expect a member of the staff to match the room décor?

Della had been privy to these silly conversations for as long as she'd been princess, and they felt more and more juvenile and hyperbolic with the passage of time. She knew that after rescuing the young maid from her supervisor's abuse two days ago, the noblewomen were bound to tread more heavily on her nerves today. Not only did these women get a personal boost from building up each other's superiority, they refused to take responsibility for their own households. They likely hired staff with no instruction, assuming the poor souls would magically know what their mistresses wanted at all times. If they didn't, they were useless, lazy, and insolent.

Della examined the teacup on the small table before her. It was pretty and delicate. The miniscule chip on the top of the handle wouldn't be noticeable to most eyes, but as a young girl, Della had been beaten into learning to see and to remedy the smallest imperfections. The women in this group were just like this teacup—pretty, delicate, lovely to look at, but with little nasty chips that one had to look closely to see. Della saw every flaw, though she wished she didn't.

She wished she were sitting here with entertaining and joyful Thea, or sweet-hearted Bry. Or even Neve, for though she wasn't much for socializing, she was unmatched in intelligence, and Della appreciated her intolerance for nonsense.

Gervaise was still drumming on about her horrendous pink-aproned maid. Idalia patted Gervaise's shoulder in sympathy.

Della was done. "I daresay if each of you had a staff as effective as mine, you could have avoided your headache," she said.

"We'd love to," Idalia said. "Wouldn't we, ladies? Alas, it seems the most efficient and seasoned staff in the kingdom work for you, Your Highness. You have a talent for choosing the best of the best."

"Or you must punish them so severely, they are afraid to cross you," Gervaise said.

"I've tried that," Petra said. "I've boxed ears, I've brandished a switch, I've denied them meals, and I've fired the worst of them with a promise I would make sure they remain unemployed for years."

Della winced.

You don't like cleaning? Go out into that wide world and see what happens to a girl who has nothing.

Is this floor clean? Is it? Perhaps if we hold your head down like this, you can lick the floor and tell us if it's truly clean.

Lick it, Cinder-slut!

"Nothing works," Petra added. They all murmured agreement.

"I don't severely punish. I don't punish at all," Della said.

"Then ... what—?" Petra started.

Della cut her off. "I haven't had cause to be displeased with even one member of my household. Not in all these years." She took a small bite of a tea cake. *Hmm, delicious.*

The women stayed silent until Della swallowed.

She now had their full attention. "They don't work for me out of fear. They work for me with pride in their good work. Do you know why?"

They went quiet, and all shook their heads. Waiting.

"Because I see to it that every new person is thoroughly trained to my specifications. That they know what to do and how to do it all before their first day." *Also, because I'm not a gargoyle. And because I treat them like people.*

"Who trains them?"

"Yes, who do you send them to?"

Della paused. She could not tell these shrews that she trained the staff herself. The last thing she needed right now was to remind them that she was the princess of ashes and dust bunnies. Not when Neve had just ascended to the throne. Not when Colby had played the fool the day his father died.

"I know someone," Della said, sitting forward and lowering her voice into a conspiratorial whisper.

All seven women brought their heads toward hers, their eyes wide.

"She's a marvel, a genius," Della added. "I've been—working with her for years. You've all seen my home."

"Yes," Gervaise said, a little breathlessly. "The gardens, the public halls, the ballrooms, the dining room. All impeccably decorated, gorgeous, spotless—"

"And maintained by a harmonious staff," Della finished.

"You must tell us who this magic woman is," Idalia said.

Della leaned back and raised her brows at Idalia.

"Er ... um," the noblewoman stammered. "What I mean is, if it pleases Your Highness to share the name with us, we would be most grateful."

"Most grateful," two women echoed. The rest leaned in, ready to receive.

Della hesitated theatrically, then sat back. "No. I can't tell you her name," she said, picking up her teacup. "That won't do. No. She takes on a very select few clients. Only royalty. Even if she knew you were interested, she wouldn't take you on unless ..." She allowed her voice to trail off.

After a full minute, Gervaise prompted, "Unless—"

"Unless I personally recommended you." Della circled her spoon leisurely in her half-empty cup. "Besides, she's rather—expensive. Exclusive. It would be worth it for you only if ..."

"If—?" Gervaise prompted again, after less time.

"*If* it were that important to you to have your staff

properly trained. Of course, you ladies wouldn't want to spend your gold on that." Della shook her head and held her cup in her lap with both hands. "For noblewomen to spend that kind of coin—it would just be a silly, shallow status thing. You're all above that nonsense."

"Y-yes," Petra said.

"Of course we are. It's not ... crucial," Idalia said.

They all looked at one another. Della gazed beatifically out the window, watching a bluebird on a branch.

"But ..."

Della looked at Gervaise.

"It would be ... a way to make Foreverness more beautiful. As a whole," Gervaise said quickly.

"Yes," Idalia said. "It would not be an indulgence as much as a ... charitable donation. The more beautiful homes there are in Foreverness, the ... the ..." She paused, trying but unable to make her weak case.

"The more the Charming family has to be proud of!" Petra finished triumphantly, and they all nodded, their heads bobbing like hens'. "It would be a community effort, truly."

"All in favor of donating to make Foreverness more beautiful?" Idalia said, and all the women raised their gloved hands, their heavy jeweled bracelets sliding to their elbows. Keeping their hands aloft, they looked at Della, their faces hopeful and expectant.

Della smiled, though they had no idea her smile was one of relief. Relief that she was clearly still a role model for them.

"I *suppose* I can broker this for you," Della said with false hesitation. "She works in secrecy, only for royalty and our closest friends. I will ... give her your names."

"Thank you!"

"Thank you, Your Highness!"

Della went on. "Choose one person in your household

who will be trained and able to train the others in your household when she returns."

Idalia had stars in her eyes, likely imagining the future sparkling windows and floors in her home.

"You will be sent a bill," Della said with confidence, though she was making it up as she went along. "When it is paid in full, I'll arrange for them to be transported to the training."

"Soon, I hope?" Gervaise asked.

"I'll see to it you receive the bills in two days' time so this can happen right away."

Idalia squealed.

"How long does training last?" Petra asked.

"Er, three weeks?" Della said, the wheels turning in her mind. That should be enough time to train seven people, if they came every day, and train them to train others. "Yes," she said with confidence. "Three weeks."

The thrilled women excitedly chattered amongst themselves, and Della sat back, nervous but satisfied.

She didn't intend to keep their payment for herself; she had no need for money, and it wouldn't be right to take theirs, even if they were insufferable. Rather, she would reinvest it in this training. She'd need brooms, soap, dusters, aprons, a full dining set, a full tea set—and she wouldn't want to have to explain these expenses to Colby. Colby was—well, Colby, but one thing he was excellent at was keeping books. He cared nothing for how much she spent on clothes and jewels and household staff, but he knew where every penny went. And she'd need a place to train—

Her mouth went dry, and her heart missed one beat.

She already had a place.

She shook her head. She'd think about that later.

Della watched the delighted women around her chat and

laugh and realized what she had done. She had identified a problem these women had, convinced them it was worth it to spend their gold, and sold them a solution. At the same time, she now had a chance to make workers' lives better, and much better than hers had been.

She was a princess, but perhaps she could also be a clever merchant.

BRY

"I don't understand," Bry said the next evening, sitting on the edge of her feathery bed.

"I don't understand, either," Lucan said, sitting beside her. "How do you know this woman Thomasina?"

"I told you, Dawn and Thea and I recently had tea with some of the ladies in the village." She didn't take her eyes off his as she brushed her hair harder than she normally would.

"Commoners?"

"Yes. So?"

"So nothing. I'm just trying to make sense of what you're saying. You made some new friends, and this woman Thomasina doesn't want her brother-in-law to take her late husband's land?"

"It's *her* land! She worked it with her own hands. And he doesn't want to just take her land. He's going to take—*her.*"

Her kind Lucan winced in sympathy, but Bry wanted him to be shocked. Angry.

"I admit it's not an ideal situation," he said, slowly and carefully.

Bry stared at him for a long moment, her brush frozen in her hair, before saying, "I don't think it's an overstatement to say that is the biggest understatement ever uttered."

"I wish it weren't this way for your friend. But inheritance laws are a tradition that my father insisted on upholding during his long reign, like all other Foreverness traditions and laws."

Bry stopped herself from saying, *He no longer reigns.* Her husband was grieving. But she did say, "Brockton is a good man, and I have faith he will be a good king."

Lucan smiled. "As do I, my love."

"Good. Then you won't mind speaking to him on Thomasina's behalf."

Lucan stood and went to the window to look out into the night, though he could likely only see his own reflection, backlit by the candle beside Bry's mirror. "I can't do that, Bry."

"Whyever not? He's your brother, and he respects you, and if you'd just explain Thomasina's predicament, I'm certain he would—"

"Bry," Lucan said quietly. "I'd like to help, but I'm afraid it isn't possible. I met with the king today, and I'm under the strong impression that he won't be making any immediate changes to law."

"Maybe your strong impression is wrong. If he only knew—"

"His very words were, 'I won't be making any immediate changes to law.' "

Bry frowned.

"He—and I—think it's important to maintain the peace and contentment of the kingdom," Lucan added.

"But he doesn't know what's happening. If he could be made aware—"

"Tradition is tradition because it endures. This tradition of inheritance of lands and titles is one of the oldest we have, and the unusual situation of one commoner woman won't change it."

Bry stood, every inch of her body priming to explode. "It isn't just Thomasina. The other women told me—"

"It's not the time," Lucan said, gently but a bit more firmly this time.

Bry decided to try a different approach. "My husband, you have daughters. Doesn't it bother you that Dawn was born entitled to less than Della's sons are, or that Thea had to give up birthright to her entitlements to live as she was meant to?"

"Dawn and Thea are princesses who lack for nothing," Lucan said, closing the heavy drapes.

"You're correct," Bry said. "But what if we were not royalty? What if we were commoners, and we couldn't give Thea or Dawn what we do have? What if they were at the mercy of these laws?"

"But that's not the case," Lucan said patiently.

"Not for them, no," Bry said, slamming her brush down on the table, lifting her candle, and setting it on the smaller table beside her bed. "Very well. If you will not speak to Brockton, I will."

Lucan moved to the bed and slid under the blankets. "You will not."

"I'm a princess of this land and the wife of his beloved brother," Bry said. "I will petition for Thomasina first, because her situation is the most dire and imminent that I heard today."

"He will deny you," Lucan said, and though no anger had crept into his tone, it had finality. "You will gain nothing, and he will ask me why I allowed you to approach him with this petition. I don't want him to think I'm abandoning our father's ideals."

Bry blew out the candle, plunging the room into blackness.

"You will not, Bry," Lucan repeated.

No, she would not. The last king who was angry with

her was her father, who let her leave for a new life without saying a farewell. She couldn't risk the anger of another king, another shaming, another may-as-well-be-banishment.

She yanked back her soft purple velvet blanket and slid in on the side of the bed that Lucan wasn't occupying. She slammed her head against the pillow, but it was ineffective as a show of anger—it only poofed up on each side of her head. She stared up at the gilded ceiling rather than at her husband. Repose hopped silently onto the bed and curled his body against hers. She laid her hand on his comforting iridescent fur. He'd been a gray striped tabby when they'd fallen under the spell together, and he'd awakened with her a century later with his swirly, hypnotic fur and long lifespan.

"None of this is meant to offend you," Lucan said softly. "Or Thomasina. It's just the way things are. And I am certain your new friendship with her will go a long way toward her contentment someday. You are a generous friend to all."

She was angry at her husband, the king, and herself, not necessarily in that order.

"I need to sleep," Bry informed the ceiling. "I spent the day organizing and hosting a birthday celebration for one noblewoman, and I met with the Eterne Castle kitchen staff with some ideas I had for the coronation feast, and while I was there, I was asked to hear some musicians audition for the same feast. I'm exhausted."

"Why do you tire yourself so?"

Because it wouldn't do to say no to anything she was asked. Saying yes kept her in everyone's good graces. Why didn't Lucan know this? She wasn't in the mood to explain, so she merely muttered, "Good night."

She flipped onto her right side and curled around her cat, her back to Lucan.

A moment later, Lucan rolled over and spooned his body

around hers, and snaked his arm under the blanket to caress her waist through the silk of her gown.

She took his hand and he stilled. Then she shoved it away. "No."

She heard a hitch in his breath. "No?" he asked.

His surprise was expected. Bry never refused her husband in bed. Even on the nights she didn't feel much like amorous activity. She loved Lucan dearly and was always willing to give herself to him when he desired it, even at the end of long, busy days. Even when they bickered, because it was a fun way to make things right—and a way to ensure she wouldn't lose his love. People could so quickly and easily change overnight.

But tonight was different.

"No," she repeated. "No. Go away."

Lucan, stunned, didn't move.

Bry looked over her shoulder at him. "Take yourself out of my bed and retire to your own chamber. Or go to the kitchen for leftovers. Or stroll the grounds and enjoy the moonlight. Just go. I'm not—I'm not in the mood for this."

"Not—in the mood?"

"I said no."

He still didn't move.

"Shall I call a healer to check your ears?" Bry asked. "Perhaps a beetle crawled into one?"

"No ... no need," he said, but he rose slowly, as if expecting her to change her mind.

Instead, Bry turned away from him again. She heard him pause, as if trying to think of something more to say, but then he left, closing the door softly behind him.

Only a moment later, she regretted her harshness. She could never be outwardly cross with anyone, lest it come back at her.

Sleep. Sleep was what she trusted, and it never let her down. Sleep would clear her mind, like a wave of saltwater over a crude sand drawing. She would sleep, and in the morning, she would do something with her disappointment.

Bry's lids half-closed as she watched Repose. The swirls in his fur mesmerized her, confusing and blurring her vision until she could no longer keep her eyes open, and she fell into her beloved sleep.

NEVE

N eve cleared her throat softly, and in the Great Hall, the sound magnified and echoed to twenty times its size.

She'd not spent much time in this hall as princess. When Brockton had first brought her to Foreverness, she'd walked down the long chamber to face King Hopkin and Queen Eira at the end of it, on thrones draped in silk and velvet. She'd dropped to her knees and Brockton knelt beside her, asking the king for permission to marry. The king and queen welcomed Neve into their royal family, and the king sent word to Goldenstone that she was their child now, under lifelong protection, and was not to be sought out. He didn't want conflict in his kingdom.

Fina didn't honor his wish, and she died.

The Great Hall was where men of Foreverness were granted audience with the king twice a week, mostly to settle disputes and petition for needs and desires. Each Tuesday and Thursday morning, the line of men began at the door at dawn, and grew and grew, winding like a sea serpent out the door of the castle.

Brockton now sat where his father had sat, but the silk and velvet covering his throne was black in mourning. Brockton didn't feel right celebrating his ascension, not quite yet.

Neve's throne had been placed at his left hand, but before she could sit in it, Brockton told his councilors to move her throne to his right, with the four seats of the council moved to his left. Neve wasn't sure if Brockton had seen their briefest of hesitation, but she had. She was the person with the second-highest public status, but when it came to the Great Hall, his councilors were "above" her in terms of word and deed, and traditionally sat at the king's right hand.

As the chairs were dragged about, the sound echoing painfully within the walls, Neve murmured to her husband, "Are you sure? You said it's your priority to keep to tradition, with few exceptions."

"I discussed this one change with my father before he died. I told him you are my right hand, and I would like you there. He agreed, as long as proceedings go as always."

Neve squeezed his hand. It was a small gesture but also a grand one. "Thank you. I admit I'm nervous."

"No need," Brockton said. "The people who come here to seek my help and counsel are far more nervous. It's difficult enough for the lords we'll see today. Imagine being a common man, facing the king and entering a request. The queen's presence is to calm everyone with her constancy and kindness. All you need to do is make eye contact and smile, if it pleases you."

The councilors took their seats with a flurry of coats and papers. "They are rather frightening and stern to look at," Neve said. "Even for me."

"They are just men. Men who know our laws and can help me if I need it. But yes, they do manage to keep an air of—untouchability."

"I don't know how anyone could be intimidated by you, though," Neve said with a grin. "Perhaps when the crown is laid on your head, you'll look more regal. Right now, you just look like Brockton, a boy who tripped over his own feet and accidentally found himself a bride."

Brockton took her chin in two fingers and tilted her lips up to his. He touched them softly and said, "It was a timeless and legendary moment. And I thank God every day for making me a clumsy oaf."

The trumpets blared, startling both king and queen out of their light embrace. Honestly, someone needed to do something about the dreadful acoustics. Neve would be hearing the trumpets ringing in her ears for the rest of the day.

The coronation was delayed, but the monarchs needed to wear their crowns to perform this duty, so an abbreviated working version of the ceremony commenced.

Neve stood, along with everyone else present, as the king's crown was brought into the room on a velvet cushion—also black, as requested by Brockton. Brockton ascended the half-dozen steps to the platform and sat on his throne. Many words were said in Latin, trumpets sounded, and eventually, the crown was placed on Brockton's head. Everyone in the room bowed low. As the weight settled onto his skull, his shoulders opened, and his neck seemed to lift an inch.

He'd been preparing for this moment his entire life.

The lead councilor, Lord Everard, gallantly gestured for Neve to sit in her smaller, black-wrapped throne. It was the softest seat she'd ever been in, yet she could not relax.

More Latin, more trumpets, and the crown was lowered onto Neve's head.

She couldn't breathe. She couldn't—

When Lord Everard bowed and backed away, she reached up and touched the golden crown with one finger, tracing it over the filigreed edge and rounding it over an amethyst.

She wondered what she looked like—then, realizing that may have been the exact thought Fina might have had at this moment in her own reign, she took in a shaky breath.

No. Neve was not that kind of queen. She didn't know what kind of queen she was—but she was *not* that.

"Let's begin," Brockton—King Brockton—said, and the double doors were thrown open wide. A line of men walked in quietly along the dark-blue runner until the first man stopped in front of Brockton. The line went still, stretching out the door and beyond.

The first man bowed and addressed the king.

* * *

Neve heaved a sigh. They were only an hour in, and her scalp was perspiring under the crown. There was a chill outside, but the number of people inside elevated the temperature in the Great Hall to unbearable. Brockton noticed and sent for a lady-in-waiting to fetch Neve a paper fan. The lady took a small, cushioned seat behind Neve's right shoulder, in case Neve might require something else.

Despite the heat, the proceedings were engaging. Neve listened carefully to all the requests and petitions, and silently agreed or disagreed with Brockton's solutions to each. Most of the time she agreed, but after she disagreed three times in a row, she began to, instead, mentally resolve each situation in her head. She knew the laws well and was pleased to see that there were two times the king turned to his councilors for advice, and when he came back with the resolution, it was exactly how Neve herself would have decided it.

As a merchant made his case, Neve noticed a slight, elderly man in line sway a bit on his feet. Neve jumped from the throne and hurried down the steps, causing gasps. Neve caught the man in a half-faint. "Please," Neve said to the council, "get a chair for this man and a cup of water."

The councilors looked at Brockton, and Neve snapped, "Now."

A chair was procured, and Neve helped the man into it, guiding the cup to his lips. "Your Majesty," the man murmured once he caught his breath, and the blood returned to his cheeks. "I'm so sorry."

"Don't be," Neve said. "I assure you I almost fainted myself earlier. Rest until it passes." She gave the man her fan and stroked his arm.

Neve hurried back up the steps to her seat. Brockton was looking at her with a smile. "Forgive me," Neve said.

"Nothing to forgive," Brockton said. "This is why you're here. To show goodness."

Neve smiled, and Brockton asked the merchant to continue his case.

A few petitioners later, two frazzled men in commoners' clothes knelt before them. Though they appeared to be together, they kept a distance between them. "Your Majesty," one said. "I am Robert, and this is my despicable, thieving neighbor, Elric."

Elric bristled. "Robert, you son of a whore's—"

"I remind you," Lord Everard interrupted sternly, "that you speak in front of a queen."

Neve leaned in to murmur to her husband, "I've heard worse from Uncle Forwin."

Brockton's lips curled, restraining a laugh.

"We know who you are," Lord Everard said to the two men, unable to hide his disdain. Which he should, Neve thought, as all these people were here for help. "Your disputes have brought you here often. It seems that pattern will continue with the new king."

"It's all right, my lord," Brockton said. "My good men, what is troubling you?"

Elric and Robert both rushed to speak, talking over each other, until Lord Everard banged his fist on the arm of his chair. "If you can't speak in turn, you can go home and resolve your nonsense on your own."

The two men snapped their mouths shut.

"Robert?" Brockton prompted.

"I have a herd of cows," Robert said. "One of the handsomest herds in Foreverness, and if I were not tending to my modesty in front of the fair queen, I would say *the* handsomest."

Elric snorted, sounding to Neve quite a bit like a cow himself.

Robert narrowed his eyes at his neighbor and continued. "Occasionally, one of my cows will wander over the property line onto Elric's land. The last two times it happened, he seized the cow and took it for his own. He put it in his own shed! The man doesn't even keep cows and wouldn't know how to care for it. It was merely for spite. I had to steal my own cows back both times."

"Why are you doing this?" Brockton asked Elric, with the patience of a saint.

"My land, my cow," Elric said.

"That's not the law," Robert sputtered.

"It should be," Elric retorted.

"Why not build a fence?" Brockton asked Robert.

"I don't have the money to do so," Robert said. "The property line is several acres. I'd have to hire men, buy materials ... I don't have the resources for it. And if I may say, Your Majesty, it wouldn't be necessary if I had a law-abiding neighbor."

"What's your issue with a cow occasionally wandering on your land?" Brockton asked Elric.

"A cow doesn't just come over to smell the flowers and

enjoy the sun. It eats my grass. I have bare patches all over the area that they wander onto."

"I ask Your Majesty to order Elric to leave my cows alone. It's just grass."

"It's my grass. It's my land, left to me by my father, who didn't intend it to be gobbled up by your smelly beasts."

"And you think if a cow finds itself on your land ..." Brockton said.

"It finds itself at my mercy," Elric said. "Just like the other animals that wander onto my land and end up feeding me and keeping me warm as I see fit."

Neve winced.

"I understand," Brockton said. "I will discuss this matter with my councilors." He leaned to his left and put his head together with his men.

Neve was familiar with the law in this case—Robert's cow didn't cease to belong to him, no matter where it wandered off to, unless he sold it.

Robert and Elric glared daggers at one another. Neve was certain that Brockton would state the law, Elric would leave unsatisfied and resentful, another dispute would arise between the neighbors, and they would be back in this hall, as was their pattern.

Was the most important thing to uphold the law case by case, or would it help to find a long-term meaningful solution?

Dozens before her shuffled uncomfortably in the long queue in the heat of the early afternoon. No one dared to sit on the floor for relief, not in the presence of the king. Brockton and his councilors were consulting a large book.

Neve cleared her throat. "Um, Elric?"

He bowed low. "Your Majesty."

"Robert?"

He also bowed. "My queen."

"I am wondering," Neve said. "Elric, what is your work?"

"I am a cobbler, Your Majesty."

"Ah, a cobbler. I wonder if you are acquainted with Princess Della."

"I am acquainted with some pairs of her shoes," Elric said.

Neve smiled. "Well, it is a noble vocation, and a gentlemanly one. Tell me true. Did you intend to slaughter the cows you took?"

Elric shuffled his feet. Lying to a queen was out of the question. "No, I didn't."

"So, it was just to inconvenience your neighbor as retribution for his errant cows?"

He sighed. "Yes."

She turned to Robert. "Sir, do you sell the milk of your cows at market?"

"I do," he said.

"May I guess that the handsomest cows in the land produce good milk?"

"Your Majesty, modesty prevents me from telling you that my cows' milk is the—"

"Handsomest?" Elric said.

"—most *delicious* milk in Foreverness," Robert finished.

"I have no doubt," Neve said. "Just as I have no doubt that two clever and accomplished men such as yourselves can come to a gentlemen's agreement on this matter, one that will satisfy you both."

She realized that Brockton and the councilors had ceased conferring and were listening to her. As was everyone in the Great Hall.

"I see two options here," Neve said. "The first is that we ask Robert's cows to kindly not wander past his property line. But something tells me that might not work as well as we'd hope."

Chuckles erupted down the long line.

Even Robert and Elric both smiled. "They are handsome," Robert said, "but not skilled in conversation."

"Then instead," Neve said, "let's assume the cows will occasionally wander. Robert, would you be willing to ensure your cows' freedom by offering Elric ... one bottle of milk a week? Is that something you could spare without much hardship?"

"Well ... yes, Your Majesty, I could. If I knew I didn't have to worry about cow abduction."

"And Elric. Would a weekly bottle of the most delicious milk in Foreverness compensate for some munched-on grass?"

"It ... it would."

The men looked at one another.

"I could bring you a bottle every Saturday," Robert said to his neighbor.

"That sounds reasonable," Elric said.

"Indeed, it does," Neve said.

"Thank you, my queen," Elric said. "You are as wise as you are lovely. And thank you, Your Majesty."

"Yes, thank you, Your Majesty," Robert said.

Both men bowed to Brockton and Neve, and walked out—not quite hand in hand, but perhaps not as careful to keep a resentful distance.

Neve smiled, then turned to Brockton, and his expression wiped her smile away. It wasn't anger, but there was confusion and—disappointment? He'd often sought her counsel, and she wouldn't have interfered if it were a matter of state. But this was just a foolish disagreement, and Neve had known she could clear the matter and move the line along a bit faster.

Brockton turned away from her. She felt her face redden under Lord Everard's glare.

The king was composed when he said to the next in line, "My good man. What is it you need help with?"

"Well ..." The man twisted his hat in his hands. "Perhaps Queen Neve would be willing to help me."

* * *

"I cannot believe you would humiliate me in such a manner."

The Great Hall was cleared. The queue had dwindled to zero, the councilors had left, and the sun had dipped below the horizon. The room was getting as dark as Brockton's tone.

He wasn't shouting. He never shouted. Not at Neve, not at anyone. But he was as irate as she'd ever seen him.

"Brockton," she said. "It was never my intent to humiliate you. It was a trifling matter between two men with, according to Lord Everard, a history of wasting the Crown's time. I happened to have an idea how to be done with it, by providing a solution that could possibly help to repair their relationship."

"You are not a ruler," Brockton said through gritted teeth.

"I wouldn't presume to be. I only acted as a mediator."

"You proposed a solution."

"I proposed a gentlemen's agreement. To help them."

"After that, a lot of people wanted you to help them, didn't they?"

Neve said nothing for a moment. Yes, after hearing her help Robert and Elric, several people requested that the queen be the one to entertain their requests and petitions. To several of them, she said that the king should be the one to resolve their particular matter, but there were others whom she knew she could help. She was careful to look at Brockton before each one and wait for his nod before she did. Only commoners had asked Neve for help; it hadn't escaped her notice that the noblemen in line weren't interested in her opinions.

"I am sorry. I didn't mean for any of that to happen," Neve said.

"Now it will continue to happen. People talk, and now they are likely to talk about the wise and clever queen."

"Is that so terrible?"

Brockton stared straight ahead as she shifted in her throne. "I'd prefer they talk about the wise and clever king and the constant and beautiful queen."

"Of course they will talk about you. You were wonderful with them today."

"When you let me speak."

Neve bristled. "It was a very long day, during which I spoke for a not very long time." She stood, realizing her royal rear end was numb. She wiggled around a bit. "You are the one who insisted upon my education. Your father agreed. He told me—and in fact, it was the last thing he said to me—that I was to counsel you."

"In our chambers. In private. Not in the Great Hall."

"Well, here's some private counsel. We need chairs in here. People are exhausted waiting all day. We need to provide fresh water for people in the queue over all the long hours, and maybe some fruit."

Brockton paused. "That is excellent advice."

Neve crossed her arms. "Thank you."

"Shared the way I expect you to share all your advice with me: alone together. Not in front of the council. Not in front of my family. Not in front of my subjects."

"Are you ashamed of me?"

"Do you suddenly want to be the object of attention? Because that's not like you, Neve."

"I—"

"It's like you to sit with your back to the wall, facing all doors, allowing me, your sisters-in-law, everyone else to shine brightly so that you're not noticed—and not targeted."

It was true.

But for just a little while today, while she was helping people, everything had seemed in the right place. She'd forgotten to sit in fear, exposing the bull's-eye on her chest. She'd given all her attention to the people who'd asked her for it.

And even though she'd felt Brockton seething beside her the whole time and knew this unpleasant conversation with him was imminent, she'd enjoyed herself. She'd enjoyed sharing her knowledge, her cleverness, her gained wisdom with people who wanted to hear it.

What good was all her education and experience in a tiny, locked room?

She'd finally found something that could make this all bearable—the death, the pain, the fear of it all happening to her again—and Brockton was ordering her to keep herself locked inside.

"I'm asking you to be admired and loved," Brockton said, "but you need to do it as a lady, as a genteel and benevolent woman, as a queen. Not as a king."

He was her loving husband, and she could argue with her loving husband.

He was also her sovereign as much as he was anyone's in the kingdom, and she was bound to obey, like everyone else.

"I am truly sorry, Your Majesty," she said.

He opened his mouth, perhaps to tell his wife she didn't need to address him formally. But he appeared to think better of it and closed his lips again.

* * *

Neve pulled the tapestry off the dark mirror and watched it swirl to life.

"My queen," the mirror said. "What a wonderful surprise

to gaze upon you. May I tell you who is the fairest of them all?"

"No."

"Er," the mirror said. "Has the cover fallen again?"

"No. I want to talk to you."

"As you wish. You begin, 'Mirror, mirror, on the—'"

"Can we not talk in riddles? Can we just talk, woman to … mirror?"

There was a long pause. "I suppose," the mirror said slowly.

"All right. Well, how are you?"

"I am well, my queen. How are you?"

"Confused."

"I am sorry. Would it help your confusion to know who the fairest is?"

Neve sighed. "I almost wish I were that simple. If you know who the fairest is, you must know all the women who live, correct?"

"I know all the women who live in Foreverness and its neighboring kingdoms."

"Then perhaps you can help me …"

"It is my existence to serve."

"Excellent. I'm looking for a woman."

"Your Majesty, I don't—"

"She is quite beautiful, so it wouldn't surprise me if you know of her. Maybe not the most beautiful in the land, but she could be near the top."

"Very well."

"Her name is Rowan."

"Do you have a last name?"

"No, but she is known as Rowan … the Wolf."

"Rowan the Wolf?"

"Shh, please keep your voice down. I'm asking you this in confidence."

"I understand," the mirror said in an exaggerated whisper.

Neve rolled her eyes. "I believe she lives in The Unfathomed."

"An unconventional place for a beautiful woman to live," the mirror pointed out.

"To be sure," Neve said. "But I need to know if she is alive or if she is ... either dead or maybe never was alive to begin with—just legend."

The mirror swirled furiously, changing colors from green to blue to bright pink to deep orange. The mist and smoke slid through the glass, winding in wisps through the room.

"She is not the fairest of them all," the mirror finally said. "Be assured you are fourteen fair ranks above her. Above you are—"

"No, no, no," Neve said. "Never mind that. Rowan the Wolf is real? She's alive?"

"As alive as you are."

Neve sat on the edge of her bed and took a deep breath. Rhyannon was correct; her spell was accurate. "She is in The Unfathomed?"

"I see her deep in The Unfathomed," the mirror confirmed. "Though I regret my abilities can't provide you a more specific location."

"Thank you. You have been ... quite useful."

"I—I have?"

"Yes, you have."

"I see," the mirror said. "You are welcome. Perhaps we could ... talk again tomorrow?"

"I'm not really interested in knowing who the fairest is."

"But perhaps ... I'd be good for something else. I was not expecting to be able to help you a different way."

A pang of guilt stabbed at Neve's conscience. She'd ignored this mirror for years, not considering it might have ... feelings. "Very well. We will talk tomorrow before bed."

"Good night, my queen." The smoke in the room sucked back into the black surface, and the mirror went still.

Neve tossed the tapestry over the top of the frame.

* * *

The next morning, before dawn broke through the trees, the queen slipped from the castle, saddled and mounted her mare in the dark, and rode fast, unescorted by the King's Protection. Sparrows, crows, and doves flew alongside and above her. Deer, rabbits, possums, and foxes raced alongside as Neve's forest guard.

When she arrived at the cottage, Uncle Bart was exiting the outhouse. "Little love," he said, blinking the sleep out of his eyes.

Biscuit pulled to a stop, as did all the furry escorts.

"Uncle Bart," Neve said. "I need your help."

DELLA

ella's heart pounded painfully as she looked around the living area.

For years, she'd lived in this home with her mother and father. It had been warm and tastefully decorated, and the lord and lady of the home entertained guests often, guests who played lutes and recited poems and brought little Della dolls and sweets and other surprises, exclaiming over her thick, shiny hair and her delicate singing voice and her creative storytelling. Della's mother loved dresses and jewels and loved just as much to get on the floor in those dresses and play games with Della as long as she liked. Della's father danced with and read to his only child, and called her clever when she demonstrated a talent for doing sums.

When her mother died, her father died too, even though it didn't seem like it to most, because his body still walked around, and his eyes still blinked. He didn't dance any more, or read. Not for a long year.

When he remarried, he came to life again as his new bride, Claire, and her daughters, Isabella and Javotte, moved into their home. "We're a family now," he said to Della. "Share your pretty clothes and toys. They didn't grow up as privileged as you, so be a generous sister with a great heart."

Javotte and Isabella borrowed without asking, and broke things, but Della remained ever patient to keep her father happy.

Until one day, he passed from this world to the one where her mother was.

Claire plundered Della's mother's closet, and when Della accused her of taking her mother's things, she'd slapped Della hard across the face twice, and the second blow sent Della to her knees. Claire gave Della a choice: Live outside as a beggar or live in this house as a servant from now on. She slammed the broom handle against Della's skull before tossing the broom to the floor at her feet, and Della began to slowly sweep, blood trickling into the corner of her mouth, her ears ringing, her head throbbing.

A head that would one day hold a crown.

Now, Della sat in a chair, and a bit of dust puffed up into the air around her. These chairs hadn't held anyone since Della had left in a prince's carriage wearing crystal slippers and arranged for her stepfamily to be sent to faraway kingdoms. Everyone in Foreverness spoke of Della's generosity in finding good marriages for her stepsisters, but the last glare Claire had given her before leaving with Javotte told Della she was well aware what her stepdaughter was doing—ensuring the women were forever below her station, below royalty. Della had raised a regal eyebrow and turned away. She vowed to never speak with them again, which was easy since they'd vowed the same.

It seemed so small now, the house. It was quite a grand noble home by Foreverness standards, and it took Della so long to clean it. Hours and hours, day after day. But now, accustomed to life in a royal castle, this home seemed like just a quaint little cottage, too tiny to hold the memories of sobbing and succumbing to the physical and verbal blows.

Sunlight streamed in through the leaves outside, and a spot on the hardwood floor gleamed, even under the dust that Della would never have allowed there.

She gripped the armrests, closed her eyes for a moment, and opened them again, trying to perceive the room as someone who had no emotional stake here, as someone assessing its suitability for a task.

It was perfect.

The home was oddly not in complete disrepair despite three decades of vacancy, but the thick dust over everything, the grimy windows, the stale air, was all ... perfect.

"Hello!" Eda called, and Della waved her in.

"Thank you," Della said. "I just needed a moment here."

Eda's soft eyes reflected understanding—not complete understanding, as Della had kept her abusive childhood to herself, but returning to one's childhood home was emotional for anyone.

"Let's begin," Della said, pleased that she could trust Eda with her secret so that she could have some assistance.

She and Eda, with the help of her driver, began dragging all the supplies into the home. When everything was inside, they created scenarios for learning.

They set the table with mismatched and backward place settings and tragically droopy floral centerpieces. They lit a fire and let it burn down without sweeping after it. Plenty of dust had already gathered on the shelves over the unoccupied room, and she flung a pile of hopelessly rumpled bedding in the corner.

It went against everything Della was to create such domestic chaos, but soon, the act of flinging things around the room with impunity was liberating, and even fun. "Just be pretty," she muttered, stomping mud from outside onto the floor. "Just be pretty," she growled, blowing to scatter cinders in the fireplace. "Just be pretty," she practically shouted, crumpling and wrinkling the bedding in her arms before tossing it on the floor and falling into it, thrashing around.

Then, sweaty and with loose strands of hair falling into her mouth, she'd closed the door on Eda, instructing her to return at midday with lunch and tea.

No sooner had her coach rounded the corner and out of sight, two carriages passed it and pulled to a stop in a neat line. Della retreated so the women alighting from the carriages didn't see her right away. The carriages had picked up each maid from her employer's home. Della had imagined few, if any, of them had ever been in such grand carriages before, and hearing their excited chatter amongst themselves, she knew she'd been correct.

She didn't know why she was nervous. She'd made grand entrances in ballrooms—sparkling, heralded entrances—and she'd felt in her element. And now, about to step before seven maids—so much like she once was—she felt her heart pounding through the bodice of her simple day dress. Della no longer owned raggedy, drab cleaning clothes, so she went with the simplest dress she had—still grander than anything these maids had ever seen, with complicated embroidery at the neck and cuffs. Her hair was swept up and pinned underneath a kerchief. She touched the top of her skull, where her smallest, subtlest crown graced her covered head with tiny yellow sapphires. She couldn't possibly be seen without a crown, but there was no reason to be ostentatious.

She kicked up her hem, then held her foot aloft, admiring the plain brown boot. She'd sent Eda to market to purchase all the training supplies, and when Eda had had some coins left over—knowing that not one of Della's hundreds of pairs of gorgeous shoes was fit for this new venture—she had bought the simplest pair of boots for her employer.

Della turned her ankle this way and that. She'd expected to be horrified at the way the brown suede boots looked on her feet, completely covering her ankles and the top curve of her foot, but they were ... strangely comfortable. Satisfying, even.

She cleared her throat loudly, and when the magpie chatter died down among the maids, Della stepped into the sun.

"Welcome," she said.

The women wore their hair in simple braids and buns, held with pins and torn cotton ribbons. All were in old dresses, and some wore aprons while others carried them in one hand, the long ties dangling, the ends brushing the dust at their feet. All wore shoes nearly identical to the ones on Della's feet. Blond women, brunette women, fair-skinned women, dark-skinned women, women barely older than girls, women Della's age and older. All of them with eyes as round and wide as skipping stones, some with their mouths hanging slack.

"I am Prin—" Della paused. "I am Della. Each of you has been sent here for domestic training, is that correct?"

No one said a word.

"I understand your mistresses are ... demanding, but surely they haven't cut your tongues out?"

"Your—your Highness," an older blonde stammered. "We are sorry, we didn't expect—rather, we were told we would be training with someone you recommended. We didn't expect to meet you."

"No, you didn't, because your mistresses couldn't tell you. They don't know the trainer is me."

Several gasps had Della quirking the corner of her lips up. "I personally train my staff, a staff that is renowned for their talent and good nature, but that's none of your mistresses' affairs, so they know nothing of it. I ask you for two things. One, that you keep my identity as your teacher a secret. I'm not ordering that you stay silent. I'm merely requesting that you tell no one—not your husbands, not your mistresses, no one—about my role here. You would gain nothing from spilling this secret, to be sure. But if you agree to comply with my request, you will be rewarded. Can you all agree?"

All the women nodded, the youngest one nodding so hard it seemed her head would pop off. Della, amused, patted her shoulder, and the maid stared at the princess's hand.

"Second, I ask that you do your best here. You need not be perfect. I only ask that you do your best. Are you amenable to that?"

One by one, they all quietly said yes. Della detected the faintest of smiles on a few of their faces. "Very well. I will learn your names, and we will work for a few hours before lunch, which will be provided for you. Do you have any questions?"

"Why?" a woman around Della's age asked. "Why are you doing this?" She immediately dropped her gaze to the dirt. "I am sorry. You asked—"

"I did ask if there were any questions." Della took a breath, and her chest rose and fell dramatically. "Cleaning is—an honorable profession. You might have heard otherwise."

Some of the women giggled. Others looked skeptical.

"Yes, I said honorable. The natural order of the Earth is chaos," Della continued. "Left on their own, vines will grow out of control, rivers will overflow or freeze, dust will gather, dirt will accumulate, children will make messes you can't have imagined. Cleaning is bringing order to the chaos of nature. You are alchemists and sorceresses. Cleaning is the power to harness nature, to bend it to your will, to impose order, and bring it under your spell."

Looking at their surprised faces, Della said, "Who better to help you with that power than a princess herself? Come. Let's begin."

Della led them inside.

* * *

Three hours later, the room was alive and bright with activity.

Two maids were kneeling on the floor, scrubbing at mud prints. One maid was bustling around the table, laying down place settings. One maid was arranging a rainbow of wild-flowers. One was brushing dust off shelves. One was folding piles of bedding. And one maid was kneeling before the fire-place, tasked with cleaning the cinders.

Della stood in the corner, arms folded, watching all the women.

One of the two women on the floor scrubbing sat back on her heels, squinting at her work, then glanced up at Della. Della lifted her chin toward her, examined the floor, and offered her an encouraging wink and a smile. The woman grinned back and bent over her scrubbing again, this time with confidence.

It was so easy to give them confidence and puff their pride. Someone who worked with pride did so much more with less effort than someone who labored under fear.

Now, as Della supervised the room, the maid by the fireplace caught her attention. The woman peered into the ashes and grimaced as if she were looking at a corpse. Della expected her to take up the brush, but she hesitated, then dropped her hands. Della pushed herself off the wall she was leaning against and kneeled beside the maid. She looked to be perhaps twenty-two years old.

"Molle, is it not?" Della asked.

"Yes, Your Highness."

"Molle, you seem to be having difficulty starting your task. Do you need help?"

Molle began to nod, then shook her head. "No, I don't need help. I—"

Della laid her hand on Molle's arm. How many times

had Della knelt before a fireplace under Claire's raised hand clutching a leather belt? "Tell me."

"I am not a scullery maid!" Molle burst out. "I am a housemaid! I handle silver, crystal. I don't wallow in dirt. I make things pretty. I could do Amee's work over there easily." She gestured toward the table, and Amee turned from the place settings to look at them. "But this—this is beneath my station, lowly though mine may be. This is not what I *do*."

The bustle in the room silenced as all the women looked at them, stunned by their fellow maid's insouciance in the company of royalty. "Molle," someone whispered urgently, but Molle lifted her chin, defiant.

Della looked at the woman for a long time, at the unruly curls at her hairline, at the line between her brows that she was far too young for. Molle knew she deserved more. Likely all the women here knew it, deep down, but Molle went so far as to demand it—from a princess. It was the kind of audacity that women in Foreverness rarely showed. The kind of audacity that encouraged one to create an illusion of finery and attend a ball one wasn't invited to.

Molle's chin never lowered, but her shoulders inched up bit by bit, as if expecting a blow for insisting on keeping what little dignity she'd been allowed in her life.

Finally, Della said, "My sweetest girl, will you listen to me?"

Molle was taken aback. "Of course, Your Highness."

Della smiled gently. "For a household staff to operate properly, harmoniously, every member must be willing to do all the jobs beneath their own. Of course, they often don't have to. But the willingness needs to be there. If someone is ill, or is needed at home, or if there is any other reason someone needs to take up for someone else, they do it competently, knowing someone else will step up—or down—for them when the time comes."

Della put her arm around Molle. "These are just tasks. These are not a measure of your worth. They are just things we do, not who we are."

"But—"

Della stood. She put her hands to her crown, hesitated for just a moment, then removed it. The sudden lightness was disconcerting. She turned her head from side to side. Usually, she moved through her day with complete awareness, stiffly controlling and minimizing her head turns through her chin to keep the crown from sliding or tilting. Now she could move freely, unconsciously, the way she did alone before bed. Perhaps this should have felt a relief, but it was quite the opposite. Della felt—powerless.

But she still had the attention of the room, so she shook her head like a cat and turned and handed the crown to Amee, who spread a cloth napkin on the table and set the royal head-piece on it with suddenly responsible, trembling fingers.

Then Della got back on her knees and crawled to Molle. "Here. We will do it together." She took the brush from where it leaned against the stone and crammed herself into the fire-place, slipping her derriere through gritty dirt.

Suddenly, panic gripped her heart.

Do you dare to call this clean? Clean enough for you to sleep here?

Della clenched a fist, digging her fingernails into her palm. Then she slid in a little deeper, surprised at how small and tight this hearth was. She didn't remember it as so—

She almost laughed out loud. No, it wouldn't have been a tight fit for an overworked, undernourished teenager. But it was a tight fit for a well-fed, middle-aged, cushion-sitting princess.

"Your Highness ..." at least three women protested. "You don't have to—"

Della began to sweep the cinders.

All the women huddled around them.

"Do you see how I'm doing this?" Della asked Molle. "Do you see how I'm holding my wrist like this? If you hold your hand this way, it's quicker and more efficient."

"I ... I do see," Molle said.

A clump of ashes fell from somewhere over Della's shoulder, and she felt it plop on her neck, covering her skin with dirt. She handed Molle the brush, her jeweled and polished hand closing around Molle's rough and ripped one. They held the brush together, gazing into each other's eyes. "I've cleaned many a fireplace," Della said. "Admittedly, I ... no longer do. But if my entire staff was felled by illness tomorrow and I wanted to keep warm, I'd do it again. Do you understand?"

"Yes," Molle said. "I do." She bent over her task and began to brush under the princess's watch.

"Excellent," Della said. "Moving with care is important, and you're doing just that."

She patted Molle's shoulder blade as Molle kept moving with intention. "Wonderful work," she said, then stood. She brushed her hands down the front of her now-filthy dress and looked up. The women were all watching her—but they weren't looking at her the way everyone looked at her when she greeted her subjects in town. The wonder, the awe, the stars in their eyes were all gone. Instead, they looked at her earnestly, with warm smiles.

"Let's continue," Della said. "Shortly, we will have a break for sweets and tea, and we can all have a chat. Does that sound agreeable?"

The women assented with delight and went back to their tasks with new energy and fervor. Della went from maid to maid to offer first praise, then suggestions.

Dust mote by dust mote, dish by dish, scrub by scrub, the maids alchemized chaos into order.

NEVE

Neve, accompanied by Uncles Bart, Terric, Forwin, Anselm, and Gerard, as well as various woodland creatures—deer, rabbits, and an ambitious porcupine—rode toward The Unfathomed.

"I'm sorry, Your Majesty," Uncle Gerard said from behind her, "but can you tell us why we're going to The Unfathomed?"

"For the love of dirt, Gerard," Uncle Forwin grumbled. "Did you not listen?"

"Stop calling me Your Majesty," Neve said. "Why didn't some of you stay home? You didn't all need to come."

"I will call you Your Majesty," Uncle Gerard said, "for you are the greatest queen who ever lived."

Neve didn't feel like the greatest anything—except maybe the greatest fearful fool.

"Neve needs to find someone in The Unfathomed," Uncle Bart said patiently. "It would be irresponsible for a queen to ride there without guard, but she doesn't want to tell the king or his soldiers where she's going, so we are acting as guard."

"They'll notice I'm gone, no doubt. Perhaps they have already," Neve said. "But they certainly wouldn't think to look for me in a place Brockton knows I would never go."

"Interesting," Uncle Anselm said.

"What's interesting?" Neve asked.

"All of it. Now that we're on the road, how about telling us why you are on your way to the darkest place in Foreverness—a place you would never go, as you said—when you have a nice castle to sit in? Find someone in The Unfathomed? No one is even there. Not voluntarily. So, what are we helping you with, exactly? We would never say no, but the truth would be appreciated."

The Unfathomed hadn't always been the darkest forest in Foreverness. Once upon a time, the Everlasting Emerald Woods had been green and full of life—maybe with small pockets of darkness where the not-so-nice creatures dwelled. But then twelve-year-old Princess Neve of Goldenstone had vanished there and was presumed dead. Visitors to Everlasting Emerald began to dwindle, and those who'd built lovely, quiet cottages there abandoned them and went back to the towns. The trees grew larger and darker, blotting out the sun, and a new name was unofficially coined: The Unfathomed.

The princess was eventually discovered alive, but a tale had already begun to circulate about another girl who went into the woods and never returned, not to this day. Those who insisted the tale was true said they'd seen the young teenage girl heading into the trees, wearing a red cape over a simple shift dress and boots, armed with daggers and poison, and dragging a too-heavy sword behind her. She'd been muttering about killing all the wolves. She'd never been seen again—if she'd ever been seen, really. If she'd been real, she had been just a poor girl of the village. A girl named—

"Rowan," Neve said. "I'm going to find Rowan."

"Rowan the Wolf?" Uncle Anselm asked. "Rowan is a fairy tale, little love. She's not real. She's a story. You know that."

"There was no Rowan," Uncle Terric agreed. "It was a story some people made up to explain an innocent girl's disappearance."

"Rowan is dead," Uncle Forwin said. "If there was a Rowan, and she confronted a bunch of wolves, then she became nothing but wolf lunch. Those wolves are not like the ones we see around here. They're a different breed altogether. More human than wolf."

"She *is* a wolf, little love," Uncle Gerard said. "That's why they call her Rowan the Wolf. Girl by day, and at night, she grows fur and a tail and large teeth, and runs with the pack. She's one of them, I tell you."

"Gerard," Uncle Forwin said, "Neve isn't a foolish child. She's not going to believe that. I don't know why you do."

"What do you think about the Rowan the Wolf story, Bart?" Uncle Gerard asked.

They rode along in silence for a moment. Then Uncle Bart said, "I don't think she's dead, but I don't think she's a wolf. There's something in those evil woods that's keeping it from taking over Foreverness. That place got real dark, real fast, but it's contained. I have to believe there's something keeping it in line. It could be Rowan. She'd be an adult now. A man would join the darkness, look for glory, and seek to lead. A woman, though—a woman would keep the darkness in check. I don't know what's keeping The Unfathomed in its place, but it could very well be a woman."

All Uncle Bart's long stories turned into jokes; he loved to make others laugh. Neve waited for the funny quip, but it didn't come. After speaking his piece, he just sat silently on his pony.

They rode for a while longer, the sunshine eventually beginning to fade. Neve looked up, expecting to see a cloud drifting across the sun, but instead, she saw the tree line of The Unfathomed looming closer. She forgot to breathe for a few moments.

Her birthday gown. Pink and purple wildflowers in a field. The careless singing of birds overhead. The scraping of the huntsman's sword as he unsheathed it behind her back. Turning and seeing his hesitation and falling on her knees to beg for her life. The angle of his chin toward the thick trees, telling her silently to flee. Running. Running. Hungry. Scared. Alone. Running.

Uncle Anselm, leading their party, halted his pony, and the rest of them followed suit. Under Neve, Biscuit shuffled her weight from hoof to hoof. They were on the edge of the woods. The border was almost a clear line where the path, covered in dirt and short grass, stopped and the long, wild, unkempt grass began.

None of them moved for a few moments. Finally, Uncle Forwin said, "Is there a plan, or—?"

Her uncles, the ponies, and all their little wildlife companions turned to Neve. "I—I'm not sure," she said.

"The Unfathomed is large and deep," Uncle Anselm said. "Even if you knew where Rowan was—even if you knew Rowan existed—it would be challenging to find her. But if you don't know where to start …"

"We know the woods," Uncle Forwin said. "We lived there much of our old lives. I don't mind wandering a bit."

"We lived there when it was the Everlasting Emerald Woods," Uncle Bart pointed out. "Neve moved us as it was growing dark. We don't know it anymore."

"And it doesn't know us anymore," Uncle Terric added.

The silence enveloping them was disconcerting. Neve remembered the Everlasting Emerald Woods, and how, as a child, she'd never felt alone there because the wind in the leaves, birdsong, cricket chirps, chipmunk rustles all reminded her she was in good company. Here, however, the silence was all there was, as if everything inside The Unfathomed was still, stealthy, and secretive.

"We should make some noise," Neve said loudly. "Perhaps

we can draw the attention of someone who can help me."

"What if we draw the attention of someone who can eat us?" Uncle Gerard asked.

"I'll take that chance," Uncle Forwin said. "We're armed."

"We are?" Neve asked.

All five of them drew weapons from their pockets and saddlebags: daggers, throwing knives, axes. Uncle Gerard brandished a kitchen knife Neve was pretty sure they used a few weeks ago to carve their dinner pheasant. She raised her brows at the assortment.

"We may be old reprobates, but we are guarding the queen of Foreverness," Uncle Forwin said. "Did you think we would be wielding pillows and pastries?"

Neve felt for the dagger in her sleeve and checked that her wooden sword with an iron tip was still at her side. Then she said, "Let's sing a song."

"We only know drinking songs," Uncle Forwin grumbled.

"Well, that's all right," Neve said.

"We haven't got any ale," Uncle Forwin said. "With drinking songs, the song isn't the fun part."

"Uncle," Neve said through her teeth. "You're deliberately missing the point."

Uncle Terric began to sing.

They all joined in, though, to be fair, the tune lacked the mirth that drink—and the safety of home—would have lent it. They finished the song, then sang another, and suddenly—

"Sssilenccce."

Two large snakes, one golden green, the other greenish gold, had sneaked upon the party, and they began to wind around the ponies' hooves. The group stopped singing mid-word, and the uncles' mounts danced in fear. The snakes twisted around each other in an elaborate knot, then slid it apart. Neve's rabbit, deer, and squirrel friends backed away several steps, eyes wide, watching every move the snakes made. The porcupine stood its ground and flashed its needles. The snakes regarded it, and wisely kept their distance.

"Your sssong is disssturbing the peaccce of the woodsss," the golden snake said slowly as it separated from the other and slithered up Biscuit's front leg, then Neve's right leg. Neve tightened her hands on the reins to keep nervous Biscuit from rearing. The snake coiled on her thigh and its head swayed side to side right in front of hers, its forked tongue sliding out every few seconds. "But I sssuspect you know thisss."

"You want our attention, yesss?" the green snake said, even more slowly than his companion. It slid up Biscuit's other front leg, ignoring the horse's shaking protest, and slid up Neve's left leg to also settle on her thigh. "Ssspeak."

Out of the corners of both her eyes, Neve saw her uncles ready their knives and daggers, but they'd have to fling them at their own child to try to hit the serpents, and she knew they wouldn't dare as long as the snakes remained on her body.

She tried not to move a muscle. She needed respect to get their help.

"I am Queen Neve of Foreverness."

"You are a waysss from home, Queen," the green snake said. "With only sssmall men and fluffy creaturesss. Do you need sssomething?"

With all the calm of a woman who did not have snakes sitting on her lap and staring into her face, Neve said, "I need someone."

"Interesssting," the golden snake said. "Who isss this sssomeone?"

"Rowan the Wolf."

The snakes stilled their swaying and fixed their yellow eyes on her. "A queen needsss Rowan the Wolf," the golden snake finally said. "Why isss thisss?"

"Yesss," the green snake said, still unmoving except for its tongue. "Enlighten usss."

"You know her, then?"

"Everyone knowsss her," the golden snake said.

"Are you afraid?" the green snake asked.

"Why do you ask me that?" Neve said.

"Becaussse you are here asssking for help insssstead of going into the woodsss to find her."

"Yes," Neve said. "I am very afraid of The Unfathomed."

"Why?" the golden snake asked. "Ssscary ssstoriesss?"

"No." She looked each snake in the eyes, one after the other. "I died there."

The snakes paused to take that in.

"Yet," the golden snake said, "you return."

"I don't want to go in there," Neve clarified. "I never want to go in there again. But I have a destiny, and I am told by a vision that Rowan the Wolf has answers for me."

The green snake slithered up Neve's left arm, curved around the back of her neck, and rested its head on her right shoulder. Neve heard several of her uncles gasp softly. "You are not afraid of usss?" it whispered into her ear.

The hair on her skin stood up. "Oh, I am," Neve said. "I'm afraid of everything."

The golden snake wound up Neve's right arm and slid its head to her left shoulder. "You ssseem rather courageousss and relaxxxed."

"I am good at hiding my fear, I suppose. I've had my whole life to practice."

The snakes remained there for a moment, breathing in both her ears, their tongues flicking her earlobes. She tried to catch any one of her uncles' gazes, but they were frozen, holding their weapons aloft, staring only at the snakes.

The serpents reversed position and returned to her lap,

swaying again. "We like you, Queen," the golden snake said.

"Yesss, we do."

"And we will find sssomeone to bring you to the one you ssseek."

"Ssstay here," the green snake said. "And wait."

The snakes slid to the dirt path, maneuvering carefully around the porcupine. The golden snake slid into the tall grass of The Unfathomed, but the green snake first turned its head to look at all of them. "By the way, niccce sssong. But ssstay sssilent until we return. The nexxxt creaturesss you attract may not be as sssweet as usss."

Then it vanished.

Her uncles all exhaled heavily and lowered their weapons. "Those two slimy bastards just took ten years off my life," Uncle Anselm mumbled. "And at my age, I can only afford one, maybe two."

"I didn't know what to do," Uncle Gerard said. "They were *on* you."

The porcupine relaxed its quills against its body and sighed. The other animals crept closer again.

"I'm all right," Neve said. "Thank you. All of you. I would not have been so brave had you not been here beside me." Though her guards would have been able to do nothing but stand by had the snakes decided to bite and poison her.

"Guess now we just wait," Uncle Bart said.

Wait they did, for about two hours, keeping their voices down. They shared some oranges and grapes that Uncle Gerard had thought to bring. They slid off their mounts and sat in the dirt and played cards, though as Uncle Forwin kept emphasizing, cards without coins or ale were a useless pastime. Uncle Anselm said that it was unlikely the snakes would ever return, but Neve trusted her instinct that they would come back. Most of their furry forest companions curled up and napped in the high sun of the early afternoon, and Uncle Terric lay on the ground with them to whittle a small boat, his hat shielding his face. After a while he gave up and dozed also, a rabbit curled in the crook of his arm. But they all began to stretch and wake as the sun dipped lower.

Neve's absence at the castle would be noticed by now. Brockton would have the King's Protection searching for her. She'd left a note for Brockton with a lame explanation that wouldn't hold up for more than a few hours, but he was likely still cross with her.

Her uncles were getting restless, and Neve was hungry for a real meal. Maybe she'd been wrong. Maybe it was time to stand up and brush off and go home. She'd already put everyone here in danger just to chase a foolish vision.

A shadow slowly crept over Neve and she looked up.

Into the faces of two wolves.

Huge wolves. One was gray as flint, the other a rusty red. They stared into Neve's heart, through her eyes.

Everyone else, human and beast, froze in place. Waiting.

Neve licked her very dry lips. "Did the snakes tell you I'm looking for Rowan the ... Wolf?"

The gray wolf dipped its head. Neve took the gesture as a yes.

"Are you Rowan?" she said to the first, then, glancing at the second, "Or you?"

The two wolves looked at one another, and Neve didn't need to speak wolfish to understand they were saying, *Is she an idiot?*

"Right," Neve said. "Of course not. She's a human." Neve stood up slowly and smoothly. At her full height she was taller than the wolves, but only just. And they were each far wider than her. She looked between them into the distant dark trees. "Is she coming?"

The wolves both turned away from the group and toward the trees. Then one angled its head back at her.

"You want me to—go with you?"

The rusty wolf dipped its head.

No.

She couldn't.

She could run right now, just hop on Biscuit and gallop with her family and friends away from here, and pretend this day never happened.

She looked at her uncles, one by one. They were all watching her. But they were not just watching the little girl they raised and protected.

They were watching their queen.

"Very well," Neve said, and briskly secured Biscuit to a nearby tree. Her uncles did the same with their ponies. "Guard the horses," she said to the rabbits, squirrels, porcupine, and deer. They huddled close.

"Let's go," Neve said, and set foot onto the tall grass of The Unfathomed—for the first time since she was seventeen.

Her five uncles gathered around her, and they all moved forward, but after a few steps, the wolves turned, lowered their heads, and growled at the men.

"They don't want us to follow them," Uncle Terric said.

"They want Neve to follow them," Uncle Anselm corrected. "Not the rest of us."

They all looked at Neve.

Running in the darkness. Alone. Hunted.

Scared.

"Wait for me here," Neve said.

"We will," Uncle Forwin said. "No matter how long."

Uncle Bart took her hand and kissed it. She turned to the wolves, but they growled once again, their eyes on the metal-tipped sword. She unsheathed it and placed it on the dirt.

She did have one concealed weapon, small though it was. She didn't want to lose this opportunity. Or her will.

The wolves began walking again toward the dark trees, and Neve followed.

She'd worn one of her simpler gowns, but she'd inherited a new wardrobe in the last few days—one fit for a queen. So her simpler gowns were still more elaborate than others' finest. She clutched the material to hold it up as she stepped through overgrown weeds with her luxuriously soft riding boots. She didn't glance down to see how they were being ruined; she instead kept her eyes ahead, her heart pounding faster as they reached the thick pocket of trees.

The midafternoon here was as black as midnight. Sinister branches pierced the sky and blocked the daylight. Rather than soft pine needles, they walked on crunchy dead leaves, every step an announcement of their presence to whoever might be interested in royal prey.

A pair of red eyeballs peeked out of a hole in a tree trunk, and a yellow pair blinked from another. Neve kept moving, her hands tightening on the front of her dress. She stumbled over a huge root, and another one a few minutes later, but the wolves didn't stop or slow. Were they walking in circles? Every dark tree resembled the next.

Neve didn't take long walks in the woods and hadn't since she was twelve, so she couldn't estimate how far they'd come, but they walked for at least an hour. Finally, she heard—waves?

The sky began to brighten, and they emerged from the darkness to overlook a beach with waves crashing. They had come out of The Unfathomed on the east coast, and this was the Silvering Sea. Neve could see the Silvering Sea from the highest point of the castle, but it was just a speck in the distance. Now her nose was filled with salt air and the scent of fresh fish. A dolphin, then a second dolphin, leaped into the air, sun sparkling on their smooth skin before they dove back into the water with barely a splash.

Neve's stance was unsteady on the sand, so when the wolves nudged her to sit, she stumbled and broke her fall with her hands, fingers failing to grab at the fine grains of sand. They stared at her, and she got the message to stay put. They walked down the beach, toward a jetty. At the very end of the jetty was a person who stood when the wolves approached. Their long black hair blew in a tangle in the sea air. The wolves looked back at Neve, and the person followed their gaze, paused a full minute, then walked toward her, the wolves flanking.

It was the woman in her vision. She wore trousers and tall boots and strode toward Neve with the confidence of someone comfortable in her surroundings. The arms of her shirt had been torn off at the shoulder, baring strong biceps and forearms.

Neve scrambled to stand. She brushed the sand off her dress and stood as tall and as dignified as she could manage. The woman stopped a few feet before her. She was a few inches shorter than Neve, but her presence somehow made Neve feel small. Her bright eyes were like sun sparkling through two perfectly round pieces of sea glass. When the wind calmed a bit, her hair fell to her elbows.

Fastened to the woman's side, a long sword gleamed in the light through the break in the trees. Two daggers graced her other side. Her fingers casually dangled a third dagger under a swatch of red velvet tied around her wrist.

The wolves settled on their haunches, then the rusty one fell on its side and rolled around in the sand like a giant puppy. The gray wolf jumped on his companion's belly, and they nipped and yelped at each other before taking off in a game of chase to the water.

The woman watched them fondly, then turned back to Neve. Still, she said nothing. Her expression wasn't unfriendly, nor was it particularly welcoming. It was clear she was waiting for Neve to speak first.

"I am Queen Neve of Foreverness," Neve said.

Silently, the woman ever so slightly cocked her head to one side as she examined Neve's face.

Neve blinked and stammered, "It is customary to bow—er, or curtsy—to a queen."

A ghost of a smile graced the woman's lips. "I don't bow to titles. I bow to character, and I don't know what yours is yet."

It shouldn't have surprised Neve that a woman in trousers wasn't much interested in custom or etiquette. "You are Rowan the Wolf?"

The woman did smile then. "That's what they call me."

"What do you call you?"

"Rowan will do."

Neve wanted to ask her if she was the child who'd gone into the woods to kill the wolves, then disappeared forever. She wanted to ask where her clothes came from. She wanted to ask what she did in the woods and on the beach by herself all day, every day, every year.

Instead, she said, "You have something for me?"

Rowan's gaze dropped as she patted her pockets. She looked back at Neve. "Er, no?"

"You came to me in a vision."

"Oh?"

"Yes." Neve wanted to stomp her foot in frustration. "I need insight, knowledge, something to—"

To her credit, Rowan was listening intently. "To what?"

The woman had come to her in a vision. Neve might never see her again. Might as well be honest. "I am a new queen, and I am—afraid. I have had a bounty on my head my whole life, even before I was a queen. And I sit beside the king, who rules, and I—"

"Don't?"

Neve said nothing.

"You want to rule," Rowan said.

"No, I—"

"You don't?"

"No, but—"

"I'm not sure I can help you if you don't know what you want. Frankly, I'm not sure I could help you even if you did, but you're not offering any clues."

"I sit on a throne, but I am powerless," Neve burst out. "Powerless to protect myself. Powerless to help others."

Rowan looked out to sea. "Ah. Now I see." Her hair whipped across her face, and she brushed it out of her mouth. "You are a woman in society. Even when you have power, you don't."

"I don't know what I'm doing."

"Is power what you seek?" Rowan asked. "Is that what you're here to ask me? Do you think I have the secret? Because perhaps I do."

Neve nodded.

"I live free," Rowan said. "I live here, in nature. I do as I please. I make my own decisions. I choose my own family. I fight my own battles. My life is my own, and no one tells me what to do. You can do this also, you know. You can toss your pretty gown into the sea and live in The Unfathomed."

"I can't live here. I can't stay here. I don't even want to be here right now."

"Why?" Rowan asked. "It has all you need. Food, shelter, company—"

"I can't."

"Of course you can't," Rowan said. "You are here, blathering about expectations and powerlessness and how hard it is to be royalty, but you'd never leave it. It's so comfortable and mushy and soft."

"No, that's not it. This place ..."

Neve's chin trembled. Rowan took three steps forward, and Neve pulled her dagger from her sleeve and pointed it at Rowan.

"It's like that, is it?" Rowan asked. She flipped her own dagger in the air, caught it by the handle, and pointed it at the queen.

Neve lunged first with one leg, extending her arm toward Rowan's shoulder, but Rowan easily sidestepped it. Neve recovered with a side turn to keep Rowan in front of her. She feinted a few times, then arced her arm with a fierce cry. Quick as a fox, Rowan stuck her knife between her teeth like it was a gentle flower, dove onto the sand, wrapped both arms around Neve's legs to buckle her knees, and dropped the queen to her back. She wound her legs around Neve's waist so Neve couldn't hit her with her feet.

Neve had learned to use a dagger and a sword, but she hadn't learned to grapple on the ground—no soldier would teach her, fearing inadvertent impropriety with the princess. She wished now that she had commanded it.

Rowan gripped Neve's wrist and somehow slid her other hand under Neve's elbow, gradually pushing up. Neve feared her arm would snap, but she didn't want to open her hand.

Rowan spit the dagger in her mouth into the sand at their side, and said, "Release your weapon. Breaking your arm would destroy all my good will with the Crown."

She applied just a bit more pressure, and Neve opened her hand, releasing the blade.

The two women stared into each other's eyes and after a moment, Neve gave up. She knew this place was dangerous, and she'd come here despite that, but maybe it was time to let go, time to surrender ...

Rowan's blue eyes widened.

"You," she said. "You are like me, aren't you?"

Neve took a shaky breath.

Rowan whispered, "You are a child of the woods. Destroyed by the woods."

"Yes," Neve whispered back.

Rowan leaned back and rolled off Neve. Neve sat up, shaking sand from her hair, her eyes, her ears. No telling how much sand was in her bodice.

They sat for a moment in silence, but the tension was gone. Finally, Rowan put a hand on Neve's shoulder.

"What happened to you?"

Rowan's hand was warm through Neve's gown, and she pressed down in assurance, or in urgency. "He spared me," Neve said, "but I died."

Rowan dropped her hand. "I died," she said. "But he spared me."

"Who?"

"You tell me."

They said at the same time, "The huntsman."

They stared at each other for long moments.

Rowan whistled to the wolves, who bounded out of the sea and trotted toward them. The two women stood, and Rowan gently backed Neve up a few steps just a second before both wolves shook an ocean of water off their coats. Neve squinted at them until they were done.

Then Rowan turned toward the darkness of the trees again. "Come," she said to all of them.

Neve hesitated.

"I think I know why you're here," Rowan said. "I think I know what I'm supposed to give you."

* * *

They traveled through the dark woods again. But Neve felt slightly more reassured with Rowan at her side. When she'd traveled with the wolves, she'd had half a thought that they could turn and devour her at any moment. But no harm could come to her with this woman beside her. She felt safer than she did surrounded by soldiers of the King's Protection.

"You were looking out to sea when I arrived," Neve said. "Were you meditating?"

"What are you talking about?"

"Er, getting into your own mind," Neve said. "Following your own breath. My Uncle Anselm once showed me how."

"Showed you how to stare into space?"

"Yes."

"What's the sense in that?"

"I'm afraid I don't really know," Neve admitted. "I wasn't very good at it." She stepped carefully over a large root, steadying herself on a dark tree without realizing it. She glanced at the tree in apology. It didn't swallow her whole, so that was a good thing. "You seemed ... deep in thought."

"We keep watch," Rowan said.

"For what?"

"Pirates."

"Pirates?" Neve poked a loose lock of hair back into place above her ear. "I hope you don't waste too much time with that. Pirates haven't come ashore here in years."

"You would think that, wouldn't you?"

Neve paused. Rowan's strides were long and sure, and Neve wished she had trousers, too. Her big swishing skirts were becoming a nuisance. "What reason would I have to not think that?"

"You wouldn't," Rowan said. "Because pirates do come ashore every few months or so. And you and all the other comfy residents of Foreverness don't know a thing about it because we stop them before they reach the kingdom to plunder and pillage. Which is, of course, always their intent."

Neve walked on silently, taking in this information. Rowan didn't seem like the type to tell tales. If this were true … "How do you stop them?"

Rowan patted her sword fondly.

"You—fight pirates?"

"I do find it's more effective than dancing with them."

"You said 'we.' Who are 'we'?"

"The wolves."

"The wolves fight the pirates?"

"The wolves—and I—defeat the pirates." Rowan gestured at the two huge wolves, who'd bounded ahead. "Look at the size of them. You wouldn't want to encounter one of them alone in the woods, much less two or three packs of them at one time. Most of the men turn and run. The ones who stay and fight—well, they don't last long."

"Why do you do this? Why would you care if they made it to Foreverness? Why not just let them do as they will?"

"We have an arrangement with the king."

Neve stopped. "My husband?"

"The arrangement was originally with your father-in-law, but I insisted upon written law, so yes, your husband is bound by his father's agreement. We protect the kingdom from threats that come through The Unfathomed. In return, we are given fruits and vegetables—food that The Unfathomed can no longer grow. We have plenty of meat there—particularly in pirate season." She grinned at Neve's horrified look. "I'm jesting. Well, I'm jesting for me. My family isn't so discerning. But the Crown does provide some meat we can't get, like chicken. And, of course, they kindly provide me with my clothes."

"I'm surprised they'd rather make a deal with you than post King's Protection soldiers in there."

"Those delicate little daisies would wilt in the face of what we fight," Rowan said with a laugh. "They wouldn't last a week."

They walked for a time in silence. If it could even be called walking. It seemed more like a slow run. Every now and then, Neve hit her toe on a little hill or stumbled over a large root. Each time she tripped, she noticed Rowan didn't even glance in her direction. Perhaps it should annoy her that this woman—this warrior—couldn't be bothered to assure the physical safety of the queen, but it didn't. Instead of rushing to help her, as anyone else in Foreverness would have done, Rowan acted as though Neve were nothing special, just a woman she expected would be able to keep up the pace on this long hike over rough terrain.

It was refreshing.

After a while, the brush got denser, and the familiar fear crept into Neve's heart, but Rowan drew her dagger and hacked through branches, opening space for them. They went about a quarter of a mile like that, and then the trees gave way to a small clearing. In the clearing sat a little log cabin with a warm light burning in two windows.

"Wait here," Rowan said.

Neve reached under her skirts and drew out her own dagger, holding it point down at her side. Rowan lifted her brows. "Very good."

Neve watched Rowan walk toward the house and knock so lightly on the door that Neve couldn't hear it from where she stood.

The door opened and a man stood framed in the backlight. His features were in shadow. He hugged Rowan in the kind of fond way—including hearty back pats—that signified they'd hugged many times before. When they parted, Neve could see Rowan talking to him, her head close to his, gesturing in Neve's direction. The man put a hand on her arm briefly, then closed the door. Rowan walked back to Neve.

"He has agreed to see you. Come."

"Who?" Neve asked, but Rowan was already walking back to the cabin. Neve tightened her grip on her little weapon and followed.

This time, the door opened before Rowan could knock, and they stepped into the warmth inside. Neve smelled fragrant lentil soup in the pot in the fireplace. The inside air was devoid of the dampness of its inhospitable woods. Neve's shoulders sagged in relaxation.

Rowan stepped aside, and Neve came face to face with the man.

He was about sixty-five, and though his shoulders were a bit stooped with age and his hair had fully grayed, his body was still muscled, and his green eyes were still sharp.

He didn't look surprised at all. He seemed as though he'd accepted long ago that this reunion would happen someday, that he'd have to say something to the child he'd been tasked to slaughter.

"Princess," he said quietly.

"Queen," she said.

He got down on one knee with just a bit of creaky effort and bowed his head. "Queen," the huntsman repeated.

He stayed there, possibly waiting her permission to stand, but she didn't give it.

Rowan shifted uncomfortably.

He finally looked up at Neve. "I take it you remember me,

though you were—so small."

"I will never forget your face," Neve said.

"I most humbly beg your pardon. I—I was—"

"Please rise."

He got up and pulled his one small wooden chair away from the little wooden table. "Sit, Your Majesty. I wasn't expecting company. The only one who visits me is Rowan. But I have some soup to share."

"Don't go to any—"

"It's no trouble." He rushed to the fireplace and removed the pot of simmering soup, ladling it into two bowls. He pushed them toward Neve and Rowan, along with two spoons.

"But what will you eat?" Neve asked.

"Never mind that." He crossed the room and sat on his small sleeping pallet. Rowan settled in beside him and dove into her soup with enthusiasm. Neve ate a few bites as well before the huntsman said, "I am Darren. I don't know if you ever knew my name."

"Darren," Neve repeated. Strange to give her memory a name. He'd always been just the huntsman. "Fina told you to kill me."

"Fina was the queen, and I was a fine hunter, known in Goldenstone for providing the best game for the royal table. She summoned me one day, and I thought it was to ask me to provide something for the banquet that week. Venison, or maybe pheasant. But she told me I was to take you into the woods and—"

Neve swallowed. "You disobeyed her."

"I did. You were so tiny. You were wearing a lovely little dress, and skipping, and picking flowers, and as we walked deeper and deeper into the woods, I was desperately asking God to forgive me, that my queen demanded it, that there must be a reason for it, that maybe you were possessed by evil that I wasn't told about, that my own life would be in danger if I didn't do what I was told to do."

Neve couldn't look at him anymore. She ate a few bites of soup but couldn't taste it any longer. She placed her spoon down. "There was a deer. I remember. I showed you."

Darren smiled. "Yes, a little fawn who came so close. You said *look!* And you grabbed my arm and held it as we looked at the fawn together. You—were so trusting. You thought I was your friend. My heart twisted."

Darren's eyes watered, and he swiped at them. "You turned away from me and I silently drew my sword and said a prayer over you. Before I could move, you knelt and began pulling flowers from the earth. You said you wanted to pick a bouquet to take to the queen. 'So she will love me,' you said."

Darren dropped his face into his hands. Rowan put an arm around his shoulders and murmured into his ear.

"I suddenly knew," Darren said into his hands, "there could be no reason Fina could ask me to do this—no reason except for hate. The moment I realized I couldn't do it, you turned and found me with my sword raised."

He lifted his head. "You begged to be spared. There was no need for your beseeching. I'd already decided to let you go, but I wasn't sure what to do. There was no one I trusted to whom I could bring you. But I suddenly remembered meeting two men in the woods several weeks prior. Two miners. They were good men, funny and smart. They said they lived in a cottage, and I hoped perhaps you could find them if I sent you in the right direction."

"You told me to run north."

"Yes. And when you ran, I saw the fawn run after you, then its father the stag leaped from the trees to follow. I trusted they'd watch over you."

"They did. They still do. And I did make it to the men's home."

"I know," Darren said. "I went looking for their home a week later and when I found it, I lurked in some shrubs. I saw you in the kitchen. One man brought you a cup of milk while another man wrapped a blanket around your shoulders. You were laughing at something, and your laugh sounded genuine. I left, feeling as though I'd done something right."

"What did you say to Fina?" Neve asked.

Darren sighed. "After I sent you running, I shot a wild boar, cut out its lungs and liver, and took them to the queen to show I'd done as I was commanded."

No one said anything for a few moments until Rowan said slowly, "That's ... grim."

"She'd ... asked me to."

Neve blinked.

"I'm sorry, Your Majesty, for the cold truth, but she'd asked me to kill you and bring her the body parts as proof. I took the chance that she'd never seen human innards—although with someone like Fina, one never knows—and that she wouldn't guess she'd been deceived. She did believe me, and gave me a small bag of gold, but she had a magic mirror, and she had spies everywhere, and I knew that when she eventually discovered you were alive and well, she would demand my death next. I trusted your new family would protect you, but I had to protect myself, so I fled Goldenstone."

"You built this home?"

"Not at first. I moved around for years, never staying in one place more than a few days. I kept to the wooded areas and stayed under cover of darkness."

"You must have been quite resourceful, for Fina is—was—persistent in her hatred."

"I was. After about six years or so, I was camping for a few weeks near an old woman's cottage. Not too many people lived in the woods, and the woods were beginning to fall into darkness at that time, but Agnes was so sweet. She refused to leave her home. I looked in on her from time to time, chopping wood for her, bringing her meat, and she was kind enough to cook meals for me and give me blankets. She was"—he looked at Rowan—"a wonderful lady."

Rowan dropped her gaze to her lap.

"Agnes was the one who told me Queen Fina had died," Darren said. "Her daughter lived in Foreverness, near the border with Goldenstone, and word was going around that the missing princess was found alive and had married a prince of Foreverness, and Queen Fina had died in captivity."

"That was the end of your own captivity to a nomadic life, I presume," Neve said.

"Yes and no. Fina was dead, but her council lives on, even now. They are old but powerful men, and I'm sure if they got a whiff of me, several of them would want to kill me just for revenge. But no one comes into The Unfathomed anymore, so I was able to build this little house, close to the old woman so we could continue to look after one another."

Rowan stood abruptly. "I'll go fetch some wood," she said, and moved with purpose toward the door.

"We have plenty, girl," Darren said.

"Then I will hunt something for your dinner."

Darren protested again. "I have what I"—the door slammed with Rowan on the other side of it—"need."

Outside, Rowan whistled to the wolves, and the three of them retreated from the cabin.

"What was that?" Neve asked as Darren also stood and cleared Neve's bowl and spoon.

"Rowan doesn't like to hear this part of her story."

"Her story?"

Darren brought Neve a lumpy pillow and placed it behind her back for comfort. "The old woman, Agnes, was

Rowan's grandmother. One day, not long after my house was finished, I was rounding the corner of her house, coming to ask if she needed anything, when I heard clattering, screaming. I burst into her home to find a wolf in Agnes's bed. A huge wolf, you know. Dressed in her flowered nightclothes and cap. I thought I was unconscious and in a fever dream. It growled at me, and its distended belly was *moving*. I realized it had swallowed my friend. I had the advantage because the wolf was full and reclining, so I killed it right away, cut open its belly, and out fell my old friend Agnes—and her young granddaughter."

Neve covered her mouth with her hand. "Rowan!"

"Yes. The wily creature had charmed Rowan on the path to visit her grandmother, and she unwittingly led him here."

Neve shook her head. "That poor child." She paused. "But why was the wolf in nightclothes?"

"I don't even know. I asked, but Agnes and little thirteen-year-old Rowan were both so traumatized and ill, I brought them to Rowan's mother."

"Rowan recovered well."

"Her grandmother didn't. It seems she was in the wolf's belly a lot longer than Rowan had been, and her breathing was no longer right, and she died two weeks later."

"Oh, no."

"And Rowan's mother died of a broken heart two weeks after that. Her husband was dead, and now her mother. She couldn't pull out of her grief, even for Rowan."

Neve widened her eyes. "Rowan was left all alone?"

Darren nodded.

"So that tale is true?" she asked. "Rowan went into The Unfathomed to seek revenge against the wolves?"

"She did. They took her family."

Neve paused again. "But they're her family now. She lives

among them. How could that have happened?"

"That part of the story is not mine to tell. You can ask her that."

"She doesn't seem to want to remember all this. Not that I can blame her."

"Maybe ... maybe she never had a friend to talk to."

Neve's heart ached for the child who lost her family.

"She looks after me now," Darren said with a soft smile. "The way I used to look out for Agnes. My back is not what it was, nor is my strength. But Rowan is young and strong, and she brings me food, water, wood. She even brings me a handsome shirt every now and then, though I'm not sure where she gets them."

Neve didn't know if the clothes came from her deal with the Crown or off the bodies of unfortunate pirates, but she didn't venture a guess.

"If you don't mind me asking, Your Majesty, why ... why are you in The Unfathomed? What could there possibly be for you here?"

"Rowan came to me in a vision," Neve said. "I didn't even know she was real. There are lots of stories about her. But the vision was true."

Darren sat on his pallet again. "A vision about what?"

Neve gazed out the window at the dark woods, a little less dark now. "I lived my whole life like—well, like you. Like someone hunted. I fear large rooms of people and outdoor crowds, I fear not sitting with my back to the wall, I fear closing my eyes at night. As a princess, this was difficult. But I'm now a queen. I'm even more fearful of being killed, but—it's now compounded because I'm not even doing anything meaningful to help the kingdom. I'm not permitted to do anything more than support the king, my sovereign, my husband.

"I thought he respected me, but he respects me as a woman,

not as a … not as a person. Not as a ruler. Because I'm not one. And I don't know how much more I can take—all the fear and impotence. I don't know how to sit on my throne and be content, and I can't even feel how I feel without guilt, because being queen is a privilege that no one else has."

"You're supposed to be the happily ever after."

"Yes, and I'm sure I look that way, but I'm fearful ever after. And useless ever after."

"That's why you came here?"

"I learned much from you, to be sure," she said, "but I'm still baffled at how to move forward."

They sat in silence for a few moments together, thinking. Rowan swung into the room with a clatter, startling them, and didn't apologize. "I brought you some dinner," she said to Darren. Then, to Neve, "Have you gotten what you came for, then?"

"I don't know."

"How will you know?"

"It would seem to me," Darren said, "that you have some more information now about what happened to you. With me."

"It's true I no longer have to worry you're coming for me."

"You worried about that?" Rowan asked. "This man is a cream puff."

"I did worry," Neve admitted. "I didn't know why you spared me. I thought it was because I'd begged, but Fina came back to finish the job, after all. I thought, why wouldn't you, if you were loyal to her?"

"I was never loyal to her," Darren said. "I thought she was a foolish, vain, and cruel monarch. I merely worked with her cooks to provide food, and my good reputation reached her ears. Why she'd thought I'd regard killing her little stepchild the same way I'd regard killing a wild turkey, I have no idea."

"I didn't know."

"You know now. Does it help you any?" Darren asked.

"Somewhat. But I'm sure there are others out there who would harm me."

"I'm sure, too," Darren said.

And at the same time Rowan cut in, "But as queen, you are well protected by men who'd kill and die for you. That must be a comfort."

Neve shook her head. It was no comfort to think of others dying for her.

"Maybe you also had to tackle your fear of The Unfathomed," Darren said.

"How did you know I had one?"

"How could you not?" Darren said. "All of Foreverness's citizens fear these woods. But you—you almost died here. Then you *did* die here. Then you came to life with a kiss and left here forever, and you saw to it that your adopted family was moved out of here. The Unfathomed only got more and more dark and treacherous in the years since. It would make sense that this was the place of nightmares for you. But you walked through it, yes?"

"I walked through it."

"And it was frightening, but you did it, and Rowan will see to it that you'll walk out unharmed."

Rowan watched him, listening intently.

"Maybe that's the lesson of the vision," Darren suggested. "Maybe it is telling you a life as queen is frightening, but you now have allies to help you. With anything you might need."

"I feel," Rowan said to Darren, "as though you just made a vow of loyalty and honor on my behalf."

"You already have an alliance with the Crown," Darren said, putting an amicable arm around her and squeezing her shoulders. "And you and Neve have a unique bond with The Unfathomed, which makes you … sisters, in a way."

"Maybe let's not go that far," Rowan said.

Neve silently agreed. "But ... we share the man who saved us. We wouldn't be alive if not for him. And impossibly, we're all here now."

Rowan stood. "Yes. Very well." She looked Neve in the eye. "Neve, I pledge a bond with you. If you need my help, you can call on me."

She didn't swear an allegiance to her queen. She didn't drop to one knee and bow her head. She pledged her help to a fellow woman. She waited for the same.

"Rowan," Neve said. "I pledge a bond with you. If you need my help, you can call on me."

Rowan reached for her and before Neve could wonder what was happening, she felt the cold dagger along the back of her hand as Rowan quickly slid it out of her sleeve and stood. Neve resisted the instinct to fight; she was with allies.

Darren's eyes widened when he saw the firelight glint along the silver.

"Right?" Rowan asked. "I didn't see it coming either." She swiped the blade across her palm and gestured at Neve's right hand.

"I—" Neve said, starting to lift her hand slowly. Rowan grabbed it and drew the blade across it so quickly, there seemed a good three seconds before Neve felt the sharp pain.

Rowan clasped her bleeding hand in her own and they shook solidly.

Darren grinned.

Neve wished for a handkerchief. "I need to go home now," she said. "My uncles are waiting for me at the edge of the woods." She peered out the window. "It's as dark as night here all the time. I can't tell the hour."

"It will be dark by now in Foreverness," Darren confirmed. "Take her to the edge of the woods, Rowan. Then come back and we will share dinner."

He kissed Rowan on the top of her head, and she smiled at him with genuine affection, then moved toward the door. He moved toward Neve and made as if to kneel before her again, but she wrapped her arms around his shoulders. "Thank you," she said into his ear. "Thank you, my friend."

"You're welcome, Your Majesty," he said, patting her on the back before they separated. "You are welcome any time. I know The Unfathomed is less than friendly, but you are welcome any time in my cottage."

Neve took a breath and a final look at the huntsman and left with Rowan.

* * *

The wolves led the way, knowing where they'd left Neve's uncles. She was worried that they'd be hungry by now, and frantic. It had been hours.

Rowan walked easily at Neve's side, while Neve again stumbled and tripped along, though admittedly less than before. "How did you come to live with the wolves?" Neve asked after a while.

"Darren didn't tell you?"

"He said the story is yours to tell."

"True enough."

A few minutes went by.

"Tell it, then," Neve insisted.

Rowan turned and regarded Neve, then rolled her eyes. "You do know we're not really sisters now? We don't need to have a cozy little chat over tea."

"If you had tea, I would be ecstatic."

"I haven't had tea since I was a child."

Neve stopped. "The king gave you clothes and food, but not tea?"

"Why do you sound so horrified? It's not like I have a lovely little tea set for myself and the wolves to sit sipping and gossiping."

Neve thought of Rowan civilly asking a wolf to pass the cream and the wolf passing it with a small toe lifted, and she laughed. Rowan's mouth twisted in an attempt to hold back her own mirth.

"I will ask Brockton to make sure you get—"

"No," Rowan said, and stopped. "Don't ask Brockton anything. Don't tell him you met me, that you know anything about this."

"Whyever not?"

"You haven't been queen long, have you?" Rowan sighed. "I'm no court advisor. But I do know there's a benefit to you having secrets, having allies and resources that others don't know about. Even," she added, louder, as Neve opened her mouth to protest, "your husband. You've experienced the treachery of your stepmother. It hurts no one to keep this meeting to yourself in case—in case you ever need to call on me."

Neve opened her mouth once more, before Rowan said, "The king knows you're here now, then?"

Neve closed her mouth.

"As I thought. Otherwise, you'd have an entourage of soldiers and weapons. Or you wouldn't be here at all, as your king and husband would likely have forbidden you."

"You are correct."

"It also benefits me to be merely a fairy tale and not a real woman. I can slip in and out of Foreverness in secret to fulfill my end of the contract without nonsense."

"I understand," Neve said. They began walking again. "So, you were telling me about the wolves?"

"I was not."

"Your queen commands it."

"The queen can go to the beach and pound sand."

They walked in silence a bit more. An owl hooted from what seemed like two feet away, and Neve startled so that she fell over a rock. Rowan helped her to her feet.

"I went to the woods," Rowan said as they walked on. "I wanted to find the family of the wolf who took mine, and I wanted to slaughter them all." She laughed dryly. "Word got around pretty quickly in the woods that a girl was dragging weaponry around, muttering about killing all the wolves. The wolves found me. I told them who I was. I told them what their kin had done to me, to Grandmother. To Mother."

She paused. "A female wolf stepped forward. Elisande. She said I was welcome to try to kill them, but as it seemed I couldn't lift the sword off the ground high enough to swing it, I was likely to die quickly. I told her I was ready for that. That I'd already died once."

"So, you've always had your hubris," Neve said.

Rowan half smiled. "I suppose I have. But I was weak, and they knew it, and I knew it. This would end in my death, but I didn't care.

"Then Elisande told me they'd disavowed the wolf who attacked us, their brother, years before, for his unethical behavior. He would steal into Foreverness and drag away a farmer or a shepherd for sport. He wasn't hungry, because his kin hunted wild boar and other larger animals. He wasn't a good creature. Elisande said his attack on a little girl and an old woman was not what wolves do. Wolves hunt to eat, but they don't hunt for sport, and they don't hunt the defenseless and pitiful."

"I'm surprised."

"So was I. The pack apologized, asked what they could do to help me. I told them nothing, that my family was dead and gone, and I was alone. I turned to go, and they stopped me, and Elisande said I could live with them. They would teach me how to be strong, how to take care of myself, and when I came of age, I could return to town stronger, able to fend for myself."

Neve said, "But you never returned."

"I never did. This is my family. This is my home."

The red wolf turned and stopped, waiting for Neve and Rowan to catch up. It rubbed against Rowan's leg, and she knelt to hug it. "You understand," Rowan said. "Darren said you also have a family you chose."

Neve felt the gray wolf nudge her hand, and she didn't pull away, even when she felt it lick her fingers.

"They—we—suffered, too," Rowan said, "when the woods crumbled and darkened and became The Unfathomed. Prey was harder to find. Edible plants and berries dried up and yielded to harsher greenery. We found ourselves almost wishing for pirates to arrive. I often found food for myself on their ships. But on my hungriest day, I had the idea to approach the Crown with a bargain. That was twenty-five years ago. Foreverness has been quite generous in payment for our protection services since." She grinned. "And I've been quite satisfied. We all have."

"You are how old?"

"I admit it's hard to keep track, and I care less about my age now than when I was around eighteen, but I estimate I'm about forty-four."

"And you don't want to—marry? Have children?" She shook her head even as the words left her mouth. Rowan was a wild child of the woods.

Rowan laughed, as Neve fully expected her to. "No to children. As for marrying—that's not possible. I don't have much opportunity to meet people, much less a person I could stand every day for all my days. But if in my adventures I one day meet her, I'll figure it out then."

They emerged into the clearing after some time, and in the moonlight, Neve could make out the figures of her uncles and their ponies. One of them saw her and waved both arms, though she couldn't tell from this distance who it was.

"I'll leave you here," Rowan said.

"Come and meet my family."

"I'd rather not," Rowan said. "I didn't wear my gown for visitors."

Neve stopped herself from insisting. Rowan was a wolf, not a woman inclined to social mores.

"Thank you," Neve said.

"Can you whistle?"

Neve pursed her lips and blew out three unsteady notes.

"Very good. If you need me, ride up to the edge of the trees, and whistle like this." She blew two short notes and one long note, three times. "It's how the wolves find me if I need them. They'll find you."

"I just tell them I need to find you? They can understand me?"

"We can understand you," the gray wolf rasped. Neve nearly fell over.

"I told you Elisande spoke to me," Rowan said, grinning.

"Why haven't you said anything until this moment?" Neve asked the beasts.

"What did you want us to say?" the red wolf growled. "None of this was about us."

"Fair enough." She turned to Rowan. "Thank you, friend."

Neve didn't know what kind of fond farewell she expected, but Rowan only nodded once, then turned and disappeared into the black of the trees.

Neve hurried to her uncles. "Little love," Uncle Anselm said. "The hour is late, and we were ... well, we were a bit worried, and—"

"What Anselm is vastly understating," Uncle Forwin, "is

that we were wondering where the hell you were."

"We need to ride, and quickly," Neve said. She untied Biscuit and swung up onto the mare. Most of their escort animals had left for their homes for the night, replaced now by their nocturnal neighbors: foxes, coyotes, raccoons, and possums. Several bats flew in erratic circles overhead, wings snapping. "Will you ride with me all the way to the castle?"

"Of course," Uncle Bart said. A raccoon chirped.

"And you'll back up any fib I tell about where I've been? You'll maintain you never let me leave your sight?"

"You ask as though we'd say no," Uncle Bart said.

"Who was that woman?" Uncle Terric asked as they rode toward Foreverness.

A child of the woods, Neve almost said.

But instead, she said, "She was me."

BRY

At the banquet following the official coronation, Bry and Lucan moved with grace from couple to couple, complimenting and making sure no one was in need of anything. Occasionally, Bry glanced down at herself, enjoying the way her silver gown caught the light like a flood of fireflies, and she was certain her tiara did also, sparkling with white sapphires. Lucan was dashing in his uniform, identifying him as Lord of the King's Protection.

Neve's five uncles were seated at a table together. Bry and Lucan had visited them briefly, and she'd wished she could stay longer, as the men were refreshingly jovial. They confided in Bry that they planned to slip out of this banquet early and join the rest of the kingdom out on the grounds, picnicking and dancing and celebrating with no heed to propriety, now that they'd seen their "little love" crowned queen.

The trumpeters brought their horns to their lips and played a smart cadence. "Her Royal Highness, Princess Della!" one shouted.

The trumpeters had done the same when Bry and Lucan walked in, and it always made Bry self-conscious and embarrassed. She wished she had Della's confidence.

And Della walked in as she always did, chin lifted, lips smiling. But she was alone.

There was applause, but Bry, ever vigilant for criticism, heard the whispering. "Where is Prince Colby?" "Why is Princess Della alone?"

Della approached the new king and queen, tucked her proud chin in deference, and dipped into a low and lingering curtsy. When she stood, Brockton smiled, and Neve put her hand on her heart and cocked her head at Della's beauty.

Bry smiled, watching her sister-in-law. Della would have attracted the kingdom's curiosity even if she weren't *Della*—she was the only princess who wasn't born to the title. But Della embraced her role as if she *had* been born to it, and inspired admiration with her stunning wardrobe and her willingness to befriend all who asked for a moment of her time.

The cut of Della's gown was simple, the sleeves forearm length, the bodice plain, the hem sweeping around her ankles. Della usually went for far more elaborate details, even for an afternoon tea or a carriage ride in the country, so it was clear she'd tried to downplay her charms because it wasn't her day. But the color of the dress—pale green at the neckline and bodice that darkened to deeper and deeper green in the center and finally a dark blue at the bottom. In the sun beaming through the high window, she was sky and sea. Her tiara featured just one large emerald in the center of her simple twist of hair. Everyone in the room took two steps closer to her. She began to move through the crowd, touching an arm here, a shoulder there, acknowledging the friends and strangers nearest to her.

Bry hurried over to her and put a light hand on her elbow. "Della, you are a goddess among mortals."

They kissed each other on both cheeks, and Della relaxed her shoulders. "I'm so happy to see you."

"You need to see the cakes," Bry said. "They're the only things in this room that come close to your exquisiteness."

"But we haven't eaten yet."

"What is the use of being at a party if we can't eat dessert first?"

Della chuckled. "Indeed."

A servant swept by and offered them golden goblets of wine. Bry went to lift two, but she gasped in laughter. "They're so heavy! Surely one is not meant to drink all of this."

Della took one from her and said, "I certainly will, and hold onto yours, for if you don't finish it, I will."

The servant stepped away and Bry said, low, "Where is he?"

"I wouldn't know. He sneaked off after the ceremony. Likely he's sulking in a corner, sucking his thumb and rattling a toddler's toy."

"It must be difficult," Bry said carefully, "to be in line for the throne and live with the knowledge that it will likely never come to pass."

"He is a grown man," Della said. "Not only that, he's a prince. He should act like one. It's not as if you and I don't have responsibility or disappointments in life. Yet our comportment remains flawless."

A waltz began to play, and couples swung onto the dance floor even before the first notes had faded away. "I'd be happy to not see his fool face right now," Della said, watching the swirling gowns and twirling gloved hands. "But sadly, he is a wonderful dancer."

"Aunt Della!"

Thea glided past them, resplendent in rosy pink and gold, her arms around a King's Protection soldier—who didn't take his enraptured eyes off her face to even acknowledge Della and Bry.

"You're the most beautiful woman here!" Della called as they waltzed past.

"I knoooow," Thea called, her voice fading as they

disappeared again into the crowd of dancers.

Bry and Della clutched each other to keep from falling to the floor in their laughter. "I love everything about that child," Della said, wiping her eye.

"And she is your most fervent admirer," Bry said. "Let's sit."

Two hours, two meat courses, and two goblets later, Bry, Lucan, Dawn, Dawn's husband, Leo, Della, Della's eldest son, Prince Bertram, and his wife, Princess Honora, and Della's younger son, Prince Emil, and his wife, Princess Filippa, were telling jokes at their table. The jokes had turned quite bawdy, particularly when Neve's five uncles had joined them for a time before heading outside. Thea only stopped dancing long enough to eat and picked it right up again with her handsome soldier.

Bry looked at Neve, sitting at King Brockton's side yet looking alone. Brockton was visited at his seat by a parade of well-wishers and behind-kissers, and they bowed to the queen, and some gave her a small gift, but otherwise Neve was—alone.

Della stood after Leo's punchline sent everyone at her table into hysterics. "I'm going to sit with Neve."

Bry stood also and leaned in to say quietly, "I'm not sure ..."

"Oh, etiquette be damned. Look at her. She's miserable."

Bry looked at their new queen and tilted her head in sympathy. "You are right. I'll come with you."

They began to move toward the head table when they heard a loud clatter, followed quickly by another.

Two wooden chairs had toppled over and between them, lying on the floor, his legs twisted around the chair legs, was Colby.

Della's nostrils flared. Hundreds of people turned to look at the pathetic princely heap.

Colby laughed and laughed. Guests chuckled and shifted

on their feet a bit. Two men rushed to help the prince stand, but he waved them away. "Stop," he said, still laughing. "This is what they all expect. This is all I'm good for."

Bry and her family were a bit floaty, but Colby was drunk. Bry glanced at Della, who seemed torn between wanting to go to him and wanting to be anywhere else.

Colby was—oh, very handsome at nearly fifty. His face still appeared cut from glass. But he was doing an excellent job at drawing the room's attention from his face to his behavior.

As it turned out, there was no need for Della to move, because a woman knelt over Colby, one of the commoners who'd won the kingdom-wide lottery to be at the coronation feast. Though, she seemed very familiar with Colby—she whispered something in his ear, and he pulled her down into the chair tangle. She shook with mirth, her full breasts nearly falling out of the top of her inappropriate gown.

Gasps echoed throughout the room. The woman called to a friend, who joined them. She fell face down on top of them, and Colby took a generous handful of her rump and squeezed it. "Prince Colby!" she shrieked, and the other woman mimicked, "Prince Colby!" before she grabbed his other hand and pressed it into her cleavage.

Bertram and Emil rose from the table. Bertram's face was red with rage. Emil bit his lip, uncertain, glancing between his frozen mother and his beyond-inappropriate father. Neither seemed to know what to do.

Bry couldn't take her eyes off the spectacle of the second royal son, now heir to the throne. Then she did—and saw the room's embarrassed gaze not on the debauchery, but on Della.

The music continued to play, but the dancing had slowed.

Colby peeked between his two companions then, caught his wife's eye, and winked at her.

Della turned her back on her Prince Charming, walked to the back of the room, pushed open the door, and left.

Bry, Thea, and Dawn went after her. Della ran about ten paces before she broke down. She waited for the heavy door to shut on the banquet before she screamed long and loud. She took off one beloved shoe and threw it as hard as she could against the door.

Bry and her daughters exchanged glances as they hurried Della down the hallway and around the corner, to give her privacy from anyone who might decide to peek out the door.

Della sank to the cold stone floor in her watercolor gown and sobbed. Thea and Dawn crouched on each side of her. Bry pulled out an embroidered handkerchief and gave it to Della, who blotted her face and wiped her nose before starting with fresh sobs again.

The handkerchief was an heirloom, but so were women's tears, weren't they? Their sorrow and defeat and unspoken anger passed down generations—without anyone stopping it.

"Prince Colby." Bry spat on the floor, away from their skirts. "Prince Cockroach is more like it."

She'd anticipated surprise from her children for her harsh words and unladylike spit, but Dawn only nodded. "Cockroaches wouldn't even have him."

Bry smoothed a hand over Della's hair and set her crooked emerald tiara straight. "Did you know?"

"About those women?" Della snuffled into the soggy handkerchief. "Not about them specifically. But about women in general?" Her sigh was ragged. "Yes, I've known."

None of them said anything for a while.

"What could I do?"

"Nothing," Bry said, and she'd meant it to be comforting, but it made her grit her teeth. "There was nothing you could do."

"He gives me everything I need. Everything I want."

Except common decency. Bry held her tongue.

"You make him look noble and good. Charming, even," Thea said with a grimace. "He knows that. You are his greatest asset."

"Why would he do this, then? Humiliate her in front of the entire kingdom?" Bry asked her.

"He's a mess," Dawn said. "He hasn't dealt with his anger, I suppose. Though his anger at his father or at Brockton is misplaced. It's neither of their faults he was merely the second son."

"So he acts like a child and expects his wife to bear it?" Bry asked. "When she's not taken one misstep since marrying him?"

"Don't misread me—I'm not condoning it," Dawn said. "What I saw out there is unbecoming of any man, much less a prince of this land."

Bry noticed Della had stopped crying and was listening to the women talk about her marriage as if she weren't there. "I'm sorry, Della."

"It's no one's fault," Della said. "Except perhaps mine."

Dawn and Thea began to protest, but Della held up a hand. "We've just pretended between us that everything is rosy and gay. Because we were united in that we wanted others to see us as perfect. It worked for both of us."

She leaned her head back against the wall. "He doesn't have everything he wants, but I can't see any reason for him to destroy what he does have."

Because he's not destroying it. Bry gritted her teeth. Prince Colby was a prince first, and a man second, and both those titles entitled him to behave any way he desired and not suffer a consequence. Only Della would suffer consequences, privately and publicly.

"I can't go back in there," Della said.

"You must," Thea said. "You mustn't let him ruin the night."

"He already has."

"He's caused a scene, to be sure," Bry conceded. "But

you must hold your head up high. He's drunk, and they can all see that. You must show you're above his foolish actions because they mean nothing to you."

Bry lifted her chin and called, "Rhyannon?"

"She can't help me," Della said. "I've already asked her to make Colby a decent person."

Bry was undeterred. "Rhyannon? Rhyannon! Call her, Della."

Della put a finger to her temple and closed her eyes. "Rhyannon," she whispered.

And she was there, smelling like fresh pine needles and wildflowers. "Della," she said, her smile fading as she placed both hands on Della's wet cheeks. "My poor child."

Thea's mouth hung open at the sight of the fairy. "You are the most remarkable creature I have ever seen," she finally managed.

"These are my daughters," Bry said. "Dawn and Thea. Rhyannon, could you create an illusion for Della? Something whimsical and magical that will delight the guests?"

"Why?" Della asked.

"So you can do as I said," Bry told her sister-in-law. "Walk back into the banquet with the magic you always have about you. After this day, people might say Colby was disgraceful, but they will also say you were, as ever, a wonder."

Rhyannon examined Della's gown. "Beautiful."

"Dawn made it," Della said.

Bry gasped as suddenly the blues on the gown were— *moving* in sun-sparkling waves, like a river. Clouds floated across the green sky of the bodice. The simple bangles on her wrists had changed into fresh bright green seaweed, winding around her forearms. Her diamond ring was now a royal blue sea star, gently curving the tips of its legs around Della's fingers.

Della lifted her hem, and they could see her one gold

slipper had been transformed into two slippers of glass—blue and green iridescent sea glass.

Rhyannon shrugged. "I couldn't help that. Glass slippers are—your signature."

"Wonderful idea," Dawn said. "Colby's childish display will be a hazy memory tomorrow, while everyone will talk about Della forever."

Della wiped her eyes and tucked loose strands behind her ears. "But this will surely take attention away from the queen."

"Neve won't mind," Thea said. "She saw what happened."

"I agree," Dawn said. "Neve would be out here with us right now, saying the worst about Colby, if she weren't obligated to remain by Brockton's side."

"How can I thank you, Rhyannon?" Della asked.

"Go in there and create legend. Just as you did last time. And remember—"

"Midnight. I know."

Rhyannon shimmered away.

Thea offered her arm to Della, and Dawn offered her hers as well, and their aunt took hold. "Coming, Mother?" Thea asked.

"I need to take a moment."

Dawn rubbed her mother's shoulder before they left.

Bry crouched on the cold floor and tried to gather her thoughts.

They'd promised the late king, she and Della and Neve, that they'd continue to uphold a standard for the women of this land. But did that truly mean they had to smile and accept mistreatment?

Was that the right example?

Even through the closed door down the hall, Bry could hear the incredulous gasps and shrieks of the guests at Della's illusion. Della was likely walking slowly, inviting the admiration and talking to everyone, making them feel special.

Guilt wound around Bry's soul. She'd meant to do the right thing here—she always meant to do the right thing. If she'd been in Della's position, with Lucan openly acting the disorderly cad in front of an entire kingdom, Bry would have done what she'd counseled Della to do: Create a diversion, smile, and push away the pain. Because she wouldn't have wanted anyone to judge her harshly.

She loved Della, and she'd be unable to bear witnessing a kingdom condemning her for something that wasn't her fault. Bry knew well how that tore one's soul from her body and shredded it.

But her solution tonight didn't sit as comfortably with her as it once would have.

Would the right thing instead have been for Della to throw a pitcher of water at Colby's face in front of everyone present, call him a swine, and step over his body on her way out the door?

All those women out there, surely some of their husbands were like Colby—or worse. Did it help them to see Della smooth it all over like a glass lake? Or would it have helped them more to see the wrath of a wronged princess—a wronged woman?

Bry tapped the back of her head against the wall two, three times. Something was happening. Colby's childish antics, Lucan's refusal to speak to Brockton about Thomasina, Brockton's holding fast to traditions that he could easily change—it was all banging around in her head and jumbling around in her heart, and she didn't feel much like being the perfect woman anymore.

DELLA

Della watched herself in the mirror, passing the comb through her hair. She'd counted strokes for a while but stopped when she got to two hundred. Her enchanted gown was just a regular gown again—spectacular though it was—and she'd tossed it over a cushioned chair.

She startled at the soft rap on the door and sat up tall, regal, in her seat at the vanity, but she slumped her shoulders when Catelina poked her head in. "Your Highness? Are you sure there is not something I could bring you?"

"No, I am fine. I will be awake for some time yet. Please retire for the evening."

"But who will turn your bed down?"

Della had to smile at the horror in Catelina's voice. "It won't be the same, to be sure, but I think I can manage this one time."

Catelina sighed. "Very well."

"Did you have a wonderful time at the lawn party?"

"I did!" Catelina said, her face lighting up. "I danced and I ate so much, and there were jugglers and bards and—and ax throwing!"

"You threw an ax?"

"It stuck in the wall!"

Della clapped her hands together. "How amazing! Tomorrow I will dismiss my guards since you have shown yourself capable of protecting me."

Catelina giggled. "I wouldn't, Your Highness."

"I'm glad you had fun."

"I'm sure it wasn't as fun as the banquet inside. I heard—" Catelina paused. "I heard your dress was magical! Not just magical, but truly enchanted."

"You heard correctly." Likely Catelina had heard other things as well, but she had enough manners to keep them to herself.

"Are your sons staying long?"

"No, sadly, they leave in the morning. Duties call them home." Though Emil and Bertram had wanted to speak to their mother about what they witnessed from their father, Della had waved them off, telling them not to worry, that Colby couldn't hold his drink like he once could. She was certain they didn't believe her. "Good night, Catelina."

"Good night."

Catelina left, and Della looked at herself again. In the lateness of the evening, and the flattering glow of a few candles, she could almost pretend she was looking into her twenty-years-younger face.

She didn't know why she was waiting up. When was the last time Colby slept in his own home, much less came to visit her?

She stood and began to blow out candles. She only had two left when her door swung open again behind her. "Catelina, I'm fine. I don't need—"

"Catelina?"

Della whirled and found Prince Colby Charming leaning against her door frame. She could smell the ale on him from across the room.

"Is this Catelina joining you?" Colby slurred. "Could be fun."

"Catelina is my maid." Della straightened and walked over to him. "Which you'd know if you spent some of your time here."

"You don't need me here at all."

Della crossed her arms. "I don't know what you're about to try," she said. "But don't. I've tolerated too much for too long."

"*Tolerated*?" Colby kicked the door shut and closed the space between them. "Forgive me, because I may have had a touch too much to drink—"

"If by 'touch' you mean an entire cask full."

"But I thought I heard you say *you've* tolerated *me*."

Della ignored the warning tone. "I cannot believe how you acted this evening."

"You're surprised? Come, darling. You've known for years."

"Yes, of course I've known for years. I'm not a bloody idiot. But the entirety of Foreverness didn't know. Because at engagements, you and I present as a couple, a picture of perfection. That's what we *do*."

Colby laughed but it turned into a hiccup.

"Your antics tonight—did you think you were making a point?" Della asked. "Did you think you were showing the kingdom what a better king you would have been? Because it seems to me all you did was draw out their sighs of relief that this land is under the control of a man of honor and temperance, instead of a child."

Colby reared back—to hit her? He never, ever had. But whatever his plan was, it was foiled when he tripped over his own ankle and landed on her bed. He giggled and rolled over. "Why *don't* I stay here more often? The bodies I find might be soft and willing, but most of the time they sleep on nothing better than scratchy straw." He rolled side to side. "This is heavenly."

"Are you listening to me?"

"Not really."

She picked up her pearl-edged comb and flung it at him, and it bounced off his jaw.

He sat up, a hand on his face. "You—what *was* that?"

"You embarrassed us! You embarrassed me!"

With a roar she'd never heard from him before, Colby sat up and reached over, grabbing tight to her small wrist. He yanked her arm so hard she cried out, and she fell on the bed beside him. He rolled on top of her and pinned both wrists above her head. Then he lowered his face to hover an inch above hers. A spot on his jaw was pink.

"*You* tolerate *me?*" he asked, his voice low and dangerous. "*I* embarrassed *you?* It seems you don't understand what any of this has been about, all this time."

"What are you talking about?" She tried to pull away. "Take your hands off me."

"I will not," he said. "You are my wife, and that's what you wanted to be—so badly, in fact, that you lied to trap me."

"What do you mean, *I lied to trap you?*"

"You lied all those years ago at that ball. My father said it was time I had a wife, and I didn't feel as if I'd met enough women yet. So I held a ball to bring all the qualified ladies to me."

"I know, and—"

"Qualified," he said through his teeth, shaking her wrists. "It was invitation only, for women who were of noble families."

"I *am* of noble birth—"

"Your father was dead, and you were a maid for your stepfamily. How is that noble?"

Della said nothing.

"You deceived me with enchantment. You bewitched me."

"I did no such thing. I was myself—only in a lovelier gown than any in my real wardrobe."

"I thought you to be a princess." He shook her wrists again in emphasis on the last word.

"I never told you I was a princess."

"You arrived in a gilded coach, with a half-dozen horses and that many footmen. Your gown was spun of glittering magic. Your shoes were crystal. Everyone thought you a princess."

He hiccupped again. "You bewitched me so that I proclaimed to all the land that I would find the owner of the shoe and marry her." He laughed, but it was ugly and ragged. "All the ladies were in throes of excitement. I tried the wealthiest homes first. Then the lesser ones. House after house, I began to wonder, if she's a princess, she may not be staying here in Foreverness. She may have gone home to—where? Goldenstone, perhaps?"

He shook his head. "Then I found you. How could I back out? I'd already told the entire kingdom, and if I went back on my word—after my brothers kissed some damn princesses and got engaged, how could I be the one to not follow through on a fairy tale?"

"You—wait. You didn't want to marry me?"

"I took you to the castle. Then I *begged* my father to proclaim publicly there had been a mistake, that you had tricked me and were a witch. It wasn't right. But by then, he'd met you and was charmed by you, and you and your story were already beloved by all our subjects, so the king refused me, and I had to keep my promise. Because that's what a Charming does."

He pressed her hands harder into the bed and bit her earlobe. Della tried to pull the other way.

"I was already a useless son," he said, "born too late to inherit. To add insult to my story, I was forced to marry a *scullery* maid."

Della winced as drops of his saliva hit her face.

They stared at one another for a heated moment, then he relaxed his grip, rolled off her, and pulled her up by her shoulders, not roughly. "You see, Princess, *you* embarrassed *me*."

Della's neck, face, and scalp heated up.

Colby kept his hands on her shoulders, brushing them downwards a few times as if to smooth away wrinkles in her silk nightdress.

"But you surprised me, I confess. You were—and still are—the most beautiful, elegant, fashionable, and compassionate princess this land has ever seen. The people love you, and that's not merely an expression. Any commoner—hell, any nobleman—would willingly lie down in front of a stampeding wild boar if it would save your life. People look at me differently since our marriage, as if I'm more valuable now that I possess you. So, that is why ... I tolerate *you*."

Della felt as though it was her turn to speak, but had nothing.

He smiled. "We work well together," he said. "You are perfect on my arm. To be honest, I didn't think you cared much for where I go at night."

"I don't, really."

"It's not as though you're suffering from heartbreak."

"It's most certainly not that," Della said.

"I give you everything you could want, don't I? Do you lack anything? You, with closets as deep as a bear's cave and jewels that the stars above covet? Is there anything else I could bring or buy to adorn you or give you joy?"

"There—isn't."

"Correct," he said. "But not to worry. I will continue to fill your closets and your jewel boxes. And when I make a mistake, as I do confess I did tonight, you will smile and be pretty. Create a diversion—such as I heard you did tonight. Smooth it over for us. You're so good at it. But then you are to say no more to me about it. Don't ambush me in the evening. Remember that in the end, we do help each other—and you need me far more than I need you."

Della sharply inhaled. "Is that a threat?"

"No," he said, taken aback. "No, of course not. Merely a fact you seem to have forgotten over the years. But I've just reminded you. So we're all right now."

Della's back teeth crashed together, and she squeezed so hard it was a wonder they didn't shatter and explode tiny white shards into her husband's face.

Colby patted her hand in dismissal and stood. He was a bit steadier on his way to the door; arguments had a way of sobering people up. He put his hand on the knob but paused. "Oh," he said, turning back to her. "Are you running some sort of cleaning school?"

Della startled and put a hand on her chest. "Wh—how did you—"

"One of your students told me."

"Who?" Della demanded.

"I'd rather not say," he said. "I'm sure she's a fine worker, and a nice girl. I wouldn't want you to hold it against her. She simply let it slip—on the pillow. She was horrified she told me when I didn't know what she was talking about. She thinks the world of you."

"I—" Della swallowed. "I—"

"It's a bit of a strange project, and I don't know what your reasons are, but you didn't have to keep it secret from me. Though I do understand why you kept it a secret from everyone else." Colby grinned. "You're royalty. Do whatever amuses you. That's what I do, after all."

Della nodded but didn't return the smile.

He opened the door to go to his bedchamber—or to leave the castle again for the night. Who could say?

"Let me know if you need anything for your little school," he said over his shoulder. "I'll have it brought in. And not to worry—I asked her not to say anything to anyone else."

NEVE

Neve crossed and uncrossed her legs, squinting at her hand of cards. After a few moments, her opponent began whistling—softly at first, then a bit louder and a lot more annoyingly.

"Do you mind?" Neve asked, switching two cards' positions and reassessing them.

"No, I don't mind getting older as you consider your next play," the mirror intoned.

Neve glanced up. "What? What do you care what year it is?"

"I get bored. Just like anyone else."

Neve pushed away the guilt of having allowed her bored mirror to hang on her wall alone for decades and looked back down at her hand. "Just give me a minute."

"I've given you—"

"Yes, yes." Neve turned over a card on the small table she'd set between the edge of her bed and the mirror. She'd lined up a few small vases in the center and set the mirror's hand facing away from her so that it could play. They'd done this a few evenings now, and though Neve found his company a mostly pleasant experience and their games a fun diversion, the mirror's ability to win every time was tiresome.

As was the mirror's tendency to gloat about it.

"Ah," he said.

" 'Ah' what? Was that the wrong move?"

"No. Not for me, it wasn't."

Neve rolled her eyes, clutching her cards.

"Please play the card to my furthest left, your furthest right," the mirror said.

Neve flipped it over, then threw her hand on the table.

"Another game?" the mirror asked happily.

"Why am I even playing cards with an all-knowing entity?" Neve asked. "You probably know my hand every time."

"I *could* know your hand every time, but I deliberately don't allow myself to access that information. The games are fair."

"I have to take your word for it."

"If you're going to take anyone's word," the mirror said, "it might as well be mine, as my enchantment doesn't allow me to lie. Every word I speak is truth."

"Yes, well, even if you were a liar, I'd still play."

"Because you like me?"

Neve paused. "Yes. I do."

"I like you too, Neve."

"I'm glad. My own husband isn't overly fond of me as of late."

"His loss."

Neve paused, surprised, then snorted. "Maybe."

"You have other allies now. Darren and Rowan among them."

"That's true. But that can't make up for a problem in my marriage."

"No," the mirror admitted. "But Brockton has always been wise enough to seek your intelligent counsel. He's simply new to doing it as king."

"Are you saying he will come around?"

The mirror's smoke swirled orange and yellow like a sunset on a lake. "I don't predict the future. I only see what is happening now, and only what I am directly asked."

"I didn't really ask for you to answer magically. I asked you as my friend."

The smoke cleared, and Neve looked into the mirror's inky depth. "If the past is any indicator, then yes, as a friend, I believe that he will come around."

Neve sighed. "But will I come around to being his queen?"

Swirls of purple ran along the mirror's oval perimeter. "Perhaps a short walk in the fresh air will clear your head," the mirror said after a few moments.

Neve stood. "Excellent idea. Next time, let's try a different game."

"Wonderful. I will look forward to besting you at whatever game you choose."

Neve narrowed her eyes as the mirror made a little choking sound. "Are you laughing?"

"Yes," the mirror said, unable to lie.

Neve stood and touched her fingers gently on the mirror's frame. "Till then."

* * *

Neve had never intended to make escaping the castle a habit—particularly now that Brockton had tipped off the King's Protection that the queen had a new and frustrating propensity to wander—but the mirror was right. The solace of the quiet and still-dark early morning was refreshing. It was a mere forty-eight hours after the shouts of "Long live the king and queen!" and she hadn't completely calmed.

Solace was not her destiny, however. Almost the moment she let the heavy door close softly behind her, two strong hands grabbed her arms from behind.

"Please, Your Majesty," a man said into her ear, "don't cry out. We mean you no harm." He hurried her around the back corner the castle, so swiftly her feet nearly floated off the ground. She was hustled into a dark group of cloaked figures, who closed in on her from all sides and walked her into the trees ahead.

When they were far enough from the castle to not be seen, they stepped away from her in a wide circle.

Neve whipped the dagger from her sleeve, and another smaller knife from her bodice. The cloaked figures exchanged glances, and all stepped back farther, giving Neve more space.

Then there was a growl, and another, and the cloaked men backed up to reveal several coyotes baring teeth, two hissing possums—and a large brown bear.

The bear stood on her hind legs, ambled awkwardly toward the group, and roared. The cloaked men pulled swords and daggers—but cowered with chattering teeth.

Neve had no idea why these people were there, but it wasn't to fight or cause harm; that much was obvious now.

"Be calm," Neve said to the bear. "Be still, my friends. All is well."

The animals sat back, insisting on keeping watch.

Neve slid her dagger up her sleeve but kept her knife in hand. "What is the meaning of this?"

No one said anything for a moment.

"Out with it," she said. "Who are you?"

One by one, the half-dozen men—and three women— pulled their hoods down to reveal themselves. Two men pushed a third forward, and the man cleared his throat. "Your Majesty Queen Neve of Goldenstone," he said, and all the men and women fell to one knee.

"You are little Neve," one woman said softly. "My eyes know it now, but my heart always did."

"Please stand," Neve said, and when they all got up, she added, "I am Neve, and I am queen, but I'm afraid you have misnamed my realm. Tell me who you are."

"I am Henry, the—the master of, er, head covers."

"You make hats." Neve tried not to smile. "A worthy profession."

"I think so. Well, I used to make hats," Henry clarified. "Before—before now."

"You sold hats in Foreverness?"

"In Goldenstone," he said, then swept his hand to encompass the group. "We're from Goldenstone."

Neve's heart flattened, and she wasn't sure why. "Why do you travel to Foreverness? Why do you spirit me away to the woods?"

"We've come in desperation to ask for help," Henry said, "from a queen. Who better to come to our aid?"

"Goldenstone has a king, as I understand. Could you not seek help from your own sovereign?"

"No. He is not the rightful heir."

Neve started to get a sour feeling in her stomach, and hoped it was due to her decadent dinner, rather than a foreshadowing. "Your king is not a usurper, but the next in the bloodline, yes? A grandnephew of the king?" *My cousin.* "Three years ago, I was told the transfer of power was peaceful. Unchallenged."

"King Gawain is twelve years old," Henry said.

"That is sometimes the circumstance of new rule," Neve said. "But there is a council in place, is there not? Until he comes of age?"

"The council, yes," a middle-aged woman said, and quickly curtsied. "I am Cecilia, Your Majesty."

"Speak your piece, friend," Neve said.

"The council who rules for King Gawain is made up of former lords of Queen Fina."

Neve tried to breathe. "Fina is gone."

"Yet her cruel legacy lives on," Cecilia said. "Through these men who puppet the child king into signing disastrous laws."

"You are the rightful queen," Henry said. "You are next in line by blood, not Gawain."

Neve's breath caught in her chest.

"I am sorry for you to have wasted your time traveling here," she said after a moment. "But I decided a very long time ago that I am dead to Goldenstone."

"You decided that?" Cecilia asked. "That's not what we know. We know your father decided that, long ago. That you are dead."

"I don't understand," Neve said.

"The kingdom was told you disappeared into The Unfathomed," Henry said. "Your father declared you dead and ordered that Goldenstone mourn its young princess. We all did. You were dead and gone, torn apart by animals." He glanced nervously at the bear, possums, and coyotes. "He said he sent soldiers to search for you, and you were nowhere to be found. We believed it."

The Goldenstone military had been renowned. If her father had sent his men into the woods, they would have combed every inch of it and found her within two days. But no—her father had cowed to Fina and whatever she'd told him, then lied about everything to everyone, willing to give up his child for his wife's happiness.

"But years later," Cecilia continued, "word spread in Goldenstone that little Princess Neve had been found alive— by the prince and heir to Foreverness, and you were on your way there to live. We thought—we thought you might come back. You were royalty there now, of course, but we were your home."

"We thought perhaps our kingdoms would join somehow," Henry said. "Now that you were all family."

"No," Neve murmured.

"That's right," Henry said, "because the king formally declared Princess Neve of Foreverness an imposter."

"What?"

"The citizens of Goldenstone were informed that an imposter met Prince Brockton and convinced him she was our long-dead princess."

"My fath—your king said I'm not who I said I am?"

Heads around the group nodded.

"I don't think many people believe it," Henry said. "It's a crime to say the sovereign is lying, of course, so no one challenged the official story."

Neve's father had allowed his wife to send his daughter to her death. Then when she was found, he denied her? He couldn't have believed she was an imposter. Surely he'd sent men to Foreverness to investigate. Men who must have seen her face and reported it to their king.

Any guilt Neve might have felt at never offering an olive branch to her father before his death—and she'd had precious little guilt—dissolved.

"I am true," she said.

"You don't need to tell me," Henry said. "I am only a few years older than you, but old enough to remember your face."

"Surely you didn't come all this way to inform me of this," Neve said. "The king lied, to be sure, but it was a long time ago, and he is no more."

"No," Cecilia said. "The trouble is the child king, sitting on the throne with Fina's men moving his hands and lips. Goldenstone is—it's—"

"It's hell," another man burst out. "It's a place of nightmares."

Neve blinked. Goldenstone was a wealthy kingdom with a fearsome and legendary army, strong farming, and robust commerce. Foreverness's reputation was that of the perfect place of dreams and harmony, but Goldenstone was a formidable neighboring land—hardly the stuff of nightmares. "I don't understand. How can this be?"

"The money in our kingdom is badly mismanaged," Henry said. "The farmers are underpaid, and the Crown seizes so much food for their own nightly banquets and parties that the people are left to starve."

"The Crown doesn't purchase the goods?"

Henry shook his head. "No. The Crown says it owns whatever is produced there, and they don't need to pay. They seize so much that farmers must drive their prices high to make a living—too high for the neighbors to afford food. The other merchants are suffering as well. Without money, people cannot buy other necessities to make the products they sell. Shops are closing."

"The army no longer serves the people," Cecilia said. "The Crown uses the army for protection not against any who would invade the kingdom, but as protection against its own people—who are now revolting. In the past fortnight, the army has gone from home to home, seizing anything that could possibly be used as a weapon, even large spoons and horseshoes."

"People are hanged daily," another man added. "For stealing to feed their children, or for begging in the roads."

Neve covered her mouth, then dropped her hand to her side, making a fist. "Stealing is not a capital crime. And begging is not a crime at all. If anything, if there are beggars, the Crown has only itself and its laws to blame."

"Women who can't feed their children are forced into unspeakable acts by the soldiers," Henry said. "Pardon me, Your Majesty, for saying such things. But the soldiers hurt women, then toss them a crust of bread or a stale hunk of cheese."

A woman fell to her knees, crying softly. Neve crouched

beside her. "My lady, my friend, what is it?"

"My boys," she said. "They took—they hurt—"

"Who?"

"The soldiers. They burst in one day, said my eldest son was old enough to serve, and took him away. He's eleven. As they pulled away, my youngest child, seven years old, threw a rock at their backs." She collapsed into sobs. "They jumped from their horses and beat him so badly, he will never be the same. He can no longer even speak."

Neve held the woman, rubbing her shaking back through her dark cloak until her sobs subsided. Then she stood, wiped her own wet eyes, and walked back to Cecilia and Henry. "You must all come with me, and we will speak to my husband at once," she said. "We don't have an alliance with Goldenstone, but we also don't have animosity. King Brockton must hear of this, and he will help."

Everyone dropped their chins, and a few shuffled their feet.

"What?" Neve asked. "I don't understand. Is that not why you have come?"

"Foreverness is aware of our plight," Henry said slowly. "Several groups—like us—have come here to ask for assistance in the last year. They kneeled before your father-in-law, who heard them and then sent them home, saying he didn't want to involve Foreverness. Upon arrival back in Goldenstone, they were all hanged by the council as traitors."

Neve leaned against a tree trunk, trying to take in what she was hearing. King Hopkin hadn't been a cruel man—but how could he have done that to them? To anyone? "I can't speak for the king who has passed about why he wasn't sympathetic to your plight," she finally said, "but Brockton will hear you, and help you. I know he will."

But even as the words left her mouth, she wasn't certain of them. Brockton had been privy to all his father's decisions, often present for them. Brockton would have known of all this when it happened, and though he wouldn't have defied his father, once he became king, he could have taken immediate action to help the suffering people of Goldenstone—negotiate with the king's council, propose a mutually beneficial alliance, or, if all else failed, declare war and charge in.

He'd made the decision not to.

At the very least, he'd made the decision to not tell any of this to his wife and queen, the daughter of Goldenstone.

No one responded for a long time, until Cecilia spoke. "No one wants to say this, Your Majesty, and I beg your pardon, but trusting King Brockton—would be a risk for us."

"Yet here you are," Neve said. "I assume you had to pass through a dangerous gauntlet to cross the border. If the Crown in Goldenstone thinks people will flee here, I'm sure it's heavily guarded."

"Yes," Henry said, but gave no details as to how they'd succeeded. "But we came not to entreat your husband. We came to appeal to you. Our queen."

"You are queen of Goldenstone," Cecilia said. "You are our rightful queen by blood. We are here to ask that you take the throne." She looked down at her feet. "And save us."

Neve swallowed.

Return to Goldenstone?

Return to the home that killed her?

"We have heard," a man in the back of the group said gruffly, "that you are temperate, fair, and intelligent. We can see that."

"There are people," Henry said, "who recognize you as our true sovereign, and not Gawain. There are rumblings among many men who would march and fight for you."

"We all will," another said, and several echoed him, one quietly adding, "Long live Neve, Queen of Goldenstone."

"We can't fight for you," Cecilia said, "and we can't recognize you as our queen, and we can't overthrow Gawain, if you don't come."

A sharp wind blew through. The animals huddled into their own skin, and the men and women around Neve tightened their grips on their cloaks, never taking their eyes off her.

She looked at the woman whose children had suffered. She was at least fifteen years younger than Neve, but her face was permanently creased with pain. Everyone here had surely lost as much, or they wouldn't have risked death to find her.

"We can see by your face," Henry said, "that you knew nothing of this."

"No," Neve whispered. "I didn't."

"Foreverness laws are different," Cecilia granted. "You don't rule here."

In Goldenstone, you wouldn't be a consort. You would be a queen regnant. Uncle Forwin's words roared through her mind.

They all stood in silence against the wind. It bit through Neve's light bedjacket, but she barely felt it. Her mind was galloping erratically through the brush, over logs and under branches.

"Very well," she finally said. "I want you all to stay here. Do not go back to Goldenstone yet." She couldn't bear to know of their deaths after this conversation. "Am I understood?"

"Yes, Your Majesty," they chorused.

She broke through their circle to where the bear and her smaller furry friends were sitting. "My friends, I ask that you protect this group of good people from anyone or anything that might harm them. They will make camp here."

The bear groaned in assent, lumbering to her feet. All the cloaked people took two steps back.

"They will see that you are all safe," Neve said.

"The queen is of the angels," one of the men said in a hushed voice. "She commands the beasts of the forest."

Neve smiled. "I don't command them at all. But they are my friends, and sometimes I ask their help." She looked back at the castle. "I would far prefer to bring you all inside for warmth and soup and beds, but if there is someone, anyone, in there whom we cannot trust, whom I cannot trust—"

"We understand," Cecilia said. "We thank you."

"I will bring you breakfast tomorrow."

"Then what?" Henry asked.

Neve didn't know.

"I have heard you, with deepest compassion for your situation," Neve said. "I—we will discuss this again soon. But until then, please stay here."

The group fell to one knee, heads bowed. "God save and keep Queen Neve," Henry murmured.

"God save and keep you all," Neve said. She rushed back to the castle before they got to their feet again.

* * *

Neve hurried into her bedchamber. "Mirror," she said. "Mirror!"

The mirror swirled with color and smoke. "My queen. You called?" He sounded entirely too delighted about that.

"Shh," Neve said. "Please lower your voice. Everyone is still asleep."

"Shall we play cards again?" the mirror asked in an exaggerated whisper. "It's a most enjoyable pastime. Though you may need to get some rest."

"I do," Neve agreed, sitting on her bed. "But I have a tiny little suspicion that you saw the Goldenstone rebels coming to talk to me. That's why you suggested I walk outside."

The mirror said nothing.

"It's all right," Neve said. "I'm not cross. You did the right thing. I need you to see Goldenstone for me, right now."

"See what, specifically?"

"I've been told the conditions in the kingdom have deteriorated badly. I can't see for myself, but if you can see it for me, it would help me."

"Do you seek someone in particular? Someone who is the fairest, perhaps?"

Neve shook her head, smiling. "You never give up, do you?"

"It is my purpose and my desire to serve my queen in the way I'm most qualified."

"I appreciate that. Now, if you could see the situation in Goldenstone ..."

"My pleasure," the mirror said, and the colors swirled into a tiny point in the center of the mirror.

A few minutes later, they grew larger again, encompassing the whole surface. "Your Majesty, I have seen ... what you meant."

"Tell me."

The mirror paused.

Neve's heart began to beat faster. The mirror wasn't one for hesitation. "Tell me," she said again.

"To view such a large area is easier when I have a target to find, like Rowan in The Unfathomed," the mirror said. "I could picture her, then just look for her. But you asked me to see Goldenstone as a whole, so I could only flash in and out on things that happened in the last day or so."

"Go on."

"I see a little girl crying and her mother screaming as her father is dragged away by soldiers. I see a teenage boy stealing crusts of bread. I see a farrier clearing his belongings out of his shop, closing his business for good. I see beggars in the streets, cowering as the soldiers ride by. I see—"

He stopped.

"What?" Neve asked.

The mirror sighed. "It's nothing good, Your Majesty. I can see nothing good. The kingdom is in great distress. Except for the men in the castle. I see them drinking and eating to excess. I see them laughing behind the child in royal velvet robes."

"It's all true," Neve said, rubbing her temples. "Everything they said, it's all true. I didn't doubt them, of course—I only needed to hear it from a neutral party."

The mirror was silent for a few moments, and so was Neve.

"It's your kingdom," the mirror finally said.

"Not anymore. They threw me out."

"You can change what's happening there."

"That's what they said. The people who fled Goldenstone to find me. They want me to save it, to save them."

"Then you must."

I can't. I—

"I don't know how."

"Your husband saw to it that you were educated to know how," the mirror pointed out.

"To help him."

"Perhaps that's what he intended. But neither a king nor a husband can change someone's destiny."

"My destiny is here," Neve insisted. "In Foreverness."

"Is it?" the mirror asked. "It would seem to me that your destiny, the destiny you were born into, was as a daughter and future queen of Goldenstone. Everything that happened after that—the huntsman, your uncles, your assassination, your royal marriage—happened as a direct consequence of Fina's need to stop your destiny. But, as you are beginning to see, destiny has a way of course correcting. And your destiny has always been to rule Goldenstone. Just as it's always been your destiny to be the fairest in the land."

"This again," Neve said, punching her fists into her thighs. "This. Again. To think, for a minute there, I was actually taking your words to heart, as if you—"

"I'm not saying what you think I'm saying," the mirror said slowly. "To be the fairest in face is what your stepmother wanted. And I confess that though you remain beautiful and will be until the end of your life, you are no longer the fairest in face. I don't fear your wrath in telling you that, because that was never what you wanted. To be the fairest in temperament, however—that is another matter."

Neve clenched her fists tighter and leaned forward.

"A queen needs, above all qualities, to be fair," the mirror said. "To be fair in making law and in interpreting it. To be fair in conflict. To be fair when confronted with disparity and cruelty." The mirror's dark colors gave way to pink and yellow and sky blue. "I know this to be true: In temperament, you are the fairest in the land."

Neve's bottom lip trembled.

"Now," the mirror added, "your land needs you to return home."

DELLA

The noblewomen chattered happily amongst themselves, sitting at the exquisitely decorated table in Della's father's home.

The flowers at the center of the table were warm and glorious—but not so tall as to block anyone's view of a friend sitting across from her, and not so fragrant as to detract from the scents of the hot lavender tea and enticing orange-ginger cakes being prepared in the kitchen. The sunlight beamed in through sparkling windowpanes, picking up the shine in the golden outlines of the dishes on the table. A fire roared in the fireplace consistently and was tended to every few moments so a guest wouldn't feel any chill.

Della watched from the kitchen, unseen. The maids had done a masterful job of transforming Della's long-neglected house into a cozy, clean, and commendable home.

Della had given them the day to themselves at their own homes. There was still some serious learning left to be done, but it wasn't theirs.

Their mistresses were smiling, engaged, excited to meet the "trainer" who had promised to improve their dwellings and their lives.

"Your Highness," Eda whispered at Della's shoulder. "Is it time?"

"Yes," Della murmured, moving another two steps away from the doorway so the guests wouldn't see her in the kitchen. "In fact, I'd say it's long past time."

A few maids from Della's own castle staff were here, and they bustled about, preparing to serve. Della had asked them to work as quietly as possible.

Eda stepped out into the room and stood beside the table. She wore a maid's gown, but her demeanor was commanding, and after a few moments, the women began shushing one another. Some looked at Eda with curiosity; others, impatience.

"Ladies," Eda said in a manner that suggested she'd addressed many rooms filled with wealthy women before, "I am Eda. I'm delighted to report that the maids you sent for training are making excellent progress. In fact, they prepared this very room. I trust you are satisfied?"

"It is lovely, to be quite sure," Petra said. "Er, whose house is this?"

"Are you the trainer?" Idalia asked.

"I am not," Eda said. "The trainer prefers to work in secrecy. She is in high demand and cannot bear what would be constant requests for her expertise."

"Why are we here?" Gervaise asked.

"There are some ... practices that the trainer would like you to put into place in your own homes to ensure a smooth transition," Eda said.

Still hidden in the kitchen, Della raised a brow. Eda was good.

"But first," Eda said, "tea and cakes. Then we will get to more important matters."

"Tea and cakes *is* the most important matter," Idalia quipped, and all the women giggled.

Della glanced down and smoothed her hands over the

crisp white apron covering a simple brown dress. She wore her practical work boots. She patted the white bonnet that covered her hair—and her crown.

Her heart thumped at the sight of herself wearing what she'd vowed she'd never wear again. But they were just clothes, and she soothed herself silently with the words she'd said to Molle: *These are just tasks. These are not a measure of your worth. They are just things we do, not who we are.*

She spun, took a tray of cakes, and followed another maid out to the table.

The ladies, of course, didn't spare Della or the other maid a glance as they laid the trays of cakes on the table. "Excuse me, my lady," Della said quietly, deferentially, to Petra as she reached across the table to snatch up two petals that had fallen from the flower arrangement. Petra leaned away from her but said nothing at Della's tidying.

Della whisked the empty tray to the kitchen again and procured a hot teapot. She carried it with care to the table and expertly poured cup after cup. No one thanked her, no one acknowledged her, not even when she leaned so close that she could inhale one lady's rosewater perfume.

Halfway around the table, she went to fill Gervaise's cup and subtly pushed it forward an inch, toppling the bit of tea she'd poured onto the table.

"What is wrong with you?" Gervaise snapped.

Della tucked her chin. "I am sorry, my lady."

Gervaise scoffed and caught the eyes of several others at the table. "I'm sure you are."

Della hurriedly set the teapot on the table, blotted the spilled tea with a cloth napkin, and set the little cup upright in its saucer. She refilled the cup and said, "May I serve you a cake, my lady?"

"Did I speak to you?" Gervaise snapped.

"N-no," Della stammered. "I just thought I'd—"

"Just stop talking," Gervaise said. "I'm not interested in what you thought, if you can even think at all. And yes, give me a cake. It's the least you can do."

Della picked up the tiny silver tongs and lifted a small cake with honey icing. She knew how to set it onto the plate with care, but instead, she feigned slipping her foot on the hardwood floor, and the cake landed on Gervaise's sleeve, honey side down.

"My lady," Della gasped, "I—I—"

Gervaise slapped the side of Della's head, hard, with her open palm. "*That's* your apology? I am a *lady* of this kingdom. You're a clumsy *idiot* with the wit of a pig at market. I don't know who employs you, but—"

Della blinked the sparkles out of her vision, shook away the ringing in her burning, red ear, and wiped the bit of saliva from her chin that had flown from her throat at the impact of this woman's merciless hand.

She lifted her head, and looked Gervaise straight in the eye as she pulled off her bonnet.

She was certain the blue topaz in her revealed tiara gleamed like a summer sky.

Whatever Gervaise was going to say next lodged itself in her throat and emerged only as a wet strangle. Scarlet heat spread over her lace neckline to cover her chest and rose up to heat her neck and face.

"Your Highness!" someone at the table cried.

"Your Highness," they all repeated, and pushed their chairs back so quickly, one toppled to the floor as they all dipped into curtsies and held them low, not daring to rise. Not now.

Gervaise was frozen in place, her princess looming over her.

Della leaned in so she could speak low, but the room was so silent, so free of even the smallest breath, that every woman could hear every word.

"How *dare* you," Della said. "How *dare* you speak to any-one that way?"

"I—I didn't know it was you!" Gervaise defended. "You—you were dressed as a maid, acting as a maid—"

"Yes, you thought I was a maid. And you felt free to speak to me as I assume you speak to all women who work for you, who serve you. You felt free to *strike* a woman serving you, and it seemed to come very naturally to you. Did it?"

Gervaise, sensing she was caught in a verbal trap, said nothing. Her teeth chattered. She had committed a capital offense, physically assaulting a member of the royal family. It had been unwittingly done, of course. But why should strik-ing a princess be an offense punishable by death and striking a maid be an everyday accepted occurrence?

Della glared. "You are a privileged woman," she said to Gervaise. "And for you to speak to another woman the way you did just because of her station is—"

Della paused. She wouldn't let herself say the words she was thinking, for to teach kindness, it must be offered. "Well, it is behavior that isn't worthy of you, Gervaise."

Gervaise's face crumpled, and she looked at her lap.

Della glanced around the table. "Get up. You could stay in your curtsies until midnight, and I would not be less dis-pleased with your behavior today."

The women slowly rose and reseated themselves, shifting uncomfortably.

"But—" Petra began, then thought better of it, but it was too late. Della went around to the other side of the table and towered over her.

"But what?" Della asked, even more quietly than before.

"But—but none of us spoke to you so insolently. None of us slapped you."

"No," Della said calmly. "None of you did. But neither did any of you thank me when I poured you tea or spare me a smile. None of you looked at my face, for if even one of you did, just for a bare moment, you would have known me right away. There was no sorcery here. It was my face all along."

Della paced the length of the table, and back again. "Your maids work for you, and they don't have the wealth you were either born with by circumstance or married into by luck, but they are women just like you in every other way. How does it benefit you to act so uncaring at best, and cruel at worst?"

She turned to Gervaise. "I believe your behavior is learned and can be unlearned. We will begin today. You will learn to reciprocate your staff's hard work with the respect you would afford to me." Della looked at Eda, who'd retreated to a corner of the room to let events play out. They caught each other's gaze for a moment before Della readdressed the room. "We will practice together. If you are as successful at making progress as I hear your maids have been, you will earn back the right to be their employers."

Della softened her voice. "I want us to all treat one another as friends."

As she said it, she thought of her grand entrances into every room, the crown she wore every day, the curtsies and bows she accepted everywhere she went. She swallowed uncomfortably.

The noblewomen nodded slowly.

"And speaking of mutual respect," Della went on. "The next matter I am to discuss with you is their compensation."

"We pay our staff," Idalia said, a bite of defensiveness between her teeth.

"Of course you do," Della said. "But I will be sending these maids back to your households with the highest training available in the kingdom. Now that they have these qualifications, each of these women is to become the head of your staff, and you are to raise her pay by fifty percent."

Petra began violently coughing, and Eda rushed over with water and ready pats on the back until Petra relaxed.

"Since each of these women will be training the rest of your staff, and their efficiency will rise, you are to raise the pay of the other members of your staff by twenty-five percent each," Della said.

After talking with the maids over several days, she'd learned that all of them were embarrassingly underpaid, so much so that even with the wage increases, these families should have no difficulty paying them. Della knew these noblewomen and what their husbands had inherited. The low wages were a manifestation of the noble households' stinginess, nothing more.

No one wanted to openly argue with their princess, but the shifting and shuffling told Della what she needed to know. "I will be summoning each of these women to speak to me privately, on occasion, at my leisure. If I discover that any of them have been mistreated, or if any of them have not had their pay raised the required amount, I will place them in households that are worthy of them. I can find many with both gold and kindness to spare."

The noblewomen exchanged looks with one another.

"Is this not what you wanted?" Della asked, very gently. "It was my understanding that you all wanted homes that raise the standard in Foreverness. Homes that show that you are most noble. Homes like mine. But if you find you can't afford to have such a home—"

"We can," Idalia said quickly.

And Petra followed immediately, saying, "We can."

"I am sure of it," Della said. "Now, please enjoy your refreshments, and we will begin work."

The chatting was hesitant at first, with several glances at Della, but she kept her expression benevolent, and soon enough the women were back to talking, though perhaps with just a little more thought before each word.

Della wondered very briefly which of the training maids was familiar with Colby's bed. She could narrow it down to the younger, unmarried women—Molle, perhaps? But it wasn't worth her thoughts. In the end, it was no matter, for it wasn't about the maid who was sleeping with Colby, but more about Colby's *sleeping* habit in general. Every maid she'd trained was industrious and reliable, and every one of them deserved their new pay and respect, despite the choices they made in their private lives.

Frankly, any poor, deluded young woman who got herself mixed up with Prince Colby Charming would eventually find him punishment enough.

After a few minutes, Gervaise tentatively approached Della. "Your Highness," she said with a small curtsy. She turned to Eda. "I'm sorry, I don't recall your name."

More likely she hadn't bothered to hear it, but Della let it go. Gervaise was making an effort now.

"Eda, my lady," Eda said.

"Eda, would you mind terribly if I spoke with Her Highness alone for a moment?"

Della smiled.

"Of course," Eda said, slipping into the kitchen.

"Your Highness," Gervaise said. "I am so very sorry."

"I know you are," Della said.

"My mother taught me that staff should be dealt with harshly. She said that otherwise, they get lazy."

"Have you witnessed that happening yourself?"

Gervaise thought a moment. "No. But I also never saw her being good to them. Or even … just decent."

"Are you willing to learn a different way?"

"Yes," Gervaise said. "I am. And I deserve to be severely punished for what I did—"

Della laid a hand on her shoulder. "I was certain I could trick you all, and I did. It was to make a point. I put myself in the way of your hand. What's important now is to do better from this day on. Make me proud. Be a genuine example to the other noblewomen in the kingdom of how to conduct oneself."

"I will," Gervaise said, and made a move to go back to her seat, but she turned back. "It's very generous of you, Your Highness, to act as the trainer's go-between like this, when I'm sure you have more important tasks to attend to."

Gervaise's eyes here honest, her smile humble, and Della could tell her question was genuine.

Della lifted her chin and looked at the ceiling—the same ceiling she'd looked at when her stepmother had beaten her with a broomstick, when her stepsisters had yanked her hair out by its roots and pushed her face into barely cooled cinders—and she blinked away the same tears she'd fought so hard to blink away then.

Della smiled at Gervaise. "I don't."

BRY

Bry rapped on the little wooden door quickly and urgently.

Giselle opened the door and, upon seeing Bry, dropped low into a curtsy.

"My friend," Bry said, "that isn't necessary. I wanted to—"

Her words stuck in her throat as Giselle straightened up, holding a sewing needle between two fingers.

Bry's vision clouded over for a moment. Her face went cold, and her palms dampened.

"Your Highness?" Giselle asked. "Bry?"

"Could—could you—" Bry stammered. "Were you—"

"I was just mending my husband's pants," Giselle said. "Nothing important. I'm happy to stop for a bit." She reached her other hand and took hold of Bry's stiff arm. "Come and sit. You look as though you've seen a spirit."

No, not a spirit.

Bry stayed away from needles. There were no sewing supplies anywhere in her home. Her castle staff knew that all mending work was to be sent off site.

One touch of a needle, one tiny pinprick, and she could—

Giselle steered her into a chair at the table and walked across the room to put her needle into a basket with the pants, and Bry relaxed.

"I'm sorry to intrude," she said when Giselle sat across from her. "But I can't stop thinking about what all the women said to me when I was here. I'd—I'd like to know more. Will you accompany me to visit other neighbors? Other women?"

Giselle tilted her head. "Why do you trouble yourself with this?"

"Because no one else is," Bry said, and the words surprised even her.

Giselle thought a moment, then placed a hand on her heart. "As you wish."

* * *

They spent the afternoon traveling by horseback from home to home. Most husbands were out, working the fields or selling at market, and the ones who were home shrugged and left the women alone, unable to recognize Bry with her hood up, and uninterested in the useless chatter of hens.

And the hens chattered. Bry spoke to a blond teenager who said her father decided to repay his debts by agreeing to marry her to his debtor, a decrepit and lecherous old man, and that the wedding would take place in a month's time. She spoke to a brown-skinned woman around thirty who said she had a gift for sales, and could do sums in her head, and loved interacting with customers—but her father was leaving his clothing business to her younger brother, who wasn't smart enough to find his way out of a room with one door. And that was all because it would be inappropriate to leave it to his clever child because she was a daughter. She was sure they would be penniless in a year.

After a half-dozen houses, the stories were tumbling inside Bry's mind. All different, but all the same. Different women, same story of not having a say in their own lives and futures, and not having the freedom to keep what should be rightfully theirs, be it their lands or their businesses or their bodies or their hearts.

After seeing Giselle home, Bry rode back toward the castles, urging her horse to fly faster over rocks and fallen leaves, but soon she slowed to a stop in a familiar clearing.

She hopped off her horse and moved toward the Aura Tree.

As Bry approached, its brown branches turned blue and drooped, its green leaves going silvery thin and brushing against the earth. The strong trunk shifted into a deep, melancholy blue.

Bry collapsed at the roots of the tree, pulled her knees to her chest, and wrapped her arms around them. A translucent tear fell onto her hand, then another.

Did men do this? Did men cry under trees? Did men sulk through the forest, wondering how everything seemed out of reach?

No. Men knew their places—above women. The princes, to be sure, but even among commoners, men had some superiority, even if it was just over the female half of the commoner population.

Thomasina's life was her farm, and because her husband had the misfortune to die, his brother planned to take control of the farm—and her life—from her. The decision was his, not hers.

So many women, so many hardships, so many inconveniences, so much unfairness they couldn't overcome because the laws of Foreverness pinned them to the ground.

It wasn't fair.

It wasn't *fair*.

Bry jumped up, kicking off her slippers. She paced around the tree, faster and faster with each round. The tree trunk's blue gave way to fiery golden red.

"It's not fair," Bry said. Then, louder, "It's not *fair*."

The Aura Tree's red branches lifted high, and the now bright orange and yellow leaves crackled with tiny lightning in the thick, tense air.

Bry stopped pacing and looked out in the direction from whence she'd come. She could see her home, and in the distance, Eterne Castle. Where Brockton ruled, like all the men before him. Like all the men who would come after him.

"It's not right!" Bry yelled, imagining she were in court, with noblemen gasping at her audacity.

But they deserved to hear the audacity. They deserved to hear the truth.

Women deserved to speak the truth.

A kernel of an idea began in Bry's red head, and she let it grow.

NEVE

"I find it interesting," Neve said to her husband, "that you haven't mentioned to me any of the current unrest in Goldenstone. Not just because you do discuss many royal matters with me, but also because Goldenstone is my home."

She kept her eyes on the playing cards fanned out in her hand, but in her peripheral vision, Brockton laid his cards face down and stared at her.

"I, as well, find several things interesting," he countered. "One, that you refer to anything happening outside of Foreverness as a royal matter, when it has nothing to do with me or my reign. And second, that you've just called Goldenstone your home, when you've insisted since the day I met you that your home is Foreverness. You told me that Goldenstone may well not even exist on a map for you."

He picked up his cards again, studied them, then pulled one. Face up between them, he laid down a king.

"You do know what's happening there," Neve said, no question in her voice.

"Yes, I do. My father stayed out of the civil affairs of other kingdoms and counseled me to do the same. Foreverness remains glorious by not meddling with other realms as friends or foes."

"It's glorious, is it, that when the people came to your

father for help and he turned them away, they were immediately hanged upon return to Goldenstone?"

Brockton put down his cards again. "How do you know this?"

"You didn't?"

"Not specifically."

"You must have suspected it would happen."

"I was not king then, and it wasn't my decision. But I asked you a question. How do you know this?"

Neve laid down her own cards. "Some people of Goldenstone have appealed to me."

"Not to me?"

"You are not their sovereign."

"They say you are?" Brockton asked.

"You know I am."

Brockton rubbed his eyes, the ever-present crease between his brows deepening. "Neve," he said, still rubbing. "You undermine me in the Great Hall before hundreds of our subjects. You duck the King's Protection and disappear for a full day without telling me where you are going. Now the latest is what, you're queen of Goldenstone? The kingdom in which you've vowed your whole life to never again set foot? The kingdom that's—not doing very well at the moment?"

"You will not help them?"

"Where are these people who appealed to you?"

"Never mind that," Neve said. "It's been confirmed to me, by trusted sources, that Goldenstone is being run by a child king's council that is mismanaging the kingdom's gold. The people are suffering heavily."

Brockton leveled his gaze at her. "It's true."

"I'm not going to ask you again why Foreverness isn't doing anything, for it's clear to me that you want to carry on the philosophy of your father," Neve said. "And that is your right."

"Thank you."

"Which means I'm going to have to take matters into my own hands."

Brockton stood without breaking his gaze. "And do what?"

Neve also stood and leaned over the table toward him. "Take the throne. I am the rightful queen and heir."

Brockton's mouth hung open almost comically. "Take the throne? Is that all?"

"That's not 'all,' " Neve said. "It won't be easy. That's why I—I need your support."

Brockton paced the room. "You need my support to leave my side as my queen here, so you can ride to Goldenstone and be queen there?"

"*Rule* as queen there," Neve corrected. "With you ruling here and my rule there, we can form a strong alliance."

"Goldenstone is in shambles. It's they who need the alliance. What does Foreverness gain from it?"

"An ally if anyone were to invade. It's not unheard of. For example, pirates often come ashore and try to cross The Unfathomed into Foreverness. If not for the wolves ..." She trailed off.

"I could ask how you know that," Brockton said, "but I'm going to let it go, as we are already discussing a matter of greater importance."

"In an alliance with Goldenstone, you'd have twice the army. As for what you could gain, I was only a child when I was last there, but I'm sure that once I'm there, I could identify plenty of opportunity for trade and—"

"Once you're there, how long do you think the king's council will let you live?" His voice softened. "You have always been afraid you'd be hunted down again. A rational and justified fear, considering your history. Now you're willing to ride into that kingdom alone?"

"I won't be alone."

Brockton blinked. "I don't know what you have planned, but you will likely be tragically unprepared for what awaits you."

"There are many there who believe I am the true queen," Neve said. "I believe many men will fight for me."

"I don't doubt that. Even those who don't believe would fight for you in the hope that you would be better than what they have now. But how prepared will these men be to stand up for you if they are starving and penniless and weak?"

And without weapons. Neve remembered Cecilia and Henry telling her the army had seized all weapons they could find from the people.

"I can make Goldenstone better," Neve said. "I know nearly as much as you about ruling a kingdom."

"You don't know nearly as much as I do," Brockton said. "You know *as* much. Look," he added, sitting down again. "Even if we put aside the not-small matter of overthrowing their king, there is the matter of our marriage. What example are we setting if you leave?"

"That we don't overlook people in need. That we do the right thing."

"We need you here. I need you here."

"You don't *need* me here," Neve said. "You *want* me here."

"Yes, I do. What do you want? You always wanted to be safe and secure. You said it when I met you, that you needed me to assure your protection. Here, you are protected. Don't you still want that?"

"I'm a queen," Neve said. "It's not about what I want. It's what my people need."

"Foreverness is your people."

"Foreverness is *your* people." Neve took a breath. "I'm

going to do this with or without your support. But your support ... will make it far easier."

She left the room.

* * *

"Your Majesty!" Dawn cried, dropping into a deep curtsy. "Aunt Neve. To what do I owe the honor of your visit?"

The maid, who'd been surprised to find herself showing the queen into her mistress's sewing room, backed out and closed the door.

"I can't stay long, I'm afraid," Neve said. "I came to ask for your help."

"Anything. Please sit."

Neve sat in a cozy chair with satin cushions. "I must commission you to create something for me."

Dawn grinned. "A more pleasant favor you could never ask. A gown? Gloves?"

"Not exactly." Neve cleared her throat. "Could you make ... a banner?"

Dawn drew in her chin in surprise. "A banner? The Charmings have been using the same banner for—I don't even know. For generations."

"It's not for the Charmings. It's for me."

Dawn waited for an explanation, but when she realized she wouldn't get one, she shook her head. "Of course. What did you have in mind?"

Neve began to describe what she needed, and after a moment, Dawn said, "Excuse me, I'm going to get something to—" and she hurried from the room, returning quickly with items to sketch with. "Go on."

Neve talked as Dawn drew. A few moments after Neve finished speaking, Dawn flipped the sketch around to show her aunt. "Something like this?"

Her heart pounded as she inspected her niece's artwork. It was one thing to see it in the mind's eye—quite another to see on the page. "Yes."

"How soon do you need this?"

"I don't have much time," Neve said. "Three days, at the most."

"It will be done in two," Dawn said, "if I have to work day and night."

"I thank you." Neve stood.

"Aunt Neve?" Dawn stood also. "I don't know what's happening here, but it's clear to me it's momentous. Whatever it is, I stand by you."

Neve opened her arms, and her niece walked into them. "You can't imagine how much I needed to hear someone in this family say that."

* * *

"Rhyannon," Neve said, picturing the gossamer-like fairy in her mind as she rubbed her temples. "Rhyannon."

The fairy materialized in Neve's bedchamber in a cloud of roses that fell away from her into sparkle. "Your Majesty," she said, curtsying. "How may I serve?"

"Before I ask, I must swear you to secrecy."

"But of course."

"I will be marching on Goldenstone in a few days with a small company."

Rhyannon opened her mouth in slight surprise but didn't ask any questions. Neve appreciated her ability to listen.

"I respectfully ask that you accompany us," Neve continued. "We may need a protection spell in the event we have to turn and flee."

"I can do that," the fairy godmother said slowly. "If I prepare the spell ahead of time, I can cast it on cue and shimmer myself into invisibility as I fly beside you and hold your spell. Have you ever been the subject of such a spell?"

"I haven't," Neve admitted.

"I will warn you, it's a bit frightening," Rhyannon said. "The sphere of protection around you will be invisible, so you will think it's not there. You'll see arrows coming at you, for example. You'll need to trust it's working and keep running."

"I understand."

"How many would I need to cover?" Rhyannon asked.

"I'm not sure. Could you do it for fifty?"

"Yes," Rhyannon said, "I could even do it for more than that. But not an entire army."

"I'm afraid I won't have an entire army."

"Yes," Rhyannon repeated. "Your Majesty, you can rely on my help."

"In three days' time?"

Rhyannon's eyes widened slightly, dropping glitter from her turquoise lashes. "Yes."

* * *

Neve rode to her uncles' cottage under guard, having told the two soldiers merely that she wanted to visit her family. She pushed Biscuit into a fast gallop, expecting the men to stay close behind her. But if her urgency to see five old men raised suspicion, neither of the guards voiced it to their queen.

A pair of armored men galloping on horseback made a ruckus, so Uncle Bart, Uncle Terric, and Uncle Anselm were already outside the front door and peering down the lane when Neve arrived. She hopped off Biscuit quickly, and said, "How wonderful to see you! You all look well." She rushed them inside before they could bow to her, shutting the guards outside.

Uncle Forwin was rocking in his small chair and stopped

when they clattered inside. Uncle Gerard sat up in bed and rubbed his eyes.

"That friend of yours, the armorer," Neve said to them all. "Will one of you go to him right away? He won't have time to make a new suit, but perhaps he can make some adjustments to one he already has, to fit me."

"Armor?" Uncle Bart asked. "For you? What in the—"

"Please," she said. "If one of you could take my measurements to him and ask him to deliver the armor here in two days." She placed a purse of gold in Uncle Anselm's hand, along with the parchment of her measurements. "This should be enough."

"That's all you're going to say, little love?" Uncle Terric asked. "We will worry ourselves sick."

Neve went over to Uncle Forwin in his chair and knelt at his feet. "Remember when you told me that in Goldenstone, I'd be a queen regnant?"

Uncle Forwin leaned forward, placed his hands on her face, and kissed her on the forehead. His face was so old, so tired—so proud. "Yes," he said, and for only the second time in her life, she saw tears shining in those gruff old eyes. The first time had been when she'd walked into his house, alive again after a year in her coffin. "Go," he said. "We will take care of it. Two days."

Uncle Anselm circled his finger in the pouch. "This is far too much gold for a single suit," he said.

"Oh, yes," she said. "I meant to say I'll actually need two."

* * *

Standing at the edge of The Unfathomed, the same spot where she had first encountered the snakes who brought her the wolves who brought her to Rowan, Neve whistled two short notes, then one long note. She'd sneaked out the rear door of her uncles' cottage while they distracted her guards with ale. Her mouth was a bit parched from her ride, and her lips were dry, and her whistle didn't quite carry, so she licked her lips and tried again, but still, the whistle was pathetically weak.

"Aargh," Neve groaned.

Two little bluebirds suddenly appeared around her head. They hovered in front of her face, flapping their wings furiously to stay aloft. They both cocked their heads. Neve whistled the pattern the best she could, two short notes, and one long note, and repeated it three times.

The two bluebirds turned and whistled the pattern together toward the tree line. The whistle pattern echoed far from them as more birds picked up the pattern and carried it farther than Neve ever could. The birds repeated this a few more times, with faraway echoes, then rested for about ten minutes before they did it all over again.

A half hour later, two large wolves approached Neve. "Thank you, friends," Neve whispered to the birds before they flew away.

Not sure how the beasts were even larger than they'd been in Neve's memory, she said, "Please take me to Rowan."

They dipped their heads in a yes.

Neve tied Biscuit to a tree and asked her animal escorts to watch over her. The wolves turned to walk toward The Unfathomed, looking back once to see that she followed.

She wondered if she'd ever be able to set foot in The Unfathomed without fear. But unlike last time, she was sure she could trust—and communicate with—these wolves and was eager to see Rowan now that she knew the woman was real—and a sworn ally.

They'd only gone about half the distance east in the forest when they came to a clearing in the trees where another half-dozen wolves lounged, and Rowan worked on a thick stick with her knife, carving—or sharpening.

Neve cleared her throat, and Rowan looked up quickly. Though she didn't break into the sort of smile one of Neve's sisters-in-law would have offered upon seeing her, she nonetheless appeared pleased for a moment, then bent over her stick again. "Hello, Queen," she said. "Didn't take you long at all."

"What didn't?"

"Needing me for something."

"I—"

"It's all right," Rowan assured, not taking her eyes off her work. "I had a feeling the day I met you that something was happening, even if you weren't fully aware of what it was. You felt its energy, and it sent you here for answers and allies."

"You are intuitive," Neve said. "A remarkable trait, considering you don't seem to spend much time around humans."

Rowan chuckled and lifted her chin. "Everyone, this is Neve. She's a queen, so no rude rump licking, please."

The wolves seemed to nod at Neve, some of them grunting. Two little pups whined and moved closer to their mother.

"Sit," Rowan said, gesturing to a rock about three feet from her.

Neve perched on it.

"What service can I provide?" Rowan asked.

"I plan to take the throne in Goldenstone."

Rowan knit her brows. "You're the queen of Foreverness."

"I'm the rightful heir in Goldenstone," Neve said. "There, I have full power as a queen regnant."

"Interesting. I take it Goldenstone doesn't know you're coming?"

"My twelve-year-old cousin Gawain sits on the throne. His council rules the land, and his council is loyal to the memory of their Queen Fina, and how she wanted to rule."

"Your stepmother. I remember. They're not going to take kindly to your presence, and by that, I mean they're likely to hang you by your pretty royal neck."

"Indeed."

"Why bother? Is Foreverness getting dull in all its perfection?"

Neve gave Rowan all the details she'd been told on the state of Goldenstone. When she heard about families starving and children being beaten, Rowan's expression darkened. When she was done, Neve sat back and realized the group of wolves were all alert and listening.

Rowan said, "It seems you need... the special kind of service we can provide."

"Yes. However many of you are willing to come. This will not be—that is, I cannot guarantee your safety."

"We live in The Unfathomed," Rowan said. "We routinely clash with bloodthirsty killer pirates. Safety is not something we've ever enjoyed. How many men will Foreverness provide?"

Neve hesitated, and Rowan laid her fist on her own mouth. "So, approximately zero," she said through her hand, "from your husband."

"He is the king, and—"

"He is your husband so feel free to defend him, but I don't mind saying that he should have stepped up. But very well. We will assume no help."

"We will have help from Rhyannon—a fairy. She's an elder, a strong fairy, and she'll join us in case she needs to encase us in a protection spell."

"We won't be able to fight through that, I presume."

"No, that will strictly be for a turn-and-flee," Neve said.

"The we-give-up strategy, you mean."

"I prefer we think of it as the stay-alive-to-think-of-something-else strategy."

Rowan snorted with a grin.

"I don't know what we will find when we arrive," Neve said. "But I can't walk in alone. I need a show of force, and I'm hoping that walking in with a pack of massive-sized, snarling wolves will at least give me the opportunity to have a reasonable conversation with the council. Perhaps we could reach an agreement. It may not come down to a fight."

"I suspect it will, though."

"What else can I do?" Neve asked. "The people think I've forsaken them. Perhaps—perhaps I have. But now that I'm aware of what's happening, I can't turn a blind eye."

"Of course you can't. And now that I'm aware of it, I can't, either."

"I was hoping you'd feel that way."

"There's only one thing worse than bad men," Rowan said, "and that's bad men with power. Let's take it away."

"In three days' time," Neve said, "I will meet you at the edge of the woods at twilight, where my uncles waited for me the last time I saw you."

"Very well."

"One more thing." Neve hopped down from the rock and inclined her head. Rowan slid down also, shook her hair off her shoulders and down her back, and walked with her away from the pack.

"Would you please take a message to Darren for me?" Neve asked.

"I had planned to go this evening."

"Perfect. Tell him—tell him that he didn't do all of this in vain. He didn't give up his life so a little princess could be a queen. He did it so she could *act* a queen."

She stumbled a bit over the words, and she wished

this woman whose help she was asking couldn't see she was terrified.

Rowan laid her hand on Neve's shoulder. "I will tell him," she vowed. "Then you and I will march on Goldenstone, and the men on that king's council will need to face the two children of the woods who've come back from the dead to claim what's yours."

Neve pressed her lips together. "Yes."

Rowan put her other hand on Neve's other shoulder and shook her once. "Yes? Yes."

Neve embraced Rowan. Her tangled hair smelled like cedar and salt. "Thank you."

Rowan went still, but then patted Neve awkwardly on the back twice. They separated, and Rowan whistled. The two wolves that escorted Neve to the group trotted over.

"They will take you back."

"You are not their leader, are you?"

"Of course not," Rowan said. "We are all equals, and we help one another. The whistle is just because my howl doesn't carry all that far." She smiled. "Also, they don't like humans to know they can understand and speak, so they let me deal with that part."

"Ah. I understand. Farewell for now."

"Three days. At twilight."

DELLA

ella threw her quill down and rubbed her eyes in the candlelight. Numbers frustrated her. Her father, God rest his soul, had hired tutors to provide a formal education for her as a child, so she could do sums and other basic number functions, but no one ever taught her the skills she'd need for business.

She'd tried to figure it out on her own. She thought she had, but the numbers were a bit messy. There had to be a more streamlined way to keep a ledger for her business. She wanted to be able to do it seamlessly before she brought in her second group of students.

There was no one she could ask. Neve was extremely clever, but she didn't want to trouble the queen with something so minor. Neve's miserable expression rose unbidden in Della's mind, and Della frowned. The poor woman was clearly having a difficult time adjusting. Even Bry seemed distracted lately, and anyway, if Della asked anyone for help, she'd have to confess what she was doing in secret. She could trust her sisters-in-law, but she just wasn't ready to tell anyone about this project, not yet.

Colby knew, though, and as Foreverness tax collector, what better person to help her with bookkeeping? Della made a sour face. She was loath to ask him for help with this, even though he'd offered. She didn't really want him to be a part of her business.

However—she could get his help indirectly. She could go into his study and take a look at his books for inspiration. As usual, he was nowhere to be found, likely until morning when he arrived at the breakfast table still drunk and reeking of jasmine. But maybe his books would give her an idea of what she could do to make her own ledger more comprehensive.

Della wrapped her silk dressing gown around her torso and tied it. She slid her feet into satin slippers that would be noiseless on the stone floor, picked up a candle, and quietly stepped out of her grand bedchamber. It was late, so she tiptoed up the staircase, and silently opened the wooden door to Colby's study.

It was an impressive room, with ledgers from years past lining bookshelves and two stacked on the desk. She placed the candle down. She hefted the top ledger, labeled with the current year, but then found a smaller one, also labeled with the current year. Maybe one was from the first half of the year and the other this half? Unsure why they'd be two different sizes, she opened the large one and laid it flat.

Colby's careful handwriting was legible and clear, and she was able to make sense of it instantly: where he'd gone, whom he'd seen, how much he'd collected, how much was outstanding. It was a much different sort of business than Della's, but she could see that she was likely keeping her own ledger properly.

Satisfied and proud of herself, she went to close the ledger, but curiosity led her to open the smaller one.

Then she was confused.

The smaller one had the same dates, the same people, the same column of money collected, but the amounts were smaller, and in a separate column she saw notes like *jewls, gld, mtls.*

Della went over to the shelf and found only one thick ledger for each year. She returned to the desk and found two large chests underneath with locks. Della kneeled on the floor, the cold of the stones seeping through her silk dressing gown. She slid two fingers into her hair and slid out a pin. She inserted it into one lock, wiggled it around until she felt it click, and swung the chest open.

She'd taught herself long ago how to pick a lock, so that she could rescue portraits of her mother and father, as well as her mother's pearls and amethysts, from Claire's clutches.

Now she looked at a stack of the smaller ledgers, with years that corresponded to the large books on the wall. She flipped through a few of them and found the same: dates, names, smaller amounts than those she'd found in the large ledger, and a column of notes.

Her heart started to pound.

She picked the other chest open and flipped the lid to find piles of necklaces, rings, cuff bracelets, some precious metals, loose colorful jewels, and some rare and foreign coins.

She drew out a dark ruby, and a string of yellowed pearls. The smooth stones were cool in her palm. She dropped the pearls and picked up a tarnished silver coin that looked from a time long ago. It clinked against the ruby still in her hand. Then she drew out a small, smooth golden figurine of an eagle, wings spread in the moment before flight. A tiny work of art.

Della sat back on her heels and stared at the wall, the precious items in her fist on her lap.

Colby stole these.

He stole them. He was extorting the people in Foreverness, taking more than their taxes. She didn't want to consider what he might have resorted to in order to take their prized possessions and their extra coins and gold, but he did travel with a small group of men.

There were a lot of small ledgers here. He'd been doing this for years.

If he were any other lord in his position, someone might have found out. But he was the prince and given this position of trust by his own father. No one would have wanted to speak up. Commoners would have done anything to stay in the king's graces; their lives were hard enough as it was.

The ruby felt like it was burning through her hand as she remembered a similar ruby in a necklace Colby had given her at dinner not long ago. He'd given her many surprise luxury gifts in the course of their long marriage. Could she have possibly worn stolen necklaces, bracelets, and rings?

No, these items were not fit for a princess. But—any of these jewels could be removed from their simple settings, reset in elaborate ones, and presented to royalty.

Any number of jewels she owned might be stolen. Any number of gowns, furs, *shoes*—could have been bought with stolen gold.

She wondered how the people could have embraced and loved her with such genuine emotion over the years—and realized they probably assumed the truth of it: that the pretty princess had no idea of her husband's misdeeds and was innocent. They didn't blame her.

But no one held Colby accountable.

She heard heavy footsteps at the door, and she quickly slid her hand in her pocket before the door swung open to reveal her husband.

He didn't look drunk, just bemused to find his princess wife sitting on the floor by his open chests of stolen goods and books detailing his treachery.

"Good evening," he finally said.

"Husband."

"Couldn't sleep?"

"Something like that."

"Ah," he said, shedding his wool coat and hanging it on a peg beside the door. "I was about to sit and catch up on some work. Perhaps you'd excuse me?"

Della frowned. "Can—could we talk about all this?"

"What would you like me to say?"

"I would like to say," Della began, "that I was having some difficulty balancing my books, and not sure I was doing it properly. I came in here to look at yours, for a bit of assistance."

Colby smiled easily. "What did you find?"

Della sighed. "First, that I am doing my books correctly."

"You're very clever," Colby said. "No need to doubt yourself, but you could have asked me."

"I wanted to do it on my own."

"Understood."

"But," she said, standing, "quite by mistake, I found all this."

"You certainly did." He took in the open chests and ledgers. "Not to worry. I'll put it all back in place. Why don't you retire? You look a bit weary. Not," he said, holding up a hand, "that it detracts from your beauty."

"Colby, we must speak about all this at length."

"What is there to say?"

They locked eyes. Was he not worried?

Why would he be? He knew his wife would say nothing. She was enjoying a long, very wealthy life, and he knew she loved having everything she needed.

But.

"Why?" Della finally said. "You are a Charming and a prince. You have everything you want and need. You don't need trifles. You don't even need gold. What is the meaning of this?"

Colby slid his cushioned chair over the stone floor and sat. "I don't know," he admitted. "My men, they've come to expect it, and I throw them extra gold for taking care of it. So they don't mind. I suppose I did it because I wanted to get back at my father."

"It's not his fault you were born second."

Colby tilted his head. "No, of course it's not. But he showed no favor to me over the years."

"He gave you the role of tax collector," Della pointed out. "A position of the highest trust."

"Also the position that makes you the least liked in all the land. No one likes to see me riding toward their village, even before I—even before I started helping myself to a bit extra."

"There are a few things wrong with your argument," Della said. "First, you weren't cheating your father. You aren't skimming off the top of legitimate payments. You are extorting extra from the people of Foreverness. You are stealing from *them*, not the Crown. And second, your father is gone now, and presumably, your resentment died with him."

"My brother is merely a younger version of the previous king. He wants to change nothing."

"Be that as it may, he is the king, and you are the next in line. You might adjust your behavior to align with your station."

"It's an option," Colby said. "But I probably won't. Like Brockton, I might as well keep the status quo. It's the easier route. Besides, my men rather enjoy their bonuses, and so does my wife."

"I don't like to think that my belongings are tainted, procured dishonestly."

"Then don't think about it," Colby said. "What's the need? It didn't affect you before today. Now you can lock it away in your memory with all the other dishonesties."

Della stared at him.

"You and I both know how to get what we desire," he added. "We know how to uphold an image. We're both fifty years old. There's no reason to change things now."

"I am forty-eight," Della said, her voice sharp. Then she shook her head. *Focus, Princess.* "How can you possibly expect me to act as if nothing's changed? Everything I wear, everything I own—"

"It's not everything," Colby said. "Come now. I was already a wealthy Charming, and if I stopped taking my little extra, I still would be. But—sure, maybe it's a few of your gowns, a few pairs of shoes, a few necklaces over the years." He shrugged.

"It's wrong. How do you not see that?"

Colby regarded her as a lock of his hair came loose from its tie and fell down his temple. He twirled it idly with one finger. "Is it any less wrong," he said slowly, "for a princess to take payments from those below her royal station?"

"I don't take payments." Della bristled.

"Then what is your ledger for? Counting magic beans, are we?"

"I'm helping people," Della said. "I take none of the gold for profit. I put it all into buying supplies."

Though it was true she had some left over in her plus column. She had handily turned a profit, despite all her expenses, and she would need to purchase fewer supplies for the next group because she had plenty left over. But she had no intention of keeping the profit for herself. The only thing she'd purchased for herself were her work shoes. She'd considered a public fund of some kind, but since it was all still a secret, she'd planned to consider that at some time in the future.

Colby kept nodding, slowly.

"What do you suppose the king would say if he knew about this?" Della asked, gesturing to the ledgers.

"I'm going to hear your question as a hypothetical and not as a threat," her husband said. "But Brockton is my devoted, loving brother. He hasn't even said anything to me about my unfortunate drunken moment at the coronation. He's taking a hands-off approach when it comes to the family problem child."

"Would Neve take that approach?" Della asked, and the fire that ignited in Colby's eyes made her instantly regret saying it. He knew full well that Brockton trusted Neve's counsel, and that Della and Neve admired each other.

Della and Colby locked in a standoff for a few tense minutes. She crossed her arms over her chest. He kept winding his hair around his finger.

Finally, he said, "Very well. You do have a point that we don't need the gold or goods, and that with my father in the ground, my desire for revenge has run its course."

Della felt her forehead, her lips, her jaw soften. "You are done, then? No more? You will order your men to engage in no more pillaging?"

"I will." He reached out a hand.

She hadn't touched him in a very long time. Neither the feel of his hand nor the heated, deep kiss that followed brought any pleasure or relief, but Della allowed herself to relax into the security and familiarity of it all.

NEVE

Brockton summoned his wife and queen into the Great Hall.

Neve was surprised—and nervous—to find the king sitting under his crown and on his plush throne. He was also in the company of his full council, with his brother, Prince Lucan, lord commander of the King's Protection, standing at attention off to one side.

She walked up the blue velvet runner from the door to the throne and dipped into a deep and lingering curtsy. "Your Majesty."

"Please rise," he said. "I have consulted with Lucan, and we will be providing you with an escort of Foreverness soldiers for your journey to Goldenstone."

Neve held her breath.

"When I asked Lucan to speak to his men," Brockton went on, "to see if anyone would volunteer to ride to Goldenstone as the army of Queen Neve when she went to stake her claim for the throne there, I guessed perhaps twenty men would stand up." His mouth twisted upward a bit. "Lucan said he stopped counting very enthusiastic volunteers at two hundred."

Brockton cleared his throat. "It would seem that Queen Neve of Foreverness is beloved. Can that not be enough for you?"

"No," Neve said. "If Goldenstone held merely another chair to sit in and the opportunity to be adorned with riches, then yes. But it's a chair of power and responsibility for me, both of which I don't have here. More importantly, my power could be used to heal a suffering kingdom. Honor, kindness, and fairness demand that I take my place."

Brockton appeared unsurprised by her answer. "You may tell the council there that Foreverness supports your claim to the throne."

Neve was taken aback. "I—"

"You are the true heir," Brockton said. "It would be folly to deny it."

"Though I did ask you to. For a very long time."

"It would also be folly to allow you to march there alone. You'd be as good as dead."

Neve's heart tightened in her chest. She had been try-ing—really trying—to not think about the personal risk, but rather about the help she could provide, the kingdom she could restore.

"I hadn't planned on marching in alone, but this—I thank you."

Brockton dismissed his council with a wave of his hand, then nodded to Lucan, who bowed first to him, then to Neve, and left.

They were alone in the vast cavern of a room.

Brockton stood from his throne, stepped down from the platform, and walked over to his wife. He regarded her for a long, uncomfortable moment.

"None of this is because I don't think you capable of rul-ing Goldenstone," he said.

"I know that."

"This is not meant to stop you—for I know you can't be convinced. But your disregard for your place here, your disre-spect of me, and your disobedience to the dictates of your own position in Foreverness have made things very difficult for me."

Neve wanted to argue that she did respect him, that this was about needing respect for herself, and for fighting her own battle that had been a long time coming. But she kept her words in her throat, because releasing them would cause an argument, and he had just given her more than she could have ever predicted he would. "I understand, and I regret that my actions and my words have made you feel that way," she said carefully.

"Our marriage is in jeopardy," Brockton said.

Neve blinked. "How—how could you—"

"I'll need to tell this kingdom that their queen has left to fight for another throne in another land. Everyone will wonder why you wanted to leave. They will wonder why I allowed it. They will see me sitting in official capacities without you seated at my side. They will sense something is very wrong with you. And with me. It's untenable."

"Just tell them the truth," Neve said. "That Goldenstone is suffering, and I have the obligation to take my place there."

"Foreverness doesn't get involved in matters of state with other kingdoms."

"You just did by providing me some of your men and giving me your support."

"The people don't need to know all that."

"Perhaps they do," she said. "What can be wrong with pointing out injustice and taking steps to right the wrongs?"

"They will not understand," Brockton said. "If they hear of strife so close—"

"I have a feeling you are not only vastly underestimating the character of the people of this kingdom, you are overestimating the perfection of life in Foreverness for most people. You sit and listen to the people who come to you in the Great Hall with their problems. Some are petty, yes, but many aren't. Surely you don't believe they're all living amidst sunshine and flowers."

Brockton shook his head slowly. "There is also the not-small matter of you choosing to live away from your husband."

"It's only a two-and-a-half-day ride," Neve said. "I'll appoint a council. I will divide my time. And I'd be happy to entertain the king of Foreverness should he choose to visit."

She tried a smile, but Brockton didn't return it. "I fear for your life, Neve," he said. "I love you, and I'm angry that after a lifetime of insisting on protection, you're pushing that aside now—when your kingdom needs you."

"This is *your* kingdom," Neve said. "As you haven't hesitated to assert to me."

She thought she saw his face soften just a bit with—regret? Fear? But he set his jaw before she ascertained what exactly it was.

"Your claim to Goldenstone is rightful," he said. "Your intention is honorable. When do you leave?"

"Tomorrow at dusk."

"I will instruct my men to assemble out front. I'll have Lucan appoint a flag bearer."

"I would appreciate the bearer. But I won't need a Foreverness flag."

"Neve—" Brockton began but stopped. "Your Majesty. I wish you well."

He bowed low.

Neve returned with a deep curtsy. "Thank you, Your Majesty."

BRY

Bry was tucking a few stray strands of hair into the upswept hairdo held together by combs when Lucan came into her room and closed the door.

"Bry, I want to talk to you."

"I can't now," Bry said, looking around for her little purse. "I must leave to … visit a friend."

"Bry, I'm noticing a change in you."

Bry didn't answer as she lifted pillows and her discarded breakfast gown on the bed, searching.

"Bry," Lucan said again, and the sudden sharpness in his tone stopped her short.

"What?"

Lucan sat on her bed and patted the space beside him. She sat, watching him warily.

"Are you unhappy with me, Bry?"

She was taken aback. "No."

"We've barely spoken in days. We've haven't shared a bed in … many nights. You are distracted and … not yourself."

"By not myself, do you mean not bending over backward for everyone every minute?"

"Er, yes. That's what you do, Bry." He put his palms on his thighs. "I know you were cross with me for not talking to the king on your friend's behalf, or allowing you to do so—"

"I still am."

"You must understand I have obligations to our sovereign. It isn't anything against you."

"No," Bry said. "It's nothing against me, specifically."

"Then why can't you be happy? You have a good life, a life to be proud of and happy with."

"That's the problem," Bry said. "I shouldn't. I was born into wealth, then married into wealth. The Crown promotes the dream of marrying a prince, and women and girls are told that means this kingdom gives them every opportunity. But there are only so many princes to go around, aren't there? The rest of the women suffer injustices that I can no longer bear to witness."

"We all struggle in some way," Lucan said gently.

"Of course we do," Bry said. "We're all human. But when the law is against you, there's no winning outcome to that struggle. Women in Foreverness aren't allowed to overcome. The best they can do is endure. That's no way to live."

"We have no choice but to live according to law."

"Laws can be changed," Bry said.

"You can't change them."

"No, but I can see to it that the king, who can change them, is made aware of the negative consequences that laws bring about."

Lucan frowned at her. "How do you intend to—"

"I am on my way to see my friend Thomasina," Bry said. "Every day is a day closer to her having to wed her cruel brother-in-law. I am going to encourage her to take audience with the king."

"She can't do that. Only men can do that."

"I have faith that Brockton will not turn her away." And Neve sat at his side. She would not let him turn Thomasina away, Bry was certain.

Lucan stood and paced to the window, raking his fingers

through his hair. "No, Bry. You cannot trouble my brother in this way."

"What trouble? He sees dozens and dozens of people. What's one more?"

Lucan's eyes, always full of love and warmth, were dark with confusion and frustration. "I command you to stop this nonsense at once."

"Command me?"

"Yes, command you," Lucan said. "I am your husband."

Bry's temper flared as bright as her hair. "I don't recognize your authority over me."

"You—you what?"

"Your authority as husband. I don't recognize it."

Lucan blinked. "Very well. Perhaps you'll recognize my authority then as lord commander of the King's Protection."

Bry went silent. Lucan sat beside her again and cupped her face in his hand.

"You are my wife," Lucan said. "Dawn and Thea are my daughters. I'm sworn to protect this kingdom, made up of men *and* women. I want you to know I understand what you are saying."

Bry looked up at him, her lips parted in surprise.

Lucan kissed her slowly. When they drew apart, he pulled her close and said, "But my first duty is to my king. Our father kept tradition sacred, and Brockton wants to maintain that. What you are demanding is—too much."

Bry pulled out of his arms roughly. "A woman asking her king to help her is too much?"

"It's all too much a departure from what makes Foreverness work. It's not going to happen."

"I'm telling you Foreverness *doesn't* work."

"I'm telling you it's not going to happen," he repeated. "You think you're doing the right thing, and your heart is pure, but you'll only get their hopes up, Thomasina and your other new friends."

"Women with hope is a bad thing?"

"No, of course not. They can talk to their husbands, and—"

Bry jumped to her feet. Her hands waved wildly, wanting to tear her hair out and throw it at the feet of this stubborn man. "That's my point!" she yelled. "Waiting for a man to rescue—"

"It worked for you, didn't it?"

"What?"

"Waiting for a man to rescue you. You didn't set out to do that, of course, but it broke your spell."

Bry scoffed. "You think waiting in a deep sleep for a century is a valid plan for a woman's future?"

"I'm saying your predicament was dire, requiring a worthy man to change it. I did."

"You *think* you did."

"I certainly do think I did," Lucan said. "I fought through the brambles surrounding Sylvan Castle in Eventide to get to you."

"Did you fight through them?" Bry asked. "Or did they—oh, I don't know—part and fall away as you approached?"

"They did," Lucan admitted, "because I was worthy."

"It's my understanding that many, many men tried in that century to break through those brambles and ended up gouged to death or at the very least, badly bloodied, and none passed through before you. Do you think—do you really think—that none of those men was a worthy soul? Not one of them?"

Lucan paused. "I'm not saying that—"

"Yes, you are. That's what you believed. Just as you believed that the bolt on the castle door fell apart as you touched it because it was *you* who touched it."

"Bry, what are you saying?"

"I'm saying that it was my birthday! Exactly one hundred years to the day! To the hour, even. *Time* broke the spell, not you. It was time for it to end."

Lucan got to his feet and stared at her. "I kissed you. I kissed you awake."

"You did not. I was already awake."

"You are saying—"

"I'm saying you do not have magic lips! Your Charming man lips did not wake me! I had awakened a few minutes earlier. The best I can say for you that day was that your timing was impeccably coincidental."

Lucan began to pace. "You *knew* this?"

"Of course I knew it! I was *there*, Lucan. I heard you enter the room before you kissed me. I heard you apologize before you kissed me for not asking permission, but that you were told it was how to break the spell."

Lucan froze, his eyes wide.

Then he gripped his hair with both hands. The gray winding through it was clearly visible in the sunlight beaming through the large window. "You let me believe it? All this time?"

"You knew it was my birthday," Bry said. "You knew the curse was for a century. Deep down, you knew the brambles shouldn't have parted that easily for you when they had killed other men. You let yourself believe it."

"Everyone believed it," he murmured.

"Of course everyone believed it! This kingdom has been set up to believe men are champions and that women are ineffectual and pathetic. Everyone was primed to believe a kiss from a man woke a girl from a hundred-year-long death."

Lucan crumpled to the floor under the window, drew his knees up to his chest, and dropped his head into his hands.

Bry crouched to touch his shoulder, and he jerked away.

"It's my fault now, is it?" Bry asked. Fear tore through her—*he will hate me, everyone will hate me, they will all throw me away*—and she pushed through it. "It's not my fault," she said, and she realized she'd never, never uttered those words before, in that order. "You were so sweet and good to me, and it was such a small gift to not tell you the truth. Now that I have, the truth won't leave this room."

She turned her head and noticed her little purse on the floor by the foot of the bed. She needed to go.

"Without the kiss," she said to her husband, "you are still a prince. You are still the lord commander of the King's Protection. You hold lands. You have the favor of the king in a wealthy realm."

She leaned closer to her husband. "I'm only asking you to think of the women of Foreverness. Women without husbands are at the mercy of their fathers, who marry them to men not for love, but for gain. Women with cruel husbands are still bound to obey and serve them. Widows lose everything they once had. Most young girls have no education. Without you, I wouldn't be a princess here, and I wouldn't be a princess in Eventide, because my angry family would have cast me out. I would have been a beggar.

"Without men," she added, "women don't have much. Please understand." She was close to him as she finished, her voice barely a whisper.

Lucan stood, put out his hand, and helped his wife up. "I do understand," he said gruffly. "Were I sitting on the throne, you might have convinced me. But—" He held up a hand when Bry began to argue. "But I am not the king."

He went to the door but turned back to her before leaving. "This kingdom loves you. I love you." He left the room.

Bry didn't move, just stared at the closed door. Yes, this

kingdom loved her because she worked so hard to earn and keep that love. She was a steadying presence, ever helpful, never questioning, never contrary.

She didn't want to be shunned. She didn't want to be hated.

But then Thomasina's anguished face rose up in her mind's eye, and Bry rushed out of the castle.

DELLA

ella counted all the letters of recommendation she had received since releasing her first group of students into the hands of their mistresses. Sixteen! The women were so pleased at the quality of the work and the beauty of their households that when their friends commented on it, they referred Della's "trainer" for her inspired incentive of a free pair of shoes, and some women referred more than once. Della had spoken to four of her former students, who reported that they were being treated respectfully and their pay increased, and, for the first time, they took pride in their accomplishments every day. Della also had spoken to most of the noblewomen, and after the initial shock of Della's maid costume had worn off, they confessed they appreciated their own training. Nearly all of them had been uncomfortable with their own heavy-handedness with the staff from the start, but they thought the extreme strictness was expected of them, because that was the atmosphere in their own noble childhood homes. Della knew she would encounter noblewomen who were mean at heart and unwilling to change, and she had some ideas on how to deal with that eventually, but for now, everything was falling into place.

A satisfied smile settled on Della's face. She had used the gold coming in for this new group to replenish her cleaning supplies and buy some new items for training, which she would need now that she had more people joining her for this session.

Della pushed back from her little desk—which she'd asked her staff to bring into her cavernous bedchamber, along with the chair she sat in—and stared at the wall. Ever since her discovery in Colby's office, and her revelatory conversation with him, she'd been uneasy. Her wealth was something she was certain she deserved after her difficult life with the witch triumvirate of Claire, Javotte, and Isabella. She easily justified every gown, jewel, shoe, and crown. She'd married a prince. She'd escaped her life of drudgery at the best moments, and abuse at the worst. She'd earned her right to enjoy her life. But learning that some of the gold used to adorn her and to make her life comfortable wasn't Colby's to give—it was wrong. Instead of joy, her wardrobes and her jewel boxes were filled with guilt. If only she knew which pieces were the ones. Now she could only feel guilty about it all.

Colby had told her he was finished, but Della didn't believe one word of it. She knew him too well.

She could turn Colby in. She could speak to Brockton and Neve. Neve would believe Della without question. Brockton was trickier—he was Colby's brother, and he let Colby get away with a lot, including his coronation-day antics. But certainly, Brockton held Foreverness to a high standard—as high a standard as his father had held it. Once he had proof of Colby's treachery, he'd have to do something about it, wouldn't he? Colby would be imprisoned and she—she would still be princess. Anything she'd acquire as royalty after that would be legitimate.

But she had very little proof to offer Brockton. Colby had returned early the other evening, so she wasn't able to pilfer one or two of his smaller ledgers. She could go to his office now—she knew for sure he was out in the villages, collecting and perhaps even tormenting—but Colby wasn't stupid. He had likely hidden the evidence as soon as she'd gone back to bed that night.

Maybe she could ask Rhyannon for help. Could Rhyannon find and procure the ledgers? If she did, it was possible the spell to get them would have a time limit, and Della needed more flexibility than that.

Perhaps the best course of action was to just talk to Neve. Neve knew the law as well as—if not better than—the king himself. She'd know what Brockton would require to order an arrest.

Della let that plan sink in for a few moments, and discovered she felt good about it. She didn't feel guilty turning Colby in. He shouldn't be doing what he was doing. As prince, he had more than almost anyone in the land. His greed and his misplaced feelings of revenge were getting old, and everyone in the royal family was over it. Fifty years old and he was still behaving like a child, kicking and screaming because his brother got a larger and juicier slice of pie, ignoring all the nearby children who didn't get pie, and would never get pie.

The kingdom owed Prince Colby Charming nothing, and innocent victims paid for his frustrating sense of overentitlement.

Yes, that was settled. Della would speak to Queen Neve at her first opportunity.

Now, to the business at hand. She pulled out a sheet of parchment and made some notes. An even number of participants was ideal because she could partner them up for several activities. She would start them all next Friday, which gave her plenty of time to get organized.

She slid open the top desk drawer to pull out her ledger— but the drawer was empty.

She moved her eyes over the top surface of the desk, and turned to look at the bed across the room. She pushed her chair away, kneeled, and looked under the desk.

Where had she put it?

She opened the drawer again as if expecting it had been replaced by magic, but it was still empty. Confused, she looked out the window.

She hadn't moved it. She only worked on her ledger in this room, at this desk. It was here yesterday; she'd entered some numbers and she knew—she knew she'd put it back in the drawer. No one ever entered this room except her trusted household staff, and—

A very, very unpleasant thought occurred to her.

Why would Colby take it? Was he curious about her business? Why would he not simply ask her about it?

She jumped up, gathered her skirts in her hands, and ran from her bedchamber to Colby's office. She turned the knob and shouldered the door.

Locked. It didn't budge.

She pushed the door two more times with her shoulder and cursed. She banged on the door with her flat palm three times, though she knew Colby wasn't there.

Something was wrong. Something was very wrong.

Della walked slowly back to her room, her heart pounding. She stacked all the recommendation letters and tied them with a ribbon, but she didn't know where to put them as her desk was no longer secure. She tucked them under her arm and left the room again.

She ran out of the castle and around to the back to the mostly unused entrance. She went in and rushed to the suite where she was storing training supplies for the next session.

Padlocked. A large, sturdy lock that would require an iron key. A hairpin wouldn't open a lock such as this.

Della put a hand on her chest and tried to steady her emotions.

What was Colby doing? And why?

She needed to speak with Neve. Now.

She went out the way she came in and walked around the side of the castle again. Her head was down, and her thoughts were racing, so she didn't see Lord Everard until she smacked into his shoulder.

"Oh!" she mumbled. "Please … please forgive me, I—"

"Your Highness," Lord Everard said, and put his hands on her shoulders to steady her. "Are you all right?"

"I have—I have to go," Della said, trying to move past him, but when she looked up, she saw three men of the King's Protection standing in a horizontal line, blocking her path.

"Your Highness," Lord Everard said with a bow, "you must come with me at once."

"I can't now," Della said. "I have business with the queen."

Lord Everard cleared his throat. "By order of King Brockton, you are to be brought to The Caves."

"The Caves?" The Caves were not exactly caves, but underground quarters where prisoners were housed. Della had never seen them personally, as it was not a place fit for a commoner, much less royalty. "I—I don't understand."

An idea dawned on her. "Is Prince Colby there?" Perhaps Brockton had already learned of his treachery and arrested him, and she was being brought to him.

"No, Your Highness. It is my duty to arrest you in the name of the king."

"Arrest me?" Della echoed hollowly, but then as it sank in, she repeated loudly, "Arrest *me*? Are you mad? Step aside."

"We cannot," Lord Everard said. "You are to come to The Caves and await your trial before the king."

"Trial?" Della repeated. "*Trial?* This is preposterous. On what charge?"

Lord Everard drew a rolled parchment from his pocket

and handed it to her. She tore at the seal—King Brockton's official seal—and unrolled it. Her eyes passed over it but through her rage, all she could see were curves in ink. She shook her head to clear it and attempted to steady her shaking hands before reading it again. "Operating a business illegally?" she said. "I don't operate any illegal business."

"I'm sure," Lord Everard said without much conviction behind it, "that this is all a misunderstanding. You can explain it to the king."

"I have nothing to explain!" The three soldiers stepped forward, and Della retreated a few steps of her own. "I will see Queen Neve at once."

"Queen Neve is making preparations to leave the kingdom," Lord Everard said.

What? Della gave a little head shake. "That's impossible. She hasn't left this kingdom in three decades. Where would she go?"

"It's not my place to discuss her activity with you. My only point is that she isn't available to speak to you. Or ... help you."

"I don't need help with anything," Della said. "I've done nothing wrong. My husband, on the other hand—King Brockton needs to know what *he's* been doing."

"You will have a chance to explain." Lord Everard put a hand on her elbow.

"Do not touch me!" Della cried, snatching her arm away. "I am a princess, or have you forgotten your place?"

"I am to escort you to The Caves," he said, his politeness giving way to stern command.

Della considered turning and running, but they would surely catch her quickly and drag her to The Caves. Better to walk beside them willingly, with dignity.

"I will do as you ask," she said finally. "But I need to get my cloak and change my shoes."

"We can't do that," Lord Everard said.

Two soldiers flanked Della and one moved behind her. "Come," Lord Everard said and led the way.

Della held her head high and arranged her face into an expression of calm. The soldiers walked quickly, and Della had to almost run a little to keep up.

She realized she still held the stack of recommendation letters tucked under her arm, and she pressed her arm closer to her side. She slipped her other hand into her pocket and fingered the ruby, the coin, and the tiny eagle. They were cold but reassuring.

NEVE

Neve waited at the edge of The Unfathomed with two hundred Foreverness soldiers and the group of cloaked Goldenstone refugees.

She'd left Biscuit in her cozy stall at the castle. Brockton had given her Monarch, who was strong enough to carry an armored rider and was allegedly solid and sure in an armed conflict. She'd tried to remind herself that this was a trained war steed when a bluebird dipped low in his peripheral vision and he'd bucked like the tiny bird was an attacking falcon.

The armor was clunky and hot and noisy as hell. But when she'd awkwardly clanked out in it to meet her soldiers back at the castle, they'd all fallen to their knees in respect. She needed a hand swinging onto the stallion with all the extra weight on her, but she'd accustomed herself quickly to the feel of it as she led her company out of the castle yard to the spot on which they now stood.

The wolves and Rowan walked in silence, with barely a movement of grass around them. Neve saw the soldiers eyeing the approaching group warily. "Hold," she commanded. "These are friends and allies who will join us to Goldenstone."

Though she could easily see why the army men would be nervous. There were thirty wolves, far larger than ordinary wolves. Rowan walked among them, not leading.

When they got to the edge of the path, Neve swung off

her horse and landed with a clatter. She turned to Rowan, who was snickering.

"You sound like pots and pans," she said. "Though I admire your effort at self-protection."

"I've brought a suit for you as well," Neve said. "I'm afraid the armorer had to go by my measurements, but we are similarly built."

"I appreciate it, but I'll have to think about it. I've no doubt my foxlike reflexes will be thwarted if my arms and legs are constrained by a big tin can."

"Please consider it, for it will be a great regret of my life if you are injured—or killed—in this endeavor."

"If you are left alive to regret anything."

"It would be easier for me," Neve said, "if we kept up an air of confidence here, false as it might be."

Rowan clapped Neve on the shoulder. "I am confident, Queen," she said, shaking Neve's shoulder a bit and rattling the metal encasing her. She looked over Neve's shoulder and widened her eyes at the sight of her two-hundred-strong army. "It seems the king had a change of heart."

Neve nodded.

"It's impressive." She shook Neve's shoulder once more. "Now I am even more confident. If these Goldenstone men aren't afraid when they see us coming, they're fools. You—we—will make things right."

Neve passed her gaze over her company of men, the wolves, and Rowan—the fiercest woman she'd ever met in real life. "You are correct," she said, then to the commander of the soldiers, "Unfurl the flag."

"Flag!" the commander cried out.

The flag bearer in the center of the company raised the staff and shook out the large flag that Dawn had sent to the castle the night before. It was a white flag with a double border, the outside border ebony, the inside one blood red. In the center of the snow-white background was the emblem Neve had envisioned and Dawn brought to life in embroidery: a golden apple split through with a silver broadsword. Blood drops fell from the point of the sword.

Neve's death. And Neve's rebirth.

Rowan squinted at the flag in the low, near-sunset light. "Sends a message. Let's head out."

Neve closed her eyes. "Rhyannon," she intoned. "Rhyannon. Rhyannon."

Rhyannon shimmered into view, fluttering veiny wings holding her aloft. A shower of sparkles landed on the ground beneath her feet. "Your Majesty," she said with a curtsy.

Neve reached up to grab the reins and a handful of Monarch's mane, put one boot in the stirrup, and hopped, to no avail. Her armor seemed to have doubled her own weight. "For heaven's sake," she muttered, before Rowan grabbed her calf and hoisted her into her seat. She was grateful for Rowan withholding a smart remark.

Neve nudged her boots against the horse's sides to move forward, but before he could, she heard, "Wait for ussss."

"Yesss, Queen."

The golden-green snake and the greenish-gold snake wound up Monarch's legs so quickly that the skittish stallion didn't have time to react with more than a quick shuffle. They slithered onto Neve's thighs and both stared into her face.

Rowan drew her dagger but Neve held up a hand.

"Not much exxxcitement around here," the green snake said.

"Ssso we are coming to Goldenssstone," the gold snake said.

"Is this a jest?" Neve said.

"We like you, Queen," the gold snake said. "Perhaps we can assssisssst you."

Neve sighed. "Very well. Your allegiance and your

willingness to sacrifice for my cause is noted."

"We don't know about any caussse," the gold snake said.

"We jussst want sssome fun," the green snake added.

Rhyannon bent to the ground and opened her airy, light cloak, releasing fireflies. The snakes wound back down the horse's legs and slithered across the dirt to disappear into her deep inner pockets.

Neve gazed to her left, east toward The Unfathomed. She couldn't see the shoreline of the Silvering Sea through the foreboding tree line.

Dark as it was, The Unfathomed didn't appear so terrifying anymore. It was a deep, misunderstood place that held nightmares and scary stories in its corners, but in other places, the daylight shone on harsh truths that were far more frightening than anything in the wood.

Neve turned Monarch around so she could look at her people: two hundred soldiers on horseback, a flag-bearer, thirty wolves, a fairy godmother, two snakes, a dozen Goldenstone refugees—two bearing the weight of one large magic mirror—and one woman of legend who once wore a scarlet cloak.

Neve nodded to them all.

She turned Monarch again and clucked to him. He began to march forward, leading the loyal company south and, at long last, carrying home the child who was as red as blood, as white as snow, and as black as ebony.

BRY

"I'm frightened."

Bry rubbed Thomasina's trembling arm through her warm cloak as they approached Eterne Castle. The king would begin hearing petitions at the ten o'clock hour, and Bry had hoped if she and Thomasina had arrived at nine, they'd be able to see Brockton and Neve early, or at least be near the front, but the line was already out the door and extending into the center of the town square. Men, both noble and common alike, were shifting from foot to foot, impatient before the waiting had even officially begun.

"Don't be frightened," Bry said. "Brockton is a good man, and once he meets you and hears your story, he will help you. I am sure of it. And Neve—Neve is the smartest and most learned woman you'll ever hope to meet. Brockton takes her counsel."

Thomasina glanced at Bry. "That is ... surprising."

"And I am here with you. Even if you are bucking tradition—"

"And law."

"And law. But no one will dare say anything to you with the king's sister-in-law at your side." They took their place in line, and Bry winced at the number of men in front of them. "We have a long wait."

Thomasina pressed her lips together and stared at the castle. "I will wait. This is important."

"It is."

"Thank you," Thomasina said, grabbing hold of Bry's arm and squeezing it. "Thank you so much. You are a true friend."

"And you are a brave woman. Don't fret about what you will say to the king. Just speak true, from your heart."

Thomasina took a deep breath. "All right."

Very quickly, they were no longer last in line, but they still didn't move. A few men turned and glared at Thomasina, but after a quick glance at Bry—who'd deliberately chosen golden velvet finery and a thick gold necklace—they bowed slightly and turned back around.

Bry scowled at the backs of their heads.

When the line finally began to move, it was only two steps, then another interminable wait. Thomasina and Bry chatted in low voices, trying to distract themselves, but even the closest of friends ran out of conversational topics eventually. When they did, the sun was very high in the sky. The late-autumn air was chilly, so heat was not a problem, but fatigue soon would be. With the line moving at the pace of an elderly snail, Bry estimated they wouldn't even get inside the castle walls until mid-afternoon.

"Would you like some water?" she asked Thomasina, who nodded gratefully. "I'll fetch some. I won't be but a few moments. Do you need anything else?"

Thomasina shook her head, and Bry patted her shoulder once before stepping out of line. She hurried to the center of town, marveling at how many people were behind them in line. Surely Brockton wouldn't be done until supper or beyond.

It took her about five minutes to hurry to Moss Apothecary, at the edge of the market. "Your Highness!" he cried.

"Peat, could I trouble you for some water?" she asked. "I need to bring it to a friend. She is waiting in line to seek audience with the king."

"She is?" Peat asked, emphasizing slightly the word *she*.

"Yes, she has urgent business, and I encouraged her to do so."

Peat filled a skin with fresh water. "Last time you were here," he said, "we talked about change."

"Well," Bry said. "Maybe it's on the horizon."

"If she is waiting in line," Peat said, "it's already here."

He handed her two skins and two apples. "I wish her luck. And you."

Peat winked and Bry rushed out.

As she walked, she noticed a flurry of movement in the line snaking from the castle—right around the place where Thomasina was. Bry broke into a run, and the commotion got louder as she got closer.

Someone shoved Thomasina, hard. She planted her feet and stayed upright, standing her ground as the men around her shouted at her and mocked her.

Bry dropped the skins and the apples and tried to push her way through the men, but they blocked her way.

"Get out of line!" a man shouted at Thomasina. "You are taking up a space a man deserves."

"You have no right!" another called.

"I have *every* right," Thomasina said, though her voice shook. "My matter is urgent, and I *will* speak to the king."

"The king isn't going to speak to a speck of dirt like you."

"Get out of here!"

She was shoved again.

"Stop!" Bry cried, but everyone ignored her.

One man stood, calmly presiding over the ruckus. He was dressed regally, and his chin was haughty. Bry weaved between flailing limbs to see his face.

Lord Everard, Brockton's chief advisor.

Since the king couldn't see what was happening out here, he occasionally sent an advisor to check on the line and keep order if need be. But Lord Everard wasn't keeping order.

He was smirking.

"I am Her Highness—" Bry began loudly to get his attention, but the men's rising jeers were too loud.

Finally, Lord Everard held up a hand, and the struggling and shouting stopped.

Into the silence, he said, "Remove this woman at once."

The men all began shoving Thomasina and under their collective force, she crashed to the ground. One nobleman grabbed her by her hair, and another grabbed her arm, and they dragged her kicking body through the dirt, away from the line.

The men who had been behind Thomasina closed her space in line.

They dropped her roughly, and as they moved away, Thomasina, frustration overtaking her fear, kicked one of the men's ankles out from under him, and he landed hard on his rear.

His friend grabbed a rock off the ground, stomped over to her, and slammed her in the temple with it. She crumpled, unconscious.

The men laughed while Bry screamed. "How could you?" she cried. "Lord Everard!"

The advisor, either unable or unwilling to hear her, turned his back and walked into the castle.

As the men shuffled back into an orderly line, space was cleared for Bry to run to her friend and drop to the ground beside her. She brushed Thomasina's hair off her face.

Blood. A lot of blood.

"Please! Someone help!" Bry begged.

Suddenly, someone else was at her side. "Giselle," Bry gasped.

"I came to bring you two some food," Giselle said, trying

to loosen the top of Thomasina's dress so she could breathe easier. "What happ—"

A rock shot through the air, hitting Giselle in the back, causing her to gasp. She stood and whirled, then approached the closest laughing man and punched him in the face.

He stumbled back with a surprised cry. Everyone was stunned, which gave her a moment to step back, but that moment wouldn't last.

Bry, still on the ground, shook Thomasina's shoulder. "Wake up, *please*," she said, though she knew it was useless. "We have to get out of here."

The men advanced on Giselle, smiling, menacing.

A light furry brush against Bry's arm.

A swirl of iridescent colors.

"What—what the *hell* is that?"

"Is that a cat?"

The men all stared at Repose and the colors that hypnotically moved under his skin, illuminating him in pink, purple, green.

Bry tugged at Giselle's hem. "Look away," she instructed.

"It's a magic cat," one man slurred before falling to his knees and folding in half, landing face down in the dirt.

Dozens of men—everyone who could see Repose—collapsed to the hard ground, mouths open, in deep sleep.

Repose swished his tail, yawned wide enough to show his sharp little back teeth, and sauntered in the direction of home. Depending how tired the men were when they went under, they would be asleep anywhere from fifteen minutes to eight hours.

"Help me," Bry said to Giselle.

They both half carried, half dragged Thomasina toward the tree line, and took refuge in the shade behind a few very tall trees, out of sight of the line of men. They laid Thomasina in the softness of pine needles.

"Get Peat Moss," Bry said. "I will stay with her."

Giselle ran.

Blood trickled from the large gash on Thomasina's head, and the blood on her face had already dried into crust.

"This is my fault," Bry said. "You wouldn't be here if not for me. They wouldn't have hurt you if not for me. This is my fault. I'm so sorry."

They will all hate you.

No. She couldn't think of that right now. She needed to see to it that Thomasina was all right.

"I'm sorry," she whispered again.

After a few minutes, Peat ran up to them on four little paws and began to immediately pass them over Thomasina's head, moving her hair, probing. His tail vibrated as he assessed.

Giselle, out of breath and holding her side, caught up a few minutes later and dropped Peat's sack beside him. Bry looked at Thomasina's pale face, and when she lifted her gaze again, Giselle was gone.

Peat cleaned Thomasina's face with a cloth and a little jar of water. Then he pulled out a tiny pair of shears and cut the woman's hair short enough to see the wound, still oozing blood. He worked a balm into the wound until the blood stopped flowing. Then she stirred.

"Thomasina!" Bry said, leaning in but trying to stay out of Peat's way. Thomasina groaned, and Peat offered her water to drink. He talked softly to her before she lay her head back down with a sigh.

"Your Highness," Peat said, "I believe she will be fine. Head wounds, even superficial ones, bleed a lot so it's frightening, but it's not deep. She may be confused with headaches for a few days, maybe some dizziness, but she will be all right."

Peat reached into the sack again, brought out a folded red cloth, and unwrapped it.

A needle.

He took it out and held it up. The evil glint of it had Bry pushing her heels into the dirt and scrambling away from him.

Peat threaded it. "I do need help. Bry, you will need to sew her wound." He wiggled his little claws. "Too small for a needle this size."

Thomasina moaned.

"I need to lull her back to sleep for a bit first," Peat said, pulling out a potion and dripping it between Thomasina's lips. "Bry?" He held the needle out.

All sound stopped, all time stopped. Bry's vision narrowed into a little cave, with the needle at the dead end. She shook her head, unable to draw words from her throat.

"Princess Bry," Peat said softly. "I need you to sew Thomasina. It's nasty to consider, I know, and I regret asking you, but you're the only one here who can. If you can forget it's skin and think of it as needlework—"

"I don't do needlework," Bry whispered. "I don't touch needles or spindles. The last one I touched—"

Peat's eyes glowed with understanding.

"If I touch that, I might—we might—"

"I understand." Peat patted her knee. "Perhaps that might happen. It's an unknown. The known is that if we don't close her wound, she could lose more blood and develop an infection. Right now, she won't die from this injury. But if we don't stitch this immediately—we know there is a chance she might."

Bry's mind reeled.

Maybe she did want to go to sleep, anyway. It was only a matter of time. As soon as word got around about what happened here, how she'd gotten Thomasina harmed in the name of fruitless rebellion, she would have no friends left.

She'd refused to speak to Lucan for days, and she'd not read several notes he'd left for her, but once he learned of this, he would finally be fully angry with her. Brockton would be angry when he learned of the scene she caused, and Neve might be as well. When the wives of the noblemen in line heard about this, they would not be happy with her, either. Thea and Dawn weren't angry with her at the moment, but they were both well set in their lives and didn't need her.

What if she just—left? In another century, she'd be a fresh flower, no more problems.

But—if she fell asleep again for one hundred years, she'd take Thomasina with her. And Peat. Perhaps even everyone in line, as they were still in close proximity. When they all awoke, they would be angry at her, just like at Sylvan Castle. It would happen all over again. But this time, she'd have no Lucan to take her away to a better place.

She could walk away now, make sure she didn't touch a needle for the rest of her life, and die naturally.

But she remembered Thomasina, trembling as she waited in line, trying so hard to push through her fear to ask for the king's help. At Bry's encouragement.

Bry couldn't walk away. She'd do the right thing, and let fate decide.

Bry swallowed hard. "I don't know how to sew," she said. "You'll need to tell me—"

"I will," Peat said. "I've already threaded the needle for you."

Peat and Bry leaned over Thomasina, Peat talking Bry gently through what she'd need to do. When Peat handed her the needle, her hands were sure.

Let fate decide.

She pushed the needle through the skin, and out the other side. The knot at the end of the catgut held steady, and she began to count the stitches as she got through each. One, two, three—

She gasped at the pinch on the pad of her forefinger.

She closed her eyes.

The numbness, the paralysis, the unconsciousness—it would all come next. "I'm sorry, Lucan," she whispered, waiting to fall onto the grass.

The cold wind bit the tip of her nose, and her nose ran a bit at the chill. She felt Peat's little paw on her forearm.

Bry opened her eyes. She looked at the tiny drop of her own blood on her finger. She tilted her head up to the sun through the bare branches and closed her eyes against its brightness.

Then she opened her eyes again.

She was still here.

Peat smeared a dollop of sweet-smelling paste on her finger and nodded at her hands to continue. She bent over Thomasina's head.

Four, five, six ...

She finished quickly and gave the needle back to Peat.

Then she stood as he examined the wound. A roaring began in her ears, increasing in volume. She thought she heard Peat say, "Excellent work," but she wasn't certain.

She moved as if sleepwalking to the tree line.

"Your Highness?" Peat called in a distant part of her mind. "Are you all right?"

Her vision closed into a dark tunnel, and she saw nothing but her castle in the distance. She focused on the window of her bedchamber as she walked toward it.

They will all hate you.
You got their hopes up.
You got someone hurt.
You caused trouble.

In a daze, she entered her bedchamber. Repose, reclining on her bed, lifted his head and meowed. She drew the curtains, blacking out the sun. Blacking out Foreverness.

She got under the blankets in her gown and closed her eyes.

Soon enough, it would be known in every corner of Foreverness that Bry was a troublemaker, an instigator, an unlovable woman. She would sleep through it all, though no sleep would be long enough to give her the strength to face the hatred that was sure to follow.

DELLA

ella hated sitting on the floor.

Hours before Colby had arrived with her lost glass shoe, she'd been sitting on the stone floor in front of the fireplace, brushing ashes from the crevice where the wall met the floor.

Since that day more than thirty years ago, she'd made it her business to rest her rear on only velvet, satin, polished wood.

Except when she helped Molle clean a fireplace.

And now.

Now she sat on the cold, packed-dirt floor of her quarters in The Caves. Quarters. Della scoffed at the word Lord Everard had used when he'd escorted her in here. Cell was more like it. There was a shapeless and lumpy bed pallet and a chamber pot in the corner. She'd refrained from using the chamber pot for as long as possible, but after many long hours, she was forced to relent. At least she had privacy and quiet; when she'd been shown to this room, she'd noticed she had no neighbors. The criminals that occupied The Caves were apparently kept elsewhere, far away from their princess.

Della shuddered to think who might be sharing The Caves with her: murderers, traitors, common thieves.

Colby should be sitting among those thieves.

After a time, with nothing but her thoughts to distract her, she'd wondered how many of the others here might be like her—innocent, with no idea how they ended up here.

Operating an illegal business? How could that be?

She could see how perhaps it might be illegal for a princess, or any member of the royal family, to profit in any way from a business. She knew Dawn didn't take payment for designing and sewing gowns and other finery. She did it simply for the love of her craft.

Della hadn't intended to keep any gold for herself, of course. It wasn't about profit. What need did she have for more money? This had been about improving the working conditions of the servants in Foreverness. Yes, she did have gold left over, but she had been considering ways to use that gold to help others. She just hadn't gotten around to it yet, as busy as the project was keeping her. But maybe she was supposed to inform the Crown of her business from the start. How was she supposed to know this? She'd never had a business before.

It was an honest mistake. Surely it wasn't a mistake that justified her having to sleep on a pig's bed of straw and be trapped in a room with a pot full of her own piss.

There was one tiny window she could gaze out of if she so desired, but as the window afforded her a perfect view of *her* castle, where she should be sitting in comfort right now, she opted not to look out.

Della drew up her knees to her chest, hugged her arms around them, and dropped her chin on her arms. This was undignified. Uncivilized.

She heard footsteps at the wooden door but didn't rise. The first few times it happened, two days ago, she'd scrambled to her feet, hoping that Brockton or Neve had come to take care of everything. But every time, it was just someone bearing a tray of food that Della wouldn't feed to a dog as a proper meal. She no longer paid the door any attention.

Colby had the gall to be bitter with her throughout their entire marriage for creating one silly, short-lived illusion that gave a destitute girl a beautiful gown and one-of-a-kind slippers. Yet no one seemed at all concerned that this entire kingdom was one big illusion, spun to keep everyone in their place.

Foreverness was a beautiful package, covered in ribbons and lavender sprigs that hid a box full of mud. Bry knew it—that was why she broke her back to secure everyone's fickle love. And Neve knew it—where *was* Neve?

But even now, Della tried to hold on to the gossamer threads that held this storybook land together. Her illusion didn't end at midnight all those years ago. Rhyannon's part had expired, but Della had picked it up and prolonged it—with her thieving husband and her gilded bed and her glittering shoe collection—for more than thirty years.

Della was Foreverness's beautiful package.

She touched the crown on her head. She was wearing it when arrested and didn't plan to take it off until she was safe at home.

It was—

Hers?

Was it hers?

When nothing else really was?

She clutched her hair with both hands. She'd lectured a roomful of noblewomen about women all being the same despite their social and financial status, yet she kept this crown on her head for most of her life because she was certain she deserved it.

Didn't Molle work hard enough to deserve it? Or Amee, or any of the other maids?

Guilt edged into Della's brain and pushed toward her heart.

No. She would not feel guilty. Royalty was a fact of this kingdom. There were people destined to wear crowns.

But perhaps those who wore crowns didn't need to be adored or to accept untold riches and bows and curtsies. Perhaps that wasn't their purpose.

The idea made Della a little woozy, but she followed the thought to see where it led.

King Hopkin had expected all his sons and daughters-in-law to set an example. Maybe a princess was meant to set a different example than one of an impossible dream and the worship of perfection.

Though Della had enjoyed it so.

Perhaps the example was not in the existing, but in the doing.

In the serving. In the leading.

Della abruptly stood and looked around the dingy quarters. This wouldn't do any longer.

None of it.

"Guard!" Della called.

The wooden door opened swiftly.

"What is your name?" Della asked, standing.

"M—my name?" the guard asked, surprised.

"Yes."

"Ralph, er, Your Highness."

"Ralph, I am Della Charming."

He looked taken aback. "I—I know."

"I am pleased to make your acquaintance. Can I trouble you to bring me a few items, at your convenience?"

He hesitated. "Er, I think so."

"I'd like a large bucket of warm water and a bit of soapwort. Maybe a little marjoram, if you can find it."

"For—for what?"

"I am going to wash my bedding, of course." She rolled up her sleeves. "I'd also like some rags. Might as well clean this window while I'm at it."

He glanced at the crown on her head, then back at her face. "Your Highness?"

"Well, I don't know how long I'm going to be here, so I might as well freshen things up. And if I'm freed today, by chance, then the bedding will be clean for the next ... er, guest."

Ralph opened the door to leave.

"Ralph, do you have a family?"

He turned back. "Yes, Your Highness. I have a wife and three girls."

"You live with four women? You lucky and poor soul."

He chuckled.

"When you return, please tell me about your girls. I'd love to hear."

"I will," he said, pleased.

Before he'd closed the door all the way, Della was already stripping the bed.

NEVE

Neve squeezed the reins with her fingers to bring Monarch to a halt. She wasn't sure of the exact boundary line, so she wasn't one-hundred-percent certain when they'd crossed into Goldenstone, but they were here.

The company leader called all soldiers to a halt, and they stood quietly behind their queen, awaiting word. Horse tails swished flies away. Wolves panted softly. The cold wind snapped the banner crisply above them.

Green and brown hills rolled before them, and Castille Keep stood in the distance, on the highest hill.

The breath caught in Neve's throat.

What she remembered of her home had always seemed more like hazy recollections of old dreams than true-life memories. To see it before her now was disconcerting.

And terrifying.

She squashed down the fear by reminding herself that the castle walls no longer protected Fina. The woman who'd killed her was long dead herself, as was the father who'd denied his only child and heir.

Inside that castle was Neve's old playroom, where she spent hours caring for toy animals in cradles and reading storybooks of happily ever after.

Behind that castle had been a fragrant rose garden, filled with beautiful bees and butterflies.

At the top of that castle was the picture window where,

she had been told, her mother had gazed at the snow, wishing for a perfect daughter.

Neve had herself gazed at the snow from that window years after her mother had passed, hoping to somehow see her.

She heard a clink on her armor. Rowan, now standing beside Monarch, had just flicked her fingers against Neve's leg. Neve couldn't feel Rowan's fingers. Neither could she feel her own rear end very well, after a two-day ride dressed as she was.

"Are you all right?" Rowan asked.

Rowan was wearing her own armor now, having been helped into it by one of the soldiers' squires this morning. She somehow managed to look as if she'd worn armor daily for years.

"Yes," Neve said. "I'm gathering my thoughts."

"Do you need help?"

"No." Neve looked at the castle again. "It's ..." She trailed off, not sure what else to say.

"There will be plenty of time another day for reminiscing and remembering," Rowan said. "But for now, if you don't mind some advice, I recommend locking your emotions in a box. Right now, that castle is nothing more than your objective. It belongs to you, and it's time to evict all the men currently sitting in there."

"You are right, of course."

"Those men, they will try to trick you. They will know this is emotional for you, and they will assume that as a woman, you will act on emotion."

"I'm the rightful heir," Neve said. "It's the law of the land."

"Yes. So you're not going to let them get the upper hand."

Neve kept her eyes on the castle. "Let's go."

She nudged Monarch to walk on. Rowan whistled loudly, and the commander shouted to the company behind them.

* * *

For a little while, it felt like nothing more than a chilly afternoon stroll through the idyllic countryside (with more than two hundred of Neve's closest friends). The not-very-warm sun dappled the pine-needle path before them, and Monarch danced uneasily at dried leaves swirling in the wind at his hooves.

Everything seemed peaceful, quiet. Normal.

They passed a small thatched-roof home, then after a while, another. But the houses didn't look right. They looked—abandoned. Broken wood creaked and dangled, pig troughs were dry, and fences were splintered. There wasn't a cow or a chicken or a person anywhere.

The distance between homes grew shorter as Neve led her company toward the center of town. There were a few people, men with torn shirts and women with torn dresses, bare feet, and gnarled hair. People—children—were shivering under ripped blankets against the chill, leaning against one another, as if none of them had enough life to stand upright.

There was no bustle of commerce, no carts being pulled, no shouts from a nonexistent market. Nothing was happening at all. These people were only existing hour to hour.

Some people gazed at the company of soldiers wearily, as if they saw soldiers every day. Some people recoiled in fear. One man lurched toward Monarch and Neve, but Rowan was between them in a flash, her knife drawn.

"Easy," Neve murmured to Rowan. "He's an old man, and unarmed."

Rowan retreated a step but didn't take her eyes off the man.

"I need food," the man said. "You all look fed. Give me somethin'. Give us somethin'."

Before Neve could answer he said, "I thought not! Here

to plunder, are ya?" He cackled. "Good luck to ya. Ya won't find a drop of ale or a rotten peach for miles. It's all there." He gestured at Castille Keep, now about a half-mile away.

"Then that's where I'll have to go," Neve said evenly.

The old man came closer. Neve shook her head ever so slightly at Rowan, who followed his every move.

"Who are you?" the man asked. "You—who are you?"

Neve waited another measured moment.

Suddenly the man's rheumy eyes widened, then softened, then filled with tears. "Sweet baby Jesus. You're the little princess. Princess Neve."

He shook his head and kept shaking it. "My wife always said it was truly you in Foreverness. I thought so too, but over the last few years, I thought perhaps not. For Goldenstone's child would not abandon us in our time of need."

"I didn't know," Neve said. "I'm so sorry. I'm here now."

"Princess." He fell to his knees, weeping.

Another woman, not much older than Neve, rushed over to him as quickly as she could with a limp, and put her arm around him. "Father ..."

"It's the princess," he gasped between sobs, and the woman looked up into Neve's eyes.

"It *is* you," she said. "I remember you. I played with you once, one of those times the children in the town were allowed to come to the castle grounds. It might have been Easter, springtime. We were playing with a little golden ball. You always threw to a girl instead of a boy. You laughed when you threw it to me, and it made me laugh, too. Time hasn't changed your face much from the one I remember."

She squeezed her father tighter. "None of us believed you were dead. We knew it had to be you. But you didn't want to come home." She looked around them. "Nothing to come home to anymore."

Suddenly, she dipped into an awkward half-curtsy. "Apologies. Your Majesty."

Cecilia, of the Goldenstone refugees, came forward carrying a bushel of oranges and several waterskins. She gave them to the man and his daughter, and called to the nearby people, "It's all right. Come. A gift from your queen."

Rowan sheathed her knife and raised her brow at Cecilia's brash public statement. Then Cecilia turned and caught Rowan's gaze.

The smell of snow was in the air, but Neve felt the sudden heat exchanged in the eyes of the two women. Neve's mouth quirked into a quick smile.

She searched the small group and spied a boy of about fourteen. "Boy," Neve said, beckoning him. "Do you feel strong and well enough to make haste to Castille Keep?"

The boy looked up the hill, then back at Neve. "I do."

Neve took a gold coin from a pouch on Monarch's saddle and put it in the boy's hand. His eyes widened.

"Go now," she said. "Tell them Queen Neve of Foreverness requests King Gawain's audience. I will meet him outside."

"Outside?" the boy asked. "Forgive me, but the king and his council ... well, they never leave their walls."

"Today they must. If they wish to speak to me. And please impart to them that they *do* wish to speak to me."

The boy grinned. "I shall run!"

"Wait," Neve said. "If they invite you in for food or any other reward in kind, just thank them politely and run back to me. We will take care of you." It wouldn't do for King Gawain's men to punish the boy.

The boy ran off, and Rowan materialized at Neve's right side. "Should we have sent a soldier?"

Neve said, "A young boy appears less a threat than an armed messenger."

"Your Majesty," a young man called. "Have you come to claim your place?"

"Spread the word I am here," Neve said, "and that I am taking audience with Gawain outside the castle shortly."

Neve preferred a public meeting, to let the people of Goldenstone witness with their own eyes the presence of the rightful heir to the throne with her flag, her men, and her formidable wolves. She hoped it would rally support, though the manner in which she'd been received by this small group of people suggested they would support anyone who wasn't in Gawain's court. Anyone would be better than what they'd suffered the last three years.

"Doggy!" A little girl pushed between the knees of the adults and broke through to the front, rushing to one of the giant wolves, apparently oblivious to its massive jaw.

The wolf stepped slowly, menacingly, toward the townspeople. He bared his teeth and growled low. But before the little girl's mother could stop her, she reached out a tiny hand and touched his red snout. "Doggy." She giggled and squeezed her fingers into his soft fur.

The wolf paused.

Everyone held their horrified breath.

The wolf collapsed onto his back and rolled side to side in happiness. The little girl fell on him and buried her face in its fur. "My doggy! What *big* eyes you have!"

Everyone sighed in relief, except for Rowan, who looked disgusted. "Seriously, Leofwine?"

Leofwine rumbled happily and licked the girl's arm.

"Not the message we're trying to send," Rowan muttered, then looked into the distance. "Speaking of messages, it appears our boy has just delivered ours."

The large front doors of the castle were open now, and the boy was running back.

"How did you fare, boy?" Neve asked when he returned, panting. Rowan passed him a waterskin. He gulped twice and wiped his mouth with his ragged sleeve.

"It was a man," he finally said. "He just thanked me and closed the door."

Neve's heart thumped in her ears. It was time.

* * *

They all stood outside, silent and at attention, for quite a while. Even Monarch was still and calm underneath Neve. She hadn't thought through what she'd do if Gawain's council refused to see her, but she didn't like her few options.

Fortunately, the decision was made for her as an entourage of soldiers circled around the castle from the back. Neve did a headcount estimate—about four hundred. Of course, they'd want to appear more formidable than her for their first meeting, and the presence of twice as many soldiers helped them to do that. When the men made it to the front of the castle, the large double doors opened, and Neve's cousin Gawain rode out on a finely turned-out chestnut stallion. He sat well on the horse, regally, despite his age. His short cap of hair was as black as Neve's, though without her gray strands.

Neve tried not to smile. Gawain wasn't her enemy; he was a puppet of his council. She couldn't help feeling some kinship with him, no matter what his demeanor with her would be.

Behind him, under a black flag with gold stars, rode the five men of his council. Three were older men, two perhaps in their late sixties, and one even older. The other two men were younger than Neve, in their mid-thirties—perhaps sons of two older men of Fina's original council.

Neve squinted and searched her memory, but she couldn't place the faces of the older men. It made sense: She was twelve when she'd been taken away, too young for any real interest in the political players at court.

Too young to die. Too young to be forsaken by her father.

They will know this is emotional for you. Rowan had been right. Neve needed to lock the past in a box and concentrate on the present.

And in the present, she was queen.

Gawain stopped in front of her. Three of his councilmen flanked his right, the other two his left. The soldiers fell into many lines behind them.

"Your Majesty," Gawain said, tucking his chin for a moment.

"Your Majesty," Neve said back, nodding her acknowledgment as well. "And cousin."

Gawain seemed to want to smile, then he seemed to think twice about it. "My council will speak to you. When I am eighteen—"

"When you are eighteen," Neve said, "we shall have tea together and chat like old friends."

Gawain urged his horse to walk backward several steps, and the young king's council closed in protectively in front of him. The men, like Gawain, wore outfits of rich dark velvet and luxurious fur capes and collars. They were outfits of leisure that suggested they did nothing but sit by the fire and—judging by the difference in their sizes from that of the people in the town—eat more than their fill daily.

"Your Majesty," each said in turn before supplying his name: the young lords Cassian and Brian, and the older lords Justus, Morcant, and Novel.

Neve met the eyes of each, in turn. "My lords. You address me in a manner that suggests you recognize my sovereignty."

"That we do," Lord Brian said. "You are wed to King Brockton of Foreverness, so you are the queen of that realm.

And here, you will be treated as any visiting sovereign from another land."

"So you recognize me as queen," Neve said. "But I have heard that you do not believe I am Neve, daughter of King Eustace."

"You do look very much like—" Lord Novel, the oldest of them, began before Lord Cassian cut him off.

"Your weak eyesight can't tell an emerald from a four-leafed clover," Lord Cassian said. "If your horse didn't know to follow ours, you'd still be in the castle."

Neve was startled at the insolence shown the older man, but Lord Novel only chuckled. "'Tis true," he said. "I remember little Neve in my mind, clear as a sunny day. But my eyes can't distinguish fine facial features any longer."

Lord Justus inclined his head toward the older man but kept his eyes on Neve. "My eyesight is still as sharp as a cat's, and I assure you I'd know Princess Neve of Goldenstone." He didn't go so far as to accuse Neve of being an imposter in as many words, but the implication was strong.

"I am Neve of Goldenstone," Neve said. "I have proof of my identity, and I am here to claim my throne from my cousin Gawain. I am the rightful heir."

"The king named his young cousin Gawain to the throne before he died," Lord Cassian said, "because he had no living heirs."

"He knew I was alive," Neve said. "Foreverness sent word that I'd been found and went there to live and to marry."

"He had no proof," Lord Cassian said.

"He never sought proof," Neve said. "If he'd traveled two days, he'd have been able to see from forty paces that I was his daughter. He chose not to."

Lord Cassian opened his mouth to speak, and Neve added, "No doubt discouraged by Queen Fina and her council."

Lord Justus cleared his throat loudly, but it turned into a cough. Everyone waited for him to cease, and he then said, "I was on that council myself, as were Morcant and Novel. We don't appreciate your insinuation—"

"Did I insinuate?" Neve asked. "Forgive me. I meant to say outright that your council, my father the king, and my stepmother the queen lied to the kingdom for more than thirty years. Until today."

"Why would we do that?" Lord Brian asked with a smirk.

"Father did it out of incomprehensible love for—and understandable fear of—my stepmother. Fina did it because she couldn't bear to be the second most beautiful woman in the land. And all of you did it because she lifted her loyal men to power, and you knew that when she and my father were gone, you could rule for years until this child comes of age. I do wonder what your plan is for when he does, because I know you have a plan."

"What?" Gawain squeaked from behind his council. "What? What does she mean?"

The council ignored him.

Neve seized the opportunity of their silence to continue. "King Brockton sends word that he recognizes me as queen of Goldenstone and recognizes my right to the throne here."

"King Brockton would do well to keep to his own affairs, the way his father did," Lord Morcant said.

"A council of a kingdom such as what I've seen so far would do well to not give advice," Neve said. "I've heard of the deplorable conditions here in Goldenstone. I admit that though I believed it, I didn't want to. But now that I've ridden past the abandoned homesteads and met the starving souls in the town—what's left of the town—I see that I have much work to do to restore Goldenstone to the glory I remember well."

"It—it does look like the princess," Lord Novel said to no one in particular. "I remember—"

"An enchantment would be easy," Lord Brian said to the old man.

"Where have you been?" Lord Novel continued as if he hadn't heard the younger councilor. "All these years? Why didn't you return?"

"My stepmother assassinated me, and my father, knowing I was resurrected, still chose to deny me," Neve said. No emotion. "It was clear I wasn't wanted here. He died only three years ago, and by then—I have a grand life in Foreverness. I had no reason to return until it came to my attention that this council is tormenting its people and crushing this kingdom to dust."

"We should—" Lord Novel began.

Lord Brian sharply cut the old man off. "You are being deceived. Princess Neve is long dead. Any sorceress worth the name could put Neve's face on a common whore in a fancy dress and call her royalty."

Neve heard the slide of metal, and Rowan walked slowly toward the men, flanked by the two largest wolves. "I know you did not just call the queen a whore," she said, her voice low, turning the knife idly in her hand. "It would be a sad end for you if your last word uttered was a disrespectful one."

Both wolves growled.

Lord Brian's horse reared, dumping the man onto the cold hard dirt and zigzagging away. A page ran after the horse. Lord Brian pushed himself off the ground with some effort. "You dare to ride in here," he said to Neve, "wearing armor and bearing a flag, threatening us with your small army and a pack of grimy dogs, and you expect us to roll over in deference?"

"No," Neve said evenly. "But I do expect that as men of courage and intellect, you should be unafraid of and willing to consider my proof that I am who I say I am. When facts are introduced, a conflict is no longer merely a matter of differing opinions."

She lifted her hand, and two soldiers brought out the heavy oval draped in velvet. One of them yanked the cover and it fell to the ground. The two men struggled to lift the glass upright. Neve hadn't realized how heavy the heirloom gilded frame was.

She shifted her gaze back to the council. Lord Morcant's eyes widened. Lord Justus's jaw went a bit slack. Lord Novel leaned forward in the saddle to get a better view. The two younger men watched without the same recognition, but with fascination.

The black mirror swirled with pink and yellow smoke.

"Several of you remember this mirror," she said. "You know it was Fina's, and you know its most remarkable enchanted quality—it can't lie."

"A fake," Lord Cassian said.

"The recognition on the faces of your fellow councilmen would speak otherwise," Neve said. "This mirror knew Fina, it knows you, and it knows me. It is all knowing. When I was a child and in hiding from Fina's death sentence, it told Fina I was alive, though it didn't want to expose me. It has an enchantment of truth."

Neve looked at the dark mirror. "It shall bear my witness now. Ask it if I am Princess Neve. Ask it about Fina. Ask it whatever you may."

The mirror shimmered. "May I tell you who is the fairest of them all?" it boomed. "Or ... anything else?"

Neve smiled.

Lord Morcant kicked his horse hard with both heels. Startled, the horse bolted at the two soldiers bearing the mirror.

Rowan ran toward the two men to help, but she was too far. The soldiers, not wanting to be crushed, instinctively jumped out of the path of the wild animal, but one ran left and one ran right, releasing their hold and letting the heavy, fragile mirror fall.

"Queen—" the mirror gasped before it smashed to the ground.

The black glass shattered into sparkling golden dust. Hundreds held their breath as the particles hung suspended, tinkling in the air before raining down on the dented frame and disintegrating into the dirt and grass.

Lord Morcant quickly controlled his frightened steed and trotted back to the rest of the smirking council.

Neve's teeth chattered. Her chest shook. She felt fire rise in her eyes and cloud her vision with angry smoke.

They'd destroyed her proof.

They'd devastated her legacy.

They'd killed her friend.

Guilt wracked her shoulders, her fingers, her stomach. In her fear, she'd ignored the mirror for so long, when all it had wanted was to serve her. Play cards with her. Chat with her. Enjoy her company. Be her loyal friend.

"That's an unfortunate mess," Lord Justus said. "But it seemed fate has intervened."

"Fate in the form of this dusty old bastard," Rowan said, gesturing at Lord Morcant with her knife. She looked at Neve and waited.

They all looked at Neve and waited.

Several townspeople began to weep. Neve wanted to jump off her horse, crawl to them, and sob with them.

What would she do now?

All this kingdom's people—in their pain—were counting on her. She didn't have enough men to wage a battle, but she'd been hoping that with the mirror, she wouldn't have to.

After some murmuring among the councilmen, Lord Cassian spoke. "We don't have any conflict with Foreverness, and you are queen there. Out of respect for your husband, we will overlook this small incident and allow you to live."

He squinted at the sky. "Dusk is falling. You may camp tonight within Goldenstone's borders—again, without threat or worry. But if you are seen in Goldenstone tomorrow past dawn, we will consider it a declaration of war, and we will kill every one of you. Am I clear, Your Majesty?"

Neve cleared her throat and willed her voice to emerge without tremor. "I ask that you let those people gathered here go home without punishment. They have shown no allegiance to me or any rebellion against the Crown by their mere presence—only curiosity."

"You are a kind woman," Lord Brian said with a mocking smile, "and we grant that request. Go home!" he shouted to the crowd. "On order of King Gawain!"

Some people ran, others shuffled, many looking over their shoulders at Neve.

Though she wasn't a fraud, in that moment, she felt like one.

The five councilmen galloped away along the edge of the army, then back toward the castle. After giving his cousin Neve a long, puzzled look, young Gawain followed them, and the army retreated, their black-and-gold flag flapping.

Rowan moved to Neve's side, taking hold of Monarch's reins. "What is your plan?"

Neve couldn't look at her. She couldn't look at any of the people and beasts who had faithfully accompanied her to this moment. She stared straight ahead at the castle she'd played in as an innocent and ignorant child. The cold air kept her eyes dry.

After a few moments, Rowan realized she wouldn't get an answer. She moved behind Monarch and spoke in a low voice to the commander, who then shouted to his men, "We will ride a mile back and make camp."

Neve heard so many hooves, paws, footsteps retreating behind her, and after a moment, she clucked to Monarch and followed.

Rowan had asked the plan, but Neve was sure the woman of the wolves already knew what the plan would be. Neve was left with only one choice, after all.

It wasn't indecision that had kept her from answering the question.

It was fear.

BRY

"Your Highness!"

"Princess Bry!"

The words were soft at first, spiraling into her subconscious, but as Bry began to emerge from the warm embrace of the dark, they got a bit louder and a bit louder.

"Princess Bry!"

"Are you there, Your Highness?"

Bry sat upright quickly, earning her a reproachful feline glare. She patted Repose's head and rushed to the window, pulling aside the heavy drapes. It was a bright morning; she'd slept through the rest of the day yesterday, and all night, waking only to change out of her uncomfortable gown into her nightclothes.

Giselle was under her window, with Maribel, Kathryn, and Anne. They all waved and gestured at her to—come down?

"Princess," Maribel said. "Can you come out?"

Kathryn looked over her shoulder. "The guards are going to chase us away."

Bry opened the long vertical glass window. "Go to the Aura Tree," she said. "I'll meet you there."

They all hurried away, just as Bry heard a guard call, "You! Get away from there!"

Bry pulled on her wool cloak over her nightgown and pushed her feet into boots. She clattered down the stairs, ignoring the confused looks of her staff as she ran out the door and toward the Aura Tree.

As she ran, she panicked. They were going to tell her how awful she was, how she'd gotten their hopes up for nothing, and gotten Thomasina hurt. They were right, and she deserved it, and she would withstand the terrible words as penance. She would offer to do anything else to make up for the harm she caused, but she wasn't sure what she could—

The Aura Tree was trembling with red rage. Its leaves were ablaze, smoking and crackling. Its trunk burned from within, glowing orange. The ground over its roots was black, sending sizzling embers into the air.

The four women standing beneath the tree were feeding its anger. When Bry slowed and approached them, the tree cooled slightly, the red and orange fading somewhat as her fear entered the mix.

"Your Highness—" Anne began.

"Bry," she corrected quietly.

"I cannot contain my rage!" Mirabel said, slamming her foot to the ground and balling up her fists. "They hurt Thomasina!"

"I know," Bry said.

"I've never been so angry in my life," Kathryn said. "Those men dared to hurt her because, what? She wanted to talk to the king? Just like they did?"

"I told them what happened. It was a disgraceful display," Giselle said.

They all stared at Bry, waiting.

As she stammered a bit, searching for the correct apology wording, Giselle said, "What will we do?"

They waited again, and Bry said, "What will ... we do?"

Giselle cocked her head as if suspicious that Bry had lost her mind. "Yes, what will we do? They can't get away with this. With silencing Thomasina at all, much less by using violence to do it."

"I hate them," Kathryn said. "If I could sic a pack of dogs on them, I would."

"We have to do something, Bry," Anne said. "We were hoping you had a plan."

"You were hoping I—wait a moment. You're angry at the men?" Bry managed to ask.

"The men, the king, the chief advisor, all of them," Giselle said.

"You're—you're not angry at me?"

The four women exchanged looks. "Whatever *for?*" Kathryn asked.

"For—for encouraging Thomasina to request audience with the king."

"How in any kingdom on Earth is this your fault?" Giselle asked. "She should have been allowed to wait her turn and request the king's help. He could have heard her, or he could have dismissed her, and she would have had to make another plan of action. In no way should anyone have hurt her. Or you or me, and believe me, we were next, if not for an enchanted cat."

"If anything," Anne said, "this proved our point even more, that the laws are hurting women, and we have no voice."

"But ... you left," Bry said slowly to Giselle. "When Peat was—"

"Yes, I went to get my son and husband so they could help Thomasina to my home. She's recovering there."

Bry's understanding "oh" didn't quite leave her open mouth.

She lifted her hand and looked at the finger she'd pricked with the needle. The tiny dot of blood was gone. Fate had spared her.

Would fate have spared her if it had meant for her to drop back into a sleep of her own making?

Finally, she spoke. "A spell was cast on me by an

uninvited guest to my birth celebration. Did you know," she added with a shake of her head, "this woman, a sorceress, was uninvited merely because there had been not enough place settings, and so someone had to be left off the guest list? I've never, ever been without extra place settings since."

The women shook their heads in sympathy.

"My entire adult life," Bry went on, "I've been afraid to anger or annoy or inconvenience anyone by saying *no* to anything. I never spoke my mind, for fear it would cause them to be displeased with me. I silenced myself. That's what women do, don't we? We speak, and when we're told enough times that what we say doesn't matter, or isn't meaningful, or isn't important, we stop speaking. Meanwhile, dragons are slain, battles are fought, and fortunes are found, all without us."

Bry pulled the pins out of her hair and threw them to the ground, an offering to the Aura Tree. Her hair tumbled down her shoulders.

"They can silence one of us," she said through her teeth. "But they can't silence us all if we speak together, with one voice. We will *demand* an audience with the king. We will *demand* to be heard. All of us!"

She didn't realize she was shouting until the others shouted their own agreement.

"Go," she said. "Get your sisters, your daughters, your mothers, your friends and neighbors. Bring them to Eterne Castle tomorrow morning. Tell them it's time for them to speak. And it's time for the king to hear."

The women cheered.

The Aura Tree spread its branches wide, as if embracing the sky. The sky descended into the tree, filling it with its eternal blue as a halo of gold encircled the tops of its highest leaves.

NEVE

In her small tent, Neve folded her legs under her in her bedroll, relieved at the freedom of movement that the armor had restricted. Even here, alone, she refused to cry. No one could see her, but she was afraid that if she gave in to tears, she wouldn't be able to stop. She had men, wolves, friends, and a kingdom to protect, and she needed to keep her mind rational and calm despite the roiling emotions in her heart.

Grief over losing the mirror, her friend.

Pain over having to fight Fina, whose evil influence outlived her.

Pity and sympathy for the people of Goldenstone, suffering at the hands of cruel usurpers.

Anger at—everything. Including herself, for waiting until she was fifty to come back here and do the right thing.

Fifty?

Neve let her head fall back and looked up at the top of the tent. Fifty. Tomorrow was her birthday.

The sound of a throat clearing stole her attention. "Neve," Rowan called softly. "Can I come in?"

"Yes," Neve said, and Rowan ducked under the flap and entered. She sprawled onto the ground beside Neve, her legs, encased in britches, spread casually like a man's.

Neve almost had to smile at Rowan's continuing pattern

of ignoring decorum. Even now, even after she'd threat-ened one of the councilmen for insulting Neve, she wouldn't address Neve as a royal. She'd told Neve when they met that she bowed to character, not titles.

But that smile faded quickly as fear clawed at her soul. Neve was about to repay Rowan's strength and resolve with death. Everyone here would be outnumbered tomorrow.

Neve would die tomorrow.

"I've talked with the commander," Rowan said, "and with the wolves and the Goldenstone fugitives. Everyone is willing to fight tomorrow. They all love you."

"Love," Neve said. "The consequence of love shouldn't be certain death."

"It's not just love. They can all see what Goldenstone has become. They want to do the right thing. The right thing isn't running from this."

"I'd love to retreat. And return with Foreverness's full army behind me. But—"

She didn't say Brockton's name, and Rowan didn't finish her sentence.

"I'll speak to the commander now," Neve said, "and we can spend some time planning strategy."

"Can the fairy help us on defense?"

"We can't fight through a protection spell. We can only hold our ground, and only for so long. The protection was merely for a safe retreat." Neve shook her head. "I keep thinking, what if we temporarily retreated? What are our options if we gave up and came back at a later date?"

So we could live.

"They'd attack us at the border if we came back," Rowan said. "It would be immediate war. They wouldn't be willing to have a second conversation with us."

"And we wouldn't have anything additional to come back

with," Neve said. "All the resources I had—I brought you all with me. Unless I traveled south of Goldenstone and tried to rally support from other kingdoms. But I have no goodwill to draw from. Other kings and queens could be as likely to shoot me with an arrow on sight as they'd be to grant me an audience. I can count on nothing more than what we have here already."

"We have strong hearts. We have clever minds. And we fight with just cause. It would only take one of us to get through and take that little king down, and then it's over."

"He's my cousin. And, if we want to get detailed about it, he's *my* heir. He has a right to the throne. But it's after mine."

Rowan looked away from Neve. "I'm sorry."

"I know," Neve said. "I know what has to happen, and what's likely to happen, and neither is easy to think about."

Neve had no idea how she kept her expression like a cool, serene pond, while under the surface, a water monster strangled every form of life in the darkness.

She didn't want to kill.

She didn't want to die.

Her whole life had been about avoiding this moment.

Neve got to her feet, hunched a bit under the low tent.

Rowan stood as well and had to hunch even more. "All will honor your decision tomorrow, I know it. Don't lose sleep for our choice to stand with you. Lose it for other reasons."

"Thank you. I will. Oh, one more thing."

Rowan paused at the tent flap.

"Go to Rhyannon and tell her I command her to go back to Foreverness. We are not retreating, and her purpose was to protect us if we were. She is not a warrior, and I want her home safe."

"Does she need an escort?"

Neve smirked. "No, she travels quickly. She will blink her

eyes and be safe in Foreverness a moment later."

Rowan nodded once. "I'll send her home at once."

"Rowan. I—whatever happens tomorrow. I—you—" Neve swallowed against the thick lump in her throat.

"I know," Rowan said. "I feel the same."

Rowan ducked under the flap and out into the night.

One tear escaped each eye, burning warm trails down Neve's face. She closed her eyes and allowed herself one breath to feel it all, then wiped her face on her sleeve and left the tent.

BRY

Her little mare galloped as fast as she could, and Bry leaned over her neck. The air was so cold. Her nose dripped. Her ears burned.

But she could hear the women now, as the sun rose, and she was proud.

She rounded the corner, Eterne Castle in sight. She thundered toward it, passing some of the women who were perhaps a bit more timid, standing at the far back of the crowd but still chanting.

As Bry flew by them, a cheer went up behind her. "Bryyyyy!"

The cheer drew the attention of the women in front, who saw her red hair and began to scream with joy. "Bry! Princess Bry!"

Her mare had to slow as the crowd thickened and spilled over into the path. Bry brought her sweating horse to a stop, leaped off her, and quickly tied her to a nearby tree before running into the crowd.

Women grabbed her arms, patted her shoulders and her back, and kissed her cheeks. Bry ignored the cold. Her quest hadn't stopped, not from the moment she'd been called from her bed yesterday morning. She'd spent the last twenty-four hours first riding into the furthest corners of Foreverness and encouraging the women to come. She then worked her way to the homes of the noblewomen, who were taken aback by her appearance, but touched and stunned by the stories Bry told them of women in their kingdom. A few of them had their own stories to tell, and all of them had vowed to come today. Bry hadn't been back home and hadn't had time to change. Her breasts and derriere were unconfined in their proper undergarments, and the sheer fabric left nothing to the imagination when her cloak hung open. She was gownless, crownless, jewel-less.

She was wild and free. She was a woman. Just like all of them.

"Hear us, King Brockton!" she cried. "Hear us and help us!"

The women cheered. A few howls went up.

"The Crown will hear us!" Bry shouted. "We want to be free to serve our desires, our daughters' desires, and our granddaughters' desires! Noblewoman or farm wife, we stand together in this! We will no longer be told we can't have what we worked for or be told we must accept a future we don't want! Women have voices, and we demand to be allowed audience with the king! We will not be silenced any longer! We *will* be heard!"

She moved to climb a tall rock, and two women immediately assisted her. When she straightened, she glanced down to thank them.

Dawn. And Thea.

Bry took a hand of each of her daughters in her own, and cried out to the crowd, "We will be heard!"

"We will be heard!"

"We will be heard!"

"We will be heard!"

Their cries went on for hours, during which time the crowd seemed to double in size. Suddenly, two soldiers of the King's Protection pushed through the women and stood in front of Bry, still on her rock. "Come with us, miss," he said sternly.

"I will not."

"She will not," Thea echoed.

"No," Dawn added.

"You are dressed in a manner unsuitable for a woman," he said. "Quiet yourself and come with me."

"Do you hear that?" a nearby woman shouted. "A man has decided this woman is not dressing or speaking in a manner that pleases him."

"Oh, we are so sorry!" another woman yelled. "Do you not like my hat? Let me take it off." She pulled off her bonnet and flung it at the soldier. It hit him on the chest.

In moments, aprons, bonnets, shoes were pelting the soldiers from all sides. The soldiers—armed with very large swords and dressed in solid metal—seemed to not know what to do.

Until the one who spoke to Bry first grabbed her by the wrist hard. "Look, here, woman. You are inciting a riot."

"No one here has expressed a problem with my dress or my words except you," Bry said. "I'd say you're the one inciting a riot."

He pushed his face as close to hers as his helmet would allow. The cold metal of it pressed against her chin. "Woman, I can do this the easy way, or I can do this the unpleasant way."

I am your princess! Unhand me! she almost said. *I am the wife of your commander!*

He didn't even know. He was as close to her as Lucan got, and he didn't even recognize her as the princess. Without a fancy gown, footmen, and her husband—she just looked like any woman. A woman who had no royal privilege to save herself.

Thea brought her knee up to her chest and mule-kicked the soldier in the side. Unarmored, it would have hurt, but he just stumbled and landed on his back. He didn't let go of Bry, and she was yanked off the rock, falling on top of him. The other soldier pulled her off by the back of her cloak and held fast. "March," he said, kicking her ankles. "You are under arrest."

More soldiers appeared and began to grab women, including Bry's daughters. They pushed them toward the castle. Women screamed, pushed back, and threw sticks and rocks.

DELLA

ella leaned her head back against the cell wall and mentally shuffled through her garderobe for a suitable outfit to appear before the king.

Dark-blue brocade? Maybe.

Shimmering pink satin? Not quite.

Ah, yes—of course. It would have to be the deep forest-green velvet, long-sleeved with brown fur cuffs. A large emerald brooch to nestle in the center of the brown fur collar. Gold drops to hang from her earlobes, and her largest, heaviest golden crown, crusted with jewels of every color. Delicate slippers the exact green of the gown to step into the Great Hall with the confidence of a woman sure of her place.

A knock on the door, and the guard stuck his head in. "Miss? Er, Your Highness?"

"Yes, Ralph?"

"The king commands your presence."

Della stood and ran her hands down her front, smoothing not her green velvet gown, but the blue casual day gown she'd put on several days ago. It was rumpled and smelled like her armpits. She reached up and adjusted her crown to hopefully cover her treacherous gray part.

She lifted her chin. "I am ready." She'd *been* ready for days. It wasn't too hard to imagine Colby allowing her to lie here in her own filth for days on end, but she'd have thought her brother-in-law would have done right by her and seen her immediately to correct this situation.

Della walked toward the door regally, as if she'd been properly dressed, jeweled, coiffed, and perfumed by Catelina and Eda.

"I don't know anything about anything," Ralph said as he stepped aside for her, "but whatever they say you've done, I don't believe it. You're a real lady."

Della smiled. "Hug those beautiful daughters for me. And be kind to them, always."

"I will, miss—er, Your Highness." He closed and locked the door of her disgusting cell. She'd harbor no sentimentality for the time she'd spent there.

He waved her ahead of him but followed close behind as she wound through the tunnel of The Caves. The tunnel ended abruptly at a large door, and when Ralph unlocked it and pushed it open, Della's eyes were assaulted by the sun she hadn't seen in a few days. She shielded her brow with one hand. She was grateful that her goodwill with Ralph had led to his apparent decision to not bind her hands, though she was sure at this point, no one would recognize their princess anyway, given her droopy hair and her shabby dress.

She could hear … shouting?

Yes, shouting and chanting got louder as she and Ralph approached the castle. When they rounded the corner, the castle came into view—surrounded with people.

No—with women. All women. Hundreds of them, screaming. Shouting. Chanting. Their arms were wrapped around one another as they swayed. The King's Protection rode along the perimeter of the mob, yelling, "Get back!" and "Silence!" but the women paid them zero mind.

Della's eyes widened. Women ignoring the commands of men.

"What is happening?" she asked Ralph.

"Ladies," Ralph said. "Unhappy with things."

"What things?"

"Everything," he said simply.

Ralph led her off the path so they could move unseen in the brush to the rear doors of the castle, where Lord Everard waited as they emerged. He had the nerve to lift his nose and sniff, but his opinion meant less than nothing to Della. "I will see His Majesty now," she said, as if she hadn't been summoned here.

Lord Everard waved away Ralph, who tipped his hat and left. He ushered Della into the castle, and she tamped down her urge to run to the Great Hall. The sooner this was cleared up, the better.

But when the large doors swung open to King Brockton sitting on his throne at the far end, Della's confidence swan-dived to the soles of her feet. Still, she walked the blue runner with dignity, and when she was at the king's feet, she curtsied low.

"Your Majesty."

"Princess," Brockton said.

"There seems to be quite a commotion out there."

"Just a little unrest." Brockton waved his heavily ringed hand. "The King's Protection has it under control."

"Pardon me for asking," Della said, "but have you been out there? That's not just a little unrest. That's possibly every woman in the kingdom."

"It's under control." Brockton's voice was easy, but his eyes cut to the large window. "I'm sorry you were made to wait overnight. There have been some urgent matters for me."

Della immediately realized Lord Everard had not told the king exactly when she had been arrested, and that he had allowed her to sit in a cell for days. She turned to glare at Everard, but he'd left.

"Where is Her Majesty?" Della asked.

Brockton's expression remained neutral. "As I said, urgent matters. But you have my full attention now."

"Thank you," Della said. "It seems I've been imprisoned for running a business and failing to pay taxes to the Crown. Please understand that I never intended to break the law. I was simply not aware of the law. I should have sought guidance, I confess, and I am truly sorry, but I started this venture unsure if I could do it. I am happy to pay whatever I owe to the Crown."

"I believe that you didn't run afoul of the law deliberately," Brockton said. "You have always shown yourself to be a woman of honor. What I need to understand is why you are running a business at all. Your place is to be a woman for other women to look up to. An ideal, an aspiration."

Just be pretty.

No.

Instead, Della told the king everything. She told him about finding the elder maid berating the young maid the day after her father-in-law died and her idea to help servants improve their wages and work environments. She explained that she also taught noblewomen to be honorable and respectful employers, and that several maids had already sent her letters thanking her for changing their lives. She told him how she wouldn't keep the profit but would continue to reinvest it into supplies and equipment, and that she would eventually use the money for programs to help women in need. She showed him all the recommendation letters from her previous clients.

When she stopped to take a breath and to consider if she'd left anything out, she realized Brockton was—staring. "Er ... what?" she asked.

"I didn't realize it was so—"

The double doors banged open, and Della started, turning to find Lord Everard making his way down the length of the carpet. His face was a placid lake, but his forehead was damp with perspiration. She narrowed her eyes at him, not ready to forgive him for the indignity of her arrest.

"What is happening?" Brockton asked his main advisor.

"Nothing of importance," Lord Everard said, quickly shaking his head and offering a half smile. "Women. Commoners. Shouting about nonsense."

"Nonsense?" Brockton tilted his head.

"Women's nonsense," Lord Everard said.

"In this kingdom," Della interrupted, "the royal family is revered and respected. I imagine it would have to be some rather important nonsense for them to be demanding the king's attention in such a large, vocal gathering."

Lord Everard frowned at her. "I'm sure whatever it is, *they* think it's important."

"Whatever it is?" Della said. "You haven't even asked them? Is it not your responsibility to advise His Majesty on matters of state? This is a state of disarray and unrest, yet you are saying you know not what is happening."

"Your Highness," the lord said, his tone dripping with condescension despite her lofty title, "I'm sure—"

"Have you spoken to their leader?" Brockton asked. "This event seems planned, and if it was planned, someone is responsible."

"Maids, farmers' wives, and seamstresses are demanding to speak to the king," Lord Everard said. "Now, Your Majesty, with your sister-in-law under arrest—"

"It's been sorted," Della said.

"—and your queen invading Goldenstone, you need not worry about this peasants' revolt. They're not even armed men, but weak women with trivial complaints."

Neve was *invading* Goldenstone? That couldn't be. But when Brockton didn't correct his advisor, Della realized it was true. Neve was the heir there—they all knew it—but it was something she never talked about. Della had no idea what could have changed her sister-in-law's mind after all these years, but she clenched her fist at her side. Good for her.

"Find out what they want," Brockton said.

"I beg your pardon, Your Majesty," Lord Everard said, "but what could they want? Here, in Foreverness?"

"Where everything is perfect?" Della asked, but her sarcasm fell flat on the blue carpet.

"Men provide them with everything they need," the lord said.

"If you believe that," Della said, "you're a blind and deaf man, and you should step down and let someone else advise His Majesty."

Lord Everard sputtered.

"Enough," Brockton said mildly. "My lord, I trust you will speak to the women leading this mob and discern if this is an issue that deserves my attention. If not, disperse the crowd."

Lord Everard bowed deeply to the king and bowed far less enthusiastically to Della before leaving.

Brockton looked at her for a long minute. "You know your husband turned you in."

"I figured that out rather quickly, yes."

"Why?"

"He's been stealing from the people of this kingdom for years. He collects ... more than their taxes. I very recently discovered his secret. He thought I would tell you, and he wanted to strike first."

"*Were* you going to tell me?"

"I was going to tell the queen. And ask her to talk to you."

She couldn't read his expression.

She reached into her pocket and pulled out the little items—the gem, the coin, the little eagle. Trinkets to a prince, but valuables to a commoner.

She gave them to Brockton. "These are stolen goods. There were more. There were ledgers of them. But after I found them, he locked his office."

"It's your word against his." He sighed. "But I believe you. Colby is … a problem. He always has been. And I've heard rumblings about this kind of illegal behavior for years—rumors and stories, nothing more. This is helpful, but I need proof from someone other than the woman he jailed."

"You're the king," Della said. "What do you need to prove? You could say the grass is pink, and the kingdom would be obliged to agree."

"He's my brother. He's a Charming. If I'm to disillusion the kingdom—"

He stopped and angled his head toward the window. The chanting was louder. Della couldn't hear the exact words, but she could hear there were even more women than before.

"I don't think," she said, "this kingdom is holding onto illusions the way you thought they were."

The king's eyes and lips softened.

"Neve is invading Goldenstone?" Della asked.

His expression hardened again, though maybe not much. "I will investigate Colby."

"But—"

"But what?"

"No one will turn against Colby. The people of Foreverness he extorted would have come to the Crown long before now, so they must fear his retribution. No one wants a royal vendetta exacted upon their family. The men who work with him will never turn against him, for likely they are being handsomely rewarded for their nefarious activity. They'll see no reason to put an end to it and, at the same time, make a royal enemy."

"You're not wrong," the king said. "I will have to hope someone has the moral conscience you have. Go home now, and let me try to find that someone."

"I can't go home," Della said. "I—I don't know what he'll do if he finds me there. He will know I told you." Colby wouldn't hurt her—of that she was almost sure—but she didn't want to return home and face him without a plan. He would surely have another plan in motion already, and she didn't want to be near him while she was at a disadvantage.

"Stay here, then. Send for your maids and your clothes and whatever else you need. My staff will show you to the guest rooms and see to your every need. And, Your Highness, I will need you to hand over all your business profits to the Crown and cease operation. As a member of the royal family, you can't continue your business, despite the good I'm sure you are doing."

Della curtsied, though her heart dropped lower than her body did. "Thank you, Your Majesty."

She calmly walked the carpet and opened the double doors, but her mind raced like a runaway stallion.

NEVE

Morning slid into the sky between dark clouds, with pinks and golds that heralded life.

Covered in armor, her sword at her side, Neve and Monarch circled her company, lined up in the same place they'd lined up the evening before to meet the king and his councilmen. It appeared no one had deserted overnight, despite what awaited them this morning.

"My friends," Neve called so they could all hear. "If this were about me, and which royal cushion I sat my royal arse on, we would not be here. I would not put you in peril's way for vanity.

"We are here because the people of this kingdom suffer injustice at the hands of those who should care for them and protect them. They've lost their livelihoods. They've lost their children. They've lost their lives. These are my people, and I say, no more."

Rowan, standing at attention, her hands clasped behind her back, nodded.

"We are many years late, I confess," Neve said. "But now we are in this kingdom, and we fight for every man, woman, and child here. We fight because no one else will. We fight for goodness and kindness. We fight because we are the fairest of them all, and we will restore Goldenstone to health and prosperity."

"Huzzah!" a soldier cried.

"Huzzah!" they all chanted. "Huzzah!"

"May God be with us all," Neve said, and everyone bowed their heads.

Neve moved to the front of the army and faced the castle.

They all stood in silence; the only sound was her flag snapping above them in the sharp wind.

Neve waited for her panic to rise—for her fear to bubble up and boil over.

Not dying had been her one goal for so long. Avoiding conflict, hiding in guarded rooms, traveling with soldiers. It was her whole life.

Beneath her, Monarch let out a huff. Neve tilted her head as she realized something: Skittish, jumpy, high-strung Monarch had been a solid rock from the moment they'd set foot in the open field.

He knew his role: to be steady and firm, to follow orders, to gallop into a fray without hesitation or fear.

He waited now, willingly, as everyone behind her did.

Neve stared across the field of browned grass at the home from which she'd been expelled.

She closed her eyes and lifted her face to the sky.

Fifty years to the day from her birth, standing on a frigid battlefield, she finally accepted her role. She accepted her task.

She accepted her death.

A wet drop kissed the tip of her nose. Then on the soft skin just under her right eye. Then her bottom lip. She opened her eyes.

Snow.

And the Goldenstone army, easily one thousand men, marching toward her.

Neve reached to her hip and, with a long metal scrape, drew her longsword.

"Ready!" the commander shouted behind her.

The Goldenstone army came to a stop a hundred yards in front of them. The five councilmen approached.

"Queen Neve of Foreverness," Lord Cassian said loudly. "You remain here after daybreak, and we must assume you choose to fight."

Neve said nothing.

Lord Brian continued, "This is folly. You should—"

"You do not advise me, my lord," Neve interrupted. "Nor shall you advise me after I take the throne, for you will be arrested and tried while I make my own council."

Lord Morcant chuckled. "Strong language from a woman facing death."

"You might have heard," Neve said, "death and I once lay in a coffin together."

Lord Morcant stopped smiling. Neve lifted her hand, a signal to her men.

Even the snowflakes seemed to freeze in the air, for a moment. "Stop!"

The councilmen knit their brows and looked at one another.

"Stop!" They all heard the call again—and the approaching hoofbeats.

Neve tried to catch Rowan's eye, but she looked shocked. She knew the voice, then? Should Neve?

A horse flew up the right side of Neve's army and skidded to a halt at her side.

"Stop," shouted Darren. "I know Queen Neve, and you know me … well, some of you do."

He hopped off his horse and held up his empty hands. "It was I whom Fina asked to kill young Neve. I took her to the forest, and I couldn't do it. I just couldn't. She was a little girl. I let her go. You behold Neve of Goldenstone. She is no false princess."

His arms still raised, his palms facing the council, he walked slowly to the oldest man. "Old Lord Novel, you remember me. You must. We dined together frequently. It was you who introduced me to Fina as the huntsman who brought her the best pheasants and boar. The whole staff knew me."

Lord Novel squinted. "Darren? Is that you, boy?"

"Not such a boy anymore," Darren said. "Not if these knees have anything to say about it."

"Where have you been?"

"I disobeyed Fina," he said. "So I disappeared."

"A wise decision. Come closer," Lord Novel said. "Let me look at you."

"No," Lord Brian said. "Stay where you are."

"I will see the man for myself," Lord Novel said. "For if it is my friend, I will know him, and I will take his word for this woman's identity."

Lord Cassian said, "But—"

"My lords," Lord Novel said slowly, and coughed. "Can you act on faith, slaughter an army, slaughter *her*, if she is the true heir? If this man can prove it?" He crooked a finger at Darren. "Come here, friend. I will see you."

Darren walked slowly, a bit painfully, toward Lord Novel's horse.

Until an arrow in the chest stopped him, and dropped him.

No. No. Nononononono ...

"No!" Rowan screamed. "Darren!"

Two of Neve's soldiers took Rowan's elbows to keep her from charging Goldenstone's army. She raged against them, trying to get free.

Neve had no idea who'd shot Darren as she'd been watching only him.

"What have you done?" Lord Justus rasped to the other lords.

His other smirking lords.

Lord Brian stepped forward and yanked the arrow from Darren's chest, a spurt of blood fountaining up behind it. He threw it on the grass.

Rowan screamed again—a raw, hoarse, long cry of pain. The other wolves echoed her with sorrowful howls.

Oh, God. Oh, God.

Neve raised her hand again, signaling her company.

She would fall dead beside Darren, but she would kill as many of these bastards as she could before she did.

Before her command could leave her lips, she heard, "Sssssssssssss."

"Sssssssssssss."

The two snakes slithered out from the grass behind her, one on each side of Monarch, to the neutral center of the field, then slid onto Darren's body.

The greenish-gold snake opened its mouth and completely covered the wound. The golden-green snake opened its mouth and covered Darren's nose and mouth. Then it lifted its eyes to Neve's.

We have ssspecial ssskillsss. The voice bounced off the walls of her mind. *SSStay ssstill.*

The snakes contracted and released, contracted and released.

Lord Novel quietly slid off his horse and moved closer to his old friend's prone form.

Neve saw a soldier in the front line nock his arrow and release it at Darren's body in an effort to hit one of the snakes, but the arrow stopped a foot above them and ricocheted away in a shimmer of yellow sparkle.

Rhyannon's protection spell.

The snakes' contractions got faster. Soldiers on both sides backed up a little more, even while craning their necks for a better view.

The snakes glowed then—brighter and brighter, changing gold to green to gold. The falling snowflakes around them caught in the invisible shield and burned out with pops like fireworks.

With wide eyes and an open-mouthed gasp, Darren sat up.

The snakes slid off him and flanked him, coiling up and swaying their heads side to side.

Lord Novel knelt before Darren, put his hands on the huntsman's shoulders, and peered into his eyes. "It is you, my old friend," he finally said. "I've missed you."

Darren put one hand over one of Lord Novel's and gestured his other hand toward Neve. "May I introduce you to Neve, the queen and protector of Goldenstone?"

"Men!" Lord Cassian shouted. "In line!"

No one moved for a moment. Then the Goldenstone soldiers threw their swords, their shields, their bows and arrows into the dusting of snow on the ground.

"In line!" Lord Brian shouted in rage.

"She commands the beasts of the forest," a soldier shouted.

"She resurrects the dead," another called. "We will not fight. She is our queen."

"Your king in the castle commands you to fight!" Lord Morcant screamed.

The Goldenstone soldiers circled quickly around the four councilmen, trapping them, leaving them no way to attack Neve. They were hidden from Neve's sight, but she could still hear their outraged shrieks.

Rowan, released by the men who'd held her back, ran to Darren, fell onto the snow beside him, and hugged him hard.

From out of the darkness of the trees, people began to emerge. Neve turned Monarch around to look at them. They were tired people in dirty, ragged clothes, wielding sticks and branches. They wound into the lines of Neve's soldiers and bravely waited, watching the woman they now knew to be their queen.

Neve opened her mouth to tell them they would not have to fight today, but before she could utter a word, she heard the two-note blare of a trumpet. One short, one long. One short, one long.

And the full Foreverness army, hundreds upon hundreds of shouting men led by Prince Lucan, thundered onto the field from behind Neve's army, swords at the ready, armor clinking. Discovering they weren't riding into the thick of active battle, they slowed to a stop, flanking Neve's men on three sides.

Neve closed her eyes and mouthed "Thank you" to Brockton, still in Foreverness.

Those on horses dismounted, and all lowered to one knee before her. Even the wolves stretched their front legs and bowed their large heads.

She turned to Goldenstone's army, and every man was already kneeling—except for the few soldiers holding the bridles of the sputtering councilmen's horses.

Rowan finally released Darren from her relieved embrace and turned to grin at Neve.

Neve blinked.

Goldenstone was hers.

"Long live Queen Neve!" someone shouted.

"Long live Queen Neve!"

Neve removed her helmet. A snowflake dropped into her eyelashes, melting into the one warm tear that fell from her eye. She cleared her throat.

"My people," she said, and began her reign.

DELLA

The royal guest suite was suitably opulent, and Della would have thought so even if she hadn't spent two days in a cell not fit for a boar. The bed was shaped like an elaborate snow sleigh, and Della reclined against no fewer than four silk-covered pillows, her arms behind her head, as she considered what to do next.

Was she afraid of Colby? Not especially. She didn't think he had it in him to physically harm her. She didn't want to return home and face him without a plan. But she couldn't avoid him forever.

Brockton had said he would investigate Colby's illegal activity, but no one would turn against Colby. The people of Foreverness whom he'd extorted would have come to the Crown long before now if he hadn't struck fear of retribution in them—and no one wanted a prince exacting revenge upon their family and home, particularly commoners. No one who worked with him would turn against him, for likely they were being handsomely rewarded for their nefarious activity. There would be no reason for them to put an end to it and, at the same time, make a royal enemy.

Della pounded her fists on the bed, though the lush bedspread prevented her hands from feeling any sting. Colby's arrogance, his certainty that he could get away with anything, was beyond belief. But why wouldn't it be—he'd never suffered a consequence in his life. Not for his behavior at the coronation, not for stealing, not for sleeping with half the women in Foreverness. Back when she was sleeping with Colby regularly, his tongue would be loosened by orgasm. While they lay together, heads sharing a pillow, he would brag about many things—

Della sat up abruptly. Perhaps there was someone.

She paused a moment, listening. She'd heard the chanting and the yelling for a few hours now, but it was getting louder and more insistent.

She swung her legs over the side of the bed, pushing her feet into her blue slippers. In her determination, she almost didn't glance at herself in the elaborate gilded mirror that hung opposite the bed. But habit won, and she did.

She froze. And stared.

She'd changed into a clean gown as soon as her clothing had arrived from her castle, but wanting some privacy to think, she'd sent the maids out of the room and put on a simple blue gown that didn't require assistance to fasten or lace up. But it had been days since her appearance had been tended to. Her face was unmoisturized and unpainted. Her hair was wild and unkempt, the streaks of gray glaringly prominent without the oft-applied dandelion to hide them or an elaborate updo to twist around them.

She looked … plain.

She looked … like any woman her age.

The longer she stared, the more she relaxed into what she saw. And just *what* was wrong with her the way she was now? She was Della without finery and sparkle and polish, but she was Della with wisdom, and the anger that came from that wisdom, and the determination that came from that anger.

"Who cares?" she muttered. "Who really, really cares?"

She grabbed her cloak and dashed for the door. Then she

stopped, blew a huff of air out her nose, and muttered an unsavory word. She ran back into the room, grabbed her crown off the bed, plopped it on top of her mess of hair, and left.

NEVE

"I am sorry, Your Majesty," Rhyannon said, placing her palms together in front of her heart. A bud bloomed into a flower on each fingertip. "I know you are busy here in your new realm, but you should be aware of what's happening in Foreverness."

Neve, seated in a high-backed chair at the head of a grand table, dismissed her new advisors, and the men and women quietly vacated the room.

She raised a brow at the fairy. "Did I not send you home before the battle?"

"I am willing to accept punishment for disobeying Your Majesty," Rhyannon said. "But I was aware of the snakes' skills. I thought the protection spell might be prudent if they needed to bring you back to life. I cast their spell, and I stayed easily out of sight. I didn't want to burden you by asking permission. You had enough on your mind that night."

Neve sighed. "I did. I thank you. You saved the man who saved me. You saved many, many lives."

Rhyannon dipped her chin modestly as butterflies circled her purple hair.

"But you have been back to Foreverness," Neve prompted.

"Yes," Rhyannon said, "and I bring you news of unrest."

"Unrest?" Neve asked. "In Foreverness?"

"Yes. Concerning—well, your family, mostly."

Neve leaned back in her chair, her heart beating a bit faster. "Go on."

"Princess Della has been arrested," Rhyannon said. "For operating an illegal business. The king dismissed the charges but has ordered her to cease operation. Her husband was the one who turned her in."

"That—that's preposterous. All of it."

"Hundreds of the kingdom's women are being held like pigs in pens on the royal premises, for disorderly and unwomanly behavior."

"What?"

"They were participating in a vocal revolt on Eterne Castle grounds. Demanding their right to take audience with the king so their grievances can be heard, as well as men's. Their leader is ... Princess Bry."

Neve covered her mouth with one hand; she was horrified, but even more horrified at herself that what she was hiding was a smile.

"She is among the imprisoned, along with the princesses Thea and Dawn."

The smile quickly left Neve's face. "Brockton is allowing this?"

"I'm not entirely sure the king understands who was arrested. He's been preoccupied by what's happening with his brother, and his other brother—who'd normally be commander in a situation like that—is here with you. Brockton's council is feeding him information. Mostly misinformation."

"How is he handling it?" Neve asked.

"He's—overwhelmed."

"Of course he is," Neve said. "He long believed his father's tale that Foreverness is without problems and full of subjects living happily ever after. I believed it too, of course. Until I didn't."

Rhyannon nodded.

"Did Della ask your help for herself or Bry?"

"She didn't. My illusions and protections aren't what they need now."

"I don't suppose you could magically teleport me there?"

"I'm not a sorceress," the fairy said. "I could get you to the other side of this room with haste, but that's about it."

"I understand. Please head back to Foreverness and stay watchful. Come back to me if things worsen."

She would speak to the council, choose a chief advisor, and prepare instructions for her absence. Then she would send for Lucan and have him return with her at once to Foreverness.

King Brockton might not want her advice any longer, but he needed it now.

He needed her.

And her sisters needed her.

BRY

"We are women!" Bry shouted. "We are not farm animals!"

"You can't keep us here!" Dawn yelled.

The other women in the pen with Bry and her daughters—dozens of women—pushed as one unified wave against the wooden gate. The gate creaked promisingly but held fast.

Several pens holding several hundred women were bursting with prisoners. Bry had no idea what King Brockton's plan was, but they'd been here since last night and it was now approaching midday. She was thirsty, hungry, and really, really angry.

"These fools have no idea who we are," Thea had muttered when they were first shoved into this sty.

"No," Bry had said, "they don't. And don't say it. Here, we are all women and equal. We want fairness for all of us, not just the ones born into privilege."

"Even the privileged women don't get what the privileged men get," Dawn had added.

"Tell me about it," Thea had said. And they'd all gone back to yelling again. The women had quieted down for a few hours in the late night, encouraged by Bry to get sleep because who knew how long they'd be there.

Despite the fires built around the pen to keep the prisoners warm, Bry's nightclothes—now damp, dirty, and torn at the seam in several places—provided her skin no protection from the wintry wind under her cloak. Her daughters had stayed close throughout the night so their body heat could raise hers, like a pair of robins caring for a featherless hatchling.

Bry's throat was hoarse and dry. A few flasks of water had been passed around, but she hadn't seen one since daybreak.

The strength the women's voices were losing, however, was bolstered now by new voices—those of men. Men whose wives, daughters, and servants had not come home. Each hour more men showed up—some angry at the Crown for penning up the women, but angrier at their women for their joining in the fray. The shouting and arguing was escalating.

If the king would only hear them, this could all—well, Bry wouldn't fool herself into thinking things would be resolved, but it would be a step in a positive direction for the women to be heard. Bry couldn't understand why Brockton hadn't emerged, or why his council wouldn't speak to them. They'd come out one by one to peer at the ruckus yesterday and today, including that pinched, constipated-looking Lord Everard, but they only surveyed the scene. They hadn't talked to the women. They hadn't asked questions. They hadn't cared.

And where was Lucan?

The women around Bry had held their ground, insistent, never yielding, occasionally patting Bry on the shoulder for encouragement.

"We will be heard!" Bry screamed now, but her voice didn't carry as far as it had yesterday. She hung her head. So cold. So tired. So … useless.

"*What* am I witnessing?" cut a fierce voice through the hubbub, and the crowd quickly hushed.

Bry pushed to the edge of the pen, gripping the cold wood with both hands and peering through the slat.

The men outside the pen parted a path and bent in bows as Princess Della made her way to the dirty, exhausted, penned-up women. She walked as regally as if she were at a royal ball, her uncharacteristically sedate blue gown setting off the aquamarine jewels in her crown. Her elegant slippers blessed the packed dirt as she walked.

Della locked eyes with Bry. Della froze, her eyes widening to saucers.

She whirled on the nearest soldier. "You! Who is in charge here? Clearly it isn't Prince Lucan, because if it were, I wouldn't be witnessing such a travesty."

"Your Highness," the soldier sputtered. "I—"

"Shut up and find me your commanding officer. Now."

The soldier scurried away like a scolded toddler. Della approached the pen, reached her hands between the slats, and took both of Bry's hands.

Frustrated and exhausted tears fell from Bry's eyes. "Della," she said. "Thank God for you. I'm—I'm in over my head, I think."

Della looked around them for a moment, then back at Bry. "You are not. We are not."

"Aunt Della!" Thea cried, and she and Dawn pushed forward to touch their aunt's arm, her gown.

"Where is Brockton?" Bry asked. "Why isn't he here?"

"Lord Everard told him this rebellion is nothing, just a mob of angry peasant women with trivial complaints."

The red haze fell over Bry's vision. "How dare he! We—"

"I know." Della squeezed Bry's cold hands in her soft leather gloves. "He was talking so much manure to the king earlier, I was surprised to not see a stable hand come into the Great Hall with a rake. I must say, though the seriousness of the situation is just what I expected, I didn't expect to see you."

"Where is Neve?" Bry asked.

Before Della could reply, Dawn said proudly to Della, "This is all Mother's doing."

"She was the one who encouraged them to come and insist on being heard," Thea added.

Della raised an eyebrow at Bry.

"I was angry," Bry said. "At Brockton. At Lucan. At your bastard of a husband. At this kingdom's false pretenses. All of it."

To soften the bluntness, Bry almost added *I'm sorry.* But she didn't.

Because she wasn't.

Della smoothed her hand over Bry's hair. "I knew there was a fierce woman in there all along," she said, tapping Bry's forehead.

A soldier came up behind Della's shoulder and cleared his throat. She turned and he bowed. "Your Highness, I am Lord Benedict, acting commander."

"Where is Lucan?"

"The prince is in Goldenstone with Queen Neve, Your Highness."

Bry blinked. Lucan was in Goldenstone with Queen Neve?

"In his stead," Lord Benedict continued, "I am at your service."

"Very good. You are to release every single one of these women at once," Della said.

"I—I can't do that," he said. "The king has ordered us to detain the women."

"The king ordered you directly?"

"Lord Everard did."

"Indefinitely?"

"We are to make them uncomfortable," Lord Benedict said, "until they show remorse and compliance."

"I see." Della raised her voice so that all around them could hear their exchange. "Lord Everard has willfully given misinformation to the Crown regarding this revolt. I heard it myself."

"Your Highness—"

"Will the Crown be pleased," Della asked slowly and loudly, "to learn you imprisoned his royal sister-in-law and her two royal daughters, and penned them in overnight in the frigid cold along with all these other good women, like common livestock?"

"I don't—"

Della jabbed a finger onto the armor covering his chest. "I will hold you personally responsible for this. My brother-in-law loves Princess Bry—this entire kingdom loves her—and we will not see her or anyone she cares about treated this way."

Bry's two tears turned into a small waterfall. She covered her eyes and let out a small sob.

Della went to Bry and drew her head and shoulders through the wide slats. "This is Princess Briar Rose, you jack-ass," she said to the commander. "And with her are Princess Dawn and Princess Thea."

Gasps and murmurs spread among the crowd.

Lord Benedict went pale, and hurriedly fumbled with the latch on the gate, ushering out Bry, who tugged her daughters out behind her. He slammed the gate on the other women, but none of the other women in the pen made a move.

Bry realized they were waiting for her to speak.

She turned in a small circle to see everyone.

"Open the gate, and release *all* these women at once," Bry said to Lord Benedict, then raised her voice. "Let it be known that every one of these women is now under my personal protection, and any punishment or chastisement that should befall them because of their presence here today will be considered a royal offense."

The husbands and fathers gathered nearby took several steps back. Some turned and left.

"These women are here because they have lived in silence. They have legitimate grievances, and they want to be heard by the king," Bry said. "As it happens, so do I. We were born with voices, just as men were, and so we will use them without permission, just as men do. These women will speak. And *I* will hear them."

"And *I* will hear them," Della echoed.

"We will petition the good king on their behalf," Bry finished. "He deserves to have the opportunity to help them, and Princess Della and I will give him that opportunity."

Lord Benedict paused, his mouth open.

"Open the gate," Bry commanded.

"Open the gate!" a woman in the crowd outside the pen cried.

Several others took up the cry, until the entire crowd was chanting, "Open the gate!"

"Open the gate!" Thea and Dawn called.

"Open the gate! Open the gate!" the crowd outside the pen sang and began to push forward.

"Open. The. Gate," Della ordered through clenched teeth.

"Open the gate!" Lord Benedict called.

NEVE

Monarch picked up his pace as his home came into view. Prince Lucan and a half-dozen other soldiers rode behind to protect the queen, but she'd insisted on not having a full entourage. Every additional person required extra minutes on the road, and more stops for rest and water. Haste was key for Neve, upon learning Foreverness was in upheaval, and Lucan's urgency matched her own once she'd filled him in on his wife's apparent activities. His love for Bry was a fierce lion, and a gentle fawn.

As for fawns, Lucan and the soldiers were a bit disconcerted at first by the animal escort that had begun in Goldenstone, galloping and hopping beside them and flying overhead, but they grew accustomed to it in time.

They made good time, just over a day and a half. They skirted the borders of Foreverness rather than dashing straight through, and when they came up just east of Eterne Castle, Neve slowed Monarch to a walk, then a halt. The men stopped with her, and they listened for the sound of unrest: shouts, chants, scuffles.

Nothing. Just a lone bird's sweet morning call.

Neve squinted into the distance and saw no unusual or frenetic movement.

She sighed with relief. More than wanting to ride in as

the hero, she had wanted this—to find that peace already had been restored.

But Rhyannon hadn't reported back to her, which meant there must be business still left unfinished.

They rode up to the front doors, and stable boys immediately approached to take the horses. The large wooden doors opened slowly, and a long carpet was thrown through.

She hopped off Monarch and hugged his neck. "Good boy," she said. "Good, brave boy."

He snuffled into the collar of her warm cloak, and she smiled, breathing in his sweet horsey smell.

She turned to Lucan, who had already dismounted. He offered his arm gallantly, but his smile was tight.

"All will be well," Neve said to him. "Don't fret."

"It's my job to say that to you."

They entered the castle and were shown to the Great Hall. The doors were already open and there was a line of people waiting. Neve tried to recall what day it was—was Brockton seeing the public today?

But no—this line was made up of only women.

The women at the back of the line gasped when they saw Neve and dipped into low curtsies.

The herald cleared his throat and shouted into the cavernous room, "His Royal Highness, Prince Lucan, and Her Royal Majesty of Foreverness, Quee—"

Lucan put a hand on the man's shoulder and leaned in to whisper. The man widened his eyes, then called out, "Her Royal Majesty of Foreverness and Goldenstone, Queen Neve!"

Neve and Lucan stepped into the room. She looked up, expecting to see her husband on the throne.

His throne was empty.

The council seats were occupied, however, but not by Lord Everard or any of the other councilmen. Della sat in the right-hand seat, and Bry sat on the left. They had parchment and quills on the table. A woman was before each princess, where they clearly had been conferring before their queen entered. Lucan escorted Neve calmly to the platform, then rushed to Bry, who nearly knocked her heavy seat over in her rush to rise and embrace him.

Della began to stand, but Neve held up a hand. "No, please, sit. What—what is happening here?"

The sudden silence began to fill again with the sound of all the people—all the women. Most commoners, but there were some noblewomen here and there.

Della deferred to Bry, who untangled herself from her husband's devoted embrace. "These women," Bry said, "are having difficulties with the law. They want the king to take up their cases. So we are hearing each story, each problem, and making a plan for each woman. And we are making up a list of complaints that could translate into changes in law—if His Majesty is willing."

"Um—oh," Neve said. "Did he—did he indicate he is willing?"

"He allowed us to use the Great Hall to hear these good people," Della said. "Seems like a step in the right direction."

"We've been here for two days," Bry said. "There's—quite a bit going on in this so-called perfect land."

"Yes," Neve said. "I've come to realize this myself."

Lord Everard approached the table, bowing low to Neve. As he rose, Neve did not miss the dirty look he bestowed upon both Della and Bry. Bry ignored him and went back to writing. Della, without moving one tiny muscle in her face, managed to look at him with such contempt, he had to cough a few times before speaking. "Your Majesty, Your Highnesses, the king will see you all at the four o'clock hour in his Council Room."

Bry looked at the enormous grandfather clock in the corner. "Very well. That gives us about two hours. We will see as many as we can before then." She turned to her husband. "If you would be willing to excuse us?"

"Of course," he said. His shoulders were relaxed, and his smile was bright. The tension he'd been holding during his journey with Neve dissipated.

"Fetch a chair, small enough for you to carry with ease," Neve instructed a nearby servant girl, who hurried away to find one. Bry raised a questioning brow at Neve.

When the girl brought the chair in, Neve dragged it to the table and sat between Bry and Della. "Now," Neve said. "Tell me how to help."

Her sisters-in-law grinned at her. "Next!" Della called, and a woman in an old dress and scuffed boots moved slowly to the table.

"Er—I—" she started.

"It's all right, my friend," Bry told her. "We are all women here. Tell Neve what troubles you."

Neve reached out and placed her hand on the woman's shoulder. "I am here."

The woman broke into tears as Neve's heart broke for her. Then she told her story.

The princesses and the queen heard, and consoled, and recorded, and discussed.

* * *

When they had seen the last of the women in line, they had just enough time to freshen up and dash to the king's Council Room, which was much like the one Neve had just left back in Goldenstone. A large wooden table took up most of the space, surrounded with large, comfortable, cushioned chairs with armrests. The chair at the head of the table was encrusted with raw amethysts, rubies, and golden topaz. Lucan was already seated at the table.

Della took her seat at the left hand of the king's chair, leaving Neve her place at the king's right. Instead, Neve went to the other end of the table and dragged the last chair to the empty spot facing Brockton's seat.

Della didn't bother to hide her grin.

"Are we expecting Colby?" Neve asked.

"I haven't expected him for thirty years," Della said. "I doubt he will suddenly follow decorum."

Bry sat opposite Della, and beside her husband.

For about two minutes, they all looked at one another.

Bry's skin was candlelit from within, the glow radiating from her bright eyes and blush skin. Her red hair burned across her shoulders and down her back. Bry had tamed her long curls into a knot for so many years, Neve had nearly forgotten its original startling color. Bry's chin was lifted with purpose, an acknowledgment of her own significance at this gathering—and in all of Foreverness. She was so—awake.

Della closed her eyes and let her head fall back against the seat. She rubbed her face with one hand, then smoothed the hand into her hair, idly threading her fingers through.

To greet her husband as a new queen of two kingdoms, Neve had dressed like a queen. Her golden-and-cream brocade gown was the most elaborate she'd owned. Her crown, placed on her head in a hurried Goldenstone coronation, was the heaviest she'd owned. Almost heavier than the weight of her troubled marriage.

"His Majesty of Foreverness, King Brockton!"

The king walked in, but his confident stride faltered as he took in his family around the table. It was brief; he recovered quickly, and Neve thought she might have been the only one to notice. He took his seat at the head of the table and looked down the length of it at his wife.

She nodded in respect. So did he.

Silence reigned in the Council Room for a moment or two, before Della finally said, "This is awkward."

Brockton cleared his throat. "It is, sister. It is very awkward, a feeling I don't enjoy in my castle or my kingdom. I—I miss my father."

Della's mouth set in a tight line. Bry looked down.

Neve's heart broke a little bit for the young prince she'd married, who'd wanted to be a good king to the land he would inherit.

Brockton exhaled loud and long and gave each of them a pointed look in turn as he spoke. "Though it felt unreal when it was happening, I always knew I'd be king. I watched my father preside over this enviable, legendary, perfect kingdom and learned how to rule as he did to preserve our kingdom's perpetual happiness."

He shook his head, quickly at first, then slower and slower. When his movement came to a stop, he went on. "I thought, I have a reliable council, I have a devoted wife, I have two admired brothers, and I have two much-loved sisters-in-law, all of whom can support me during this transition by continuing to serve this kingdom the way they always have."

He stared into the distance, somewhere over Neve's left shoulder, his eyes hardening. "One of my brothers has always been trouble, and now, he's a bigger liability than ever. My lead advisor, I find, is not quite supplying me with the accurate knowledge I need to make decisions. And it seems my father was not as—effective as I'd thought he was. Or as he could have been. I expected none of these problems this early in my reign. But surely, I thought, I can manage these issues, and maintain this kingdom's reputation for happiness."

Neve startled when Brockton slammed a palm on the

table, so much so that her rear end lifted off her seat. The burning candles on the table wobbled from the impact, and Lucan put out a hand to steady the tallest one.

"Instead," Brockton said, his voice low and dangerous, "my life is further complicated by my own family. Not just family, but *women*!" He shouted the last word. Neve didn't flinch this time.

"You royal women have been paragons of temperance and virtue for decades. The women of Foreverness have looked to you for guidance, and you choose now to fight the law, to operate an illegal business, to abandon your home and claim a throne in another land. You choose *now* to rebel, to break laws, to make my new reign a hot hell."

Bry muttered something.

"What did you say?" Brockton roared.

Neve expected Bry to hunch her shoulders, dip her red head, blush, and apologize. Instead, she lifted her chin and stared straight at her king as she spoke in a voice as clear as a vespers bell. "I said, it's not about you."

Neve was certain the king's head would explode into flames and ash. Lucan gazed at his wife in lovestruck wonder. Della snorted delicately.

"Would you have been so bold as to say that to my father, Princess Briar Rose?" Brockton asked, leaning forward.

"No," Bry said, "and that's not a disrespect to you, Your Majesty. I loved your father, the king, and he was kind in many ways. But as a ruler, he was rigid, unrelenting, unwilling to see problems anywhere. You—you are not him."

Brockton didn't move, but the stiffness in his arms, his shoulders, his fingers, dissolved. His lips parted as his jaw softened. He sat back down.

"We have a lot to go over," he said. "I am committed to us resolving all your concerns here and now. I want the

Charmings united in purpose, so we can spend the rest of our days making this land one that future generations will remember for all the right reasons."

Everyone murmured assent, but Brockton was looking only at Neve. "Your Majesty? Are you amenable to that?"

"Yes, Your Majesty," Neve replied, putting both hands flat on the table.

"Della," Brockton said, turning to his sister-in-law. "Let's sort this out."

Della lifted her chin. Not for the first time, Neve admired her queenly composure. She'd been arrested and spent time in The Caves, yet her confidence never wavered.

Brockton gestured to the guard, who opened the door to a young, nervous maid, who curtsied quickly and stood in a far corner.

Then, a few moments later, in walked Prince Colby—and his guard. Colby, though unshackled, was clearly in custody. Neve was surprised, but not. She stole a look at Della, but there was no change in her face. God, she was good.

Colby walked toward the table, the guard staying close. Della pushed back her chair and stood, and prince and princess were eye to eye.

"My husband," Della said. "You look as heartbreaking as ever."

"My wife," Colby said. "You are the pinnacle of loveliness. Roses wilt in your presence, unable to compete with you."

"Indeed," Della said.

"Della," Brockton said, "your husband is being investigated for high crimes against this court and against the good taxpayers of Foreverness. Crimes for which, if he is found guilty, would carry the consequence of a lifetime of imprisonment, or worse."

Then the king sighed. "He is my brother and blood. And, despite his years of reprehensible behavior, I know I would be unable to condemn him in such a way."

Colby smirked at his wife.

"However," Brockton said. "Though he has yet to be found formally guilty, there is sufficient evidence for me to do one thing now. I am removing him from the line of succession."

Neve held her breath. The room was silent for a moment.

Then Colby roared and leaped at Della. He managed to tear her sleeve at the shoulder before the guard seized his right arm, and Lucan his left. Then Colby's attention was on the king. "You can't do this!" he shouted.

"You will find there is very little I can't do," Brockton said evenly.

Bry rushed behind the king around the table to Della, drawing her away from her screaming husband. Lucan wrapped his cloak around Della to cover her, though only her upper arm was exposed.

"You do not have sufficient evidence against me," Colby said to his brother. "My own men will not speak against me. And no taxpayer I've ever dealt with will say a word that is anything other than in my defense. You have no one."

"That's not true."

The young maid in the corner stood and twisted her hands nervously. "I will speak against you." She swallowed. "I will."

Colby spun his head quickly to look at her. He clearly hadn't noticed her until this moment.

"And who are you?" the king asked.

"This is Molle," Della said. "One of the women I trained in my cleaning business. I asked her if she might have anything to say to you, Your Majesty."

"I'm so sorry, Princess," Molle said, and two tears fell out of her eyes. "I shouldn't have—you were so good to me—he—he—he came to me and—"

"I've known of no woman able to deny the seductions of Prince Colby Charming," Della said gently. "I've fallen for it myself, and I consider myself quite clever."

"I'm s—s—sorry."

"You are forgiven, my sweet," Della said.

Molle let out a sob of relief, then said to the king, "He told me everything—his stealing, his extortion, his—"

"Molle," Colby said, his voice honey on a hot day. "There's no need for lying. I'm sorry it was just that one night, but I'm married."

Bry snorted.

"He gave me this bracelet," Molle blurted, opening her hand to reveal a gold bangle encrusted with blue-sky jewels. "He said he took it from a woman who was short on taxes, and she begged him not to because it was her late mother's, but he—"

"Enough!" Colby shouted.

"Yes, enough," the king said. "Molle, I appreciate your candor with your king. I will speak to you in the morning." Then, to the guard at the door, "Please show Molle out and keep her under your care."

"She's lying!" Colby yelled as Molle dropped the bracelet on the table in front of Brockton and scurried away.

"She has no reason to lie," Della said. "She gains nothing from giving back a valuable bracelet and telling the truth."

"She's doing it for *you*," Colby spat.

"Perhaps so."

The king cleared his throat. "Della, with your permission—"

"With my permission?" Della interrupted. "You're the king. What permission could I give?"

"The only permission I can't give—a mother's permission. I'm taking your husband out of the line of succession, which would take your sons out as well. But, since I have no interest in punishing your children, my nephews, I'd like to formally adopt them."

Della did look flabbergasted then, as flabbergasted as Neve felt. "What?"

"That way I can keep your sons in line for the throne. With Colby out, and Neve and I with no children, your eldest is the heir. I request your permission to do this because they are your children."

Della took a deep breath and recovered quickly. "Of course. They are grown men, so it's merely a legality. I give you permission."

"I don't!" Colby said.

The king ignored him. "It will be done."

"I can't do much, can I?" Colby asked no one. "I've been backed into a corner. But I can do one thing." He looked at Della. "I can throw you out into the street. You are no longer my wife. I renounce you. I renounce this marriage that I begged my father to cancel before my wedding day. No more Princess Della. No more jewels, no more crowns, no more servants or carriages. No more shoes. No more gold. You are finished."

Della slid Lucan's cloak slowly from her shoulders and handed it to him, never taking her eyes off Colby. She moved slowly over to him, a lioness with a hapless goat in her sights, and she didn't stop until they were a hand's width apart.

"Now you're nothing but a graying, wrinkling peasant. Your spell is finally over," Colby said, his voice low but clear. "You've been at the ball long enough."

"Silence, brother," Brockton said. "What happens with your marriage is between you and Della, but she will retain her title and holdings. She is beloved in this kingdom, having bestowed her grace on its people for decades. She earned it."

There was a subtle, collective intake of breath at the table.

"She is not royalty, *brother*," Colby said, still staring his wife down. "*I made* her a princess."

"The law made her a princess," Brockton said. "Now, I am the law."

Neve's love for her husband had doubled, then tripled, in the time she sat here. This was the man she'd married and the king he'd wanted to be.

The fairest man in the land.

Neve looked at Della, who refused to break eye contact with her husband. At the king's words, her composure cracked just a tiny bit, at the corners of her lips. Then her face iced over.

"I've been at the ball long enough? That's the truest thing you've ever said, husband," Della said. "Yes, I have. Long enough to see everything is a fake. The spoiled, drunk, debauched prince; the stolen jewels; the ill-gotten wardrobe. It's all a pretty illusion and a story to tell hopeful little girls."

She turned to Brockton. "You honor me deeply, and I am grateful for your benevolence. But I don't want to be a princess any longer. There are other ways to be an example, make a difference."

She paused and pressed her lips together, and Neve was certain it was because the words were painful in her mouth. No princess in Foreverness legend had embraced her royal station more than Della had, or had been more admired and loved.

She stepped one dangerous inch closer to Colby. "You're done with *me*? I'm done with *you*. Because as it turns out, I'm pretty good at making my own money. And since I'll not be a princess anymore, I can reopen for business."

Neve wanted to throw her arms around Della.

"See His Highness out," the king said, but Colby was already storming out the door, his guard on his heels.

After the door slammed, Bry said, "You can live with us,

Della. You are my dear sister, princess or not."

"Of course," Lucan agreed.

"Oh, I don't need a house," Della said. "I have my father's home. It was always meant for me, after all. He'd intended for me to be a comfortable and resourceful noblewoman, like … like my mother. Now, I can do that."

Della sat in her chair, brought her hands to her head, and hesitated only the barest moment before lifting her crown and placing it on the table in front of her.

Neve couldn't recall the last time she'd seen Della's head without a crown. It was possible she never had.

Della's face was calm, her breath steady. She lifted her gaze to Neve's, and her small smile was content.

"Bry," Brockton finally said. "My sweetest sister. It turns out you have quite a bit to say."

"Yes," Bry said. "Everyone does."

"I understand you have many, many petitions for me to consider. Petitions from women who suffer under current law."

"Yes."

"There are things that my father didn't see. Things that he didn't encourage me to see, either." He looked at Neve. "I'm sorry for that."

He took a sip from his jeweled cup. "He was crowned at age fifteen, and so I trusted in his wisdom. But I'm finding you don't gain a lot of wisdom sitting on a throne for decades and ignoring what happens outside castle walls. The wisdom comes from speaking to the people."

He dipped his chin at Bry. "You've done that."

Bry waited.

"It will take some time to go through all these petitions—to give each the attention it deserves and to rewrite laws that might resolve a number of them," the king continued. "And it would take extra time with one fewer person on the council, since Lord Everard has been dismissed to early retirement."

Della caught Neve's eye and they shared a smirk.

"With all this work to do, I've no choice but to fill that council position quickly," Brockton said. "And I do hope, Bry, that you're willing to begin tomorrow."

Everyone at the table gasped. Bry froze with her mouth open.

"Your—Your Majesty?" she asked.

"Is there a problem?"

"Only that a—a woman has never held that position before."

"Indeed, that is a problem. This should take care of it."

"I'll be—advising you?"

"Yes," he said. "I'll expect you to keep finding the problems in Foreverness. But instead of taking off your clothes and screaming about it, you'll go into a room with your fellow council members and create laws to remedy them, and then you'll recommend those laws to me."

As queen consort of Foreverness, Neve had no legitimate power or recognized influence in this kingdom. But as a council member, Bry would. A woman would.

Lucan beamed at his wife and squeezed her hand. She squeezed back but she didn't look to him for encouragement or for agreement before she said, "I accept."

Everyone at the table clapped and cheered.

"Also," Brockton added, "from this day forward, every person residing in Foreverness will have the right to seek audience with me at the appointed times, regardless of gender."

Bry grinned.

"Wait a moment," Della said to the king. "If you knew you were going to resolve our issues the way you did, if you were going to help us, why did you yell at us first?"

"I'm the king," he said. "Big softie is not a good look."

* * *

The family filed out to dress for dinner, leaving the queen alone with the king.

"Thank you," Neve said, "for sending the army."

"I couldn't let you—" He stopped and cleared his throat. "I promised you the day I met you that I would see that you were protected."

A sudden lump rose in Neve's throat.

Perhaps there was a lump in her husband's throat as well, because he cleared it. "I'm told there's quite a bit of a feast waiting for you in the Great Hall."

"For me?"

"It's not every year a beloved queen turns fifty. A celebratory feast is in order. And despite all that's been happening, your sisters wouldn't let the occasion slide without festivities. They gave detailed instructions to the staff."

"They are kind."

"Indeed. They are the bright jewels of Foreverness."

An awkward moment came and went.

"I'm sorry you rode back here," Brockton said, "when I had our family matters in hand. When I couldn't be in Goldenstone to help."

"I was going to come back shortly anyway. For you."

"What do you—"

"I rode into Goldenstone to claim my throne," Neve said. "And I rode back into Foreverness to claim my husband."

Brockton blinked.

Neve stood and looked down the length of the table. "The people of Goldenstone needed me and still need me. Helping them was the right thing to do, but I refuse to do it at the expense of our marriage."

"I—"

She walked down the table, pulled out the chair at his right hand, and dragged it to his side. Then she grabbed the arm of the chair he was in and tugged until it squeaked on the wooden floor, turning. After a moment, Brockton helped her, and they sat facing each other.

She leaned forward. "I understand that an alliance with Goldenstone would benefit us far more than you, so I don't ask for that now. But I intend on rebuilding our kingdom into a prosperous, proud kingdom. At that time, I will formally ask you, for I am sure Foreverness and Goldenstone can then mutually benefit from joining forces and resources."

She paused, then went on. "Goldenstone is not a long journey. I've done it twice now. I've appointed a council to rule in my stead so that I can travel back and forth when I like. Perhaps you'd like to make some of those trips with me, and counsel me and—spend time with me."

"You can do this without me," Brockton said. "You have the knowledge, the strength, and the fortitude to be a queen. A great queen."

Neve laid a hand on Brockton's cheek, and he turned just slightly into her palm. "Yes. I can do this without you," she said. "I'm certain of it. But I love you. I have loved only you, and I will not give you up. And I will not *let* you give me up. If you send me away now, I will only keep coming back to convince you."

Brockton rushed to press his lips onto hers, and they lingered there. When they separated, Neve chose not to mention the tears she saw glistening in his lashes. "This is a timeless, legendary moment," he finally said.

"Not our first," Neve said, and pressed her forehead to his. Her crown slipped forward a bit, as did his, and they clinked against each other. "We will be great. Together."

AFTER HAPPILY EVER

Bry tried to remember the last time she had slept, but her exhausted brain couldn't figure it out.

She wanted to sleep—but not to escape. She wanted to sleep so she could wake up rested and get started making changes. Making laws.

She held onto Lucan's arm as they emerged from the castle. Thea and Dawn were suddenly there, hugging their mother.

"I'm so proud of you," Dawn said.

"You were wonderful," Thea agreed.

"If you're proud now," Lucan said, "you'll be even prouder to learn that your mother is now a member of the king's council."

Dawn and Thea froze for a moment with wide eyes, then both jumped up and down and screamed. "You did it!"

"A woman on the council!" Dawn said. "It's—it's such a big thing."

Bry swayed on her feet. "Can we rest a moment?" she asked before bringing herself down on the front step. She extended her legs and wiggled her toes. Lucan sat to her left, her daughters to her right.

"Can you believe it, Father?" Thea asked.

"I wouldn't have believed it a year ago, or a month ago," Lucan said.

Bry tried to run her fingers through her red hair but too many tangles impeded them. "I must look a fright."

"You've tied that red hair back your whole life so you wouldn't be too loud," Lucan said. "But now you're strong, and angry, and willful—and loud. I have never loved you more."

Bry closed her eyes, and Lucan placed a kiss on each eyelid. "What year is it?" she whispered, her eyes still closed.

"I have no idea," Lucan whispered back. "I've been asleep for so long. Thank you for waking me up."

* * *

That evening, Della walked into the visitors' wing of her castle.

Or, rather, it was the castle she'd lived in for more than three decades. The castle she was vacating.

Colby was being held in The Caves and would likely be moved to another location. Della had told the distraught staff that she was leaving, but she would see to it that many would remain to maintain the grounds and that Brockton would reassign the rest of them. But it became clear the staff was more upset that Della herself was leaving; they loved her so.

The large room was dark, and Della used a small candle to light a few lamps so the room glowed golden. Her most famous gowns displayed on the walls—her wedding dress among them—didn't look nearly as impressive in the cover of night.

She walked to the showpiece in the center of the room—the glass box containing her legendary crystal glass slippers, nestled on a velvet cushion. Even in the dark, the slippers' enchantment sparkled pink and blue and yellow. There was a faint and distant tinkling sound.

So many mothers had brought so many little girls to gaze upon these shoes. To build hope upon an illusion. They represented a dream that no one would live, not even the one who'd worn them.

The box was locked with magic, sealing away the shoes from anyone who would touch them. Only Della could open it, but she hadn't ever tried. She placed both hands on the glass, and it dissolved away.

She lifted the pair, one shoe in each hand. They were lighter than she remembered.

She walked to the large fireplace, where the late evening's fire was in its last dying embers. She held up one slipper, admiring the light of the lamps playing off the delicate crystal.

Then, one after the other, she sent the slippers smashing onto the hearth with all the strength and rage she had in her.

She stood still for a moment. Then she calmly took a small dustpan and brush from beside the fireplace and began to sweep up the glass. She swept and swept until she thought she got it all, then brought the candle close to the floor to find the last of the tiny shards. She piled all the glass in the corner of the hearth, then replaced the dustpan and brush. She slid off her gold wedding ring and used two careful fingers to place it on top of the glass pile.

Then Della moved back to the display case and sat at the foot of it. She tilted one ear toward her shoulder, releasing her muscles. How nice to have full range of motion of her neck because she wasn't trying to keep a crown from sliding off her head. She pulled all the pins out of her hair and shook it out. It looked grayer, but her loose hair felt more comfortable. Freer.

She'd spent much of the day packing. Brockton was giving her all the time she needed to move out, but Neve had asked her last night if she would return with her to Goldenstone to sit on her council. Neve needed to get people back to work and was certain Della could assist. Della said yes immediately. It was funny; once she'd gritted her teeth in jealousy of Neve's position, and now she couldn't imagine anything she wanted to do more than serve her new kingdom.

She'd told Neve it would be temporary, but as she considered it, she thought maybe she'd stay in Goldenstone for some time. She could offer her childhood home to Bry to house women and children who needed a refuge.

She extended her leg, and unlaced and removed one of her shoes, then the other one—the practical boots she wore to train her students. They were the first thing she'd ever bought for herself with gold she'd earned.

She stood and put the shoes on the velvet cushion. The shoes were dirty, dusty, with frayed laces and worn-down soles. The cushion welcomed them as easily as it had the more famous and ethereal pair.

Della put her hands where the top of the box would have been, and it re-materialized under her hands, enclosing the boots. Then, in her stocking feet, Della went back to her bedchamber.

Tomorrow's visitors, and all the ones after that, would be disappointed, but truth could look disappointing at first—before you realized it sparkled so much brighter than the most exquisite tiara.

* * *

Neve approached Castille Keep. She'd ridden back with a soldier escort, but it wasn't Lucan—he'd stayed in Foreverness. Della would be here in a few days; she wasn't much of a horsewoman and had elected instead to come by carriage. Uncle Anselm also would be escorted here in a few days to stay for a time—Neve needed all the best minds she knew, and he was wise beyond measure.

There was no grand fanfare at Neve's arrival—she'd told her council not to waste gold, resources, or time on anything unnecessary.

She hopped off Biscuit, handed her reins to the stable hand, and leaned back to look up at the castle.

Her castle.

It was familiar and it was not. It was her childhood, but a childhood she'd tried hard to forget. It was new and old at the same time. She'd get accustomed at some point.

A man approached her, bowing low. "Your Majesty," he said softly and straightened.

He was young, in his late twenties perhaps, with dark hair and dark eyes topped by thick dark brows. He was dressed like a lord, and she'd never seen him before.

But—had she?

She blinked. "Do I—do I know you?"

"Yes," he said, his voice still low.

Neve waited. "Well?" she prompted after a moment.

"I don't suppose you'd recognize me."

Did she?

Then his voice boomed out. "Would you like to know who is the fairest of them all?"

Neve's hands flew to her mouth. "What? What? *Oh!*" She threw her arms around him and hugged him tightly. "I thought you were dead. I thought you were dead. I thought you—were a mirror! What—how—?"

"I was enchanted into a mirror when you were an infant," he said. "When the mirror smashed, the spell broke and I was released. But I was released into the place I'd been standing when I was imprisoned into it, quite a few miles away at the home of one of your cousins. He's long dead and his house is gone, so I found myself standing in a field of cows. I began to walk here, but it took me days. By the time I got here, you'd left for Foreverness. So I waited."

"You were at the home of my cousin when you were enchanted?"

"Yes. I—I knew Fina for what she was. She heard I'd been talking about her and was furious I was turning people against her, so she imprisoned me into the mirror and ordered me to serve her for eternity."

"But who are you that Fina—cared what you said?"

"I'm your mother's brother. I'm your Uncle Easton."

Neve's mouth fell open. "Why—why didn't you tell me?"

"The enchantment wouldn't let me tell you my previous identity—or how to release me."

"I'm so sorry."

"I'm not," he said. "For I'd be a very old man, or even gone now, if I weren't in that mirror. I got to see you grow up, and now I'm young enough to offer my assistance in any way I can—even if that's simply by being a loving uncle."

"I have quite a few of those," Neve said, "but I welcome another uncle, even an oddly young one who's become very dear to me. Come."

They linked arms and walked into the castle together. She asked a servant to show Uncle Easton to an unoccupied apartment of rooms, and with another hug, she told him she'd see him at dinner.

Meanwhile, she had much to do. Today and every day in the foreseeable future.

The staff bustled around her, but she waved them away as she walked briskly to the door of her chief advisor's chambers. She knocked once and opened the door.

The advisor's back was to her, chair turned, to study a large parchment on a far table. But when Neve opened the door, the advisor turned and strode to her, wearing leather pants and a cape. A warm, deep scarlet cape.

A wolf unfolded itself from under the table and stretched.

"Your Majesty."

Rowan bowed deeply.

Neve's heart bloomed open. "My lady."

Rowan straightened with a smirk.

"If you need to return to The Unfathomed for a time—" Neve began.

"No need," Rowan said. "The wolves secured the Silvering Sea shores for many years before I joined them. Darren will take my job of reporting their activities to Foreverness. Perhaps we can discuss a similar arrangement with Goldenstone." She grinned. "When you are able to afford us, of course."

"I intend to be able."

Rowan glanced back at the table and its towering stack of parchments. "I know you just arrived, but we have a great many things to do."

Neve didn't hesitate. "I am ready."

THE END

Enjoy more about
After Happily Ever
Meet the Author
Check out author appearances
Explore special features

Photo by: Mark Karlsberg / Studio Eleven

ABOUT THE AUTHOR

Jennifer Safrey lives in the Boston area with her novelist husband, Teddy, and their two cats, Kimura and Potus. She's a longtime freelance editor, as well as an adjunct professor at Emerson College, where she teaches a graduate course on romance novels. She grew up on Long Island. *After Happily Ever* is her seventh novel.

Please visit Jennifer online:
www.jennifersafrey.com
FB: JenniferSafreyAuthor
IG: @JenniferSafrey_author
TT: @JenniferSafreyauthor

ACKNOWLEDGMENTS

I have no sufficient words to effectively and effusively thank Vicki DeArmon, Julia Park Tracey, and the entire staff of Sibylline Press. Their mission of publishing books by women fifty-plus is beyond admirable, and I am continually humbled by their support of and enthusiasm for *After Happily Ever.* Thank you. Thank you. Thank you.

I thank the Brothers Grimm and Charles Perrault for their enduring fairy tales, particularly *Little Snow White, The Sleeping Beauty, Little Red Cap,* and *Cinderella.* I like to think they'd smile at the middle-aged versions of their heroines.

Mimosas, chocolatey brownies, and crackling fireworks for The OG Art Friends: Roberta Lerman, Shelagh Braley Starr, Dottie Grant Cohen, and Michelle Bermas. Thanks for seeing me through those moments when I doubted my ability, and for encouraging me every day to put myself out there.

Applause, sprinkled cupcakes, and sparkling champagne flutes for The Unos: Jenni Jenks, Emily Battaglia, Kat Hankinson, and Kathlene McGovern. Every writing and critique session with you four is worth a queen's fortune (so I'm glad it's free!).

A golden MVP trophy to Laura Apgar, who helped me carve this manuscript into a tighter, richer, shinier story.

Elaborate flower arrangements and large New York pizzas for Mom and Jim; Dad and Angela; Liz and Seth and Juliette and Nate. Having so many talented and ambitious people in my family tree is daunting—and inspiring.

Cheesecake with cherry compote and hours of joyful Greek music for Vicky and Constantine Kechris, who welcomed me into their family and provide lots of laughs and support.

Adoring scritches, tummy rubs, and chicken treats to my cats, Kimura and Potus, who nap quietly near me for every word I write.

And as always, endless and eternal love for Teddy. You are braver and more gallant than a thousand honorable knights. Thank you for escorting me into Foreverness, and crowning me the luckiest and happiest queen.

AFTER HAPPILY EVER BOOK CLUB QUESTIONS

1. In your opinion, what's the most significant turning-point decision that Neve makes in this story? How about Della? And Bry?

2. Which of the three main characters do you identify the most with? Why? What do you think was that character's strongest moment and weakest moment?

3. Does any member of the Charming family do something that surprised you? Why?

4. What does "midlife rebellion" mean to you? Which character best exemplifies your definition of "midlife rebellion", and why?

5. Which secondary character of Foreverness has the most impact on the story and why?

6. How does the presence of the three Charming prince brothers create obstacles for their wives, and/or how are they an impetus for the women's positive growth and change?

7. King Hopkin is gone, but how did his past actions (or inactions) have lasting repercussions for the kingdom, and for each of his three daughters-in-law?

8. Now that the story is over, what do you think Foreverness will look like going forward? What do you think Goldenstone will look like?

Mortal Zin: A Mortal Zin Mystery
BY DIANE SCHAFFER

MYSTERY
Trade Paper, 412 pages (5.315 x 8.465) | $22
ISBN: 9781960573933
Also available as an ebook and audiobook

A crusading attorney's death. Sabotage at a family winery...As threats mount and the winery teeters on the brink of ruin, Noli and Luz must navigate a treacherous landscape of greed, revenge, and long-buried secrets. Can two fearless women from different worlds unravel the truth before it's too late?

Charlotte Salomon Paints Her Life: A Novel
BY PAMELA REITMAN

HISTORICAL FICTION
Trade Paper, 392 pages (5.315 x 8.465) | $22
ISBN: 9781960573919
Also available as an ebook and audiobook

This historical fiction depicts the encroaching terror of the Third Reich and the threat of psychological disintegration of the artist Charlotte Salomon as she clings to her determination to become a serious modernist painter, to complete her monumental work "Life? Or Theater?" and get it into safekeeping in a race against time before capture by the Nazis.

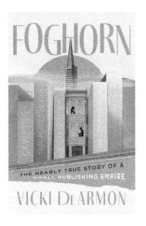

Foghorn: The Nearly True Story of a Small Publishing Empire
BY VICKI DeArmon

MEMOIR
Trade Paper, 320 pages (5.315 x 8.465) | $20
ISBN: 9781960573926
Also available as an ebook and audiobook

The heyday of small press publishing in the San Francisco Bay Area in the 1980s and 1990s lives again in this never-before-told story of how small presses—armed with arrogance and personal computers—took the publishing field. Vicki Morgan was an ambitious young woman publisher, coming-of-age while quixotically building Foghorn Press from scratch with her eccentric brother to help.

Little Great Island: A Novel
BY KATE WOODWORTH

FICTION
Trade Paper, 356 pages (5.315 x 8.465) | $21
ISBN: 9781960573902
Also available as an ebook and audiobook

When Mari McGavin flees with her son back to the tiny Maine island where she grew up—she runs into her lifelong friend Harry, one of the island's summer residents, setting off a chain of events as unexpected and life altering as the shifts in climate affecting the whole ecosystem of the island...from generations of fishing families to the lobsters and the butterflies.

For more books from **Sibylline Press**, please visit our website at **sibyllinepress.com**